THE VULTURE

AND

THE NIGGER FACTORY

GIL SCOTT-HERON

The Vulture and *The Nigger Factory* were first published in individual editions in Great Britiain in 1996 by Payback Press, an imprint of Canongate Books Ltd, 14 High Street, Edinburgh EH1 1TE.

This edition first published in 1999 by Payback Press.

10 9 8 7 6 5 4 3 2 1

British Library Cataloguing-in-Publication Data

A catalogue record for this book is available upon request from the British Library

ISBN 0 86241 901 8

Typeset in Minion and Serif Modular by
Palimpsest Book Production Limited,
Polmont, Stirlingshire
Printed and bound by Caledonian International
Book Manufacturing, Bishopbriggs, Glasgow

THE VULTURE

*To Mr Jerome Baron
without whom the 'bird'
would never have gotten
off the ground.*

Standing in the ruins of another black man's life.
Or flying through the valley separating day and night.
'I am Death,' cried the vulture. 'For the people of
   the light.'

Charon brought his raft from the sea that sails on souls,
And saw the scavenger departing, taking warm hearts to
   the cold.
He knew the ghetto was a haven for the meanest
   creature ever known.

In a wilderness of heartbreak and a desert of despair,
Evil's clarion of justice shrieks a cry of naked terror.
Taking babies from their mamas and leaving grief beyond
   compare.

So if you see the vulture coming, flying circles in
   your mind.
Remember there is no escaping, for he will follow close
   behind.
Only promise me a battle; battle for your soul and
   mine.

The Bird is Back

It would not be much of an exaggeration to say that my life depended on completing *The Vulture* and having it accepted for publication. Not just because it placed more money in my feverish hands than I thought I might ever see at one time, but also because I had bet more than I had a right to on that happening and it was such a long shot.

In 1968 I was a second-year college student at Lincoln University in Oxford, Pennsylvania. I had put up all the money I had earned plus a small grant from the school to follow up what had been a less than scintillating freshman year.

Six weeks after school opened I quit. I dropped out. The reason was the same one that had brought my first year crashing down around my ears. I had an idea for a novel and wanted to write it. I thought I could find the proper rhythm and could balance my schedule between class-work and work on the story, but there was no way. I was getting nothing done. There's a story I heard once about a jackass that was set down squarely between two bales of hay and starved to death. I was just like Jack. When I opened a textbook I saw my characters and when I sat at the typewriter I saw my ass getting kicked out of school for failing all my subjects.

What I asked the school for was similar to leave of absence. I would remain on the campus for the rest of the semester since I had paid for room and board, but I would be at work on the novel and would receive **I** (Incomplete) for all my final grades. The advantage was that when I finished the book and if I wanted to apply for re-admission to Lincoln or elsewhere, I would not have a complete set of failures to overcome.

The Dean reacted as though I had taken leave of my senses

and asked me to get the school psychiatrist to approve. That read like a challenge and perhaps a bit of 'C.H.A.' by the Dean. (In traditional institutions when someone makes a request for extraordinary consideration the person responsible for approval likes to 'cover his ass'.) The Dean must have thought I was crazy. It certainly seemed crazy that someone as poor as I would bet his last money on a first novel.

My plan was to finish the book before the second semester began in February. That showed how little I knew about what I was doing. By January I had little more (that I felt good about) than I had when I saw the psychiatrist in October and gained his approval. And I still had no ending for the damn thing.

January brought me the idea for the ending I needed and a method of connecting the four separate narratives to the book's opening. Now all I needed was a chair and my typewriter.

That was damn near all I had. Over the next two months I worked in a dry-cleaners about a quarter-mile from the school. The owner and his wife both needed to work elsewhere and wanted someone to mind their property. I slept in the back and took meal money from the small income generated by the students.

The miracle that got *The Vulture* accepted by a publisher, along with *Small Talk at 125th and Lenox* (a volume of poetry published simultaneously), consisted of a series of cosmic coincidences and intervention by 'the spirits' on my behalf. Let it suffice to say that the interest in the book of three brothers at Lincoln I will never forget; Eddie 'Adenola' Knowles (a percussionist on four of our first six albums and founding member of The Midnight Band), Lincoln 'Mfuasi' Trower (Eddie's roommate, who also missed a good deal of sleep as they sat up reading the manuscript instead of doing their school work), and Lynden 'Toogaloo' Plummer (my best customer at the cleaners who never failed to sit down and read a few pages when he came in with his things). Those three friends probably have no idea that they were the barrier that saved me from being pulled into the discouraging blank pages that I faced occasionally when a scene or an idea about the plot, the characters, the connections, something, would not work. I will always owe them.

I must also say here that I came from a family that zipped through college much like high school and kindergarten. My mother and her two sisters and brother all graduated from college with honors, literally at the top of their respective classes. I set quite another precedent by being the first one of their line to ('Ahem') 'take a sabbatical'.

To say the least it was not a popular decision but my mother had faith. In a telephone conversation we had after the deed had been 'undone' she said that she '*didn't think it was the best idea I'd ever had*' but to '*go ahead and finish it and promise that, whether it was published or not, I would go back to school somewhere afterwards and get my degree.*' She finished by saying that '*I would always have a home with her and that she loved me.*'

I did not dedicate *The Vulture* to my mother. I dedicated *Small Talk at 125th and Lenox* to her instead because she always appreciated the poetry so much and helped me with lines and ideas (including the punch line for *Whitey on the Moon*). And there was a special man, a very gentle man, the father of a high-school classmate of mine, who was the person I believe 'the spirits' helped me connect with somehow.

I did go back to school. I have a Master's degree from Johns Hopkins University in Baltimore that was sent, sight unseen, to my mother upon my completion of the work, and I have since dedicated many accomplishments in my career to the person who brought me no further grief at that time of stress and need for a kind word, Mrs Bobbie Scott Heron. She is a helluva person and a good friend.

I hope you enjoy *The Vulture* as much as I enjoyed the thrill of writing it. My experience of putting it together was my way of doing the high-wire act blindfolded, knowing that if it didn't work, if it wasn't published, there was no safety net that I could land on and no hole that I could crawl into, no way to face the other folks at Lincoln and no money to go anywhere else. In retrospect, I think it has held up remarkably well.

The major task of a murder mystery writer is to conceal the identity of the perpetrator while not getting caught yourself. It's a bit like a puppet master who must not be seen pulling the strings.

I admit that as a 19-year-old I had never put on a puppet show in my life. I knew that I was controlling the characters connected to each other. I knew that as the story progressed I had to advance the reader toward the identity of the killer(s), but not that each revelation had to shed new light on all of the suspects.

I was also caught in a language and culture trap. I was writing a story for anyone/everyone to enjoy and guess about as they read, but my characters and their way of speaking and language had to be true to the neighborhood and the murder had to be true to the underworld culture and its symbols.

The Vulture might work as well (or better!) on film as it does on the page. My biggest problem setting it up was how *to show you* the murder of John Lee without showing you the murderer. Hence, the autopsy report in the opening section.

Some people accused me of using that and a half dozen other devices as 'red herons'. Why they are so adamant about that is 'a mystery to me'.

I do hope you enjoy 'bird watching'.

Gil Scott-Heron
New York, September 1996

Phase One

John Lee is dead
July 12, 1969 / 11:40 P.M.

Behind the twenty-five-story apartment building that faces
17th Street between Ninth and Tenth avenues, the crowd of
onlookers stared with eyes wide at the bespectacled photographer firing flashbulbs at the prone body. The hum of
conversation and the shadows of the rotating red lights cast
an eerie glow and kept the smaller children tugging at their
mothers' cotton dresses.

From the apartment windows high above the ground, faces
with no visible bodies scanned the darkness and listened to
the miniature confusion below.

A young white policeman stood next to the curb leaning
into the patrol car, ear to the receiver, listening to the drone
of the dispatcher. Suddenly he placed the receiver down and
yelled something to the photographer, who cursed and yelled
that he *was* hurrying.

The police ambulance driver stood next to his wagon and
chatted with a second officer, a kinky-haired black, waving
occasionally at the body. The two ambulance attendants, both
in their early twenties, sat on the hood of the prowl car smoking
cigarettes.

'You through, Dan?' the white officer asked the photographer.

'Keep your shirt on,' came the irritated reply.

The crowd of passersby inched closer to the corpse, trying
to get a better look. Here and there women turned their heads
and shielded their children's eyes as they noticed for the first
time the red ooze that trickled from the base of the skull.

The photographer limped away muttering, and the wagon
attendants moved in with a flexible stretcher. With some

difficulty they hoisted the bulky frame of the deceased onto a hammock-style death rest and pulled a sheet over his head. Then they loaded their cargo into the van, and within seconds they were whistling down the block toward Eighth Avenue.

The black policeman was asking questions of the group of pedestrians and receiving negative replies to all of his inquiries. He walked back to the patrol car and slid in under the wheel.

'What do we have?' his partner asked.

'Nothing but the wallet.'

'What about the woman who found the body?'

'Nowhere to be seen. She's prob'ly somewhere pukin' her guts out.'

The prowl car lurched toward Ninth Avenue. The whine of the siren bit into the heavy silence of the night. The neon midnight beacons summoned the restless for beer and whiskey. The youngsters, knowing the Man as they do, followed the prowl car's progress up the avenue with suspicious stares.

'Does the name John Lee mean anything to you?' the black finally asked.

'No,' the rookie replied. 'I donno what to think.'

'I know what you mean. At first I thought some junky had taken another overdose, but when I saw that blood comin' out the back of his head, I figured somebody did him in ... But he wuzn't robbed.'

'Shit!' the rookie exclaimed. 'I don' give a damn. It's outta our hands now. Let the others worry about it.'

'Yeah. But these Puerto Ricans piss me off.'

'What?'

'Talk a mile a minute all day an' cain' answer one simple question for me.'

'They got so many junkies they probably identify.'

'We oughta bury 'um all in the gutter.'

'Can't.' The young white laughed. 'Against the law to bury a man at home.'

In accordance with the Act of April 16, 1907, P.L. 62, as amended by the Act of July 12, 1935, P.L. 710, 16 P.S. Sec. 9521, and on section 503 of the Vital Statistics Act of June 29, 1953, P.L. 304, 35 P.S. sec. 450, 503, I hereby request that an autopsy be performed on

the body of _____John Lee_____ at the expense of the County of New York and send a report to me or the coroner of the County of New York.

Melvin A. Diggs

Deputy Coroner

Date: July 13, 1969

Witness(es): Arthur T. Randall

BIRTH NO. 46703171

CERTIFICATE OF DEATH
DEPARTMENT OF PUBLIC HEALTH
DIVISION OF VITAL STATISTICS

FILE NO.

DECEASED — NAME				DATE OF DEATH (MONTH, DAY, YEAR)
1. _FIRST_ John	_MIDDLE_	_LAST_ Lee		2. 7/12/69

RACE WHITE, NEGRO, AMERICAN INDIAN, ETC. (SPECIFY)	SEX	AGE — LAST BIRTHDAY (YEARS)	UNDER 1 YEAR MOS. DAYS	UNDER 1 DAY HOURS MIN.	DATE OF BIRTH (MONTH, DAY, YEAR)
3. Negro	4. Male	5a. 18	5b.	5c.	6. 5/8/51

COUNTY OF DEATH	CITY, TOWN, OR LOCATION OF DEATH	INSIDE CITY LIMITS (SPECIFY YES OR NO) Yes	HOSPITAL OR OTHER INSTITUTION — NAME (IF NOT IN EITHER, GIVE STREET AND NUMBER)
7a. New York	7b. Manhattan	7c.	7d. 427 W. 16th St. (Rear)

STATE OF BIRTH (IF NOT IN U.S.A., NAME COUNTRY)	CITIZEN OF WHAT COUNTRY	MARRIED, NEVER MARRIED, WIDOWED, DIVORCED (SPECIFY)	SURVIVING SPOUSE (IF WIFE, GIVE MAIDEN NAME)
8. New York	9. U.S.A.	10. Never Married	11. None

SOCIAL SECURITY NUMBER	USUAL OCCUPATION (GIVE KIND OF WORK DONE DURING MOST OF WORKING LIFE, EVEN IF RETIRED)	KIND OF BUSINESS OR INDUSTRY
12. 154-30-6657	13a. Student	13b.

RESIDENCE — STATE	COUNTY	CITY, TOWN, OR LOCATION	INSIDE CITY LIMITS (SPECIFY YES OR NO) Yes	STREET AND NUMBER
14a. New York	14b. New York	14c. Manhattan	14d.	14e. 306 W. 15th St.

FATHER — NAME	MOTHER — MAIDEN NAME	INFORMANT — NAME	MAILING ADDRESS
15. Hamilton Lee	16. Cassie Johnson	17. None	

18. PART I. DEATH WAS CAUSED BY:	[ENTER ONLY ONE CAUSE PER LINE FOR (a), (b), and (c)]	APPROXIMATE INTERVAL BETWEEN ONSET AND DEATH
IMMEDIATE CAUSE (a)	Overdose of Heroin	None
DUE TO, OR AS A CONSEQUENCE OF: (b)	Inflicted blow to the skull base	2 min.
CONDITIONS, IF ANY, WHICH GAVE RISE TO IMMEDIATE CAUSE (a), STATING THE UNDERLYING CAUSE LAST DUE TO, OR AS A CONSEQUENCE OF: (c)		

PART II. OTHER SIGNIFICANT CONDITIONS: CONDITIONS CONTRIBUTING TO DEATH BUT NOT RELATED TO CAUSE GIVEN IN PART I (a)	AUTOPSY (YES OR NO) 19a. Yes	IF YES WERE FINDINGS CONSIDERED IN DETERMINING CAUSE OF DEATH 19b. Yes

ACCIDENT, SUICIDE, HOMICIDE, OR UNDETERMINED (SPECIFY)	DATE OF INJURY (MONTH, DAY, YEAR)	HOUR	HOW INJURY OCCURRED (ENTER NATURE OF INJURY IN PART I OR PART II, ITEM 18)
20a. Homicide	20b. 7/12/69	20c. 11:30 P.M.	20d. Inflicted by unknown party

INJURY AT WORK (SPECIFY YES OR NO)	PLACE OF INJURY (AT HOME, FARM, STREET, FACTORY, OFFICE BLDG., ETC. (SPECIFY)	LOCATION (STREET OR R.F.D. NO., CITY OR TOWN, STATE)
20e. No	20f. Street	20g. 427 W. 16th St.

PHYSICIAN — CERTIFICATION I ATTENDED THE DECEASED AND DEATH OCCURRED AT THE PLACE, ON THE DATE, AND, TO THE BEST OF MY KNOWLEDGE, DUE TO THE CAUSE(S) STATED. 21a.	SIGNATURE Hollis Farmer M.D.	DEGREE	DATE SIGNED (MONTH, DAY, YEAR) 21b. 7/13/69

MEDICAL EXAMINER — CERTIFICATION ON THE BASIS OF THE EXAMINATION OF THE BODY AND/OR THE INVESTIGATION, IN MY OPINION, DEATH OCCURRED ON THE DATE AND DUE TO THE CAUSE(S) STATED. 22a.	SIGNATURE Fortis Billings	TITLE Coroner	DATE SIGNED (MONTH, DAY, YEAR) 22b. 7/13/69

CERTIFIER — NAME (TYPE OR PRINT) 23a.	MAILING ADDRESS (STREET OR R.F.D. NO.) 23b.	CITY OR TOWN	STATE	ZIP

BURIAL, CREMATION, REMOVAL (SPECIFY) 24a. Burial	DATE (MONTH, DAY, YEAR) 24b. 7/16/69	CEMETERY OR CREMATORY — NAME 24c. Woodlawn	LOCATION Woodlawn Road, Bx., N.Y.	CITY OR TOWN	STATE

FUNERAL HOME — NAME AND ADDRESS (STREET OR R.F.D. NO., CITY OR TOWN, STATE, ZIP) 25. Calton Funeral Home / Bx.	REGISTRAR — SIGNATURE 26. Carol Dollars	DATE RECEIVED BY LOCAL REGISTRAR 26b. 7/18/69

Spade

'Name: Edward Percy Shannon; age: eighteen. Nickname: Spade. Born on October 6, 1949, in Cambridge, Maryland. Mother and father died last year in auto accident. May 19, 1967. Lives with cousin named Calvin Shannon. High-school grad, George Washington High School in Manhattan. Swimming team. Fourth in class at Osaka-Kyoto School of Defense and received green belt, ninth degree. Has broken toe, left foot. Broken rib, left side. Shall I go on?'

'I know it all,' I said.

'Ha! That's good! You know, of course, what all of that was about. That was a little demonstration as to how thorough I am. That's exactly how thorough I demand my men to be.' He paused long enough to offer me a cigarette from a gold case. I accepted. 'Drugs is a very serious topic around here . . . I see that you have no previous police record. That's another essential. An ex-convict is a constantly hounded man. I need nothing that can tie me to illegal activities.'

He looked up from the paper he had been reading about my life.

'Have a seat,' he suggested.

I sat down and watched him go over the typed papers from his filing cabinet. This was the first moment of quiet in the room. There had been the initial darkness when I entered, during the showing of a home movie. Then there was a brief conversation between my host and my friend Smoky. A minute later the projector was switched off, and the lights switched on, revealing the den, a working office for the man who controlled a major part of the drug traffic in the city.

'Tell me. You smoke reefers?' he asked.

'Yeah, I . . .'

'Snort?'

'No.'

'Skin pop?'

'No.'

'Good,' he said, adding that information to the sheet. 'I don't mind my men getting their kicks. In fact, I sponsor a thing or two now and then, but a man who takes drugs regularly is unpredictable . . . You know any junkies?'

'A few.'

'What do you think of them?'

'I don't know jus' what you mean.'

'They're animals!' he said. 'All of them. I know that you're probably fed up with that term, as much as a man's exposed to it nowadays, but I'm damned if it's not adequate. The men and women you'll be dealing with are desperate sometimes.'

I could tell that he was really gone now. His hands were waving in the air, and his eyes took on the deep concentration of a man who's really enjoying his own rap. I wasn't really interested in what he was saying as much as the way he said it.

Frank Zinari was his name. From all indications, he was one of the top men in the drug game in the Bronx and Manhattan. Of course, I knew that there might easily be a hundred or more top men, but this guy really lived the part. Smoky, an old high-school friend of mine, who had dropped out in his junior year, had seen me one night and through the conversation asked me how I would like to make some easy money. I said I'd like it fine. He told me that his boss, a man named Zinari, was looking for a man; and now I sat in a fabulous crib drinking Johnny Black from a swing-out mahogany bar and sitting on clouds that some furniture maker had captured and shaped like chairs.

'. . . the women will offer you sex, and the men will try to cheat you or rob you or maybe even kill you . . . Now, I've been having trouble with Sullivan charges.' I frowned, not understanding. 'I mean that some of my men have been bothered about carrying concealed weapons. That's why I was particularly interested when Smoky brought your name up. You know a type of self-defense, and there's no telling when you might be called on to use it. If at all possible, avoid this type of confrontation, but if not, do your best to teach the motherless bastards a lesson.'

He was grinning a bit. Proud of his colloquialism, I guess. I looked past him through the glass doors that led to the indoor swimming pool and recreation room. The man himself, Zinari, sat before me with bulging cheeks, struggling with the wrapper of an expensive cigar.

'So what do you say, Spade?' he asked without looking up.

'Sure,' I replied.

'Good,' he said, removing the cigar from rubbery lips. 'Now, I want to make sure that you and Smoky are together on everything.' He paused and beckoned Smoky from his vigil by the door. 'Each night except Sunday and Thursday you will meet these people at these places.' He handed me a sheet with fifteen names on it. 'They are all in the same area, but they don't know each other, so don't try to make any adjustments that might be easier for you. I have it the way it should be. You and Smoky get together on a meeting place where you will turn over to him what you collect from the pushers. Now, the people you work with know better than to be late, but the schedule allows for you to wait twelve minutes. After that, move on to the next spot. Clear?'

'Sure.'

'Oh, one more thing. You will see me only when I send for you. Our only contact will be Smoky. He will pay you each week on Friday. Naturally, he'll see you every night and relay any messages that we have for each other.' He stood and offered me his hand. I shook it.

'What about bread?' I asked.

'Two hundred per week.'

Zinari turned toward the projector and started rewinding his film. I took that to mean that our business was finished. I followed Smoky through the den door, still watching Zinari out of the corner of my eye. I hoped that he would not disappear and I wake up thinking of the money I might have had.

'yeah man! zinari iz aw ri'; no trubble at all. less you try in mess wit' hiz dus'. you know, dat cat iz allatime uptight 'cauz a purty boy muthuhfuckuh think he kin git away stealin' from the man. try if'n you wanna, but if he ketch you, yo' ass iz grass.'

'Two hundred a week,' I said, thinking out loud.

Smoky and I were cruising down the West Side Highway, caught in a mild stream of rush-hour New York traffic. The real crush was opposite us, where motorists were sardined together trying to escape uptown to the suburbs and to Jersey by way of the George Washington Bridge. Smoky handled the big black Cadillac easily, weaving in and out of traffic like a puppet master with the huge car as a mechanical extension of himself. His eyes, hidden behind thick sunglasses, and his hunched posture as he sort of drooped over the steering wheel, displayed his relaxation. He muttered again. His language was a combination of street slang and high-school intellect that he seemed to whistle through a LeRoi Jones beard. Having been a friend of his for so long, I had learned to interpret it.

'yeah, man,' he said, 'thass a good pil a dus' you makin'. i'ss s'pose t'keep you from gittin' greedy ... look, fergit that animal shit! jus' deal wit' de muthuhfuckuhs when you have to, an' don' git involved, ya see? all whi' people think nigguhs iz animals anyway. he didn' say dat shit jus' 'cauz these iz takin' a l'il hoss ... anyway, you meetin' a lotta fine street foxes an' dey gon' promise you a l'il dis if dey kin git a l'il dat, primarily dey gon' be after dat green stuff you be carryin'. all you needa do iz lean wrong one time an' nex' thing you know, you all fucked up.'

'Where are we gonna meet?' I asked Smoky.

'what time you say you gon' be through?'

''Bout twelve.'

'i be near harvey's on 129th street.'

'Good. I'll meet you there.'

Smoky swung the big Caddy down the narrow runway that the city calls the 19th Street exit from the highway. He let me off on 17th Street and Eighth Avenue, pointed back uptown. I waved as he swung back into the six-o'clock Friday horde.

As you approach 17th Street on Eighth Avenue you pass the pizza shop, the staple company that went out of business, other abandoned storefronts, a grimy brownstone, and a corner group who stand in the same spot every evening whistling at the secretaries who wouldn't spit on them. It was quite a change from Zinari's Riverdale paradise. It meant I was almost home.

Midway between Eighth and Ninth avenues on 17th Street there is a park on the south side. There are blue park benches to the left and right of the entrance and a small courtyard with blue picnic tables. To the far right as you enter there is a blacktopped basketball court where teenaged Puerto Ricans run, soaked in perspiration, and call each other various varieties of bastards. In late June, just after the New York schools call it a year, the park is as crowded and lively as a small Mardi Gras.

The sun was setting when Smoky let me out in front of the park. The men of the neighborhood sat and played dominoes and twenty-card poker.

I took a seat on top of one of the picnic tables and watched the basketball game in progress.

'Hi, Spade,' someone called from behind me. I turned, to see the approaching figure of John Lee, smiling and clad in khakis and a T-shirt.

'Whuss happnin'?' I asked.

'I need to talk t'you for a second, man.'

'Do it.'

'You int'rested in some good Red?' he asked.

'Can a fish dig water?'

'I got some,' he said in a low voice.

'Come on stronger.'

'Panamanian Red.'

'You dealin'?'

'Yeah. You down?'

'You got trey bags?' I asked.

'Treys *an'* nickels.'

'Whuss a trey countin' for?'

'Ten or 'leven joints.'

I thought about that for a minute. Panamanian Red is one of the more rare variations of marijuana. Also generally much more expensive. Along with Colombian Gold, Acapulco, and the powerful Black smoke from Vietnam, it is very hard to come by in the city. At least, an amount large enough to start dealing.

John sat down next to me on the table. The sight of the Spanish boys running, naked to the waist, with handkerchiefs tied around their sparkling hair and sweat marks staining their crotches, was enough to give me hallucinations of a great waterfall of beer.

'Ten joints?' I asked, to be sure I had heard right.

'Well, the way you roll 'um, prob'ly six. Goddamn Pall Malls.'

'Lemme have a trey bag, then,' I said, sliding him three bills. 'I got to check up on Red an' find out what happened, so I can roll six joints for three dollars.'

John had on a pair of knee-length athletic socks under his

khaki trousers. He slid down the rubber band that held the socks up and found a small manila envelope in the folds of the sock. The envelope was half full, folded over and glued to the opposite side, forming a neat square. He handed it to me and smiled a bit.

'Thass some good shit,' he said.

'I don' need no goddamn commercial. I already bought the shit.'

John was a pretty nice guy, on the whole. He had worked at the food market on 28th Street all through high school and was the man responsible for many highs when the neighborhood was low on green. He was a dark, baked-bean-colored guy with a round, close haircut and a pimply face. He was heavy and slow, not much athletically, but his bulky frame indicated a physical strength.

'How long you been dealin'?' I asked him.

'Jus' a coupla days,' he said.

'Red all you got?'

'Naw. I got some straight smoke too. It's Cuban.'

'I bet it's sweet as hell,' I commented. 'All that Cuban smoke been comin' over in them sugar barrels.'

John, I noticed, was lost in thought. I had gotten interested in the action on the basketball court. Two of the Puerto Ricans had gotten into a heated argument that resulted in one of the guys banging his nose into the other guy's balled-up hand. I lit a smoke.

'You comin' t'night?' Lee asked me.

'Yeah. I'll be there, but I donno if I'd cut them niggers loose in my crib on a Friday night. School jus' gettin' out, too. You know they gon' wanna be high.'

'It'll be all right,' John said.

'Yo' folks still gone?' I asked.

'Another week. Ha! I bet my ol' man wishes ta hell he wuz havin' hiz vacation in town. Aunt Agnes, thass my mother's sister, she's a cold pain in the ass. I couldn' go see her every year. Ha! 'Bout once every ten years'd do me fine.'

I tapped the envelope on my nose.

'Ten joints regular?' I asked.

'Gar-An-Teed!' Lee declared.

John moved on toward the 16th Street side of the park. I saw Game and Nissy, two of the neighborhood characters, having a heated discussion about something. They were just outside the perimeter of a circle of crapshooters. Game was probably laying odds on Lew Alcindor scoring a hundred in one game or something. John got into the conversation, whatever it was. His wide ass was almost laughable from where I sat. I couldn't help but dig him, however, because his attitude was always: 'Spade!' – and I dug that. I suppose he was really afraid of me, but a lot of people on the block steer clear of a man they're scared of. John was one of the few who had decided it would be better to get in tight.

The basketball game was picked up again. There was a replacement for the guy with the bent beak. He sat on the sidelines with tears in his eyes and a wet T-shirt across his nose.

There was a different type of noise filling the park now. The cry of various numbers from the crapshooters as they risked their hard-earned pussy-bait on a flick of the wrist. There were shrieks as mothers decided it was time for dinner, and the traffic of small children turned toward the exit and the apartment buildings as the thought of another meal of rice and beans beckoned.

The small girls still wandered here and there with jump ropes and hula hoops, but now the night people were coming. There were the winos and phony subway blind men who had escaped the crush and the Man with enough bread to appease their Jones for one more day. The calls for Angela and Maria became more insistent as the sun slid toward the other side of the world. The victims of the street were not particular if other younger ones were fascinated by their activities and decided to give it a try. They were not crusaders for or against anything. If someone thought that they were cool because they were high all the time or trying to be, let's go and get high. Otherwise, what the hell? They had decided long ago that the game of life really was not worth playing, because the inventor of the game kept most of the rules a secret. Mothers' shrieks subsided, and those who had not responded were being yanked by the hair away from the park to safety; away from the grown animals in the playground zoo. Mother always knows best.

The name on the small label read '*Bambú*,' and under that was: 'Sobrinos de R-Abad Santonja. Alcoy.'

I lifted the protective flap and read the inscription.

'El papel marca *Bambú* es el mejor – fino y mas aromático.'

I hadn't had any Panamanian Red in a long time. It had given me sort of a festive idea, and instead of the Top brand of paper that I usually rolled with, I skirted the neighborhood to 23rd Street to secure some of the stronger, more expensive *Bambú*. I tore open the small manila folder and peeped in at the red and green leaf mixture. I took a good lungful and then poured it all into an ashtray to separate the seeds from the grain. These are the seeds that pop from the heat in the middle of your smoke and scare the hell out of you.

I pulled out two sheets of *Bambú* and folded them, forming a neat trench. Then I tapped the fine powdery grains into the paper and leveled it off. I licked the glue on the corner and stuck the sides together. Then, using my key chain, I sealed the ends of the paper off. Presto! A perfect joint. It took a lot of practice to roll a joint like that every time.

I rolled the entire bag and marveled. Six joints, and any one of them could get a man high. No wonder all the cats quit drinking once they got hip to smoke. I looked at my watch. Eight-thirty already? Time to take a shower and shave before I got dressed to go to John's party. I knew that the niggers would be out in full force. Gig time on a Friday night!

John Lee's Party / 10:15 P.M.

There's something about Friday night that reminds me of a starter's pistol. It seems to release everybody from their week-long hangups. They feel a freedom that they wish they could feel all the time. Stay up all night and get high if they want to. Stay up all day the next day and get higher if they want to. Go and praise God on Sunday if they see fit. Or ignore Him if that's what they feel like doing. You can see a whole lot in seventy-two hours in New York City. All you have to do is know what you're looking for.

Friday night in the neighborhood has always been a gas. There is always somebody throwing a private gig, or some organization willing to inhibit your delinquency for a dollar. These groups had started to flourish once it was no longer the thing to run the block with your main men and roll over anybody who didn't dig what you were into.

The parties in our area, the Chelsea district, are notoriously wild. When we had all been fifteen or sixteen, there had been a gang for every block and a chick for every gang member. The big gang fights had been often and bloody, but rarely fatal. It was a chance for every cat to go out and swing a chain with little chance of being the major concern at a Sunday funeral. That was a passing fad. As the gang members grew older, their turf and their women became more and more a part of their pride and what they symbolized. It was a *something* to hold on to. That was when the knives, razors, and guns turned up on the weekend and people started searching you at the door when you came to a dance. All of a sudden the fun of ambushing a whitey became a serious topic. Most of the gangs started to dissolve when killing became reality, but the ones who decided to stick it out were hell. Everything was for keeps. The whiteys battled the P.R.'s and the blacks, and it went the other ways around too. The gangs all wore their jackets and insignias. The Easter suits stayed in the closet. They were reserved for your burial.

The Dock Battle of 1966

I had made my reputation early. At sixteen, I was already out in the street by myself. Spade, gravedigger for all bad niggers *and* spics. I wasn't a gang member, and I fought anybody I had to. In doing a thing like that, you set yourself up as a quick target the minute you beat up a gang member. Even a punk will try to back you up if he knows he has a follow-up and you don't. It just so happened that before I became a serious problem I had a break. A friend of mine from school named Hicks, who was the leader of a Chelsea Houses group called the Berets, called on me one evening to invite me to a party. He had been trying to convince me that I should hook up with his gang for protection. They were supposed to throw this beer-and-reefer gig on the docks at 20th Street on a Friday night. I took myself for a look-see.

I went to the party, and there were perhaps thirty of us, girls and guys drinking beer and roasting hot dogs over an open fire. The girls that the Berets had invited were primarily Puerto Rican chicks. This was a guarantee that everybody would get some leg, even if a few trains had to be engineered. All of these babes were notorious for drinking like fish and screwing everything that wasn't nailed down.

Out of the darkness behind us we were attacked, caught completely by surprise. I was sitting on the edge of the rotting dock with my feet hanging over the water. Before I could even turn around, I was pushed or kicked and was plunging into the murk that lapped up around the decaying columns.

I went under immediately, taking in a great mouthful of the slimy water. The shock of the cold blasted my brain, and tears stung my eyes. As I went under, I could hear the foghorns from the drifting barges of garbage farther up the filthy Hudson. As I came to the top, I could see a fire starting to grow on the dock about twelve feet above me, and I could hear all the broads screaming and the yells of surprise and pain coming from the other Berets.

My blue jeans felt like weights around my thighs. They had somehow come loose during my fall and now were binding my legs together and hindering my attempts to tread water. I went under once more and struck my head against something. Pain flashed across the length of my mind. I grabbed out in front of me and managed to get a hold on one of the pillars that supported the dock. All of the noises that had previously been so frightening to me now attracted me. I wanted to see someone and be with some people. The wet, mossy wood felt like a snake's belly, cold and alive. The knit sweater that had been my pride and joy was ripped open, exposing my quivering skin to the snake's bosom. I started to cry, I know, but at the same time I started climbing, hoisting myself up the column.

The scum and murk of the water irritated my eyes, but still I could see the smoke rising above me in great balls. The sweet odor of the reefers had been replaced by the stink of burning wood. When I peeped over the platform, I could see the battle. My man Hicks, the leader of the Berets, was on his knees trying to fight off an attacker. He was dressed only in his bathing suit, and blood poured from a slashing razor cut on his shoulder. The towel he was kneeling on was dripping with the fluid from the head of the Puerto Rican girl who had been in his arms short minutes ago. Without really being aware of what I was doing, I seized a beer bottle and began to raise and lower it on the head of the fallen leader's attacker's skull: over and over I hit him until I felt his blood splatter against my chest and I was sure he was dead.

Hicks's eyes sought mine, but I was dazed and unsure of reality. Everything had happened so fast. The Beret that Hicks held in his hand was soaked with blood too. I watched without moving as he rolled the distorted figure of his woman over and pulled a revolver from beneath the towel.

'BAM! BAM! BAM!' Three times the sound of dynamite split the night in half. Twice it seemed that the noise had been the gun's greatest effect, but the third time Hicks had aimed at the body I had beaten into a pulpy mass. The form jerked, hung on the edge of the pier, and then dropped into a coffin of water.

The sound of sirens registered for the first time. Much of the screaming had subsided. There were no enemies left; few of the Berets remained. They had either chased the P.R.'s back toward Tenth Avenue or fled from the Man. Hicks collapsed back onto the towel with the revolver curled under him.

I touched the girl next to him. She was barely breathing, and the warmth that her body had seemed to possess before had faded as she lost more and more blood. Hicks too was in trouble. I ignored the girl completely and lifted Hicks over my shoulder. I threw the gun, which dangled from his limp fingers, over my head into the river. Blindly I started trotting, running, stumbling toward Chelsea. I was familiar with many of the back alleyways that made up the neighborhood. We would be safe if I made it east of Tenth Avenue.

I turned under the West Side Highway exit ramp at 20th Street. It seemed that the sirens were coming from every direction at once. I started thinking that Hicks and I would never make it out of there alive. The cops would beat us and say that we died in the gang fight. I thought we had escaped death, only to find it all over again.

'Hey, kid! Kid! C'mere!'

The words came out of the shadows of the storefront next

to me. It was an old black man, nearly invisible in the inky darkness of the entrance to the shoddy store.

'I wuz lookin' atcha comin' down the street,' he croaked. 'C'min an' I'll hidja.'

I didn't raise any objection at the time, but I wondered why he would do this. All of the old people I knew wanted the hoods dead and all gang members lined up against a wall and shot. I got to the partially open doorway, and the old man lifted Hicks from my shoulders. His strength amazed me. I started to protest that I could make it, but I wasn't really sure that I could.

'Close de do',' he said back over his shoulder.

I reached back for the door, but the sound of the sirens drove me to the threshold again for a final look. Fire engines and prowl cars and ambulances made red a dominant color beneath the shadows of the highway overpass. The acrid smell of the flaming pier was still wedged in my nostrils, painting my mind ugly.

'Jus' hi' long you think you kin stan' inna do' lookin' like de wrong enda hell?' the old man asked.

'I'm sorry, pop . . .'

'I ain'cha pop . . . wouldn't be pop fo' no young hoods an' thugs like you.'

He was shuffling around in the darkness with a clarity of movement. I couldn't even begin to recognize any of the hazy forms that presented themselves in the no-light of the store.

'How's my man?' I asked.

'Thass whut I'z 'bout to concern myse'f wit ni,' was the reply. 'I'm tryin' t'fin some dry close fo' you so you kin go git whut I need. He done los' a lotta blud, joo know.'

I knew. Blood had poured from the wound on Hicks's arm, all down his chest and into the waistband of his swimming trunks. A crimson blotch covered the damp knit on my back.

The old man raised from his slumped position long enough

to hand me a stiff flannel shirt and a pair of paint-stained overalls.

'This all I got,' he said.

'Thass all right,' I told him.

'Gotta be . . . you got any money?'

'Naw. I ain' got nuthin' but a wet ass.'

'. . . an' a dyin' frien'. Mebbe we bettuh take 'im to the hospital.'

'We can't!' I shouted.

His old eyes regarded me with annoyance from their sunken caves. He shrugged and reached into the front pocket of his own tattered overalls and came up with a ten-dollar bill.

'You go an' git me a big box a gauze an' some cotton swabbin' things an' some adhesive tape. I need some a them ice packets too. Evything else I need, I got . . . an' git what-evuh you need fo' yo' own patchin's. You don' look like you 'bout to fall out dead to me.'

I had been changing into the dry clothes, waiting for the instructions. The thought of Hicks laying in that back room was scaring me. More than the gang leader's death was at stake. What to do about the old man would be a problem if Hicks died. Maybe he was willing to help me as long as Hicks lived, but death would change all that. What would I do with the body? What would I do to silence the old grocer? I was thinking that I would definitely be forced to kill my good Samaritan if Hicks couldn't make it. I broke into a cold sweat and started running toward the drugstore.

The old man's ten spot was squeezed tightly in my hand. Even the dampness of my body could not overcome the warmth that came with the fear that was now a part of me. Inside my head I was reviewing the store's layout and making plans. There had to be a back way out. I had to convince Hicks when and if he recovered that he had been responsible for the death of the boy whose body the police had probably already seen floating in the river. Once I had made Hicks believe he was the killer, and not me, I wouldn't have to worry about any pressure that the Man would apply to Hicks when they caught him.

I played the part at the drugstore, listening to the druggist's jokes about winos burning the docks down while high on Robutussin Cough Syrup. I bought the articles the old man had listed and started back down Eleventh Avenue. The commotion that had been in the streets fifteen minutes before was fading. Firemen remained to hose down the blaze, but ambulances were speeding away behind patrol cars. I returned to the store.

The old grocer was waiting quietly when I returned. He had left the door unlocked for me, and I went straight through to the back room, where he sat with a wet towel across Hicks's forehead. He had ripped another towel into strips and was using it as a tourniquet. Hicks was twisting and moaning in a semicoma.

Without a word the weatherbeaten hands took the package from me and set things in order on a scratched nightstand next to the cot. A dim light cast shadows around the cubicle and distorted the crow's feet about the eyes.

'I useda be a medic back in prehist'ry times far as you concerned. I wuz a man noted fo' steady han's an' allat.' He was talking for me, not to me.

'Why you doin' this, old man?' I asked him suddenly.

'I dunno why,' he said, without looking up. 'I wuz jus' askin' me why I wuz doin' it.' He took a needle and thread from a pan of hot water on the nightstand. 'I guess it's cuz I knew them whitey police wuz gon' ketch yawl an' whup yo' po' l'il asses. I didn' wanna see no white man beatin' yawl.'

'One cop like another,' I said.

'I wanned t'see yo' poppas beatin' yawl, not no cop,' he said.

That was the last thing I remember hearing. He told me the next morning that I had passed out.

The thoughts of the Dock Battle party entered my mind as I hiked the three flights of stairs to John's apartment. Four people had been killed that night, and no telling how many beaten or cut. As Hicks got better, I began to fill in the missing details in his mind, making sure he considered himself a killer. We stayed in the back of the old man's store for almost five days recuperating, so that we would be ready when we hit the street again. The P.R.'s had been bragging that they had gotten rid of Hicks and me. When we came out on the block together almost a week later, all the black people in the area knew it within minutes.

I could hear the sound of light laughter as I approached John's door; a good time being had by all. I entered without knocking and was greeted by a startled smile from Debbie Clark.

'Hi, baby,' I greeted.

'Everything's all right,' she said. 'But you're late.'

'Thass impossible, hon. The ball don't really ball till I show.'

'Yeah, but one night you're gonna come in drag-assin' an' we all gonna be gone.'

'Aw, you sweet young thing. If I hadda known you wuz gonna be here early, I woulda been here all day.'

'Bullshit!' she said, smiling.

I chucked her chin lightly. 'Where's John L.?' I asked.

'He's further on in. I'm the hostess.' She struck a pose. 'Look for him at the bar.'

'Why don't you hostess me on back, so I can see what I can get into.'

'Wow! You do move fast!'

'I wuz jus' thinkin' over what you said, an' decided I might be a little late.'

'You ain't *that* late.'

'An' my rap ain' that good?'

'No comment.'

Someone knocked on the door, and Debbie pushed by me, muttering about leaving the door open. Her nicely built chocolate frame rubbed a part of me that I liked to have rubbed, and I plunged into the darkness looking for a drink.

Already passed out was one nigger who had had a little too much of whatever it was he had had. That was one of the good things about our neighborhood, however, among the booze brothers, anyway. When a man had too much to drink, he didn't cramp, he camped until he and the room got back on friendly terms. There was very little wine in the air, and less liquor. John had everything under control. It seemed that the people were content to sip beer and do some dancing.

I walked through the small hallway toward the living room and the two back bedrooms, where the people were doing their thing. The people were spread along the walls and jamming the middle of the floor with some wild dancing. There was only one red bulb lighting the room with the bar in it, and that was where I knew I'd be operating from. I sensed rather than saw people. I checked for a path by looking for a silhouette and then blundering forward until I hit something.

'So Debbie is hostessin' John L.'s gig, huh? Another innovation on the block.' I was thinking out loud. John had been after Deb for almost a year, but she would never give him a play. I had always told him that it was because she didn't want to be tied down to any one man, but I really thought that it was because everybody believed that John was a nowhere cat.

My eyes started focusing, getting accustomed to the light. Bodies took on form, and faces had names. I was hailed from several parts of the room, and I waved and shook hands like a politician.

My main record started spinning, and I caught a glimpse of a mini-skirt that revealed a fine pair of legs. So I said to myself: Why not? I touched her hand with mine, and she grasped my fingers firmly and followed me onto the dance floor. Somewhere out of the walls Smoky Robinson was crying '*Ooo Baby Baby.*' Our bodies touched, lightly at first, a gentle probe on my part. You can never tell when you've got somebody's Cousin Minnie from Over the Ridge, Ohio, who's going to scream bloody murder and go home telling everybody that she was raped on a dance floor in New York. This was nobody's Cousin Minnie.

'I thought I knew every fine chick on this side of the Mason-Dixon Line, but I seem to have missed someone. Who are you?' She took the compliment with a smile. I knew that at best it was only a variation on a theme she probably knew by heart.

'I'm Crystal Amos,' she said. 'Who are you?'

In truth I was Humphrey Bogart, romancing a good-looking young woman in a darkened, secluded hideaway. My voice was noticeably deeper as I went into my thing.

'Eddie Shannon,' I bassed. 'Some folks call me Spade.'

She stopped dancing. 'Eddie Shannon?'

'Yeah. Is it *that* bad?'

She relaxed in my arms again. Our bodies began to touch, rhythmically, more firmly with each beat of the song.

'No, it's not bad, but I've heard the name.' Her smile was genuine.

I let it drop and pulled her closer to me. The song was coming to its climax, Smoky begging and pleading for the woman to give him that chance he needed. Crystal flattened her hips against me, and we touched completely. The record ended, and I took her arm.

'I'm afraid you lost your seat,' I said, indicating the fact that a woozy cornerboy had fallen in her spot.

'That's all right. I was tired of sitting anyway.'

'You been sitting? What's wrong with these niggers, anyway?' I asked. 'They blind?'

She smiled a warm, shy smile. She had a cute face that a smile did things for. Her eyes were light brown, and everything was complemented by her caramel complexion and soft brown hair.

'Can I get you a drink?' I asked, discovering the makeshift bar abandoned behind us.

'No . . . I don't drink. It, uh, tastes like medicine.'

I smiled. 'I'm gonna have one,' was all that I said. I poured a shot of Scotch and threw in two ice cubes and lit a smoke. As I leaned back against the wall, I struck another pose and maintained my scowl as much as possible.

In Chelsea, Spade was supposed to be the closest you could come to witnessing a walking death mask. I had picked up the tag 'Angry Man' because I seldom decorated my looks with a grin. I thought about that and chuckled. It was just another part of being onstage twenty-five hours a day.

My thoughts shifted to the little thing next to me. She had turned down a brother's invitation to dance while I was pouring my drink. I saw her now looking up trying to catch my eye. I just wouldn't give her the satisfaction of acknowledging her attention. I was actually trying to figure her out. It had been a long time since a young lady in my neighborhood had said that liquor tasted like anything but a good time. Most of the chicks were so hung out on acting grown that they fell into the parties in worse shape than the cats. They were buying their own Bacardi Light and really struggling into gigs with too much drink and too little coherence to offer any kind of companionship. Most of the time they weren't even good for screwing, because they passed out or threw up all over everything.

'I didn't expect you to be a gentleman,' I heard Crystal say.

'What?'

'You know what I mean. Like not drinking when the young lady that you're with refuses.'

'You can only refuse for you. You can't refuse for me. What I think you're talkin' about iz some real phony shit,' I said. 'All it really turns out to be iz coppin' out on yo' manhood. What do you care if I drink or not? I'm gonna enjoy it, an' it won't get you high . . . Excuse me if I don't make a big deal out of it.'

She looked a bit deflated. I didn't know if it was because I had been so blunt with my disdain for manners that she appreciated, or because I hadn't gone out of my way to get in tight with her. She turned her head, so that only her profile was visible. She started to pay a lot of attention to the dancers.

'By the way, was I a good guy or a bad guy?' I asked.

'Nothing like that,' she said. 'My cousin Delores mentioned your name a few times during our gossip. You know how girls talk.'

'And you remembered me from that?'

'. . . And the way you came in tonight, with everybody calling you and speaking to you. I couldn't help but notice how well known you are.'

'Well, to tell the truth, I don't know yo' cousin too well. I guess she's mostly into a younger thing.'

There is a social caste system in the neighborhood. Since the Dock Battle I had been accepted anywhere I wanted to go. My running men during the corner years, fourteen to seventeen, were always all at least two years my senior. The legend reads that after you go through the corner stage you evolve into a lounge-and-bar man. That was the period I was entering now. When I hit eighteen, I went straight to the Man and got my card. I had been drinking and buying taste in the neighborhood for a few years, but that was simply because my reputation told the liquor-store man that if he didn't sell to me he might have some repairs to make on his store when he showed up the next day. Immediately after my signing to go to war if my number came up, I started hanging out at places like the Cobra on Tenth Avenue. The customers were generally bigshot whiteys. Businessmen, tourists, career women, and entertainers all flocked to the joint because it had a write-up in *Playboy* and a few other magazines that said it was 'in.'

'Delores is seventeen,' Crystal said. 'How old are you?'

'Eighteen.'

'What's one year? A lot of girls have boyfriends older than themselves. Most girls feel like they need it.'

'I can unnestan' all that, but what I mean is that she ain't trav'lin' in the same circles that I am.'

'Which means that she's too young for you?'

'It simply means I ain't got time for no lead weights aroun' my legs right now.'

'Few people can stand lead weights around their legs.'

Somehow Crystal and I had gotten into this tug-of-war thing, each of us trying to make a point.

'Yeah, but a lot of people don't see the situation as I do. To me, you're either a girl or a woman, a boy or a man. I'm not really speakin' now only in terms of age. I mean the way you dig life.'

'What decides which?' Crystal asked.

'You either live life or you don't. You either get out an' go for what you're after, or you watch the world drift away from you.'

'And?'

'And if you know what you want when you're twelve, you're grown.'

She was watching me drink, and I had a sneaking suspicion that she wanted a drink. I thought she was about to show me a little independent action to show me that she was mature. I was reaching for the bottle.

'I still don't want a drink,' she said.

I stopped in midair and smiled at her. She was watching the couples in the middle of the floor dancing and weaving in time to the beat.

In the distance, Derek Martin was singing a song called 'You'd Better Go,' and an angel soprano accompanied him, telling him that his time had run out, but he kept on rapping strong. I watched a few couples appear from the shadows and cling to each other. I wrapped an arm around Crys and led her onto the dance floor.

By eleven o'clock John's party had turned into a downhome 'sweat box,' with barely enough room between people for a man to know what in the crowd was his and what belonged to someone else. The fast records were for breathers and time-outs. All of the windows were open, but late June is no time to be looking for a breeze in Manhattan. Crystal and I were sitting on the stairs even with the next floor. I was smoking one of the joints I had rolled from John's bag, and Crys was holding a cigarette to camouflage the sweet aromatic drug.

'Take a drag,' I coaxed.

'I don't want any, Eddie.'

'Look here. I ain' tryin' to turn you into no junky or get you high so I can screw you. You ain' gonna get high the first time you smoke anyway.'

'So why should I do it?'

''Cause damn holy rollers iz always preachin' 'bout the evil a this an' the evil a that an' come to fin' out they wouldn't know a joint an' couldn't identify one if they got bit on the ass.'

'Have I been criticizing you or what you do?' she asked slowly.

'That's not the point,' I said. 'Look, what am I s'posed to be? A pusher or what? Like, I want you to start smokin' to add to my income, right?'

The effect of the liquor and the Novocain reaction that comes with marijuana had me talking and listening in slow motion. I was starting to ramble about nothing. Behind the lenses of the reflector sunglasses, tears were welling up in the corners of my eyes as I began to nod and lean on the stairs and lose parts of the conversation.

'All right,' Crystal agreed.

She took the stick from me and tried to imitate the way I had inhaled it, taking it straight down to my lungs. She only succeeded in damn near choking herself to death. I couldn't help but laugh, and in spite of everything. Crystal fell all over me, laughing at her own ineptitude.

She looked at me carefully when the laughter subsided and took the sunglasses from my eyes.

'Do you always wear these?' she asked me.

'Yeah. I wear them most of the time, anyway.'

'Why?'

'To be cool, I guess.' I started laughing again.

'I can never really see a person who wears these things. People just aren't the same when their eyes are hidden.'

Softly she wiped the tears from my eyes, tears that had been uncontrollably released when I became temporarily hysterical at her attempts to get high. Everything always seems to be a million times funnier when you're high, and I was sorry that I couldn't stop. I could nearly feel the embarrassment that Crys felt.

'I'm too young for you too, aren't I?' she asked.

'Well ... aren't you? You claim seventeen, but how old are you really? How long have you been livin' insteada just watchin'?' My eyes weren't focusing properly. I took another drag from the bush and then stubbed it out and put the roach in my shirt pocket. I felt as though Crys and I were caught somewhere in a mist between life and reality.

Her face was very close to mine. I felt very masculine and in control of everything that happened between us; lord and master of a slow-motion jungle. I draped an arm around her and looked away. The dim lights flickered at the bottom of the stairs, and the smoke fought its way across the ceiling. I turned her face to mine and kissed her very gently. I felt her lips parting under mine. Very tenderly I touched the fabric covering her breasts, and her sighs began, her breathing ragged in my ear. I touched the cloth of her skirt just above the knee. She gasped for air and clung to me. The drowsiness that had grabbed me blunted my senses and kept my mind away from her small sobs.

'No, Eddie. Please, no . . . Will that prove that I'm a woman?'

I removed my hand and touched her face softly. She kissed my cheek and mouth as I struggled to light a cigarette. There was nothing I could say.

August 3, 1968 / 4:00 P.M.

Memories of the party faded. I started working for Zinari on the Monday following John's gig, and I was raking in more money than I had planned to see for quite some time. I got involved with the job and lost sight of friends from the block. I was determined to do a good job.

At the same time, John Lee had become very involved with his job too. I heard about one narrow escape he made from the Man because Junior Jones burned up the patrol car. I knew that I wouldn't want to have my business balanced on anything as dangerous as that. I tried to act as though it was just a part of life. I told myself that it was no concern of mine, because I wasn't on the corner anymore. I still heard the news, though, and it was very strange to hear one of your basketball teammates referred to as a twenty-dollar Jones. The mainline train to hell was collecting passengers at a rapid clip. The older cornerboys had gone the way of the needle, and all I could do was shake my head and swear that it wouldn't happen to me. Sometimes in the middle of the night I saw myself in a dream world of rubber walls and straitjackets, crying and trying to free myself from insects that crawled all over me and nibbled at my privates. My hands would be so covered with ants and spiders that I couldn't determine the fingers. My hair was infested with lice and leeches. I would wake up screaming and run to the liquor cabinet, where I sat up for the remainder of the night with a drink in my hand, trembling.

It was a Thursday in August. I had worked for fifteen straight nights, and Zinari sent Smoky with a message to take a four-day weekend. He also sent a fifty-dollar bonus.

That's how I happened to be in the coffee shop on Ninth Avenue when John Lee came in. There had been very few words between us since the party. There was no static in the air. It was just that our new roles seldom crossed paths. We both mingled with the night people in different sections of town. When I was off, John was working, and vice versa.

Hot days like this gave a man an idea of what life in hell itself would be like, and made a lot of wishy-washy people think seriously about trying to find God. Inside, the air-conditioner was keeping everything together, and I kept the jukebox playing, so Tommy, the owner, said next to nothing to me.

My job had been running as Smoky predicted. The pushers I met nightly were no trouble. They were people of darkness who wanted to spend very little of their time under the streetlights where I met them. There was seldom any conversation. Maybe once in a while they would try a 'Whuss happnin'?' But after a while they saw that my answer would be 'You,' and no more. Our relationship was entirely business. I wasn't really as cold as all that, but in the eyes of the junkies there were always too many things being reflected. The death of men and women without a burial. It was as though death had paid his call and left without stamping his usual notice on the forehead of his victim. He took the heart and soul, but he left the shell of the listless survivor, discarded as worthless. The bulging facial expression, bloated features, and shaggy clothes that often disguised blue veins filled with pus in scrawny arms. The silly smiles that met your inquiring stare when they snapped out of a nod leaning on an impossible angle. All of these things were a part of the cats I had been with and of. There was no running away from the faces that were often transformed into familiarity by the dim light. There was no denying that this was an old friend with a different name and a different reason for dying before his time.

'ain' nothin' persnal 'bout nothin',' Smoky whistled through his beard.

There were often evenings when I came through the door at Harvey's near the witching hour and saw Smoky rapping with the women who frequented the place in the late evening. They were all nurses and librarians and social workers, lonely women in general who knew that respectable men often came in to eat at Harvey's because it was the nicest cafe in Harlem.

I would fall in about ten of twelve or so, and more often than not the game between Smoky and the women was already under way. I would come over, be introduced, and then lay and listen through the hum-and-giggle conversation. Smoky would say things like, 'yeah, well dadadadada,' and the chicks would 'Hee Hee!' Harvey would come out of the kitchen in the back occasionally and make up fantastic tales about the service, where he always turned out to be at least the indirect hero by pulling a fast one on some white officer. Harvey's wife would look out from behind her perch in the kitchen and wink at me as her mate rambled on.

The women who sat with us always seemed to strike a chord somewhere in the back of my mind. They were always reasonably intelligent women, with a secret storm boiling between their legs, but too much pride to get into a thing with the first man who came along with the equipment to extinguish it. The eternal longing in their eyes was for some man to make a positive effort to seduce them, so that they could momentarily imagine themselves in love and discredit the evil thought that their actions were only the timeless, rhythmic movements of a woman in heat, a woman being destroyed from within because her physical needs fought the constant battle with her mind to control the countless caresses that she eventually would succumb to and the many orgasms that she desired.

Smoky would sometimes forget that we were supposed to be working. We would be joined in the small dining area by two women, and he would nudge me in the side as though my own eyes were failing me.

'look, man! two birds come in lookin' for a play. les play.'

'What about Zinari?' I would ask.

'zinari got miz zinari an' any else he want. i wan' some too.'

Anything that would resemble a difference of opinion on my part would never be considered. He would always call the women as though he knew them and invite them to join us. If they balked, he would go over and sit with them, assuring them that we weren't drunk and that our only desire was for a little freshness to decorate our table, a little female company.

I must admit that Smoky was generally a winner. He was an ideal man to double-date with. Whereas I was a bit picky, he would rap to the girl that I paid least attention to.

'nuthin' but some leg,' he would say.

He would always bill us as clerks in the real-estate business. This is a business with a future. With determination and a few breaks, there were tremendous advances to be made by Negroes. This was all a part of Smoky's initial approach. He explained it to me very simply one night.

'wimmin in harlem jus' like whi' wimmin. they movin' becuz uv two things. firs' thing iz the body. mos' a them out that time a night cauz they can' sleep. they cain' sleep cauz they wan' a man. the secon' thing iz that they alwaze thinkin' 'bout tomorrow even if t'night iz mo' important. they ezier an' mo' quick to the sack if they think the cat iz ejucated an' got a l'il money. they know they takin' a chance they never see 'im agin, but they need a l'il romance an' all that shit they read 'bout in the movie magazines. they wanna be wined an' dined, but a cupa coffee an' a charmin' rap will do jus' as good.'

I saw the whole point. We all used each other. The women used us for sex, and we used them the same way. A double cross with no winner, because all the participants were aware of the swindle.

I was injecting my third quarter into Tommy's jukebox when John came in. His huge bulk obliterated a customer's view of the steam that rose from the smoldering concrete. I waved and indicated the booth I was parking in. He returned the wave and plopped, mopping sweat from his fat cheeks.

'Whuss been happnin', man?' I asked, sitting opposite him.

'You know how it iz, man. Same old same o.'

'Yeah, but I think this heat is some new shit.'

'That motherfuckuh is fryin' brains.'

James Brown came on doing 'Cold Sweat,' and John and I grinned. The smiles were forced, and I thought about that. It was odd that we would be forcing grins for each other. Things were changing, I had to admit. John was into his dope thing, and I was into mine. I looked back at him with renewed interest. The youth was gone, and he looked like an old man, freshness erased by some unknown blackboard cleaner. It was a new day for John Lee. There had always been a smile on his lips and a chuckle rolling over his vocal cords, ready to be exposed with only the slightest provocation. The daytime was gone from his eyes. All that remained was the night. He was dressed in a good Italian knit shirt, double-breasted, and silk pants. He was the corner fashion post. The blue jeans and T-shirt were gone, but so was the sunshine. Along with the height of fashion had come the alleys of the neighborhood and the shadows of buildings that purged the air of theater cops who would inform you of your constitutional rights. John knew all of this stuff the same as I did, but nevertheless the fame and fortune that was his as the dealer was not something that could be easily dismissed like a T-shirt. It was a type of recognition, perhaps not the applause given to a movie star, but the sort of praise you dream about. It was attention, and that was what John wanted. He wanted it badly enough to live near the junkies, who would kill him for a dollar. He wanted it badly enough to take the chance of being dimed on by some punk who would never reveal himself. Somehow I saw all of these things in the lines in Lee's forehead, and I slowly turned to face my own crumbling mask in the mirror over the booth.

I took a swipe at my hair. There were dark, curly waves that I brushed carefully in place every afternoon before going out. My nose was flat and wide, but it went with the lips and eyes that mirrored my father's Latin ancestry. I breathed on the reflector sunglasses, wiped them, and put them back across my view.

'Whuss gonna happen when you git busted, man?' I asked Lee.

'I ain' gonna git busted. What are you, Mother Nature?'

He was irritated. I took another swallow of the soda before me.

'Yeah, I am,' I said. 'How's things wit' you an' yours?'

'Who?'

'You an' Debbie.'

'We all right. I bought her a leather coat, three quarters, and a watch. One a them wide square watches with 'bout half a dozen different bands. She digs them things.'

John yelled back to the kitchen for some food, and Tommy scurried out, wiping his hands on his apron and muttering some nonsense about the Mets.

John ordered, and I got up and put another quarter in the

jukebox. A group of five girls came in and took the booth opposite John and me. One or two of them timidly faked conversation while the others watched us out of the corners of their eyes.

For the first time since I started working for Zinari there were questions rolling around in my head – questions that were important to my work and to John's. Until I looked at John and saw the circles under his eyes and the lines in his forehead, I had been unaware of everything except two yards a week. Now there were images of the things that were really involved. I was running up and down on a felt cushion with lime stripes. Next to me was James Bond and Our Man Flint and Bill Cosby. We were all wearing Dracula capes and laughing at each other but not at ourselves. In the corner was Rod Serling, watching us and speaking into a microphone. He was talking German, and the whole audience was Crystal, and she was crying because of what was being said about me. Behind me were Oddjob and Smoky – the hired killers. But I was the only one who didn't know that the play was fiction.

I saw a picture of white Narcotics detectives with powdery faces falling on Lee from a rooftop and beating his knotty head with billy clubs as long as firemen's hoses. They beat him until the shape of his head was no longer familiar and blood ran down Ninth Avenue and small children came out to sail their boats in the crimson river.

The chatter from the girls in the booth across from Lee and me became more bold as we ignored them and made small talk. They began to speak of us in the third person, just loud enough for us to hear the compliments over the din of the records.

'Goddamn teeny-boppers!' I snorted.

'Not the one in the red shell blouse,' John said without looking up. 'I saw a pair of legs on her that could wrap around a man's waist and have him begging for mercy.'

'Bet she couldn't get 'um aroun' yo' waist,' I said, eyeing John's middle.

The conversation reminded me of Crystal. I was still with her on and off, and everyone in the neighborhood thought that I was taking her down. The truth was that I had been afraid. I hadn't known quite how to deal with her freshness, her smile, her warmth, or her obvious affection for me that went beyond that idolizing that a lot of chicks had. I didn't want to lose her.

I was shaving when she knocked lightly on the door. I had opened the apartment to her, expecting my older Cousin Calvin. Calvin and I shared the apartment, and he had left only minutes before to see his girl. I thought he might have left his keys. Crystal came in, and I complimented her light blue skirt and blouse. She smiled as I ducked back into the bathroom with lather all over my face. She rambled through the stacks of old forty-five rock-'n'-roll records and through my cousin's jazz LP's and then called me. 'Can I put on some music?'

'Sure.'

Lou Rawls came on nice and easy. I could hear her humming and singing the blues rendition as I wiped the remaining foam from my face. It was inspection time. I actually needed a haircut, but Crys said that she liked long hair, so I submitted to a bit of henpecking. Also it made me look older to some of the women that Smoky and I talked to. There were chocolate half-moons under my eyes. I hadn't really been getting a lot of sleep. I got home about one-thirty most of the time, but when Smoky and I had some women, I was crawling into the sack with the sun and the big trucks, and Con Edison men were starting their noise. I just sat in the kitchen and watched TV. There was no sleep. I tilted the sunglasses over my eyes and went back to the living room.

'Hey, girl.' I smiled. 'Lemme have a kiss.' She pecked me on the cheek. 'I thought I was coming to get you at Delores' house at eight,' I said.

'I wanted to come,' she said. She pulled me to her when I was back within arm's reach. Her lips found mine, and I was taken over by the fire within her body, the sheerness of the silk blouse, and the perfume that blew my mind.

She ran her fingers through my hair and under my T-shirt. The cool touch of her palms across my stomach and chest made me gasp and crush her to me. Her breasts flattened against my chest, and I ran my tongue across her lips until they parted and gave me entrance. I began to touch her everywhere as our tongues fought each other. Her breasts, arms, and hips were all targets for my hands, and the sudden desire that I had for her alarmed me. Already I could feel myself swelling and yearning to enter her.

I began to undress her. I shed her clothes and threw them in the direction of the easy chair behind us. The couch sighed as I lay next to her and wrenched my pants down over my knees. With tenderness and all the restraint I could manage, I guided her hand to me, and she was released by her desire to touch me as she was being touched.

The ribbon that had held back her brown locks became tangled and fell to the floor beside us. Her face was framed by the curls, and I saw her more as an angel than ever. I bent to kiss her breasts.

Somewhere on the other side of the world I heard her voice break through the fog in my mind.

'Eddie,' she called. 'I'm not . . . this isn't the first time.'

I heard her and understood all of the things that the statement implied, but I couldn't stop to analyze. There was a naked woman next to me. Without thinking of what I was doing, I was on top of her. With one smooth movement we were one. She shook momentarily and then bucked under me. Our chests flattened against each other, and I could hear through my own body her rapid heartbeat as we began to match our rhythm and response. Then as quickly as I began, it was over. She shook spasmodically, and her nails dug furrows deep into my shoulderblades. I could feel the onrushing end and fought it until it all but overcame me, and I sent the messengers of my virility hurtling through her body.

I rolled off onto the floor and lay quietly. I could hear Crys trying to retain a normal breathing pattern. She was the first to move. My eyes were closed, but I saw everything clearly. She stepped over me and padded to the closet, hesitated, and then went into the bathroom. I heard the sound of running water, a splash, and then nothing.

When she emerged from the bathroom, she was wearing a pink towel around her neck and one of my bathrobes. I had put on my pants, but I still lay in the middle of the floor, smoking a cigarette.

She sat on the couch behind me as the seconds ticked away.

'What's wrong, Eddie?' she asked softly.

'Nothin', hon.'

'This *is* what you've wanted, isn't it?'

Now there was a question. My jaws started to tighten, and I could feel the blood rushing to my head. What in the hell do you think? What does a man want except to lie next to a woman and embed himself in her loins and feel her shudder? What does a man need except to know that somewhere in the world he is still the master? That nothing can take the place of the power he possesses between his legs? What is the supreme prize but the treasure that a woman carries at the base of her stomach? What is life all about except fucking?

All at once I realized that this did not answer the question.

'I don' know,' I told Crystal.

She didn't look surprised. There was neither anger nor disappointment in her eyes. The brown stare that I loved so much had clouded to a noncommittal gray.

'Is the game all over?' she asked no one in particular. 'Now that the hunter has captured the game . . . and found out that it will not go down in history as a singular accomplishment?'

'That's not the point!' I yelled.

'Then what is the point? What have I done today except the thing that you've wanted since the night we met? . . . Now I want to know if that's all you want? You've had me! Is it over? Do you want me to go?'

There was a blazing fire in her face. The smile that I wanted to see was gone, replaced with bitter disappointment. I knew then that our first act of love had been a failure. My own ego had eaten up the happiness that she should have returned to. My pride was ruined because I was supposed to dance a victory dance after breaking down all of the girl's defenses; but all I had was, at best, more empty, pointless exploitation. I was not the conquering hero. I was the runnerup. I was not Leif Ericson. I was Christopher Columbus. I had been deceived.

No! I had deceived myself. She had never told me that she was a virgin. I felt like banging my head against the wall, but instead I extended a hand to Crystal, and she lay next to me crying in my arms.

'Spade! What the hell's wrong wit' you, man?' It was John Lee.

'Oh, wow! I wuz daydreamin', man.'

'Thinkin' 'bout tryin' to git to that broad over there?' His eyes slanted toward the red-bloused teeny-bopper.

'Naw,' I said quickly. 'Thinkin' 'bout callin' Crys an' tellin' her to come over an' watch us smoke some a that mean bush you got. How 'bout a nickel bag?'

'Sounds hip to me.'

'Tell me somethin', man. Whut wuz that shit you came up with las' week about the Juneyuhs shootin' up?'

'Wuzn't what I thought,' Lee said. 'They been shootin' wine in their legs.'

'Wine?'

'In their legs,' said Lee.

January 4, 1969

When January comes to New York City, she brings traveling companions – dirty snow, forty-mile-an-hour winds, jackets, earmuffs, and scarves. As the weather grew colder in the city, I totally lost contact with everyone who had been a part of my life except Crys. She and I constantly saw each other, but everyone else was just a part of the gossip I heard about when I stopped into Tommy's for a cup of coffee. Once baseball season ended, Tommy became a radio who broadcast all of the neighborhood's misfortunes.

Usually, come winter, I make the Cobra my home. It features a three-piece jazz group on the weekends and tasty soul food all of the time.

I visited the bar on the Saturday night following New Year's Day. The collecting had been light, and neither Smoky nor I had seen any reason to sit and chit-chat in Harvey's. Fortunately, he gave me a lift down the West Side Highway and then plowed off through the slush.

I was dipping into a Jack Daniels as the group came on. The pianist did a few light chords and the group swung into Cannonball's 'Mercy.' The crowd began to warm to the strokes from the bass, and the rendition brought out the soul in the audience. Here and there you could hear a 'Git it, baby!' or 'Do it jus' one time!' The waiters and waitresses waded through the crowd serving food and drinks from trays balanced on one practiced hand.

From the dimness behind my corner table an arm reached over and tapped me on the shoulder. It was Howie, the head waiter.

'Nissy wants to see you, man. Sez it's urgent,' he whispered.

'What the hell about?' I asked.

'Man, I don' know. Might be jus' another excuse to try an' git the hell in here, but I ain' havin' none a that shit.'

I got up from the corner of the bar and waded through customers and candlelight atmosphere. Through the door that led to the small alcove I could see two struggling figures.

My mind went out to meet them. Nissy? What the hell would he want with me? He could possibly want some wine money, but he knew better than to bother me about something like that.

Nissy was a wino, a man dedicated to the pursuit of the grape. He was always either drunk or trying to get drunk. His whole hustle was shining shoes when somebody set him up with the equipment. And as soon as he had enough for a quart, he would be gone to get high, and a little kid would cop his polish and box and be gone. Occasionally he could get a job running messages for the numbers man or something, but once he got high, he'd quit. Money was only important because it furnished wine for today. To hell with tomorrow. His bloated face gave me a wild stare as I came through the frosted glass.

'I gotta see ya, Spade,' he squeaked breathlessly.

'Thass what I hear. Cool it!' I commanded, dropping the sarcasm. 'Let 'im go, Hemp.' Hemp was one of the Cobra bouncers. He was holding Nissy at arm's length by the front of his filthy overcoat, the smaller man's feet practically off the floor.

'I gotta see you, Spade,' he repeated.

I waited until Hemp had disappeared back inside. I turned and faced Nissy with contempt in my eyes.

'How menny times I tol' you not to hussle this place?' I asked. 'You gon' come by here one night when I ain' here

an' Howie ain' gonna be for no bullshit, an' he gonna have
Hemp an' Jason throw yo' ass in the river. You need a cold
bath?'

'Naw, Spade . . . Lemme tell yeh. Then we see who's right.'
I nodded. 'Somebody got to Isidro t'night. They put a bullet
in between his eyes. I swear! Paco an' Jessie went to fin'
Slothead, an' they gonna get John Lee. They said they gon'
cut his dick off!' Nissy was panting, and his eyes were rolling
in his head.

'You drunk!' I yelled.

'No! Man, I seen Seedy dead wit' my own eyes! I swear!'

I looked him over for a second and then nodded.

'Wait a second. I'll be right back.' I turned and went inside.
Howie was standing in the corner I had occupied: his face
wrinkled when I reached for my coat. I picked up my topcoat
and scarf and swung over the bar and grabbed a bottle of Jack
Daniels Black.

'I'm goin',' I told Howie. 'I'll pay you later.'

'In the street,' Howie whispered. 'Please don' start no shit in
here t'night.'

'I ain' startin nuthin',' I told him.

I slid back into the lobby and found Nissy regaining his cool,
leaning against the outer door smoking a stogie. I handed him
the bottle and started squeezing into my coat. I waited until he
took a shot.

'I need all the details you have, man,' I told him.

'Okay. Fifteen minnits ago the cops pull up at Seedy's pad
an' jump out, runnin' upstairs. You dig? Then a ammalance
come an' they haul his ass away. It's Seedy. They got 'im
covuhud but I know who it iz. There wuz a hole in the
mid of hiz head, a small 'un. Not too much blood. The
cops come out an' they ast a few questions an' then they
haul ass. That's when I hear Paco an' Jessie say then gon'
get Lee.'

'How you know I wuz in here? Where's Lee?' I couldn't ask the questions fast enough. Nissy was still pulling at the mash.

'I jus' took a chance. You know, Saturday night. Where *you* gon' be? I donno where Lee iz at. Home?'

I was already preparing myself to deal with the Hawk. My gloves were on, and the scarf was around my neck.

'Somebody hadda hep Lee. I donno who else would hep the cat, considerin' heppin' him agains' who. Them spic mothuhs gon' tear him a bran' new one.' Nissy was starting to ramble.

'What makes Paco think that Lee did it?' I asked.

'I donno. No sign I could see. Look like a clean hit. Guess he put one an' one togethuh an' got Lee.' Nissy fell out laughing at his joke.

I came out of my pocket with a bill. The little wino's eye caught the picture of Hamilton and nodded.

'You haven't seen me in a week,' I said. 'You know nothin' 'bout Seedy an' John an' none a that shit. Right?'

'You goin', huh?' he asked, pocketing the bill.

'Ain't rilly got no choice,' I said.

'Damn! Gon' be mo' killin' t'night. Wish all this could happen in the summer when it ain' too cold to go an' watch. . . . Who you wan' me to see if they git you?' Nissy asked.

'I don't give a fuck,' I snorted.

I went through the last set of doors on that note and out into the early-morning chill. My watch read one-thirty. The wind blew grains of snow up against my sunglasses, and the swirling flakes began to crust on my eyebrows and in my hair. At my feet, along the sidewalks, were stains where dogs had come along escorted by frozen masters and done their thing to help keep New York beautiful.

From the high-rise apartments that faced 17th between Ninth and Tenth avenues, there were still millions of lights hanging in the windows, fighting to aid the streetlights illuminate the corners and save travelers from muggers.

A sudden thought crossed my mind. Where in the hell could Lee be at this time of night? The answer was home, but if he was there, what would the P.R. boys do to get him out of the house? Even they weren't so bad that they were going to bust in to the man's crib and take the whole family off. That was Roaring Twenties action. I checked for cars and crossed Ninth Avenue. I was tired, hungry, and needed a drink. I should have taken that Jack Daniels away from Nissy. A wino couldn't even begin to appreciate a mellow thing like that. It was almost like handing a grade-A-1 steak to a vegetarian and watching him throw the choice meat to the dog.

I headed downtown on Ninth Avenue. John lived at 306 West 15th Street. I passed the four-hundred block between Ninth and Tenth. John lived between Seventh and Eighth.

Cars and trucks struggled through the foot-high slush with fog beams that simply flashed everywhere except through the dirty mess that children wake and marvel at. No school tomorrow, and a million games to play. Building snowmen and castles and hitting the fat bully across the street with snowballs would be the order of the day. With a little luck, the pony-tail girl from the next building would be out, and she would either be impressed by his sled and marksmanship with snowballs, or be pushed in the drifts with the other creepy things.

I ran up the stairs to John's apartment. The dim light in the hallway added to the shivers. Inside my fur-lined gloves my hands felt like icicles that couldn't be flexed. I took off my sunglasses to wipe away the haze. That was when I saw the figure standing in the corner of the hall, wrapped in a shadow and smoking a cigarette. As the smoke was inhaled, the corner was illuminated.

'Whuss happin', Paco?' I asked the Puerto Rican.

'I theen' you know whuss happnin',' he said slowly.

'No, I don', bruthuh. Thass whut I'm askin' you. You know I don't go through no bullshit thing, right?' I stopped about five feet from him. He remained in the corner dragging on the weed. I removed my gloves and slid them into my coat pocket along with the sunglasses. I pulled out a cigarette and in so doing made sure that my coat was unbuttoned and would not restrain my arms.

'Seedy iz dead, man. You know that?' Paco asked me.

'Yeah, I jus' heard. Thass a shame. You got any ideas?'

'One.' Paco grinned. 'Yo' amigo John Lee.'

'Why you think that?' I quizzed.

Paco shook his head, and a small smile took over his face. He was convinced that I was playing a game with him.

'If I gotta tell you, man, I will. John an' Seedy in the same job, an' if Seedy ain' in the job, then John get alla business. Izzit right, o' what?'

'Whuss John gotta say?' I asked.

'He ain' in here,' Paco said. 'He be here soon or late, but he gon' be here. You see what I mean?'

'I see yo' point. But how you know John did it? How cum somebody else didn't do it?'

'I know he is the one,' Paco flashed. 'He could win mos'!'

'There ain' nuthin' I can say, huh?'

Paco giggled and tossed his cigarette down. I tossed mine down too.

'You can say adios to John Lee.' He giggled. I could see now that he was high. He scratched the side of his face softly, and his head swung out of the corner darkness. His eyes were half-closed, and his teeth were bared.

'John ain' goin' nowhere, Paco. You are. You leavin' here, an' if I ever hear about yo' hangin' out near this place, I'll kill you.' I was moving in on him. All at once I realized that

Paco was not the real danger. His eyes opened at the sight of something behind me, and I had only a second to duck as Jessie's arm swung by neck-high. I caught the startled P.R. near the elbow and turned it until I heard the straight-edge clatter to the floor. I hiked the arm another notch and was satisfied by the bone-cracking snap that answered me. Rushing up from the lower landing, I heard the hurried stumbling of Slothead, so I reversed my position and flipped Jessie back down the flight, where the sounds told me he had met his bald brother head-on. There was a collision, and I heard them tumble back to the landing below.

I turned around and stooped for the razor, but it was gone. Paco had it clutched tightly in his left hand. His high had evidently deserted him as he scanned the darkness for an angle on my body. I backed up a couple of paces and lowered my arms, allowing the heavy coat to drop to the floor.

'I'm gonna kill you, Paco,' I breathed. 'I'm gonna grab you by you' neck and choke you till the blood comes through your teeth, an' then I'm gonna drag you to the Man an' swear you committed suicide.' I was almost screaming, and the echo of my shouts came back at us again and again.

'D'you hear me, Paco? I'm gon' kill you!'

He was standing there unsure of what his next move should be. Sweat materialized over his top lip. I blocked his exit to the stairs, and I didn't know if I was glad of that or not. Any man is dangerous when he's in a corner. I knew just how good Paco was with a razor, too. I had seen the chicken fights in the park on 17th Street. Paco was seldom beaten, but I wasn't bluffing at all. I had every intention of taking the razor and choking the scrawny bastard until life was only a memory.

Without the slightest warning, however, the door behind the Puerto Rican opened, and John's father was standing there with a .45 pressed against the base of my enemy's skull. Paco dropped the razor and waited for instructions. The straight-edge hit the floor.

'Go on and move!' Mr Lee said.

Paco walked slowly past me, not looking to the right or to the left. His eyes were wide open. He disappeared down the stairs, and I heard him fussing with his two brothers, who made no reply. Seconds later the echo of their slow departure faded. I exhaled.

'Goddamn spics!' Mr Lee cursed. 'Alla time with a lotta crap, even at this time in the morning. What the hell wuz that all about?'

'Oh, they followed me here,' I lied. 'Something about me not covering a bet that their brother was supposed to collect on. I told them that I paid him this morning, but I didn't have any proof.'

'Goddamn spics,' Mr Lee said. 'It's a good thing Cassie's not here. She would have had eight heart attacks.'

I was waiting for him to hint about how he was glad nothing like that ever happened to John. I wanted to hear a few words about good ol' John Lee who never did anything except pull a pigtail or two. I needed to hear Mr Lee say that John was a fine boy on his way to college and all that. I wondered silently how John had so easily blown his parents' minds.

'Come on in,' Mr Lee said. 'I bet you could use a drink.'

'Or two,' I admitted.

'Were you on your way up here?'

'Yeah,' I said. 'I got locked out, and the Hawk was howling so tough that I wuz gonna lay here for the night.'

'John's somewhere with his girl,' the big man said, pouring me a drink.

'That's good,' I said.

'What?'

'Make that drink a double,' I said.

April 17, 1969

The days seemed to disappear. Before their arrival could be announced, their departure was already a matter of fact. I saw pictures of Santa Claus on a broomstick. George Washington and Abe Lincoln rode in on a one-horse open sleigh. Suddenly, before you could say April Fool, spring was back. Small girls appeared with ropes to jump and colorful hula hoops to spin around nothing waists. Little boys popped up with new skates and bicycles to ride. The grass sent up tiny buds, like periscopes, to scout around for Jack Frost and see if he had really gone back north. Before the arrival of the scouts, everything was only an underground rumor.

I was returning home on a Thursday, trying to beat what seemed to be an oncoming spring rainstorm. The skies were just beginning to tune up for a good cry when I met Debbie Clark. She was sitting under the mezzanine in front of my apartment building.

'Where is everybody?' I asked.

'On a Thursday? Who knows? It's hard enough to find any real people around here on the weekends.'

'An' whuss L'il Miss Happiness doin' spreadin' so much sunshine?'

'Nuthin' at all,' Debbie said.

'Where's I.Q. and Websta an' all them othuh triflin' niggers?'

'Websta's workin' his ass off prob'ly, an' I.Q. is bookin'. . . . You know, thass a real oddball.'

'Wuzn't he some kind of good-student-list man or somthin'?'

'He got that college scholarship he was after,' she replied. 'An' he's a regular guy, too.'

'You find that odd?'

'Well, he's the only guy I know who quotes Shakespeare an' smokes pot,' she said.

'The pot is the regular part?'

'What I mean is that he's not . . . well, he's smart but he hangs out.'

'I see what you mean,' I said.

'And then again, he's odd. I think he's girl-shy or somethin'.' Debbie wandered back and forth between I.Q. being regular and odd. 'I mean, he's okay, but he's not like you.'

'How's John?' I asked.

She blew up.

'Why does everyone expect me to know? Am I some kinda radar, or do I have the *fat freak* in my pocket? I don' know where he is, an' I rilly don' care!'

'All right! All right! What did I do wrong today, Lord?'

'I'm sorry,' she said, like a river changing course. 'I know what you think, but I don' know where John iz, an' I don' go with him, so I get tired of folks askin' me about him like I've got him tied to a tree somewhere.'

'I didn' . . .'

'I know you didn't. That's what makes me mad. Did you ever try to find out? Everybody in this neighborhood is into the same bag. I go out with him a few times, and right away, no matter what, I'm eternally hooked to him.' She paused. Her anger faded and then rekindled. 'What kind of spell does he have on you all? Are you afraid of him?'

I laughed out loud.

'Me? Afraid of Lee?'

'That's not funny. You never asked me out, an' Delores told me that you don't go with Crystal . . . Am I that ugly?'

I had nothing else to say. I sat back and lit a cigarette. Debbie held out her index and middle finger, forming a V. and I filled it with a smoke.

'Well, I'll tell you this. I'll never go out on another date with that fat ass, if I'm in the house forever!'

'He'll still ask you,' I said.

'I jus' won't go.'

'So why did you ever go with him?'

'I never *went* with him. We dated. I like to go out. I didn't realize a date was a marriage license.'

'Okay,' I breathed.

'I had always kinda hoped that you *would* ask me out,' Debbie said suddenly.

'You always been a fine thing, Deb, but I guess I wuz jus' one a the ignorant multitude.'

'Well, you know how it is. You've always been sort of the man around here. Spade this an' Spade that. I had heard of you a long time before I met you. An' when you were nice an' everything, I had to get a crush on you.'

'John is the man aroun' here now,' I reminded her.

'Yeah, and Johnny used to be a lot of fun. I was never really strung out on him, but he was a good time, an' he was good to me. Now he doesn't have time for this an' that. Sometimes he sleeps all day an' runs all night. He was lonely before, but you know there ain't nobody aroun' here lonely with money.'

I paused and thought about that. I thought about the lines I had seen in Lee's face. The lines that were in my face. I knew that the Puerto Ricans would still kill John if they thought they could do it somewhere that I wouldn't find out. I knew that Lee must have dreams about the Narco men catchin' him with a whole bag of smoke. There was no more nice-guy John Lee that was my friend. He was dead. All that remained was for the new John Lee, the new street man, to remember the sleep he used to get, and to see clearly that the next time he closed his eyes they just might not open, or the ushers could lower him into the ground. The sad thing was that I was not much better off. I never touched the skag that the junkies were ridin' on, but I touched the money that they got together by mugging and stealing and selling their women's bodies. I did a harmless thing when taken literally, but right over my shoulder was Smoky counting the bullets he would fire into disagreeing heads at the first sign of trouble. I was just another link in the chain that was wrapped around the body of so many slaves who would soon be cast into the slimy Hudson or dumped into a niche at Potter's Field. All I had was Crystal. As long as I had her to pull me back into the good world from time to time, I would make it. I wondered at times like these why I didn't just crush her to me and say, 'Girl, you are all in the world I have, and I can't lose you.' I knew that this was the only thing that was missing from our relationship that could make her happy. I knew that as long as I played all of the hands with icy fingers, her heart would carry a section of the chill.

'So we'll go out sometimes,' I told Debbie.

'Why not tonight?' she asked.

'You got school tomorrow,' I said quickly.

'Ain't no problem.'

'All right,' I agreed weakly. 'What time?'

'Eight-thirty?' she asked.

'Punctuality is my middle name,' I said, forcing a smile.

I sat there with a lead weight in my stomach. There was a size-ten shoe in my mouth. Already, however, in the back of my mind a plan was forming to keep my candle burning at both ends. If I could get Debbie to and fro on a date, and John Lee didn't find out, I was straight both ways. The thing to do would be to take a cab up Tenth Avenue, since the gang would be on Ninth, and then come back the same way about midnight, when most of the younger cats and chicks would be in the house. I would be a two-way loser if I got caught, but a helluva winner if I got over. I cursed my ego as I realized how I had done myself in. It had all come to a head when she hinted that I might be afraid of John Lee. It had been a subtle dare, and I was always a man to accept a challenge. I had always needed to prove my bravery. Not to reinforce the image that was handed out, but for myself.

'Bye.' Debbie pecked me lightly on the cheek and skipped off through the light rain. I sat there dreaming up a device with several size-twenty boots on a rotating wheel so that I could plug it in and kick my own ass.

April 17 / 8:35 P.M.

Debbie wasn't ready when I arrived at her apartment. The rain had stopped, leaving the evening overcast, and birds returned to waterlogged trees: but they had had their audience chased. I was wearing silk pants and a Nehru shirt-jacket with my raincoat tossed over my arm.

Debbie met me at the door with her housecoat on, and I thought for a moment that our date might be off.

'I'm sorry I'm not ready, but Mom was going to a P.T.A. meeting with Dad, so I had to fix her hair and everything before I could get myself together. They didn't really want me to go.'

'But it's okay?' I asked.

'I told them it was something special, so they agreed,' she said.

'Good.' I smiled.

The thought occurred to me that Debbie and John might not have such a hot thing in bed. That just might be her reason for playing with me.

Debbie was whistling something. She asked me if I wanted a drink, and when I accepted, she came out with a bottle of Dunhill. I poured myself a small hit and threw in a couple of ice cubes. I was back in my profile bag. I leaned back against the couch and dug the furniture and interior decorating. Nice upholstery and covers for all the chairs and sofa. Some sort of thick drapes blocking out the night, and pole lamps that looked like lanterns.

'I thought we might hit a place uptown called the Night Owl,' I called in to Debbie. 'It's a totally new thing. I've only been there once.'

'What's it like?' she asked.

'Wait and see.'

'I hope I like it.'

'Oh, I'm . . .'

I was interrupted by a knock on the door.

'Could you get that?' Debbie called.

I opened the door. It was John Lee.

'Spade, what are you . . .' John began his question and then put a spot on Debbie over my shoulder, clad in only her slip. His mouth clamped shut, and he yanked the door from me and slammed it in my face.

I turned to face Debbie with shock. I found it impossible to change expressions. I don't know how, but at that second I saw through Debbie's whole facade, as easily as I saw through the sheer slip that she wore.

'You black bitch!' I screamed. 'You set that up! You called Lee and made sure that he'd catch me, didn't you? You knew he'd be working ordinarily, didn't you?'

My right hand shot out with cannon force and slapped the girl into a sitting position halfway across the room.

'You black bitch!' I repeated.

'At least he won't bother me now!' Debbie cried.

I grabbed my coat from the couch and lunged out into the empty hall. My own stupidity was blinding me, and the walls seemed to be closing in on me. I punched angrily at the button that summoned the elevator. I needed a drink.

I stepped into the trap. She wanted me. She wanted a man. She needed someone to caress her and do the thing to her she had been trying to get all that liquor to do. She wanted me to do what the fat boy couldn't do for her, if he did anything at all. Cool Spade, I thought. The man has done it again. His program is so together that not only is he getting the leg that he's after, but stuff that he didn't even know he was in line for. The main man is pulling another fast one on the world. Poor silly bitch can't resist the reputation and the coolness that this nigger wears like another vine. Goddamn! Goddamn a silly-ass Spade and all the idiocy that it represents! Goddamn motherfuckin' make-believe people! They ain' out here and they wouldn't dare try to pull all that cool shit in the middle of 17th Street with the P.R.'s on one corner and the whiteys on another and them right in the motherfuckin' middle! Goddamn! There was no point in getting into a thing about saving the princess from the fat ogre. All I had really been doing was trying to screw John's piece of tail. I had needed that just for myself to prove to me that I was the MAN, while John was just another two-bit dealer. He would never be another Spade. All Debbie had been was just another piece of ass!

I sat in the corner of the Cobra and drank a Jack D. and listened to Ray Charles sing about crying. Listen to the blind man see.

Time. The word comes through the turnstiles of your mind, ringing that bell that attracts your attention like the warning bell near the end of a line on a typewriter. Time is here; then it is gone. I remember the first day I learned the meaning of the word *gone.* I had found my grandmother dead. *Gone* meant no tomorrow. *Gone* meant over. Dead meant that you, who had been *something,* were now nothing. That was the first time I saw a body lowered into the ground while people cried. I cried too, because I realized that I would someday die, and I was afraid of death. No longer was death a shootout in a cowboy movie or Christians being eaten alive in a Roman arena by toothless lions. It was the end of everything.

Time is also supposed to be the great healer. In the weeks

that followed, I knew that John Lee would give me a chance to explain to him. I was sure that John would be man enough to sit down and listen to what I had to say, but he seemed to avoid me as though he knew that talking with me would be fatal for his ideals. It never occurred to me that he might sense the truth and just not want to hear. I never thought that he would rather believe something that was wrong than to find out the truth about the woman he called 'love,' but I was no student of the mind. John held Debbie the way I held Crystal, free of blame. To find out that Debbie never really wanted him would have been to discover that the solid ground he walked on was really only sand.

July 9, 1969 / 8:29 P.M.

I didn't travel the same roads I had once traveled. The corner Spade had become the missing link, and instead of greetings on the block, I heard whispers being thrown past, talk of my former deeds, as though I were a ghost instead of a man. I was looking down on the corner from my window when the phone rang.

'Eddie?'

'Yeah, Crys.' Her voice was shaking.

'I've got to see you,' she said.

'Yeah, baby, tomorrow, jus' like we planned.'

'Now! . . . Not tomorrow or next week or whenever. Now!'

'All right,' I said. 'I'll be right there.' I dropped the receiver and then picked it up again. I dialed Smoky, hoping that he wasn't gone for the rounds. I told Smoky that there was a family emergency and asked him if he could make my rounds for me. He said that he would, and I thanked him.

I ran out into the street dressed as I was. Blue jeans and a sweatshirt was all that I wore. Not my general street thing at all. I hailed a cab as it rolled down Ninth Avenue. All sorts of things grabbed my middle as I remembered the urgent, pleading tone in Crystal's voice. I had never heard anything like that from her, even during our infrequent arguments.

The cab made fairly good time, but nothing like the instant teleportation that I wanted. We were going down-town on Avenue D just off 14th Street when I told him to halt. I tossed him two bucks for the dollar-and-a-half lift and made it inside. In the elevator I lit a cigarette and wiped my sunglasses clean.

Progress was slow in the elevator. Riis projects had been around a long time, and the elevator was a part of the history it represented. I thought about what it would be like inside with Crystal. I'd try a 'Hey, baby,' and see how that got over.

As I knocked at the door, a flash of fear shot through me. In spite of the exterior thing that I was trying to get together, I was nervous. I could feel cold drops of sweat forming in my armpits and trickling down my side. I shivered involuntarily.

Crystal opened the door, and I stepped in, false smile in place. I stooped to peck her on the cheek, but she moved out of range. It was only ten before nine, but the house was silent and empty, like a tomb.

Crystal had been crying. The attempt she had made to straighten herself out had not been worth the effort. Her eyes were puffed and red, and the little lipstick that she used was uneven. I had been shocked to see her looking like that. I forgot the part I was supposed to be playing. She handed me a letter as we walked through the hall to the living room. I reopened it where the seal had been originally broken and read it.

I pretended to keep reading even after I had finished. My mind was gone. I couldn't even stop and focus on the written words in order to salvage the deeper meaning. Surely this was not what the author had been trying to say. It was some sort of code, some kind of trick. This was a lie!

'You believe this?' I asked Crystal.

'Why would she lie?'

'Do you believe it? That's what I'm asking you,' I yelled.

'Yes, I do. I believe every word of it.' Crystal's eyes clouded, and she started sobbing again. She stretched out on the sofa and turned her back on me. I wanted to lean over and hold her and comfort her, but my feet were embedded in rock. I couldn't pull them free of their position.

I looked around the dimly lit room. The only light was the one directly behind me that I had used to read the letter. I wanted Crystal's mother and little brother there. The only jury I had before me were the silent furniture sentinels, who could only observe. I needed people.

I saw Mrs Amos sitting in the corner easy chair where she usually sat during my visits, making small talk and waiting for Crystal to come out and entertain her guest.

'Mrs Amos,' I was saying. 'You know me. This is Eddie. Remember Christmas when we all went shopping together and I bought you the house shoes and the sweater? Don't you remember me?' Mrs Amos sat unmoving in the corner. Unmoving and unblinking and unbreathing. 'Why in the hell don't you say something, Mrs Amos? God, what's wrong with you?'

Crystal's little brother, Mack, was sitting at his mother's feet playing with a section of an electric train.

'Hey! Mack! This is Eddie. I'm like a big brother to you, Mack. I took you to the movies and the zoo, and I gave you that train. I'm yo' boy! Mack? Well, at least look up at me and act like you know me. Doesn't anybody here know me?'

I glanced down at the letter again and looked to the crying girl on the couch. I realized with a start that there was no one else in the room.

Dear Crystal,
How are you? Perhaps you are wondering already about this letter. Perhaps I should not be telling you this. Most likely the letter will make you absolutely no difference. I

am writing because you need to know that the man you are probably sleeping with, Eddie Shannon, is going to be the father of my child. When I told him this, he laughed and said 'So what?' In a few times that I saw you, you struck me as a very nice girl who would probably fall for a guy like Eddie, just as I did. You raised questions in my mind very often, but Eddie assured me that you and he were just good friends. It was only recently that I learned that he was using both of us for play toys. I am telling you all of this because you probably think that Eddie will marry you if something goes wrong. That's what I thought. My life is all messed up as a result of this. I will have to raise a child without a father. I have moved away from home. I could never live with my family after this. Please do as you see fit, but remember that I warned you of it all for your own good.

Debbie Clark

Crystal continued to lie on the sofa, sniffing. Some sort of wall had sprung up between us. I could only shake my head silently. My mind would not permit my body to do the things I needed to do. I was helpless and hopeless. I balled up the letter and tossed it to the floor. I took the envelope and put it in my pocket, and without so much as a good-bye, I went through the door and down to the street below. I cast one single glance back to her window as I started uptown on foot. The lights were out in the apartment. It was all over.

I was back on the block in twenty minutes with my head still spinning and the atmosphere of the world pressing down on me like a bleak moment in one of Edgar Allan Poe's nightmare classics.

I stopped at Delores' house on 13th Street and Eighth Avenue. Delores was Crystal's cousin, but she was also Debbie's best friend. There was another mystery involved with everything now. Delores met me at the door and ushered me through to the living room with a smile that I quickly erased.

'Where's Debbie?' I asked point blank.

'How should I know? At home, I guess.'

'Look, Delores,' I was speaking with my teeth clenched and my voice barely above a whisper. 'I'm gonna find her if it takes me the rest of my life. You had damn well better tell me if you know anything 'cause if I should ever find out you knew an' sent me huntin' turkey, I'll beat you until yo' own mama wouldn't recognize you. An' yo' boyfrien' ain't bad enough to stop me.'

'She's in Baltimore,' Delores said.

I knew that to be true. I had taken the letter envelope and seen: 'Baltimore, Maryland July 8, 1969.' I needed an address in Baltimore.

'Where?' I asked.

'I don't know.'

'Look here,' I said. 'Yo' bes' frien' gits knocked up, an' I ask you where she's at, an' you say you don' know. Girl, you mus' think I'm crazy!'

'She has friends,' Delores said. Her eyes were pleading with me not to ask her any more questions, but I didn't care.

'And that's where she's havin' the kid?'

'She's gonna have an abortion.'

I was completely out of everything. I needed a drink, but I didn't trust Delores out of my sight. I could hear her parents running off at the mouth about some TV show they must have been watching in the next room. I could barely see the girl through the sunglasses. I took them off.

'That cost money,' I breathed.

'She had almost five hundred dollars when she left.'

I whistled out loud. 'Is that enough?'

'I don't know,' was the reply.

'Who's she stayin' with?' I asked.

'She's stayin' with Faye Garrison.' The conversation was

becoming thick and weighted. Delores kept throwing suspicious stares back over her shoulder toward the door that separated us from her parents.

'Where do . . .' I began.

'Spade, stop!' For the first time Delores raised her voice, and I looked to the door. 'I don't know everything! I've already told you more than I should have. That wasn't really any of my business! I don't know how you're mixed up in any of this, but anything you're involved in is always bad and ugly. I told Crystal to leave you alone! You know how tight Crys and I are . . . Now you come in here askin' me about Debbie when I've just seen Debbie leave here four days ago with more money than I've ever seen in my life. You're a rotten bastard, Spade. I wish you were dead!' She ran from the room and slammed the door behind her. Her father looked out into the living room and saw me.

'You know how women are,' I grinned.

He didn't say anything at all. He simply sat looking through the wedge he had made until I closed the door behind me. At the corner store I bought another pack of cigarettes, a paper, and a sports book. Once inside my apartment, I showered and shaved, then donned new clothes. I checked myself out in the mirror as I made the front door. New shirt and silk pants, plus a white raincoat and alligator shoes that started at sixty-five bucks. I caught a cab to the Port Authority at 41st Street and was entering the terminal when they announced my bus; 10:15 P.M. to Baltimore.

Baltimore, Maryland / July 10 / 2:30 A.M.

Nine o'clock hits Baltimore like a nightstick. All of the facilities of the central nervous system go immediately off duty. I arrived during the time each day when morning and night are colliding just offstage. The lords of the night are not yet fully prepared to relinquish their confiscated territory. The night people on the planet Earth are sullenly aroused by a knock at the door atop the solar system. It is the sun. Several stars are involved in a mutiny, and little by little the sun robs the moon of all his subjects. The moon dreams of recapturing the stray night lights, and he fades either east or west to recall them. It is daybreak.

I stood in the Baltimore bus terminal watching the beginning of the fray near the other side of heaven. I checked the city phone book looking for the name I knew would connect me with Faye Garrison. There was only one such name, and I prayed that I could find it.

Garrison, Odom 216 N Chas	BI 6–0907
Garrison, Oliver 37 Aztec Dr	KL 8–6472
Garrison, O.T. 995 Royal St	TA 4–7299

I stopped at the name O.T. That had been Oscar Taylor Garrison's initials. Faye had been a go-go girl at a dive called El Sombrero on 20th Street and Eighth Avenue. The owner had been O. T. (On Time) Garrison, who bought another place in Baltimore, where he and Faye moved. All of this came back to me when I saw his name and address listed.

I jumped into a cab outside the terminal. The warm air assaulted me after my sit in the air-conditioned coolness of the bus. I gave the driver the address on Royal Street and then settled back, watching the sleeping city flash past the windows. Sleep was closing in on me. Lights changed: Red-yellow-green-yellow-red. The initial anxiety I had had was wearing off. The tense feeling that had choked at my bowels was releasing me to the warm womb of drowsiness and ease. I thought I might need to see Debbie because I had lost Crystal, and there was no doubt in my mind that Crystal was lost to me. Crystal had been a great part of me. She had replaced the love I lost when my mother died. My father and I had been enemies. We stood opposite in terms of everything. My mother had been sort of like a mediator who struck agreements for us, so that it was possible for us to live together under the same roof. Crystal had been my love. She gave me the kind of love that cannot be measured in the amount of fear you command, because fear cannot be a mother for true love. The love that supplements reality when your goals become hazy and obscure.

I got a tremendous surprise when I knocked at the door. I could see the whole situation turning around in my hands. Debbie did not seem surprised to see me. I was a bit let down.

'I'm watchin' a late-late-late,' she said. 'C'mon in.'

I followed her. The door opened onto a wide red carpet that needed a vacuum cleaner's services.

'I came about the letter you wrote Crystal,' I said.

'I know,' she admitted, looking back. She plopped down on the couch in front of the idiot box and stared at Humphrey Bogart, my man. She was eating an apple.

'I want to know why you did it?' I asked.

'I needed the money.'

'Well, just how much was my soul worth?'

'Tsk. Tsk. Let's not be like that. Five hundred.'

'From who?'

'John Lee.'

Of course. Why in the hell? What in the world? Why in the devil hadn't the image of that fat idiot appeared on my screen. Of course. What had I been thinking of?

'I went to John and told him that I needed money. He said he would give it to me if I wrote the letter. It's that simple.'

'You have the abortion yet?'

'Day after tomorrow.'

'Did you tell dear John I wuzn' sleepin' with you?'

'No . . . Would you believe that?'

She was perfectly in control of everything, at ease with the world. I was the one who wasn't sure what was going on. I could not even look at her.

'Pardon me,' she said in Spanish. 'Have a drink?' I nodded.

She nodded in return and went off behind me somewhere in the kitchen, coming back with Old Grand-Dad, two glasses, and ice.

'You want to mix?' she asked. I shook my head no.

'How you gon' make out?' I asked.

'Okay,' she said.

'Five hundred ain' a whole lotta bread.'

'It'll do. When I'm well I'm gonna dance with Faye down at their club. That's where they're at now.'

How much she had changed since I had last seen her. She had aged so much that she hardly seemed like the same girl. She had decided just what she was going to do, and she was making the most of it. I wondered how many girls I had known who came up pregnant and decided that life was over and started screwing for a living?

'You know,' I said, 'You're carryin' my kid, an' I never went to bed with you.'

'So?' She smiled.

'I wuz wondrin' if I gave it to you by proxy or somethin'.'

'No. Nuthin' like that.'

We both had a good laugh at that. The drinks I had originally poured were now warming our midsections and loosening the initial discomfort. I dished out refills.

'You sold me out,' I told her.

'I had no choice,' she said softly.

'You're the one who had this crush on me . . . and you sold me out twice. Once to get rid of Lee. Once to get money from Lee.'

'Don't act hurt, Spade,' she said. 'Nothin' ever really hurt you. You came to my house with one thought. That was getting into bed with me. I got you into a corner before you got me on the sheets. You know how the game is played.'

I lit another cigarette. She was so right and so wrong at once. I wanted to scream and break the silence that surrounded us. Yes! We were out to use each other the first time, and you won, but not the second time. You were wrong the second time. You swung a long way below the belt when you took Crystal from me. I noticed that Debbie wasn't kidding me. She hadn't known how much Crys meant to me. It was all part of being Spade, the man with a death mask for a face. The man with a tombstone for a heart. The man without a solitary soul who knew how he felt, what he wanted, or how much he was alone. The silly actor who could never get off-stage long enough to tell the one girl who mattered that he loved her.

But John Lee knew.

John Lee had to have known how much Crystal meant to me, or else he could never have done such a perfect job of destroying me. He was in the street just like I was, and the only thing that kept him going had been Debbie. Even though he probably knew that he was buying her love. Bought love is better than no love at all.

John Lee knew! He must have seen me on the shore with Crys, and he wanted me out there trying to swim next to him. Too far out of reach to swim to safety or be rescued. Two men who could not survive. Two men in a cave-in with no air to breathe. Two men in the desert without water, watching the vultures circle overhead.

'Let's go to bed,' I said.

'What?'

'Let's go to bed,' I repeated.

I thought for a second that I was going to be Humphrey Bogart one more time. Then I realized that I was going to be Spade again. The truth was that Bogart and Spade never battled. It was always Spade and Eddie Shannon who fought for control. Deb followed me into the bedroom, whoever I was.

July 12, 1969 / New York City

I was on my way to work. The only exception was that for the first time I really felt like I knew what my job was. I could no longer be detached. There was nowhere else to look except into the eyes of the junkies and streetwalkers and pimps. They were my people. I felt that I was killing them just as surely as Smoky would if they didn't pay. I felt dead.

It wasn't even the same type of feeling I had before I met Crystal. I hadn't known what love was then. You can never miss something until you have experienced it and have to do without. I was now a man without love.

At about ten o'clock I stood in back of the church on 127th Street and Seventh Avenue in the park, waiting for one of my men to deliver. He would be the first of fifteen. The breeze came in with token force and swirled the charred ashes of a burned newspaper around my feet. When I looked up at the sound of footsteps, it wasn't Kenton, but Smoky.

'Happnin', Smoke?' I asked.

'Nuthin' much. i come tell you they ain' no work t'night. i try to call an' git you at home. zinari give a l'il thing in his crib startin' 'bout twelve.'

'Oh? That sounds pretty good.'

'yeah, man! menny girls, much tas', l'il smoke.'

'I think I'll make that,' I said, nodding.

'want me to pick you up?' Smoky asked.

'No, I'll be getting there a little late. Could you give me a lift home now?'

'sholy, sir. my limazine iz alwaze at yo' service.'

We hopped into the Cadillac, and Smoky burned rubber getting away from the curb at 127th Street. It would be good to do a little partying. Parties do a lot for the nerves.

Phase Two

Phase Two

John Lee died last night
July 13, 1969

The squat captain was speaking into the mesh microphone of his intercom.

'You can send Mr Watts in now, Sergeant,' he said.

'Right, sir,' came the reply.

The captain turned to his partner, who sat directly in front of the whirling, three-blade fan. The office was large and comfortable, but the air-conditioning was on the blink. The working officers, confined to paperwork in the bowels of the station on 18th Street, hurried through the technical chores in order to hit the street and work on unsolved cases that would take them near coffee houses and bars where they could sneak away for a hit.

'This guy is mighty cool,' the captain said. 'If anyone in the area can give us a hand with the case, it's probably him.'

There was a knock, and a shadow was seen crossing the frosted glass that spelled out the captain's name backwards.

'C'mon in, Watts,' the captain yelled. He was ripping the wrapper off a cigar with a mouthpiece.

The man came in. He was short and black, cigarette dangling from chapped lips, and sunglasses in place. He wore a light topcoat in spite of the merciless heat. There was a sport hat with a red feather on his head, and a wedding band on the smallest finger of his left hand.

'Have a seat, Watts,' the captain said, motioning toward the small swivel chair opposite him at the desk. The second officer turned and waved perfunctorily at the visitor but maintained his seat in front of the fan.

'Hot as hell today,' Watts said, sitting down.

The captain merely grunted.

'Watts,' the captain began, 'd'ja ever see this man before?'

Watts studied the enlarged photo of a black teenager. Yes, it was the baked-bean-colored character with a pimply face and large bone structure.

'Yeah,' Watts said.

The second officer turned his profile to the fan.

'Describe him,' Watts was asked.

The police guest removed the sunglasses and wiped a dirty handkerchief across his eyes.

'A guy named John Lee. He was 'bout eighteen. Six feet, maybe less, weigh 'bout two hundred poun's. Make that height closer to five-ten. He wuz fat. Lived somewhere aroun' 15th an' Seventh.'

'You said wuz,' the captain said, flattening his accent.

'I said wuz 'cauz he ain't,' Watts said. 'He's dead.'

The two policemen looked at each other furtively. The conversation skidded to a halt. The only audible sound was the clicking of the fan as it battled to get a breeze together for the perspiring officers.

'Captain Mason said that you might have some help with this one.'

Watts grimaced at the thought and pulled out a package of filter 100's and lit one up.

'What's the word?' the captain asked.

'They tell it like suicide,' Watts began. 'Accidental O. D.'

'I ain' here for no bullshit. We know it wuzn't that!'

The phone rang at the desk, and the captain picked it up. He introduced himself and then sat in silence for about a minute. He hung up and jabbed at the intercom button.

'Yes, sir?'

'Lay out fresh shirts for me an' Lieutenant Thomas. We'll be going out in about twenty minutes. Have the car ready, too.'

'Yes, sir.'

There was a click, and the captain turned his back to Watts.

72 | The Vulture

'We need some information,' Watts was told. 'Some names.'

The black man was already sweating. His eyes fidgeted in their sockets.

'Lee wuz dealin' pills an' a few reefers on the side. You remember a Puerto Rican named Isidro Valsuena?' Watts asked. The captain nodded. 'Well, his brothers always thought that Lee killed Isidro, and they been after Lee for 'bout six months. That's all I know.'

'Was Lee shootin' dope main line?'

'No chance.'

'Did Lee kill Isidro?'

'No chance.' Watts seemed confident of both of his answers.

'All right,' the captain said. 'Keep your eyes open.'

The black informer got up and put both his coat and sunglasses back in place. He and the captain both laughed at the last line.

The intercom buzzed, and the sergeant came on.

'Everything's ready, sir.'

'Good,' the captain said. He and the lieutenant got up to leave.

'Where to now?' the lieutenant asked.

'The woman that found the body called in. She said she was too sick to talk to anyone last night, but she's ready now.'

The two men went through the frosted-glass door of the office and up the stairs that led to the dressing room. They would shower and shave before interrogating the woman who found John Lee's corpse.

'What was that thing you and Watts were laughing about?' the lieutenant asked.

The captain smiled again. 'I told him to keep his eyes open. He's one of those phony blind men you see in the subway. He does it to support his dope habit.'

'I was looking for tracks when he took that coat off, but I didn't see any.'

'The smart junkies nowadays shoot in their thighs and in the veins under their balls. A whole lot of ways to do it.'

They turned into the dressing room, and the conversation was turned off as they faced the heat and steam from the showers.

'I can use a cold shower,' the captain said.

'Yeah. This is a filthy city.'

'Bite yo' tongue.' The captain laughed. 'You s'pose to "give a damn."'

Junior Jones

July 17, 1968

'Anybody get caught?' I asked, dragging on a cigarette.

'Naw,' Cooly reported.

'Good.' I laughed, and so did everyone else.

My laugh was one of relief more than anything else. I knew I had a lot of faint hearts running with me. If anyone had gotten caught, it was a sure thing that the Man would've been knocking on my door.

'You sho save Lee's ass.' Cooly giggled. Cooly was my main man, really the only cat that I could count on. He and I had been hanging together since junior high, when stealing beer and cigarettes was a kick. I was closer to him than any of the other cats, but it still got on my nerves when people commented that he and I were both in charge of the group. I wanted everyone to know that it was me all by myself, just like it was Spade all by himself. I knew that there was really no way to have a gang and be a loner, but cats got over by themselves, like Spade, and then seemed to hold check over an entire area.

'Where'd Lee go?' I asked Cooly.

'I think he wuz headin' fo' Chelsea,' Cooly drawled. 'I seen the Man gainin' on him near the co'ner, but when the cah blew up, the cops hit the brakes an' Lee wuz runnin' jus' that much fastuh.'

'What the Man do?' I asked.

'Well, when the cah went up, they turn aroun' an' try to git back to it, but wudn' no way. The damn thing wuz hot as hell. Dey lookin' sad as hell, boy. Whut dey gon' tell the boss?' Cooly started laughing again.

I scanned the faces of the group. There were a few Puerto Rican cats, but we were primarily Bloods. There were about fifteen of us in all. Spade called us the Junior Jones boys. To call us a gang isn't entirely right, although I say it sometimes. There aren't really any more gangs in the city. It was just a thing where we all generally got high together and made sure that we didn't get bunted by a lot of goofs and old head dealers.

What had happened to Cooly and me in Harlem had been enough to tell us that we weren't as hip as we thought. The two of us got out of the IND train at 125th Street and came upstairs on Morningside Avenue. The directions we had been given were hazy, but we figured we could find our man. We went through the projects between Eighth and Seventh Avenues and came out on 127th Street.

'Nex' block up,' I told Cooly. 'If we don't see nuthin' that looks like whut Tiger said, we got to check somethin' else.'

Cooly nodded agreement. This was about a year ago, I guess. School was still in session, and a guy told us how we could get some really hip pills. Neither Cooly nor I had ever had any before, but it seemed like the next thing to try. I knew that a lot of the cats from the 17th Street park were talking about 'ups' and 'downs' and a lot of other stuff. We had run through wine and beer and cough-syrup. We had put glue down as a bad ride when I damn near fell off a roof after sniffing. So when Tiger put the word on us about pills, we were interested. We told him most of the cats who were trading on the block had gotten busted and asked him where we could cop. He told us to take the A train to 125th Street, walk to 128th and Seventh Avenue, where we would see an old amputee selling pencils and comics. We were to ask him where we could start flying, and he would tell us where to meet the dealer. The dealer met his load in a different spot every day.

As Cooly and I crossed 128th Street, we saw the old man. He was seated under an awning with the pencils and junk. We came up on him warily. As I look back on it anyone who saw us must have read the guilt on our faces.

'Batman! Superman! Archie! School supplies,' the old man said.

'We want to fly,' I said out of the corner of my mouth.

'Oh?' The old man looked at me rather sadly. 'There's the park behind the church one block down. A guy sitting in the swing with a blue straw hat – well, that's the pilot.' He managed a grin. 'Batman?'

Cooly and I turned and headed toward the park, walking south on Seventh. I didn't even look back at the old man. He was nothing but a shell. It looked like some kind of bug had gotten inside of him and eaten all of his bones and everything that had given him structure. He was burned a crisp brown from the sun, and his face was covered with hair, most of it gray. His clothes had only been shreds of torn this and that with suede patches sewn over the open pants legs that would have exposed stumps. He sat there eternally, from the looks of things. The wrinkled funny books and pencils were his only company. At a time like this, when the sun rested and ended the heat, the old man probably praised God.

Cooly and I waded through the little kids as we entered the park. There were the older cats playing ball and girls playing records and doing various dances. The guy we were looking for sat swinging slowly in the shade of a tree. It looked as though he had reserved a section. There was no one near him.

'Whuss happnin'?' he asked as we approached.

'Nuthin' too tough,' I said.

'Whuss the word, fellas? Batman *and* Superman, or choose?'

'Batman.'

He reached into an inside pocket of his lightweight jacket and pulled out a carrying case for his sunglasses. He forked a cellophane packet from the case with his index finger and thumb and replaced the holder.

'Ten dollars,' he said, throwing the filter cigarette he had been smoking to the ground and squashing it with the heel of his shoe.

I handed him a ten-dollar bill, and he passed the pills.

'Have a good flight.' He grinned. I grinned as best I could.

I shoved the packet into my back pocket, and Cooly and I headed back for the park entrance. Before we could get there, we were stopped.

'Thass good right there,' someone said from behind us. 'Now, don' neither a yawl turn 'roun. Jus han' the pills an' yo money. What I got here is a .32-caliber automatic that you can jus' think uv as a gun fo short.'

I reached into my hip pocket and handed the pills back. Out of the corner of my eye I could see a short black with a process palming a gun, with the nose buried in Cooly's back.

'Money. Money too,' he said.

I squeezed a couple of dollars backward, and he snatched them.

'Now, yawl take off walkin' slow. I'm gon' watch till you git to the corner, an' if you turn aroun', you dead.' He paused. 'It's been a business doin' pleasure wit yawl. Come agin.'

We walked with our hands at our sides, and I started counting. Just after we turned the corner I looked back to see if the thief was still in view, but he had vanished. I was sure that someone in the park had noticed, but no one was looking our way. What was even more strange was that the guy who sold us the pills was gone too. The only reminder of him was the swing, still swaying slightly. I ran back to the entrance of the park, but there was no trace of anything. We had been had.

From that time on, any pills that I bought were from cats in the neighborhood. Cooly and I were hanging with a bunch of kids who were as tired of getting bad stuff as we were. Most of the time the pills were flour and the smoke hadn't been cleaned. Because of the group, many times I had been able to get high when I was flat. The fourteen and fifteen-year-olds would do a lot to be tight with me and Cooly, just as I did to be tight with Spade and I.Q. Soon after the group began, however, Isidro, the P.R., started selling stuff. It was the beginning of 1968. Most of the big-time dealers didn't want to be bothered with smoke and pills. The first reason was that the big money was in cocaine and skag. The second reason was that mainly the younger cats smoke and pop pills, and a young cat will blow your cool when the Man applies the heat. When we found out that Isidro was dealing, we figured we were set. There would be a man on the block, and no more paying older guys to go to Fox Avenue and Tinton Avenue in the Bronx.

Isidro proved to be just as bad as everyone else. He sold us smoke that had so much sand in it nobody could get high. He gave us low-count smoke when we did get a decent bag. Maybe you could roll ten joints for a nickel bag. The pills were messed up too, and some were packed with less than others. For over six months we took that. We took it because every time we complained, the stuff would be better for a while. Then we would get beaten for a good night, like Friday, and he would have it all made back.

The end of June was when John Lee came on the scene. I was in the 13th Street park drinking beer at a card table. John walked up and sat down.

'Whuss the word, Lee?' I asked.

'I need to talk to you, man. I think we might be able to help each other out.'

'Howzat?' I asked. 'You want some beer?'

'Naw.' Lee sat and wiped the sweat off his face. 'I'm gonna be dealin' startin' tomorra, an' I thought we might be able to work sum'thin out. I know Seedy been fuckin' wit' you an' yo boys, an I know you don' dig it.'

I took a swig of the beer. 'What's the play?'

'Today is Wednesday the twenty-sixth, right? Well, I got a l'il smoke for t'night, but I rilly won't be togethuh till tomorrow. I wan' to know if I can count on you cats to deal wit' me. I got a good play from the boats, so you won' be cheated. How much you want, and how often?'

'We'll deal with you,' I said. 'Tomorrow night, not much. My boys iz primarily git-high-on-the-weekend men, you know. But the las day a school is tomorrow, so after that we'll be tightnin' up regular ... What time on Friday, an' where?'

'Early Friday. 'Bout five meet me here. I'm havin' a l'il gig Friday night. You invited.'

'Bring about ten nickels for smoke, ten red devils or purple hearts. Thass a hundred right there.'

'I'll have some smoke tomorra. Cheebo an' Panam Red. Treys, if you want.'

'You already sound like a goddamn commercial, man.' I laughed.

'Whut you say?'

'I'm tight till Friday ... Hey, wait!' I called Lee back as he drifted across the park. 'How you know Seedy been buntin' my boys?'

'Aw, he wuz high a night or two ago an' started runnin' off at the mouth about blowin' yawl's mind wit' weak shit an' that all yawl had wuz psychological highs.'

'When does he ship?' I asked.

'His shipments hit on Sundays,' Lee said. 'Somewhere near Eleventh Avenue and the pier. Maybe 9th Street.'

'How much?'

'He pulls off about sixteen hundred dollars a week raw,' John said. 'Including the coke an' heroin.'

'He ain' pullin' nuthin' this Sunday, 'cause we gonna hit him for alla his shit,' I said.

'You got a buyer if you come up with it.' Lee smiled.

I didn't say anything else. Lee waddled off across the

park, and I tried to figure out ways to catch Isidro on Sunday night.

'Hey!' I said suddenly. 'Where's Ricky Manning?' In exploring the faces of the group, I had somehow gotten lost in thought. I suddenly realized that someone was missing.

'He's wit' I.Q.,' Cooly reported.

'I.Q. iz aroun'?'

'Yeah. He wuz stannin' by the bar, but you wuz probably too busy to notice when you went by.' Everybody laughed again.

Lee had been true to his word. Friday afternoon we met him in the park at five, and as far as I could see, the pills and the smoke were both good. I ended up with some reefer.

Everything had been running smoothly for three weeks, until tonight. Lee would show up on Mondays, Wednesdays, and Fridays. We met him at a table in the park and got our stuff. Then it was every man for himself.

Tonight when Lee showed up, there was almost an omen of bad luck in the air. There were too many new cats in the way – guys from Chelsea Houses and other men I didn't know. Before anyone could get together and buy their stuff, everything was interrupted by the arrival of the Man, live and in living color from the Tenth Precinct. The prowl car hit the brakes on the corner of 13th Street and Ninth Avenue. The two cops hit the sidewalk, and everybody who had congregated to buy a high found running more interesting. The group meeting broke up and turned into a track meet, with John Lee, bag of dope in hand, leading in the hundred-yard dash. Several of us who hadn't heard the opening gun were caught in the rear of the pack. We ran behind the park maintenance house and back through the same entrance the cops used. When I arrived at the corner where the idling patrol car sat, I turned and saw the two cops directing each other in terms of who they should try to catch. They were at the other end of the softball field with their backs away from me. Parked directly in front of their wagon was a New York City Housing Authority maintenance truck with what looked like the day's refuse from some set of apartments. On the tailgate was a can of gasoline that was leaking onto the street. I pulled the can out and dumped the gas into the front seat of the copmobile, backed off, and lit a match. I heard the dispatcher's voice reach out for me as I threw the match and fled toward the docks. The car ignited with a roar and a lot of crackling like a dead Christmas tree. Just as I turned for the last glimpse of the Man's reaction, there was an explosion. Chips of metal and paint decorated Ninth Avenue. I ran down to Tenth Avenue and lay under a car away from the streetlamps, panting for breath.

Once I grabbed my wind, I took my shirt off and left it under the car. I knew that at least two or three old white checker players had dug on my red Banlon. I doubt if much more than that could be identified. Until the car went up, all the activity was at the other end of the playground.

I circled the neighborhood and turned finally into the park on 17th Street and Eighth Avenue. I knew that eventually the guys would come in. Less than half an hour after the raid, we were all huddled together again.

I lit another cigarette. Cooly and the rest of the guys were still discussing the speed I had when I passed I.Q. and Ricky at the bar.

'I.Q. wuz there, huh?' I asked Cooly.

'He seen it all.'

If I.Q. had seen everything, then I was sure that Spade would hear about it. Spade was the man around the block. The guy in the area who can beat anybody at any time and get any chick he wants. I wanted Spade to hear that I burned the cop machine so that he could tell everybody I was coming to get him. Spade told all the older cats that I was going to be the man. He would come up on us in the park sometimes when we were getting high, and all the guys would ask him about the days when the Berets were running the neighborhood. It was surprising how they talked to him like he was an old man, even though he was just a little older than we were. We all wanted to know about the time when everybody was in a gang. At that time anybody who was anybody was falling off a corner and kicking so much ass that nobody could keep score. It took a whole lot of heart to walk out on the block and get high with nobody to back you up. Everybody knew about Spade, though. He had been his own gang. Now, he said, the block had been turned over to white hippies and young faggots who couldn't tell a gang from a tea party. I always wished I had been on the scene when Spade was taking over. Me and Spade would have been too much to handle.

'You got time, Junior,' Spade would say. 'Jus' lay an' dig whut iz an' whut ain't, an' when you think you time iz here, don't ask no questions, jus make you move. Even if you got to move on me to git whut you're after. It ain't how old you are, it's how well you carry the years you have.'

I was waiting. I was waiting for the days when the older guys on the block who were running things now started to settle back and fade inside the bars. Then the street would belong to me and those who ran with me. There would be no more Spade. There would be no more of the wild rumors like there were now. John Lee was supposed to be the new man since Spade wasn't on the corner anymore. All Spade would have to do would be to snap his fingers, and John would be decoration on the stage again. When Spade walked down the block in the summertime and everybody was on the stoop, you could tell. The look in his eyes, maybe, or the way he dressed. He didn't say much, only nodded to the people he knew, but there was a certain thing happening, and you could tell if you were there. The way he moved said that the Spade was back and still the man, and anybody who didn't dig his thing could settle it in the middle of Ninth Avenue. Very few people stepped out with him, and he was paid his due respect as a man who had come the hard way. I was going to have my respect too.

'You guys gimme yo bread,' I said to the group. 'Me an Cooly gonna fin' Lee an' git the stuff.' I looked at my watch. 'It's 'bout nine-thirty, an' we gon' be back inna hour.' I looked up and down 17th Street. 'I want you cats travlin' light. No more than three cats togethuh. If you see the Man, you jus' came outside. When yawl see Ricky, tell 'im whuss happnin'.'

A hat was passed up with everybody's bills. Cooly took the money and put it in his wallet. The hat was passed back through the crowd.

'Look here,' I said before we broke, 'if the Man stops you, you don't give out no lip. Ansuh whatever he wants to know an' tell 'im you been watchin' TV an' stay on the block. Stay away from the 13th Street park an' stay in the open where a lotta old people can see you. That way the Man can't rough you up an' claim you fell while you tellin' all you know.'

The crowd started out of the park when I finished. Cooly and I strolled down 17th Street toward Ninth Avenue. We acted as though we owned the sidewalk. Even though it was going on ten o'clock, the block was still lit up with domino games, and crapshooting was on full blast. The Puerto Rican boys on the stoops were drinking beer and rapping to their little painted women. When we passed, they waved and whispered. I grinned to myself. I like to see them spreading the word about me. Soon everyone would have to know me. It would be an unwritten law.

The gambling had started right after work, and now only the beer cans and cake wrappers could say for sure how long José, the store owner, had worked to keep the games going. They kept him rich when they gambled all night, and he didn't give a damn if he had to do a little extra sweeping every morning. Most of the storekeepers didn't want the men gambling anywhere near their place, because the old ladies complained and went elsewhere to buy their cat food. José evidently had no concern for old ladies and their cats.

As we moved closer to Ninth Avenue, the sounds of the night took on a Latin beat. Eddie Palmieri and Joe Bataan were the music heroes of the neighborhood. The Met game was coming out of some window or other, and the Mets were getting their asses kicked again. The blasts coming from off the rooftops told us that a few Spanish boys were having a 'love-in' under the sky. The old ladies crowded the sidewalks in folding chairs and sped through Spanish in no time at all. All I could ever catch was Puerto Rico and something-something 'MeeAmi.' They could rap a whole book while I hung back trying to translate the first word they had flown over.

Aretha was coming from a window. She was singing 'Do-Right Woman,' and for a second I thought I heard Isidro's voice. Every time I heard that side I was reminded of Isidro, because I had been sitting in Tommy's Coffee House the day after school listening to it when Seedy barged in. I was surprised when he walked in, because I had only talked to Lee the day before and found out about my new deal.

I was drinking a Coke with a little rum Tommy had thrown in, and there was my girl Aretha building the atmosphere. It was early afternoon, and very few people were up and about. None of the chicks that I wanted to talk to were around the place, so I kept the back table busy and played sides.

'I wanna talk to you, man,' Isidro said, dropping into the seat opposite me.

'Talk,' I said. From the broken English I hadn't had to look up to identify the speaker. I was cursing under my breath for being caught off guard.

'Who you gize gon' buy you stuff from? Me o' dis odder cat?'

'We gonna deal with Lee,' I said.

'Why?'

'You know good and damn well why! You been beatin' the hell outta us for too fuckin' long! Dirty smoke! Bad pills! Fuck you!' I looked around, but there was no one near enough to hear us. Tommy was watching from up front, however.

Isidro made a gesture with the middle finger of his right hand. His eyes widened, and he pulled closer to me across the table. I could smell the wine on his breath and the odor of coffee.

'Look 'ere. I jus' wan you to know somsing. I heard 'bout dis sheet you wan pull on me. It ain' gon work. Oye? I wan you to know I ketch one pussy near my sheepment, I gonna keel 'im. I don give a fuck you got Spade to back you up. A boolet can kill Spade like any man. I'm gon carry a gun from now on. I can kill too!' Isidro leaned back in the chair. I didn't move or change expression, but my mind was working fast. How could Isidro have found out what I was going to do so fast?

I talked to Lee about it yesterday, I was thinking.

Tommy came over and asked if I wanted anything. He was talking directly about Isidro. I told him that everything was all right.

I only mentioned things vaguely to Lee, my mind went on. Then I brought it up yesterday afternoon to Cooly, and we talked about it somewhat last night. Then I told the gang my plan, and we agreed on it. We were going down to the docks about three Sunday morning when Isidro left to pick up his stuff. At least we would follow him. That's where we thought he got it. Then we were going to jump him from behind. How could he know about it the next morning? Who squealed?

'I don' know whut you're talkin' 'bout,' I told Isidro.

'I'm talkin' 'bout you motherfuckuhs tryin' to take my stuff. Eef you think you can make eet, try eet. I'm gon' kill somebody.'

'Look, man. You mad 'cause somebody beat yo' racket. Fuck you! I don' need you.'

'You don' need me now, but eef somsing happens to the fat one, don' come back to me. Comprende?'

'I dig you, amigo,' I said. 'But if Lee gets busted behind some mysterious phone call, you gon' get picked up the same way. Do *you* comprende?'

Isidro left in a hurry, and I sat in the booth trying to figure out who had turned me in. The logical suspect would be one of the Puerto Rican boys who ran with me, but that was too obvious. It had to be a brother – a twentieth-century Uncle Tom. The setup had been good. We could have robbed Seedy and taken the stuff to Lee. He could have kept us high for a while, and we would have had Seedy up Shit Creek! Now it was the other way around. I was in trouble, because I had to figure out who the rat was. If I didn't, something else might happen, and I could get blown away, and we all end up in jail or juvenile court at least.

I met Cooly about six and told him that the hit was off. I didn't tell him why, but I know he got the idea that somebody was onto our setup.

'What if Lee ain' in Chelsea?' I asked Cooly.

'We'll find 'im. He know we lookin' fo' him.' Cooly gave me a thick smile. 'Where yo min' at t'night, man? Clarice ketch you yet?'

'What you mean?'

'You been in yo' own worl' all night. Daydreamin', o' just heavy thinkin'?'

'It ain' no bitch,' I told Cooly. 'Jus' heavy thinkin'.'

We passed the projects on Ninth Avenue, walking up-town. The projects stretch from 15th Street and Ninth to 19th and Ninth. Across the street from the projects, on the northeast corner of 19th Street, I could see that the lights were out in my apartment. It meant that my mother was out somewhere, either with my baby brother and the neighbor's boy, or alone while somebody watched the brat. My older brother was in the Navy.

Across the street under the low-rise apartment buildings, the young whiteys were drinking beer and macking while they listened to WABC radio. It seemed like they drank enough beer to wash out the whole goddamn neighborhood. The way things lined up, God put black people on earth to blow bush and take a lot of shit, and white people were for drinking beer and dying of boredom.

My thoughts changed to John Lee again. Until he started dealing, he had been just another nowhere cat. The black cats had been going to Brooklyn and Harlem or buying their stuff in school. All at once John was on the street with all kinds of stuff. Most of the older cats said that they knew where John got his supply, but I was sure that they didn't know. John was a smart cat. He was seldom early or late. He seldom carried any more than he would deal. He found out in advance what you wanted and disappeared right after he gave you what you ordered.

John carried Red Birds, Yellow Jackets, Purple Hearts, and Blue Heavens in quantity. They were the genuine pops that everybody had heard of. If you wanted, he could get some depressants, or 'downs,' but black people don't dig that too tough. That stuff was for the hippie poets and folk singers who liked to go around singing the blues and talking about the total destruction of mankind and all that wild shit. They liked to feel like they carried the weight of the world on their shoulders. They convinced themselves when they got high that the message in their poems and flimsy melodies were the true salvation of civilization. It was always that nobody would listen to them. I guess that's why they wore their hair long and had freak-out sessions with psychedelic music. They felt that they might as well cram as much of life as possible into their few remaining days on this doomed planet. You could always hear them ranting and screaming when you got out of the subway at West 4th Street. I figured it was a lot of bullshit and another excuse for lazy cats and chicks to get down without getting married, and stay high all the time without ever getting a job.

John's dealing made him a big thing on the block. He arrived during a time when there was basically no man on the avenue. John started dealing at the end of June. Spade hadn't been around for a long time. You heard less and less about him. The arrival of John Lee prompted more talk. The arrival of a new adventurer. When I was twelve, the man had been Hicks, the leader of the Chelsea Berets. Spade was fifteen or sixteen and saved Hicks's life. That meant that the man owed his life. Spade captured the neighborhood. The women dug him because he never said anything to them. The older cats were scared of him because he knew karate. The old people hated him because he didn't have any manners, and his parents couldn't control him. He was so slick, though, that he never gave them any real reason to call the cops.

I thought about how Lee came to fame, and I was almost mad. I made a quick decision that I would be the man soon. I was going to deal. Then I would walk down the block, and all the girls would dig the things I did, and all the cats would stay their distance. I was going to be the 'somebody.'

Just as the word 'somebody' was repeating itself in my head, Cooly spotted Lee. We had passed the projects and all the stores between 19th Street and 25th Street. We were walking through the Chelsea Houses, another group of apartment buildings. Lee was sitting between two other cats in the play area peered down on by two high-rise apartments. He was dressed in the familiar green trench coat. There was a can of beer in his hand and a brown paper bag protruding from his pocket.

'Happnin', Lee?' I asked as Cooly and I approached.

Lee grinned his same moon-faced grin and slapped me five.

'Juneyuh,' he said, as though he still hadn't caught his breath, 'I wuz jus' tellin' these cats whut you did. That was nice as hell.'

'You the one burned the cop car?' one of the cats asked. There was a look of admiration on his face.

'He did it,' Cooly drawled. I said nothing. I just sat back and listened to Cooly and Lee describe the thing. They had to be exaggerating, because both of them were running in the opposite direction. The net result was a picture of me looking like a cross between Napoleon Solo and James Bond. Lee handed me his can of beer, and I lit up a Kool.

'I tol' you,' Lee concluded. 'It wuz jus' like the time Spade put that stretch a wire across the roof and tripped Happy Stick Kinkaid. The sonuvabitch broke his arm in two a three places and wuzn' on the block for months.' Lee stopped and related everything to me. 'Happy Stick was this whitey who tried to ketch me an' Spade allatime when we drank wine and smoked on the roof. That motherfuckuh wuz fixed good!'

There was a pause. Across the park square, teenagers loafed and pretended to wrestle so that they could sneak in a few public feels. The small kids ran around and did whatever they damn well pleased, while the oldsters listened to the Mets and played checkers.

'Can we git our stuff?' I asked Lee. I handed him the can of beer.

'Sure.' He looked around to see who was watching and then took the brown paper bag out of his pocket. He placed it on the bench between us and slid several packets of pills and small manila envelopes to me. Cooly pocketed the pills and the grass and handed John his green. I noticed that he didn't even bother to count it.

'Mañana,' I told Lee as Cooly and I departed.

Lee and the two other cats waved.

'Hey, Junior!' Lee called. 'Anybody get grabbed?'

'Naw, man,' I assured him. 'Rest easy.'

The thought of Lee hung in my mind. His fat face had been a picture of worry, perspiration dripping down his nose. Some of the Juniors called him and Spade the 'Dynamic Duo,' but I really didn't know why. Spade was six feet and muscular. Lee was short and fat. The best thing that could be said for Lee was that he smiled a lot. Spade was a very noncommittal type of cat. He rarely smiled. When he did laugh, it wasn't because everyone saw something that was funny. The older cats said that when Spade smiled, it generally meant that he had thought of another way to give somebody a hard way to go.

Cooly and I slid back into the park and rationed out the stuff we bought. Almost none of the guys had left the park, even though I told them to. I disregarded it because I had so many things on my mind.

'You gittin' high t'night, o' whut?' Cooly asked.

I looked up, and everyone was gone except us.

'Yeah, man. I got some smoke and some wine down in Tommy's cellar. I'm gon' make it down there later. I got some things to think about.'

'I kin dig that,' Cooly said. 'I git that way.'

'I'll ketch you later,' I told him.

Cooly probably knew what was going on. We had been hanging out together long enough for him to have an idea what was on my mind. There was no big issue as I could see. I was just restless. I wanted to be bigger and older and more important. I didn't care about controlling the Juniors, because they didn't really hold a lot of check. We didn't fight. We got high. I kept remembering back to the party. That was when I got jolted into another plan. Lee had invited me to this gig when I told him I would deal with him. It was the end of June, after all the high schools had closed for the summer.

John Lee's Party
June 28, 1968 / 8:30 P.M.

John's party was on the twenty-eighth of June. I remember so well because it was also my older brother's birthday and my mother didn't want me to go out. She figured he might call or something, and she'd want me to be around so that we could get on the phone like one big happy family. Matt took that seriously, because he considered himself the head of the household. I told her that I had some partying to do and not to wait up. I took off with her sitting on the sofa tuning up to cry.

I walked into the liquor store on 18th Street and Eighth Avenue about eight-thirty. The storekeeper looked at me for a second.

'Can I help you?' he asked.

'Bacardi Light in the pint,' I said through a cloud of cigarette smoke.

He reached behind him and plucked a pint of the clear liquid from a lower shelf. He reached for a bag on top of the cash register. I could see the big German shepherd that guarded the place standing at attention at the end of the counter.

'May I see some identification, please,' I was asked.

'Sure.' I went through the ritual of fumbling through my pockets and my wallet before coming up empty-handed. The dog moved closer.

'Gee! Looks like I didn't bring it with me.' I paused for a

second. 'Look, I always buy from the older cat. He don' ask me for nuthin'.'

The man began to chuckle a bit as he handed me the bottle.

'See that you bring your draft card in or something next time.'

'I'll do that,' I said.

I was wearing a lightweight spring jacket, and I hooked the bottle into the inside pocket and strolled to the park on 17th Street and took a seat.

Once inside the park, I felt better. The sun dimly watched everything progress slowly with its one hot eye. Up and down the street the night people were starting their rounds. Career women and just plain laboring hags staggered home from their nine-to-five with bundles cramming their arms and chests. The calls always started around this time. The music and the gambling that the P.R. people dig so much was off and running. A Parks Department maintenance man was picking up pieces of broken bottles and beer cans. Even the breeze seemed to know it was Friday.

I wondered idly what the gang would be into. Friday night, so they were probably somewhere high. The broads were out of school too, so they might have taken the whole thing down to the dock, where they could sip beer and smoke in peace. The broads would go anywhere as long as they could lay all over everybody and get dicks hard without going too far. Maybe there was a dance in Chelsea. I hadn't even bothered to find out the schedule. For a second I wanted to be with them, because I didn't know what John's party would be like. I knew that a lot of the girls would be my age, but they were always looking for cats older than themselves. What the hell? If it was as dark as I figured it would be, all raps would be the same. I opened the rum and took a swig. It burned a bit and left a sour aftertaste on the edge of my tongue. I was tempted to tip into José's and buy a Coke to mix with it.

One of the Puerto Rican boys came over and sat next to me.

'Hey, man! I'm su'prise to see you over here,' he said.

'Why?'

'I been tol' you at war wit' Seedy the smoke man.'

'You musta heard that from Seedy,' I said.

'Whuss wit' you an' him?'

'I ain' in no sweat, man. Seedy got tight jaws 'cause I ain' dealin' wit him no more.'

The Puerto Rican was carrying a bottle of Amigo in a moist paper bag. He took a large swallow and handed it to me. I handed him the rum, and he nodded.

'I heard you wuz gonna hit him an' he got wize.'

I didn't comment on that.

'He started carryin' a gun. 'Zat true?'

'Iz whut true?'

He took another straight shot and handed me the rum.

'Look, man, you wuz dealin' wit' Seedy until two days ago, right? Now you wit' John Lee.'

I nodded both times.

'There mus' be a reason you deal wit' one man an' then another.'

'Whussat gotta do wit' me hittin' Seedy an' him totin' a piece a thunder?'

'Ef you got another dealer, Seedy ain' necessary anymore, an' eef you theenk you wuz cheated, then you might wan' revenge.'

'Jus' like that?' I asked.

'Sure.' He took another swig from the wine bottle and grimaced when he set it back between his feet. 'This iz tough shit.' I nodded.

The thing to do was to play it cool. Seedy was a junky, and

it was his word against mine. The redeeming factor for me was the three Spanish boys I had who hung out with me. That meant I couldn't be all anti-Spic. Any sign I made that hinted that what I was supposed to have done was more than idle chatter would get me a visit from a few razor carriers that I knew.

It was an unwritten law. If a man puts a contract on another man, he really signs one on the whole community, because that's who his new enemies are. I had been caught putting a price on Isidro, and now the shoe was on the other foot. There were bounty hunters looking for me, and the bounty was community commendation. The only real factor was proof. That and my closeness with Spade kept the noose from around my neck. Anything that happened would be traced by him.

'I got to make it, man,' I told the Puerto Rican.

'You take it easy,' he said.

'I got to.'

There was nobody there when I got to John's house. It was about nine-fifteen, and I had stalled as long as I could. Debbie Clark answered the door and let me in. John was in the back filling the bathtub with beer. It appeared that since John's folks were taking a little vacation, John was setting up a real domestic thing. I lit up a cigarette and parked near the record player, shuffling through the sides and putting what I wanted on the turntable.

Already the fan was losing its battle with the heat. The breeze I had detected earlier had evidently thought better of it.

There was a heavy accent on atmosphere. Incense was burning in every corner. The only light in the front of the house was a table lamp with a red bulb, and that was nearly nothing. For a minute I thought we were going to have a psychedelic thing with filtered light and Jimi Hendrix.

Anybody who walks into one of those things, high or not, gets his mind blown.

At about ten-thirty the party was together. All the names in the neighborhood had shown about ten or so. Spade, Afro, I.Q., Websta, and everybody else had a corner or a seat. They had all brought taste, and for a minute I wished I had brought a bottle to contribute.

Evidently I had done something wrong with my head. Either I had no business mixing rum and wine and beer, or I had no business smoking half a pack of cigarettes in three hours. I had stumbled through the back of the group trying to make it to the john. There were very few people present now who were not partying. At first there had been some standing around and rapping, but that had disintegrated with a few drinks. Spade had disappeared altogether with his girl. I figured if I was going to get myself together to dance once or twice, best I not feel like the last chapter of what's the use. A couple of the younger girls had been giving me that look. I reached the edge of the dance floor and ran head on into Debbie Clark. She was leaning at an odd angle against the bathroom door and smelled like she had just bathed in a bottle of overproof rum. Her eyes lit up when I nudged her.

'Junior,' she slurred. She looked at me wide-eyed and giggled.

'Hi, Debbie,' I said slowly.

'C'mere, Juney. C'mere, baby,' she said.

'I want to get by.'

'Not now, baby, c'mere.'

I was already close enough to take a bite out of her shoulder, but evidently she was having trouble focusing. She was wearing something black and flimsy, the kind of thing with the two straps over the shoulders. Her breasts were half hanging out, and her lipstick was smeared and messy. The eye makeup was mixing with her sweat and running down her chin.

She reached for me, and before I could react, she had pulled my head down to hers, and the smell of her breath was hot as well as foul. Then her lips were on mine, and her tongue was pushing my lips away. I was so surprised that I lurched backward and shoved her against the wall. Her eyes were at first wide with surprise, and then she slid down the wall pointing at me and laughing. I couldn't help but throw my hands to my ears. Her laugh was loud, piercing, hysterically accusing. She kept pointing at me and stammering drunkenly.

'Juney ain' never been kissed,' she shrieked. The thought of that seemed to be more than her mind was ready for.

I dived at the open bathroom door and locked it behind me. The light sparkling off the soaking beer cans in the tub seemed to cool my burning face. I looked in the mirror and saw someone else. All that I could really distinguish through the tears seemed to be a painting of me when I was five and afraid of thunder. The salt from my eyes trickled down my cheeks and into my mouth. The mixture on my tongue was a combination of sweat, beer, rum, wine, and embarrassment. I fell on my knees and vomited into the bowl, while still more tears streaked my face and dried my mind.

I watched Cooly disappear around the corner and lit a cigarette. I could still feel the cold shivers that came every time I remembered the unpleasant party thing. When I came out of the bathroom Debbie was already stretched out on the bed in the bedroom, but even as I managed to smile my way through the crowd and mumble about what a great sense of humor she had, there were some people who looked at me rather oddly. I hadn't done anything wrong, the eyes seemed to admit, but what a hell of an embarrassment.

August 29, 1968

The summer just seemed to fade away. It always seems as though the things you enjoy last no time at all. I widened the gap between myself and the gang. I still went around to get high every now and then, but there was no more to it than that. I didn't feel up to the lies or the highs anymore. Once we had all sat out in the park and told tales about fantastically built chicks that wanted no more from life than to get screwed over and over by us live and in living color. I was no longer able to put myself in those lies, because I had been blown away. I had had a chance with Debbie Clark, one of the finest little asses in the neighborhood, and just because she was high, I pushed her away. I couldn't understand why people got girls high on purpose to screw them, and when my opportunity came, Debbie disgusted me. None of the people at the party had paid any attention to Debbie, because she was drunk, and none of the gang knew about it, because they hadn't been there, but I had been there and I still had my memory.

'Junior, is that you?'

'Yeah. It's me. What'choo doin' up?'

'Just having some coffee. Come in here.'

I walked into the kitchen. My mother sat in her bathrobe at the dinner table. Her hair was in rollers, and there was cream on her face and forehead.

'It's almost two o'clock. Now I told you to come in earlier this evening because you have to start getting back into that routine. There will be school next week, as far as we know. There's no use in you counting on this teacherstrike thing for keeping you up until all hours of the night. Remember, Bobby will be going to school this time.'

I sat down opposite her and lit a cigarette.

'I guess you jus' ain't gonna listen to nothing that I say, is that it?' She got up and went over to the cupboard and found two cups. She placed one in front of me and then poured both cups full.

'How come you can't say anything?' she asked.

'I'm tired.'

'I guess so. Runnin' the streets until all hours of the night like I don't tell you different. Don't half eat the food that's fixed for you. Livin' off beer, and cigarette-smokin' like you grown. Wouldn't do no good for me to tell you to do this or that. You so grown. I done tol' you, though. Don't have the Man knockin' on my door when you get picked up, 'cause I will swear that I never heard of you, you hear?'

'I hear you.' I sipped the steaming coffee. I heard her, and the people in the next block probably heard her. I had heard her before, too. She had no real time or energy to worry about where I was or what I was doing. She didn't know what she would have me do if I told her I would do anything that she wanted.

All she really knew was what she didn't want. She didn't want me in the Navy like Matt. Each day she secretly expected a letter from Uncle Sam so that she could cry some more. The letter would be headed 'We regret to inform you . . .' and she would burst into tears and run across the hall for consolation. I knew that Mrs Boone, our neighbor, must hate to see her coming. Always another tale of woe. My mother was a one-woman soap opera. She cried and cried, always on the brink of tears, but no matter what happened, she would always fall back on that same weak story about God testing her.

She couldn't tell me what to do, because she wasn't doing anything for her own peace of mind. She didn't want me to be like my father, who died when his kidneys and liver rejected his style of life. His heavy drinking had been the cause of his death and had led to a nervous breakdown for my mother. At

Junior Jones | 99

sixteen, I had been fatherless for almost eight years. The sign on the tombstone said that my father had been forty-three when he died. I remembered a man of sixty, complete with wrinkles and white hair. Alcohol had turned big patches of his skin to a bluish-purple. What the sign in the graveyard did not say was that when my father died he left behind a woman with a third son in her belly, and two older sons who had no reason to respect anything at all. It did not say that my father had been driven to his death by my mother. Matt realized all this and ran away to the Navy. Her whining and complaining had become as much a part of my life as breakfast. I inherited the position of whipping boy. From the day that my brother left, anything that went wrong with her world was my fault. I started to ask to go out more often, and whereas I hadn't cared for the neighborhood when we first moved from Brooklyn, I really started to enjoy leading my own group. I began to return later than I said I would, and instead of correcting me, she seemed to get more and more into her 'Patience of Job' thing. By the time I was fourteen, Matt had been gone for almost a year. I was riding the corner horses every night of the week. By then I didn't even bother to ask to go out; I just went. That was another source of screaming. She had raised me and loved me and given me all that I had in the world, and I had no respect for her. That was her side of the story, and it was always consistent.

'I'm goin' t'bed,' I told her.

'Goodnight,' she said tolerantly.

I wanted to leave and get out of the way of her latest kick. She complained now that I was trying to embarrass her in front of all the parents in the neighborhood. My behavior was not an indication of the way I had been raised. I was turning out to be my father's son.

I passed my little brother's bed and looked down on him. There was no question about whose son she wanted him to be. Draped over the back of the bed was the baseball shirt with the number seven. I could never tell him enough about baseball, and particularly Mickey Mantle. Once or twice he had talked me into going with him to see the Yankees. But his interest was more the thrill of going somewhere with a million people than the game. He was only seven. He had had pneumonia the year before, when it was time to start school, and missed a year. Now all I could hear about lately was starting school. No more Mickey Mantle. I was a Mets fan anyway, if I was anything. The Mets were losers from the word 'go.' The only kinds of records they set were for the most games lost and most people coming to the game. Shea Stadium was a madhouse. The people got more hits than the team did. Somebody would get high and start cursing, and the next thing you knew, whole sections were being kicked out. The Man was ruthless. The Mets were the team that the Negro and Puerto Rican people could identify with. They were the ones with the whipped heads and the kicked asses. They were the underdog on the streets of New York, like the Mets were on the baseball diamond. The fans who got drunk and swung on the Man when he tried to quiet them down were heroes, because they were striking a blow for underdogs everywhere. When they were finally subdued and beat into unconsciousness, it was a sad, proud moment. They had not given up.

Junior's Dream

'First and third, and nobody out here in the bottom of the fourth. There's no score in the ballgame. Both teams had scoring opportunities earlier, but strong defensive plays turned the tide . . . Kranepool is the hitter. Eddie's batting .274. He grounded out to Javier in the first . . . They'll be pitching away from his power, trying to make him hit the ball to left. Brock shaded toward the line.'

'So what you been into, Junior. I haven't been seein' you.'

'Nothin' much. Been too hot.'

'I heard the guys tellin' you Clarice was lookin' for you. Why don' you give her a play?'

'I ain' got time to be bothered with Clarice.'

'Well, all right. I guess you said that.'

'. . . pitch on the way to Kranepool is outside. Mets baseball is brought to you by Rheingold, the extra-dry lager beer. Also by Winston, America's largest-selling filter cigarette. Winston tastes good, like a cigarette should.'

'First and third, an' nobody out. Bet the bastards don't even score.'

'They gon' get a run,' I said.

We were sitting out on the sidewalk in front of José's store. In the middle of the block between Eighth and Ninth avenues on 17th Street, there are many walk-up apartments that open onto the street. Ricky, the guy I was sitting next to, lived between José's store and Isidro's house. I had been playing dominoes with José and a few of the other men before the game came on. Kids and old ladies had been all over the place. I knew it wasn't late, but everyone had left. Ricky asked me if I wanted some Colt .45, and we had since waded through the last two innings of the first game of a double-header, and almost four innings of the second game. We had also put two six-packs away.

'. . . there's a fly ball to left field. It's deep enough to score the run. Brock makes the catch, and Harrelson scores, with the first run of the second game. The Mets lead one to nothing.'

'I told you they were gonna score,' I said.

'It sure is a nice night. I wish we could get a breeze like this in my place every night. Last night was so goddamn hot I couldn't even move. José is gonna have to do something about that fan. I bought a fan three weeks ago, and that sonuvabitch is busted already. It never did stir up a helluva lotta air, but, damn, now I can't get a thing.'

'One to nothing,' I said. 'I shoulda bet you.'

'You want some more beer? I got more upstairs.'

'Naw, man, I'm fulla beer.'

'I'm gonna get myself another one. Don't you take my fifty-dollar radio.'

'Fifty dollars my ass! Twenty-five on Forty-second. A 42nd Street gyp joint.' I picked up the radio and looked at it closely, but I couldn't make out the name for some reason. A drop of rain hit me on the nose.

'. . . ground ball to Maxvill at short. Over to Javier for one and to Cepeda completes the double play. But the Mets got one run on two hits. There were no Redbird errors, and no one left on base. We go into the top of the fifth with the score: The New York Mets one and the Saint Louis Cardinals nothing. Now for a word about . . .'

I was watching Orlando Cepeda chase a foul ball on the TV screen. The color was great, but there was no sound. I kept getting up to turn the damn thing up, but I could never hear the description. Ricky was in the kitchen talking about something that I couldn't translate either. I kept thinking he and I were on TV too, because everything in the room was the color of something on the screen. I was drinking some Scotch from a glass that reflected my face in the bottom. I kept thinking that as soon as I finished that drink, I was going to leave, rain or no rain, but every time I tried to drain the glass and looked back, there was as much as I started with.

I was getting sleepy. 'Ricky, fix the damn sound.'

I was half-lying back on the couch, and I could hear Ricky singing in the kitchen. I wanted to sleep, but his singing kept me awake. As I hollered for him to shut up, he came through the door saying that he hadn't opened his mouth. I closed my eyes and cursed the silly bastard. Of course he had opened his mouth, or someone was in there opening it for him.

I could feel his hands on me. He was unzipping my fly, and I knew that he couldn't say he wasn't doing it. I kept thinking I was going to raise up and knock the hell out of him. You find out about people when you get high with them. They start to come out from where they really see things. Ricky was a faggot! Just a second, you scroungy bastard, trying to get me high and feel me up like a bitch! That's the only thing I knew for sure. I didn't know you were a faggot, Ricky, because I wouldn't have come up here and had a drink with you or sat outside and rapped with you if I had known you were a faggot. Ricky, you know how everyone looks on faggots, and I'm going to be the man, and I don't want nobody to think that the man is a cootie-loo. I would've drank your stuff outside and told you I was leaving when it started raining, like I didn't know what you were up to, because I *didn't* know what you were up to. You got to string them queers along so you can use them. They got money and fine cribs an' . . .

'You can dig that, can't you, Junior?' Ricky whispered. 'You got a nice long one for such a young man. Ahhhh, the youth of America.'

I could hear the rain beating against the window, but it wasn't cooling anything off. It was hot in Ricky's stuffy little place with all the colors. I didn't even open my eyes, but I could picture the dingy little room. It was dingy and gray with chips of plaster on the floor. Ricky didn't have any clothes on, and his pecker was stiff.

'I want you to touch me, Junior,' Ricky gasped.

'You're crazy!' I said, opening my eyes. 'Ricky, you a fag! I didn't know you wuz a fag! I'm gettin' the hell outta here.' I looked down and reached for my clothes that were scattered all over the rug. All of the color had come back to the room.

'You know you don't really want to go, Junior. Look at you.

You want everything I can give you. You're conditioned by society not to like the thought of a male-to-male relationship, but nobody is entirely heterosexual, because if he was or she was, they couldn't stand to sit down for a minute with a member of their sex. Junior, we're all the same!'

'Then I'm gonna kick our ass instead of just yours,' I shouted. I'm screaming and running down the hall with good old Ricky right behind me grinning.

'You like it, Junior. You like it, and you know you like it, but you think you can run away because of society. I'm gonna run with you, Junior.'

I turned and swung at Ricky and thought I had broken his face into a thousand pieces, but I had slammed into the wall and knocked a hole in the plaster. The hole revealed Ricky's grinning face. He had somehow sneaked away from me. I ran down the stairs three at a time, and when I looked up at the next landing, Ricky was ahead of me going down the stairs backwards. I tumbled down the stoop in a head-long dive and landed in the middle of 17th Street traffic. I thought it was ten o'clock at night, and it's the rush hour. There is a traffic cop. What's he doing on a side street? I think I'll ask him which way I turn to land back at ten o'clock. Everyone knows that the Man is a friend of the people and not a rotten pig like they're made out to be by hippies and militants. They aren't really the kind of men who spread Vaseline on your body and then beat you so that your body won't show any marks. 'Hey, Mr Cop, Man, Fuzz, Sir,' I said, but I felt silly. Now back inside my head the weekend man that gets in my bottle when I drink hammered away at the bass drum and said: 'But who would believe that only minutes ago you were listening to the Mets game in Saint Louis, where they were playing a twi-night double-header? Just because you think some fag is behind you or in front of you. Why don't you turn on the radio?' Okay, I think I will.

'Bottom half of the sixth inning, in case you've just joined us. The Mets are leading one to nothing. They lost the first game in ten innings by a field goal and two free throws by Larry Wilson, the Cardinal free safety.'

Well, that proves that everything I said was true, I guess. There is obviously a night double-header going on in Saint Louis right now, and the time difference is not that great, so there must be something wrong with a lot of things, so I'll talk to the cop who's ... gone. I noticed that I was in the middle of a circle of REA trucks on their way in from a day of delivering whatever it is they deliver. I was screaming because I knew they'd hit me, and they didn't see me. Ricky! What did you put in the Colt .45? I knelt in the middle of 17th Street and yelled at the top of my lungs.

'Hit me, goddamn you! I don' wanna stay here no more,' I screamed.

I peeked through my fingers and saw a truck coming, but it stopped right in front of me. Ricky was driving the truck. The word 'Clarice' was painted across the front bumper of the truck.

'I've got to find Clarice,' I said to myself.

I got to my feet as Ricky stepped on the gas, and I started running toward Ninth Avenue, trying to make it to Clarice before the truck ran over me. I turned one last time to see Ricky closing in on me. I closed my eyes and watched Ricky swerve and hit the policeman, knocking him through the air and over my head, where he bounced on a cloud with springs shooting out of his back and head. I rolled over, and Clarice reached for me. We were in bed naked together. I was throbbing. I moved to her and kissed her. She opened her mouth like Debbie did, but I didn't dodge. I kissed her as I thrust my tongue against hers in the tunnel formed by our mouths. I felt her hands running back and forth on me lightly, teasing me. She was driving me crazy on purpose, and I wanted to pull back so that I could screw her, but she continued to nibble at my lips and tongue. I was frozen and shaking at the same time. All of a sudden I felt myself tumbling and my stomach starting to twitch. I had a feeling in my lower belly like the minute you're through pissing and there seems to be more fluid in your body. It's a shivering, quivering, nervous excitement. I pulled away and rolled onto the floor. I saw the end of my dick shriveling to normal size.

'C'mon, Junior,' Clarice called. 'You got me all hot and bothered.' I heard her giggling, and her toes dug into my back. I started pounding my fist against the floor.

'You and Ricky and Ricky and you and you all set it up because you wanted me to be all fucked up in the head, but it won't work, because I'm hip to what's happening, and any girl I know that sets up a plot with a cat that everybody knows is a fag except the guy they're trying to run this game on, well, that girl has got a lot of nerve going over to all the Junior Jones boys and telling them that she's in love with this cat she's just about to make an ass of, because she's been had by everybody in the neighborhood and everybody knows she's just a slut, so she should be trying to make a good impression instead of teaming up with a faggot!'

'I can't! can't! Clarice, I'm not a faggot. I just can't.'

I woke up!

My eyes were stung with tears, and the memories of the dream closed in on me. I was tangled in the sheet, and my pillow was gone. My body was covered with perspiration, and I had come in my pajama bottoms. They felt sticky and slimy against my thighs. I got up and stumbled over to the chair and got a smoke while I pulled off the pajama pants and rubbed the cream off my thighs. I wondered if I had screamed and whether or not my baby brother had heard. Evidently he hadn't heard a sound. I stubbed the cigarette out in the ashtray and dived back into bed.

November 16, 1968

School was two weeks late getting started because of a strike by the New York City schoolteachers. I couldn't have been happier before school began. I had been hinting that I wanted to quit school altogether, but my mother wouldn't hear of it. Every time I tried to say something about not going to school but working, she'd bring up the neighbors and the jobs their sons had. All of them had been blessed with seventy-five-dollar-a-week slaves because they had their high-school diplomas. I had more of a feeling that Mom was concerned about what the neighbors would say about her if I just decided I'd had it at the beginning of my junior year.

I always drew the line when she started talking about college and that trash. She wanted me to go because she had never had the opportunity. I'd have a chance to meet a lot of intelligent women. I would also be a thing for her to lay on the neighbors for the next forty years, even if I was unhappy about the whole damn thing.

I was sitting in the schoolyard across the street from Charles Evans Hughes on a Thursday evening when Spade walked by, strolling actually, profiling for all the cats who thought they were seeing a ghost.

'Hey, Spade!' I called. 'Whuss happnin'?'

'Nuthin' that I know of,' he admitted. He came over and sat with me and Cooly. 'Could yawl stand a taste?' he asked, indicating a bottle under his arm.

'Not me,' Cooly said.

I took a swig from the bottle. It was some kind of wine.

'Man o man,' Spade said, meaning Manischewitz wine.

The three of us sat and smoked, looking across the Ninth Avenue crush. It was almost six, and the sun was gone. A gray color had taken over the evening and brought the Hawk along as a bodyguard. The children were inside watching cartoons, and I had stayed outside to watch cartoons. Old white ladies running along with TV dinners, and uneducated black soldiers from the docks heading for Eighth Avenue and the A train.

'I'm sick of this shit!' I said.

'What shit!' Spade asked.

'All this shit.' I pointed out the books between my feet. 'I feel like I'm in jail. Read this and write that. Today I do it, and tomorrow I don' remember what I did, an' it don' make no difference.'

'Schoolitis,' Cooly drawled. 'I think I got me a bad case a that too.'

Spade smiled and took another swig from the wine.

'You know what I wanna do?' I asked. 'I wanna start dealin'. I need to make me some money an' git the hell away from home.'

'Schoolitis an' homeitis,' Spade said. 'One uv 'em is named Lee an' the other is named Isidro. If you deal, you got to deal in yo' neighborhood. Thass the only way you got a chance. You got to have contacts, or one cat will try a l'il pressure, an' when he see you ain' leanin', he'll call the Man on you.'

'Those ain' the only problems I got,' I admitted. 'I ain' got no lead. John an' Seedy got a very steady lead, an' thass whut keeps bizness good. They alwaze have their stuff. I ain' got idea the first 'bout where Lee iz gittin' set up.'

'When the Man jump Lee an' beat his ass, you gon' be glad you didn't know nuthin',' Cooly commented.

'The less you know 'bout another man's thing, the better,' Spade declared. 'An' thass his woman, his job, his fam'ly, an' everything else.'

'We got a meetin',' Cooly reminded me.

'Yeah.' I guess I must have grimaced at the thought.

'Whuss the problem?' Spade asked.

'Nuthin',' I lied. 'I'm sleepy.'

'I'll see you later,' Spade said. He took off in one direction, Cooly and I in the other. Cooly and I were heading for the basement of José's store to hold a meeting. The thing that kept puzzling me was that I still had no idea who had turned me over to Isidro. No one had stopped hanging out with the group or acting extraordinary.

There were two reasons that finding the informer was important. The first was that I felt uncomfortable with the group, knowing that we couldn't plot anything significant. We used to hit a little something once or twice a month. In the summertime, more often that that would've been okay. But without knowing who I could depend on, I couldn't do a thing. The second reason was personal. The rat, whoever he was, was blocking my way to being the man. In so doing, he had almost gotten me killed.

'Only way you can be the man iz to prove that you are a man,' Spade said. 'And in order to deal with other people, you got to make sure your own house is straight.'

That was what I had to do. Before I moved in the street, I had to be sure that things were together with my men in José's basement.

January 4, 1969

The Hawk was kicking much ass when I stepped out of José's basement. The three Puerto Rican boys, Cooly, and I had been blowing a few joints, standing in a circle passing the sticks and waving at a small electric heater to keep warm. I had smoked enough to lay out and nod for a week. Somehow I just couldn't get in the mood to cut loose and laugh at all the funny shit that was happening. The guys were all moving in slow motion, and I was listening to what they said five minutes ago as though I was communicating with some little green men from Mars by way of a language disc. I never really heard the meaning, but the sounds were familiar.

It was almost two in the morning when the group broke up and headed home. I shuffled through the snow toward my crib, hoping to God that my mom was in bed so that I wouldn't have to hear no Sermon on the Mount or whatever. I walked over to Eighth Avenue and then uptown. The avenue was still lit up a bit with Christmas lights and big signs about white-elephant sales that the Puerto Ricans loved. All the P.R. and blood women had been running up and down 14th Street and traipsing off with bundles of shit.

Christmas hadn't been bad at my house for the first time in a long time. My baby brother had given up the idea of Santa Claus, but he got a bicycle with the training wheels and a few other *practical* gifts. I had given my mother a clock-radio that I stole from 42nd Street and told her I had been saving for. What I had been doing was giving my money to Lee. My mother fell for what I told her, and enjoyed the holiday in spite of herself. She didn't work because of the nervous breakdown she had had, but with money from Matt plus her check, we managed to have a tree and a big Christmas dinner and the whole family bit. As a special holiday surprise, my big brother, Matt, left Vietnam in one piece. My mother swore that it was an act of God and that the seven years of famine were over.

'Step over here an' don't move.' My thoughts about the season were cut short at that instant. I knew the voice.

'Okay, amigo, I give up. Why me?' The guy's name was Pedro. I had met him at the park the day John gave his summer party. He had had a bottle of wine, and I had given him some rum.

'Jus' step careful.' I could feel the point of the gun jammed into my back. 'What eef I tol' you Seedy wuz dead, man? What would you say?' I half-turned and then halted when I heard him cock the trigger.

'I'd say this was the first I heard,' I said.

'I don' believe you, you bastard!' He pushed me ahead of him. 'Start walkin'.'

'Whut if I say I ain' goin' nowhere?'

'Then I'll shoot you here. But you gonna die anyway.'

Isidro was dead? I had laid a contract on him almost six months ago and hadn't done anything to him now, but by the time Pedro found that out, it would be too late for me.

'What time wuz Seedy killed?' I asked. 'I been with frien's all night.'

'I would be su'prised eef you didn' have a lie worked out. I ain' sellin' time. Yo' time ran out this summer when you plotted on our man. I been jus' waitin' 'cauz I knew you couldn' be trusted. I didn' know you planned to keel 'eem.' The faster Pedro tried to talk, the more pronounced his accent became. I could see his breath coming past my shoulder in long streams.

'Look! I didn' hook Seedy. I don' know who did. I been wit' my boys blowin' bush all night. Why don't you check it out?'

'Whatever I check mean that more than the dead man knows who killed you. I can' check nuthin'. They would lie for you.' He paused. 'Start.'

We started walking slowly toward 18th Street, and then he prodded me into a left turn that pointed us west, toward the river and the docks.

'Look! I wuz wit' my men,' I said. 'I ain' seen Seedy in three months or more. He wuz the las' thing on my mind.'

'That's right,' someone else said. 'He wuz with us.'

Pedro and I turned, to see Ricky Manning right behind us. He was breathing heavily into his hands. He wore no gloves.

'When? Cuando?' Pedro moved at an angle so that he could watch us both at the same time.

'From ten-thirty till about ten minutes ago,' Ricky said.

Ricky, you stupid bastard! I was thinking. You should have come up on him with a gun. You standin' there ain't givin' us a chance. Now he's gotta get both of us out of the way.

There was silence. I watched Pedro. I was looking for a chance to grab the gun from him. He shook his head and then looked at me and gestured with the rod. I nodded that Ricky was telling the truth. Pedro turned and walked away.

'I'm grateful to you, Rick,' I managed. 'You saved my life. I owe you.'

'It was nothing, brother.' Ricky turned, and before I could add anything, he was gone, wheeling around the corner at a trot. I broke into a trot too, even though I don't know why. My nerves were on edge. The cold weather was no factor. The chills I had were goosebumps.

That's a weird cat, I said to myself.

Ricky was the quietest of us all. He hung around with I.Q., like a Siamese twin most of the time. Even when I was with them and they were getting high, they were arguing over the merits of this and that. Ricky was my age, but he had skipped a class because he was smart. That had put him only two years behind I.Q., and he seemed to thrive on the thought that even though he was younger and might not have read as much, he was as smart as the Q. In my mind, and most of the other corner cats', there was no chance of anyone being as heavy as Ivan Quinn. He had been on TV for the High School Bowl, voted to *High School America's Who's Who*. There were very few honors he had not gotten in school. Out of class, he smoked and got high like the rest of us.

There used to be a particular hangout that we don't use much anymore down on Eleventh Avenue. It was an old warehouse that had been abandoned. Whenever we wanted a little privacy, we went up there to smoke and pop pills. It was there that I first saw and heard Ricky and the Q get into their philosophical who-did-what. They were as high as two kites. When I showed up, they had already popped three 'cats' apiece. I wanted to smoke, but they told me that in order to relate to the greater realm and a lot of other shit, I had to be high on what they were with. The only thing about 'cats' that I had ever heard was that they were 'downs.' I avoided all kinds of downs, because I thought they would make me feel like I was at home.

'Look at mankind,' Ricky was saying. 'There is nothing right with the world the way it is. Everywhere you look there are bombs being dropped and people being flooded and diseased. For the advanced state that mankind has reached technologically, he has achieved nothing humanely. Discomfort and discontent. Hippies, yippies, beatniks, anarchists, revolutionists, rebels, communists . . . are there no more just plain people who believe in living life singularly and finding a separate peace?'

'Peace was created by people as a way of describing oneness with God. There are no more Thomas Mores, if that's what you mean,' I.Q. said.

'Then why must I remain in this state? I believe in reincarnation. I think that I would be much better off as another form of animal if this is the highest form. I need to know nothing of all this. Why must I conform?' Ricky turned to me. 'Do you know what the answers are? The purpose of life can't be in preparation for praising God forever. . . . Just as I can't see myself burning in hell throughout eternity, I can't see myself kneeling at the feet of an Almighty God and singing of his glory.' Ricky looked up, and there were tears in his eyes. I was thinking that this was some white-boy action. All of this conversation and these words that sounded like some kind of a book. What kind of a brother got high and ran all of this shit down? 'It simply means that I will be as well off anywhere in the universe as I am here,' Ricky said. 'The brain is made up of electrical impulses that can never be shut off. That means that when death comes it cuts off the transmitting of signals from the brain to the body. It does not mean that the brain itself desists. Electricity does not fade like breath . . . I should not have to live under oppression and something less than the ideal humane conditions when I can end this fiasco . . . I should kill myself.'

'Who, then, is free? The wise man who cannot command his passions, who fears not want, nor death, nor chains, firmly resisting his appetites and despising the honors of the world, who relies wholly on himself, whose angular points of character have all been rounded off and polished.' I.Q. made a long speech and then explained it for my benefit. 'If you have no need of life, then you have no need of death. Who knows what you may someday do to inform others of your unconcern?'

'You're full of shit!' Ricky screamed. 'You talk all that shit tonight when you're high, but what about when you need and want? I have already experienced the pains of a man who has lived twice my age, and not half of the joy that one is supposed to squeeze from life like juice from an orange. I know what you want. You want like the rest of us. The cool of I.Q. is not as notorious and impregnable to me as it might be to others. I reject life in a test tube. I shall leave you to your maker.'

The conversation continued. Ricky would tell about sixteen years of pain. That he had ached for the salvation of mankind since his first realistic look at the system.

I.Q. was the master of the quote. As he supplied quotes to explain to Ricky why life was worth living, he would name the author, the year, and the speech if he felt like it. Ricky screamed about suicide and actually looked like he was trying to jump one time. Q and I managed to control him. The pills that we took kept us up. I nodded as Q and Ricky continued, and finally cried myself to sleep as the sun rose.

June, 1969

'You workin' for John?' Cooly asked.

'Yeah.'

'Whattaya do?'

'I deal.'

'Thass why you don' hang out no mo'?'

'Yeah, I'm too busy.' I lied and exaggerated a bit.

I was working part time for Lee. It started at the end of May, when he went down to take his physical for the service. He had had some appointments to make that couldn't be canceled, so he sent me to deliver the stuff and started to use me as an errand boy after that. To no one's surprise, he didn't pass the physical and beamed on the block about his 4-F.

I spent as much time as I could watching Lee. He had become good at smelling the Man and staying out of trouble for almost a year. The closest he had ever come to getting nailed was the night I burned the car. I was learning all that I could.

'In other words, you ain' gonna be with us no mo'?'

'In other words, brother,' I told Cooly, 'I ain' got no mo' boys on the block. I'm gittin' into a thing where yawl don't fit in. In a year or so, maybe less, yawl gonna all be movin' on yo way, an' there ain' gonna be no big thing. I'm jus' leavin' a l'il early. I'm sorry if it looks bad, but . . .'

'Fuck it,' Cooly said. I watched him closely.

'I'm seventeen, man,' I said.

'That ain' no hundred,' Cooly drawled.

'Spade an' John Lee ain' much older! I got to move!'

Cooly laughed. 'You still wanna be the man?'

I didn't comment. The way he said it made it sound like a comic-book hero.

'Lemme tellya,' he said. 'Lee an' Spade may not be much older than you inna way, but in other ways they ten times yo' age. Can you dig that?'

'The only way to learn iz to find out.'

'The hard way?'

'If thass the quickest way.'

'You ain' comin' to no mo' meetin's an' tell the gize?'

'No.'

Cooly started off across the park. He turned back long enough to shake his head.

'Man, you ain' never gonna be another Spade,' he said.

July 9, 1969

'I got something for you ta do,' Lee said.

'Yeah?'

'If I can trust you . . . This is important.'

'You know you can.'

John was sweating. It seemed as though he was always sweating. Either because he was fat or because he was nervous.

'I got some pills for you to deliver,' he told me.

'Where?'

'Brooklyn.'

John reached into a brown paper bag and came out with the familiar cellophane packets. He rewrapped the packs in cloth and stapled the ends together. He did all of this on the kitchen table. His parents had left the day before to see his mother's sister in Syracuse. I had been practically living there anyway. They weren't due back for a week.

'I want you to go to a place called the Ivy Hall.' He took out a piece of paper and started to jot down directions. 'You take the A train to Hoyt and Schermerhorn and catch the bus on Hoyt, the QL, four stops. You get off on this corner. The place you're looking for has about five entrances. You want the one on the west side in the back. This is a side door that says "Personnel" on it. Ask for a cat named Immies. Tell him you got held up last night and couldn't make it. Anything. You give him the pills and then he 'spose to give you two-fifty . . . You got that?'

I nodded. I picked up the piece of paper, but he stopped me.

'Memorize it,' he said. That was smart. If I got caught, the Man wouldn't have a map of my plans.

'Now,' he said. 'I may not be here when you get back, so jus' cool it. I got bizness elsewhere.'

He handed me a jacket with stitched-in pockets under the armpits. I put the pills in these pockets and took off. John saw me to the door. I almost ran down the back stairs in my eagerness to get started, but I figured John might be looking out of the window, so I took the slow way down on the elevator. I didn't want him to think I was running off to cheat him. He'd make a call, and I wouldn't make it to the corner. I settled in the elevator and lit a Kool. This might well be my big break. I was finally getting a chance to meet the Big Boss.

6:30

I remembered Brooklyn. Brooklyn's Bedford-Stuyvesant was the new Harlem. People were stacked on top of each other, and rats and roaches were the most familiar thing about the buildings. I had lived in Brooklyn until I was almost ten. I had watched my old man drink until he could no longer hit my mother with any kind of accuracy as she screamed and yelled about the lack of this and that and the other. There was the solitude of sharing the bathroom with the families down the hall and sitting on the toilet with your ass out while the

Hawk whistled through the cracks in the wall and turned your balls to ice.

There were the radiators that fizzled and hissed and made noises that were supposed to convince you that they were heating while you watched TV after dinner in your overcoat. I watched my father beat knives out of shape signaling the landlord that we were freezing. Into the night he would sit up with his liquor cursing the white man who owned his forefathers and the white man who owned us.

Even in Brooklyn my mother had been into a fate bag. She was always predicting her own downfall through the Lord's punishment of us for our wicked ways. Our father was being punished because he was a man who wanted his wife to open her legs and close her mouth. Matt and I were doomed because we loved him and he was a wicked man.

When I was almost eight, my father died. He was a stranger to me. He was in the Veterans' Hospital for four months while the white men did this and did that to him. They did not bring back his smile. He was in pain, and I heard my mom praying that he would die. I hated her more than ever until I understood that she really loved him after all and wanted to see him out of his misery. Then I hated her for what she was without him.

When my mother had her breakdown, we moved to Manhattan. Six months after her husband's death, God sent her a third son. The city decided to finance our trip to a lower-rent zone. I noticed the changes in our new house. The street was different, too. The boys' names were Juan and Enrique, and Cuba. The way they talked was funny, and the way they dressed was even more odd. I knew the Beast when I saw him, though. My father always told me on trips to the barber shop, where we saw men leaning almost parallel to the ground, that when the Beast got us we were no longer sons of God or man. The Beast was dope.

The A train was through with the rush-hour millions that piled into each other at nine in the morning and five at night. Those who had run into the Manhattan shopping districts and Wall Street district and business areas had once again escaped to the Bronx, Brooklyn, and Queens. They were safe in their other cages.

7:10

I knocked at the door marked 'Personnel' at the Ivy Hall.

'Yeah?'

'I want to see Immies,' I said.

'I'm Immies.' It was a fat white man who blocked my way. 'You Lee?'

'Yeah,' I lied.

'Good shit! I thought you'd pull out on me. All goddamn night I'm waitin' an' waitin', ya know? Whut happened?'

'I got held up.'

Immies had on a baggy suit that just seemed to match his baggy face with the overflowing jowls and rubbery lips. He had an unlit stogie in his mouth, clenched between yellow teeth.

There were two other men in the room. Both of them were white. A squat, fireplug-looking cat with a derby on sat propped against the wall with his feet on a battered desk. The other, a short, red-nosed faggot with a casino man's dealing hat on, sat at a desk trying to write in a big ledger under the glare of a no-watt bulb.

'You got dem pills?' Immies asked.

'Yeah.'

'Lemme have 'um.'

I pulled the packets from the pockets under the armpits and tossed them at him. Immies had a small pouch in his hand which he handed me. It felt like a roll of bills.

'Cheg dem dolls,' Fireplug said.

I leaned against the wall and relaxed opposite the three men who gathered around the desk. Immies pulled the staples from the cloth and opened one of the cellophane packs. He spilled the contents onto the desk.

'Whatcha say, Nita?' Immies asked the fag.

Nita picked up a pill daintily and popped it between his index finger and thumb. The white, powdery filling spilled onto his fingers and the desk. He tasted it.

'It's salt,' he purred.

I didn't think I heard him right. I looked from Nita to Immies to Fireplug. The three of them looked at me accusingly. I moved to the desk and ran my finger through the powder. I placed it to my tongue. It *was* salt!

'It's salt!' I said.

'Thass right, you schemin' l'il black motherfuckuh, you. Goddamn salt! All these goddamn capsules iz prob'ly fulla the shit! First I gotta wait, an' then you play me like a dumb bastard, some dumb fuck in the playground!'

I hadn't been watching Fireplug. I was still trying to find out what had happened. Plug hit me across the head, and I stumbled face down on the floor, my head spinning and smacking against the wood. Immies kicked me in the ribs. That's all I know.

1:35

I woke up in a crowd of Juniors. Everything near me was pain. My eyes opened and then quickly closed as the hurt stabbed my head.

'Who done ya, Junior?' Cooly asked. 'The whiteys?'

'How'd I get here?'

'We saw them dumpin' you here. Two men threw you outta car ... Who wuz it?'

I was getting my mental and physical together. My mind

was in worse shape than my body, because the body can't hurt unless the mind is registering. There was a taste in my mouth that reminded me of blood. My brain was running here and there, never stopping, always running.

There was an echo chamber that kept repeating John Lee's name. I was ashamed to look at Cooly. I felt that he knew what happened somehow, even though *I* didn't really know. John must have known I wanted his job. He set me up to eliminate the competition, just like he might have gotten rid of Isidro. He never cleared himself of that. He had set me up by giving me phony pills and making me think he was trusting me for a big job. Immies thought that *I* was cheating him. John wanted me dead.

I stayed at home the next day. My mother got into a terrible thing when she saw me with my face all kicked in and my ribs crunched, but she was quiet long enough to prod for broken bones and patch me up as well as I would let her. John came to see me about his money. I told him that the pills had been bad and that I had gotten a bad ass kicking and no money. If he wanted anything from Immies, he'd have to go and get it. He said that he didn't know how those pills happened to be bad, since the rest in the shipment were good. I decided that my showing up alive had brought a great performance from the fat man. He was the picture of concern. When I told him I didn't have the money, he looked like he would die.

I hated the very sight of him. Cooly's words kept coming back to me. He had said that I would never be as smart as Spade or Lee. He had said that I would never be the man. John Lee reminded me of those words, and Debbie Clark reminded me of them. I supposed that Spade would make me think when I saw him, too. I didn't want to see him, though. I didn't want to tell anybody what happened. The only reason I told John was because it seemed to be one of the games we were playing.

John Lee is dead.

Phase Three

John Lee died last night
July 13, 1969

'Mrs González,' the captain said, 'I know this hasn't been a very easy thing for you, but your help could be vital. . . . I assume from your call that you are willing to help us.'

'My wife will help all that she can, sir, but she is not a well woman. She is to have another child,' the middle-aged Puerto Rican man said.

Captain O'Malley and Lieutenant Thomas sat in a cramped apartment on West 16th Street. They had refused Mr González' offer of beer or lemonade and now waited patiently for his wife to tell them what had prompted her call about the previous evening.

'Now, last night, what did you see that made you call us?' the captain asked.

'I went for the paper to the corner, and as I am coming home, I walk through this . . .' She asked her husband for the word. '*Como se dice este?* . . . parking lot? Yes. When I come through this parking lot, I see a man bending over this one, and I scream at him . . . He looked back to me and ran away.'

Mrs González was a Puerto Rican woman of about forty. She was plump and short, with long, black hair pulled into a bun. Her husband was older than she by about ten years. He stood at the back of her chair with his hands resting on her shoulders.

The two white policemen sat facing the couple, their lightweight jackets barely concealing the weapons under their left armpits. There was a small fan directly behind them spinning furiously in an effort to battle the ninety-degree New York day.

'About what time was this?'

'About eleven-thirty,' she replied.

'Could you give us a description of the man you saw?' the captain asked.

'Well, it's so fast I canno' really see. An' dark, you see?'

'Was he white, Puerto Rican . . .'

'Not a white man,' she says.

'Well, can you give us anything? Height, weight, dress, that sort of thing?'

Mrs González turned to her husband, who interpreted the question in rapid Spanish.

'Sí. He was about six feet, and very quick for running.' The two policemen smiled vaguely. 'He was wearing a white raincoat with a paper bag.'

'Beg pardon. *Como*?' the captain asks.

'While he runs, he dropped a package, an' she looked, uh, it looked like a pa-per bag. He stopped all his running to get it.' The woman paused. 'But where he was running, there was no light.'

Lieutenant Thomas was jotting down everything in a black note pad. He asked the next question.

'How about a hat? Glasses? *Anteojos?*'

'No. None of this. I wish I could help more for you, but then maybe he could see me too.' Mrs González looks at her husband.

'We were afraid to tell. About the movies, you see? In the movies the ones who see are killed. This is a bad neighborhood for killing, because of the young ones. They kill . . . We went to Mass this morning and asked the father. He told us we should call to talk to you.'

The policemen nodded.

'Well,' the captain said, 'unless you can think of something more, I suppose that will be all.'

'Nothing more,' Mrs González said.

'If you think of anything else, no matter how small, please call us.'

'And thank you,' the lieutenant added.

Mr González showed the two men to the door. Down the hall away from the apartment, they conferred on their information.

'What do you think?'

'Don' know,' the captain said.

'Think some mug shots would help?'

'I doubt it. All she could say was that the man wasn't white. There would be no reason for the mug file.'

The two officers reached ground level on 16th Street and moved to their car, parked near the corner.

'This is fourteen-six to base. Fourteen-six to base. Over.'

'We read you, fourteen-six.'

'This is O'Malley. I want to see Mitchell in Narco when I get back. That should be about four. Tell him that I'd like complete files on our district for a man named Isidro Valsuena. Over.'

'Ten-four.'

The unmarked black sedan pulled away from the curb and swung out into traffic. The kids on the corner had loosened the nozzle on a fireplug, and water banged against scrawny legs and chests and ricocheted to form a small river in the gutter, flowing to the sewer. The policemen drove by, ignoring it.

'Check this address,' the captain said, using his note pad: '357 West 17th Street. I'd like to see where Paco Valsuena was last night.'

Afro: Brother Tommy Hall

July 28, 1968

Applause.

'Thank you, Brother Bishop, for those kind words of intro-
duction . . . Brothers and sisters, I'd like to thank each of you
for coming out on a night such as this to hear us. As Brother
Bishop told you, BAMBU* is a black organization that was
founded in New York City almost a year ago. The aim of
BAMBU is to develop a collective approach to the specific
problems of black people. When we use the word "collective"
we mean that black people can only solve their problems when
they are unified in terms of thinking and acting.

'Black people have to move to a level where they begin to
push toward each other as brothers and sisters. This means that
brothers from the Bronx cannot get into a hassle with brothers
from Brooklyn. As Brother Malcolm has taught us, "We don't
catch hell because we are Baptist or Methodist, Mason or Elks,
Democrats or Republicans." In other words, we don't catch
hell because we are from Brooklyn or the Bronx. We catch
hell because we are black.

'Once you and I understand and accept this, then we may
begin to take care of business collectively. Therefore it is
necessary for us to do our homework. This means that we
must begin to equate and liberate black minds. We in BAMBU
have developed a program which speaks to this need. Not only
does it speak to this need, but also it provides other means by
which black people can deal with the system.

* Black American Men for Black Unity

'We feel that freedom will only be achieved through the *collective* efforts of black people. In other words, that we must develop our own schools and our own cultural values. In this way black people will have a knowledge of self and necessary skills to implement meaningful change for the future.

'Therefore our objectives are: (1) to provide a school system for black children that will replace the present system. (2) To become involved in a politicization of the community to the extent that black people control the governmental offices where they are most directly concerned. (3) To create the necessary means by which people stop the racist police force that brutalizes us, and defend our women and children against the other racists that exist in this country . . .'

Applause.

'(4) To foster a cultural revolution that will create new values for our family. (5) And to develop our own means for economic survival in America.'

Applause.

'What we of BAMBU plan to do is the following. On August 7, that's Monday week, we will open our fourth Community Center in Manhattan. The Community Center will be this very building you have met with us in this evening, and the children will be taught about their blackness. Black history, black literature, Swahili, and African music will be taught. This will be for the children between the ages of six and fifteen. In the evenings there will be cultural classes for the adult and young adults of you who would like to participate. Also, for the men, there will be classes in karate, judo, and riflery in the evenings and on weekends.'

I paused because at that moment I saw I.Q. get up and leave.

'Now,' I continued, 'when we say police brutality and racist police force, just what, exactly, are we saying? We mean that we want to inhibit the molesting of our people. We are talking about the lack of response and the downright indecency we receive when dealing with police. We are also talking about the physical abuse that black people have been known to receive in this city. We have categorized all of this under the heading "Police Responsibility," but it ties in with our desire to politicize black people. Through our program people will realize that the police force is only the racist arm of a racist structure, that of the United States government . . . What other country in the world would have a man such as George Wallace receiving thousands of dollars from thousands of people? What other country would allow a state like Mississippi to exist within its boundaries when the reports of countless shootings, lynchings, burnings, and bombings have been reported with black people the victims of all of these atrocities? Where else but in the United States would a man have to demonstrate to get an opportunity to *buy* a hot dog? . . .'

Laughter and applause. 'Tell it, brother!'

'Where else but the United States is the highest court in the land listening to appeals on laws written two centuries ago, in order to discover whether it's legal or not to go to school where you want to? . . . Brothers and sisters, this is a racist institution you and I live under. We of BAMBU are doing our best to prepare a program that will help black people better understand *who* the enemy is and how we can best attack the system and change it . . . Thank you, very much. If there are any questions, I will be glad to elaborate.'

Applause.

Brother Bishop got up. 'Thank you, Brother Hall,' the older man said to me. 'I appreciate your suggestion that we hold our meeting here this evening. It's not often that I have an opportunity to visit this part of town . . . As Brother Hall mentioned, on August 7 BAMBU will be opening a school here for our people, and he will be in charge of the activities in this area. Brother Hall is a recent graduate of Manhattan

Community College, where he majored in history. He will be teaching the history here for our youngsters ... You know, it's good to see the young brothers and sisters involved so heavily with the freedom of black people. It's a warm feeling to go into our centers in Harlem and see the young brothers and sisters serving as instructors for our children, teaching them what it means to be black ... You know, when I was young I was taught that to be black was to be inferior, to be something undesirable. It seems a shame to me that I would have passed so many years along before I saw the error of all this. I'm hoping that all of our youngsters will see the beauty of their blackness and stand up for it ... That, of course, is the purpose of the group programs we have begun here in New York. We have six centers in Brooklyn, two in the Bronx, and three here in Manhattan. Each one of them full of young black minds. This program has recently acquired a secretary for the Chelsea Center. Sister Mason, will you stand up?' A young girl stood near the back of the meeting room. 'Sister Mason will take the names of the students you brothers and sisters might want to sign up. Our program in this area will be able to facilitate seventy children at least ... Now, if you have any questions for Brother Hall, would you please raise your hands.'

A man to the right of the stage raised his hand and was recognized by the chair.

'Brother Hall,' the man said. 'First of all, I would like to say that I enjoyed whut you had t'say very much ... I wuz wond'rin' if maybe you could go into the types of things you will be teaching our chil'ren.'

'Certainly, brother,' I said, standing. 'We are raised in America under many contradictions and hypocrisies. America has always been known as the land of the free whites and the home of the slave. One of the greatest perpetuators of this type of hypocrisy was the Father of the country, George

Washington. How many of our children are aware of the fact that George Washington was a slaveowner and a criminal being sought by the English authorities? Not very many. And it is important that they know, because a lot of our children grow up idolizing George Washington – wanting to be like him, because he never told a lie! Never told a lie!' I repeated. 'He was living a lie! All George Washington represents in my mind is another Virginia racist who thought black people were ignorant savages. We must be careful not to let our children foster these false examples. All of this is part of the white "brainwashing" that has taken place in this country for so long.

'How many of our children know of Nat Turner? How many know that the slaves were living the lives of miserable cattle in the South? The white man has had a way of depicting things through his use of the media to make things look as though the slaves were happy in the plantation and didn't want the South to lose the war. How many know how badly the slaves were tortured and beaten? In 1831 Nat Turner led a slave rebellion in Virginia which resulted in the death of fifty-seven whites. He was a preacher, a man who walked from plantation to plantation spreading the word of God, and it was a sign from God that prompted him to burn and plunder and kill. There was no contentment for any other than the "house niggers" during this period. The black man in America has always been hounded and hunted, hungry, and abused . . .'

Applause.

'How many of our children know that 400,000 black soldiers died in the War Between the States? Fighting on the side of the Union Army to do in the master that he reputedly loved so dearly? . . . No, my brothers and sisters, we have been brainwashed. We might unify our thoughts and our actions. If two and a half million Jews can demand their freedom and hold enough check to scare the hell out of the rest of the world, surely twenty-two million or more black Americans can fight for their rights. These are the type of things I will try to convey to our children.'

Applause.

'Brother Hall, how old are you?' A young lady of approximately my age was asking the question, and the others in the audience laughed.

'I'm twenty,' I told her.

'I was wondering primarily about your background and qualifications.'

'I graduated in June from Manhattan Community College as a history major. I hold two jobs, the most prominent of which is my work with BAMBU.'

'In other words, you condone a section of the education we receive from white people?'

'I'm glad you asked that,' I told her. 'In every great revolution there have been educated men at the top. Mao went to a university. Ché went to a university. Fidel Castro and Ho Chi Minh were educated men. In this country some of our most eminent men are educated at the university level. Dr King, Ron Karenga, Stokely Carmichael, to name a few. These men were not brainwashed during their stay at their schools. They came out with more ideas about how we as a people may better combat the system. I think that it is necessary for us to learn the white man's skills. That applies to science, math, engineering, all of the major fields where we may profit and grow financially as a people.

'I think that it was important for me to gather facts while discovering how history is taught the wrong way, before I came and offered to teach what is more than history, but truth.'

'Thank you,' she said.

There didn't seem to be any more questions, so Brother Bishop stood up and adjourned the meeting. As the people began to file toward the exits, the young girl who had asked me the last question came up from behind me and touched my shoulder.

'Hello,' I said.

'I'd, uh, like to ask a few more questions, but I didn't think I should try and hold up the group. Do you have a minute?'

I nodded and turned to excuse myself from Brother Bishop and a few of the older brothers, who would probably have discussed issues for hours. They nodded and smiled when they saw the young lady behind me. I put on my raincoat and followed her toward the door.

'I haven't eaten,' I said. 'Would you like something?'

'Maybe a cup of coffee or a Coke,' she said. 'Uh, what I wanted to talk to you about concerned something rather personal. I hope I wouldn't be bothering you.'

'No,' I said. 'No bother.'

We walked from the third floor to the first and then out onto 23rd Street. The rain had stopped, and the dampness left a pleasant smell in the city streets. As we walked toward 23rd and Eighth Avenue, where I usually ate, I took a closer look at the girl. She was about my age and well developed. Her hair was done in a short afro, and it topped about one hundred and ten pounds. Her mind was evidently elsewhere while I was taking inventory.

'By the way, I don't know your name,' I said.

'Natalie . . . and yours is Hall?'

'Tommy Hall,' I said.

'I'm Natalie Walker.' We shook hands.

Natalie and I walked into the coffee shop just as the rain started again. We took a booth in the corner facing the only entrance. I took her coat and coaxed her to look at the menu while I selected a couple of records at the jukebox.

After we had ordered, she began to talk a bit more freely.

'I'm going through a similar situation to what you were discussing,' she said.

'In what respect?'

'In terms of education. I'm a student at CCNY, but I don't want to stay in school here. They're not teaching anything relevant. I told my mother I had to go to a black school and enjoy some of the things that young black people are doing in this country, but she won't listen. She absolutely refuses to let me transfer or stop school.'

'What are her reasons?'

'She says I need to be near home. She thinks all of these student uprisings will get me in trouble if I go to a black school with the type of black curriculum that I'm interested in.'

'I agree with her in a way.'

'What?'

'I agree that she needs you close to home.'

'That's not what I said. That's not what she said!'

'That's what's happening, though. She doesn't want to lose you to beliefs contrary to those of her own. Now, she was a follower of Dr King, is that right?' Natalie nodded. 'And you talk about Rap and Stokely, is this right?' She nodded again. 'In your mother's eyes she's protecting you. She believes that if she can keep you close at home, keep her finger on your pulse, that whenever you start talking a lot of that black stuff, she'll be around to remind you of all the fine things Dr King did in the movement.' I paused. 'Because most of the older black people think that this current trend toward being black and expressing your blackness is only a fad anyway.'

'What do you think?'

'I think that black people are waking up after a long hibernation, and after they do their homework, we'll be ready to make some changes in the system.'

The waitress came up with our food. 'A toasted corn muffin and coffee for the young lady, two hamburgers, French fries, and coffee for the gentleman. Will that be all, sir?'

'That's all, thank you,' I said.

'Well, that's what I wanted to talk to you about,' Natalie said.

'What is?'

'I want you to talk to my mother. I want her to see some of the fine things other young people in our area are doing. All she knows is Spade.'

'Spade? What about Spade?' I asked.

'My mother hates him and Hicks and boys like them.'

'Do you know him?' I asked.

'Who?'

'Spade.'

'Not well.'

There was a pause in the conversation. Natalie offered me a cigarette that I refused.

'Will you come?' she asked.

'I don't think I can do much good. I'm not much of an example of anything. Perhaps after the school is on its feet she will be more receptive to my ideas.'

'But don't you see? The school starts in August, and it's almost August already. I need to get her permission soon to send for transfer applications to other places.'

'You mean you haven't sent for the transfer notices and you want to be accepted for September?'

'I sent for the transfer to Howard, and they accepted me, but if I don't get her permission soon, by the time I convince her that I've written off and gotten everything back, Howard will have assumed I'm not coming. In the meantime, I can't say I am coming until my mother reacts.'

'Whew! Girl, I don't know about this situation. It's almost too confusing to even attempt to figure out. I think I know what's what, but I didn't know women did that kind of thing outside of the movies. Especially not black women.'

'I know it sounds confusing, but that's all I could do. Will you help?'

I was about to answer when I.Q.'s face appeared at the window. I leaped to my feet and ran to the door, but before I could get outside, I had a feeling that he would be gone. He had disappeared.

'What's wrong? Who was it?' Natalie asked.

'Looked like a guy I knew,' I said. 'Guess I was mistaken.'

'Well . . .' she began.

'Look, when do you want me to come and see your mom?'

'Tomorrow night. That is, if it's all right with you.' I nodded that it was all right. 'I'll tell her we're going to a movie and you're my date. Come in about eight, and I won't be ready. You can talk to her while I get dressed. Then I can go to a party they're having at my girl friend's house. Would you like that?'

'No. I'm not much for parties . . . I'm not much for lying either,' I added. 'Why can't you just tell her why I'm coming?'

'She wouldn't talk to you.'

'Okay,' I agreed. I said I would do it just because I wanted to see her one more time, without all the lying involved. I wondered what she was like. She made me realize that I had a lot of homework to do when it came to women.

I walked Natalie home and explained that I had some unfinished business to take care of. My unfinished business was named Ivan Quinn. I wanted to learn why we were playing games around the block. I left Natalie at 18th Street and Ninth Avenue and started toward the 17th Street park. The rain had been a shower, hard for a second and then gone. The streets were damp and seemed to reflect a certain calm that I felt.

All at once I realized why I.Q. was following me. He wanted to know why he received a rejection slip from BAMBU. He wanted to see me alone. I knew he had received the slip because *I* had mailed it to him two days ago. All I had to do was wait, and he would find me.

The whole thing with I.Q. started when John Lee held a

party at the close of the school year. For once I had been as anxious as anyone else to go out and do some partying. The school year had been no problem, but it seems that no matter how close you stay to the work, there are a million things to get together when they start talking about finals.

The Party

I had come in expecting a good time. The music was nice in the back of the Lee apartment. The food was cooking somewhere, and most important of all, nobody was drunk or rowdy. I plucked a can of beer out of the bathtub and slid into a corner chair.

'Congratulations, man,' Websta said, coming over and giving me the handshake. 'I hear you untied the knot today.'

'Yeah, brother. It's all over.'

'Soon as I get a l'il bread, I'm gonna go back an' do that thing. What you plannin' on doin' fo' yo'self?'

'I'm working with the organization, you know. We're gonna open a center near here in August. Up near the Chelsea projects. I start nine to three with N'Bala on Monday.'

'You in the same boat I am,' Websta said. 'Workin' two jobs. Hell, seemed like I wuz gon' need an act a Congress t'git here t'night ... You got that paper. Seem like you could git some bread with IBM or one a them initials.'

'Yeah, I could, I suppose. The only difference is that I didn't get my education so that I could run off the street to the suburbs. I want to work around here.'

'Yeah, you *wuz* that way. You ain' gonna make much with N'Bala. He ain' gonna ketch on aroun' here like New Breed did uptown. We got too many jitterbugs in the neighborhood.'

'Thass all right,' I told him. 'Nothing changes overnight. I mean, I don't expect miracles.'

'You rilly like them African clothes that N'Bala sells? I mean, the shirts like the one you got on. What'choo call 'um?'

'It's called a dashiki, brother. I think they're better than the white man's shirts. You see the way it's cut?' I stood up so that he could see the way the dashiki is stitched under the arms. 'With a cut like this, you have a measure of freedom in case of attack. In a thing like what you have on, you can be limited physically. I could run a jack on you f'rinstance.' Websta nodded in agreement. Running a jack is the street term for grabbing a man's shirt and pulling it over his head.

'It's pretty. They all are. Lotta colors an' whut have you.' He waved. 'I'm gonna have to talk to you, man. Lemme ketch this slow one.'

'I'm So Proud,' by the Impressions, came on. I touched the arm of the sister next to me, and we stepped to the middle of the dance floor. I was caught up with what Websta had said. My mother and father had been disappointed when I told them what my plans were. I suppose they had been looking forward to seeing me leap out into status-symbol-land. My father had always told my mom that the things I was doing were just a passing fancy, because he had been intent on changing the world and helping the Negro when he was in college. Sooner or later I would be out there for the buck too. I would get a haircut and start wearing white shirts and maybe even go on to a four-year college so that I could teach for the state or the city. Now that I had graduated and moved my stuff to another apartment in the same building, even he was asking questions about how long was I going to stay with N'Bala and what the hell was I doing with the organization, pulling eighty dollars a week.

First of all, I wanted to teach black history. The opportunity that BAMBU gave me to do this could never be touched by the city or state. For any government teaching job I would have to have a diploma from a four-year college, and I wouldn't be able to help shape the curriculum until I had gotten tenure. BAMBU was giving me the curriculum for my area, along with the syllabi from other centers for references. I had almost an unlimited budget in terms of books and materials.

The second job was with N'Bala. I didn't consider that a permanent position. N'Bala was an African brother who had opened an Eighth Avenue clothing shop that featured all of the finest in black wear. He was suffering, however. In opening the store he had spent most of his money and didn't have much for salaries. He had been open for a month, and business hadn't exactly been booming. The answer to that was the area. Most of the Chelsea area is Puerto Rican. From 14th Street to 23rd Street west of Eighth Avenue, the population is seventy percent Puerto Rican. The black people live just outside of this wall, in force.

I had bought the dashiki I was wearing at John's party less than two weeks ago from N'Bala, and even though business wasn't heavy, he had his hands full running up and down and trying to make sure that he wasn't robbed while he stocked his shelves.

'Where's your help?' I asked.

'He quit, brother. Yesterday he came to me and he said, N'Bala, I am very sorry, but I cannot work anymore for you because I will never have money.' I watched the little African wipe away the sweat from his face and neck. 'I told him that we will do better and I will raise him some money, but he wants to know when, as though I am God and can see tomorrow.'

'I know what you mean. Getting a business started is a struggle.'

'You think you know?' N'Bala asked. 'I have to close the door to go to the bathroom. The schoolchildren, the little ones, come here to try to steal from me. Not to mention the large high-school ones. I think I will go crazy.

The air is broken down. The air-conditioner, I mean. You don't know!'

'How much you payin'?' I asked.

'Sixty dollars a week for five days. What can I pay?'

I liked the little man. He was self-made, in a way. He had graduated from Columbia as a business major and returned to Africa. When his country became involved in a revolution that failed, he was forced to flee to the United States. With his life savings he was trying to start a little business. It was exactly what we had been asking for in BAMBU. More black businessmen, therefore more black workers in higher positions, better deals for the black consumer, and more financial stability for the black family.

'Can you last two weeks?' I asked.

'Even the dying man finds courage when he knows that help is near.' N'Bala quoted something, and I smiled at the metaphor.

'In two weeks I'll be your salesman,' I said.

'What?'

'If you can use me.'

'Of course. But you will be a graduate then.'

'Two weeks. I'll start the Monday after graduation.'

I was cut short by the record's end. The sister I was dancing with said something that I didn't catch.

'Beg pardon, sister?'

'I said thank you,' she repeated.

'My pleasure,' I said. 'You'll have to excuse me. I'm not together this evening.'

'Are you drunk?' she asked.

'No. No. I'm just doing a lot of thinking when I should be concentrating on more important things like yourself.' I smiled, and she smiled.

'That was a nice try ... That's a beautiful dashiki,' she commented.

'Thank you.'

'I was looking at them. I made one for my brother, but it didn't turn out very well. No pattern.' She was sipping a drink. 'Did you make that one?'

'No, I bought it.'

'How much are they? Aren't they expensive?'

'They come in all styles, colors, and prices. I got this one at N'Bala's Fashions on 18th Street and Eighth Avenue. It just so happens that I'll be working there starting Monday, and I can see to it that you get a well-made dashiki at a reasonable price.'

'I'll have to come in,' she said.

It was nearing midnight. The crowd was wild, but everything was under control. I didn't blame them for celebrating. School was out. The beaches were in. The weather was warm, and the beer was cold. A lot of people had paired off, but it was my misfortune to get into an intellectual conversation with a few of the brothers. I appreciate their interest and am always proud when they ask me a question that's been on their minds, but sometimes you just do not want to talk. That was how I felt.

From my initial remarks about BAMBU when one of the brothers asked about it, an argument had cropped up between several of us as to the cause of riots and the explanation of what constitutes a riot. The real issue was whether or not riots were helping or hindering the movement.

'A riot is a violent dramatization of black despair in America,' I told them. 'Time comes when you just can't stand no more. A man can have his ass kicked so often figuratively that he doesn't care what happens to him literally. A few brothers are standing on the corner, looking inside the white man's store, and their hands are closing in on the nothing in their pockets. Before you know it, they're taking what they want.'

'It's usually 'cauz somebody got high,' one brother said. 'They're all drunk, and then they start throwin' shit.'

'Drunkenness is the ruin of reason. It is a premature old age. It is temporary death,' I.Q. quoted.

'It's not necessarily due to drunkenness,' I said. 'I believe the primary ingredient is frustration and not alcohol. Combine that with opportunity, and you have a very emotional, explosive situation. What is always necessary is the spark that ignites the fuse, because black people are tired of being exploited and taken advantage of. Also of being underestimated.'

'Only the complacent are true slaves,' I.Q. quoted.

'There are very few happy people in the communities of this country that exploded last summer and that may explode again. Being drunk may pacify for a while; that's why I don't think the rioters were drunk. These were the men who had been denied the right to be men, treated like savages for three hundred years, and they suddenly decided that they may as well take what they want. They have seen the white boys' law. It works for the benefit of the white boys.'

'But if you notice,' one brother pointed out, 'the people who are killed are always black. No whitey get offed. It's really murder.'

'Murder is white justice. Livin' in America has always been murder for black people. There has been three centuries of murder. Either the quick death from a gun or a rope, or the slow death of trying to survive under inhuman conditions.' I looked over the group of naturals and beads. 'Black people aren't as foolish as they used to be, though. They ain't callin' on the Lord like they used to. They realize that God helps those who help themselves. And as for those of us in the great North, we know that a whitey is a whitey and that his bullshit is everywhere. We know we've got just as much of a struggle here as we do in Mississippi ... Maybe even more, because we're supposed to have to pick out the good whiteys from the bad ones. Down there you know who the enemy is.'

As the group began to break up, an even more frenzied dancing thing with the women began. I.Q. stayed near the window with me and continued the conversation.

'We're movin' into a new day, brother,' I told him. 'The younger brothers are talkin' black, thinkin' black, and usin' the white boy to better themselves and their people.'

'Victories that are cheap are cheap. Those only are worth having which come as a result of hard fighting,' I.Q. said.

'Don't you ever say anything that's not a quote?' I asked.

'I'd like to join BAMBU.'

'In what capacity?'

'As a teacher. I can teach practically anything.'

'All you need is a general statement. You know what I mean. A little thing about yourself in terms of biographical material. You send it in to the central office and they send it to the branch you specify if you have a choice.'

'I'll do that,' he said. 'Do you see? Everything I say isn't a quote.' With that he moved off toward the dance floor.

As he walked away, I was reminded of a quote myself. It was something very practical that Buddha had said: 'A man should first direct himself in the way he should go. Only then should he instruct others.'

BAMBU originated in August of 1967 in Harlem. That was the time when I first heard of the residents of Harlem asking for more black people to teach in the high schools. They wanted more black courses in the curriculum. Latin was out, because they thought their children should know Swahili. They wanted their children to know more about their roots and heritage. For a while there was very little response from the people to the program that BAMBU outlined. It began as a cultural organization where black dance groups did African numbers and guest speakers came in. By November, however, four older brothers and I began a tutorial program in black history at BAMBU's 125th Street Liberation School, and the community began to gather interest.

I had been working as a tutor-teacher for four months when the organization decided they were going to expand to all parts of the city. Two buildings were acquired in Brooklyn right away, and then came two more in the lower Bronx. In April Brother Bishop told me that the Chelsea area would be opened because a group of parents known as the Black Community Council was establishing a center for us. When the opening was announced formally to the neighborhood, I was set up as chairman because of my familiarity with the people. I was given April and May to get the building into working condition. Sister Mason worked with me as secretary and accountant. Between the two of us a large number of pamphlets and leaflets were distributed throughout the community and surrounding area.

We gave August 7 as an opening date because I hoped by then I would have a staff of capable workers and teachers. I was learning a lot about trying to organize. I found out how difficult it is to get volunteer help. The brainwashing of black people in America had become more serious than I wanted to believe. As a race we were suffering from taking on the white boy's value of the dollar. The white boy values the dollar over everything else that he comes in contact with, including his fellow beings. He had become triumphant over the Indians in America because he sought land and power and money to such a degree that human life was secondary.

By the end of June I had been advertising the fact that a branch of BAMBU was organizing in the community and would need volunteer help in terms of the teaching and maintenance. The maintenance was taken care of by Sister Mason's brother, who would also run the projector for the films I had ordered. The books that had been sent for were simply shoved into a corner until I got to them, because I didn't have anyone to check them and shelve them. The rest of the people who came by the office were high-school students who were willing to run errands but honestly did not have the real qualifications to do anything in the classroom. That was why I was pleased when I.Q. said that he wanted to join us. He was a high-school graduate with a scholarship to Columbia, and I knew that he was intelligent. All of the applications were handled by the same box number, but after they were screened and a check made by the central office on qualifications, they were sent to the area chairman for approval or rejection on the basis of a personal interview. I.Q.'s application would naturally come to me.

The last week of June I found it impossible to get to the office. I had my final exams and graduation practice and a million other things to do. I took a leave of absence and left things with Sister Mason. I told her that I wanted to be sure and pass the exams and get the hell away from under the white man's structure. I was thinking about that as John's party started to get mellow. The forty-fives were replaced by a few Latin jams. Eddie Palmieri, Tito Puente, Cal Tjader, and Joe Bataan took over for a half-hour, and then came Little Anthony and Smoky and grinding couples. I laid low while the women got their heads together. I don't think I'd ever seen so much rum disappear in my life. I thought of the busy weeks ahead of me. I would start with N'Bala on Monday. I would work there from nine until three and then go to the center from four until ten. This would go on five days a week. I didn't know if I was ready, but that was what was happening.

July 12, 1968

I went straight home from the center on Friday night. Sister Mason and I had painted the lobby and stopped about nine when we decided we wouldn't be able to finish another stroke before collapsing. At times I almost forgot that the sister was working two jobs like I was. She came in punctually every day and worked as long as I asked her to with no complaints, but when I stopped to think about her, she was hurrying on her way home. I got home about nine-thirty and made myself a couple of sandwiches. I had no sooner sat down to eat when the phone rang.

'Brother Hall?' someone asked.

'Yes?'

'Brother Hall, you have a possible teacher in your center by the name of Ivan Quinn.' I said yes. I had just received I.Q.'s application that afternoon. 'I don't think you would appreciate Mr Quinn's services very much if you saw the type of black man he really is. Why don't you follow him tonight? He'll be leaving his house about ten o'clock.'

The words 'ten o'clock' were followed by a click on the other end of the line. I checked my watch and saw that it was already a quarter to ten. I gave Websta a call. The phone rang four times before Websta answered groggily.

'Web, this is Afro,' I said. 'Look, brother, I was wondering if I could borrow your car for an hour or two?'

'Yeah,' he said. 'It's parked right across the street from here. You comin' over?'

'I'm gonna be in a semihurry. I'll be there in about five minutes.'

'Okay. I'll put the key under the mat. I gotta get some sack.'

'Thanks a lot.'

'No sweat. Put the key back under the mat when you're through.'

That was a beautiful brother. He was always willing to give a hand when it was needed, without a whole lot of questions. I ate the sandwich on the run and made it from my place on 22nd Street to Websta's on 15th Street in little or no time. The key was under the mat, and I found the 1962 Oldsmobile parked just as I had been told. I swung it out into traffic and circled north on Tenth Avenue and then east on 20th Street. New York streets are generally set up so that the odd-numbered streets go one-way west and the even numbers are one-way east. The avenues with odd numbers generally go downtown and the even numbers go uptown. I pulled up about five cars behind I.Q.'s parked blue Volkswagen.

I still didn't know what I was doing or why. At ten o'clock I.Q. still hadn't come out of the house. I started to think about the whole situation, and I felt a little embarrassed. Who was I to distrust another brother and follow information given me by a man who wouldn't identify himself? But, I decided, if I.Q. wasn't doing anything, I wouldn't see anything. I sat for another five minutes before he came out.

I.Q. wheeled into the street and pointed toward Ninth Avenue. At Ninth he swung downtown to 18th Street and went back to Eighth Avenue. At Eighth he started uptown. I stayed just far enough back to see him without his noticing me. It was clear now that the call I got was at least partially correct, but what was the significance?

We stayed on Eighth Avenue all the way to 59th Street and Columbus Circle. There we took a right turn and started toward the East Side on Central Park South. I was still about five car lengths behind him. At Lexington Avenue I.Q. turned into a parking space and got out. I parked a few yards back and watched. He stood on the corner of

Lexington Avenue and 59th Street smoking a cigarette. He was clean as a whistle, as usual. He was a little under six feet, dark-complexioned, with a very flat nose and thick bush. He was vined in an open-throated white shirt with olive slacks. There was a string of shark's teeth around his throat. Aside from that, he had on the usual wire-framed sunglasses.

Another five minutes passed before I saw what was going to happen. A blazing red 1968 Firebird pulled up at the corner, and I.Q. got in. I took off in pursuit, but this car would be a whole lot harder to lose than I.Q.'s Volkswagen. At Second Avenue there was a right-hand turn, and the late-evening traffic was light enough to clear a path all the way to Canal Street. I fell almost a block behind, timing things so that I still caught the lights. The Firebird gave a left-hand-turn signal between 32nd Street and 31st and swung off down a parking ramp. I was sure that the two of them would be coming back up the ramp, so I parked across the street and watched. There could be no denying anything now that I had seen things with my own eyes. But who called me and told me what would take place? The two of them came back to ground level and walked arm-in-arm through the door that led to the Festival Motor Inn. I merely nodded and drove off.

I.Q. was screwing a devil!

July 27, 1968 / 11:35 P.M.

'I got to talk to you, Afro. Wait up!'

After walking Natalie home I stopped in the park on 17th Street. I knew that I.Q. had been following me, waiting for an opportunity to see me alone. I had waited for almost half an hour when it started to sprinkle slightly, so I got up to leave.

That was when I.Q. hailed me. He was coming in from the 16th Street side of the park.

After catching him with the chick, I stalled for a couple of days before I sent back the rejection. I hadn't known exactly what I would say when I met him and he asked me about it. I decided that since he didn't know I was the one who would inevitably accept or reject his application, I wouldn't tell him anything at all.

'I got this in the mail today,' he said. He passed me the letter with the rejection notice stamped across his application. I went through the motions of reading it.

'I wonder why?' I asked.

'One cannot know everything,' he quoted. He didn't know anything at all. I had him fooled.

'What were your papers like? I mean, what were the references like?' I continued to play the game.

'I had knowledge of naught but victory, but defeat has shown me only a clearer road. It is only a detour to better things.'

'You don't mind being rejected?'

'Sorrows are like thunderclouds,' I.Q. said. 'In the distance they look black, over our heads scarcely gray.'

One of those thunderclouds opened up just then and sent us scampering for the cover of José's awning.

You're a hard man to deal with, Brother Quinn, I was thinking. It's always hard to help a brother defeat himself.

July 29, 1968

I was sitting in Natalie's room with her mother. We were talking about the 'movement' and about my work in particular.

'BAMBU is the type of organization that black people have

been after in this area for a long time. Our parents have felt it necessary that our children be taught our native language and learn more about the contributions black people have made to the world.' Mrs Walker had asked about the place I thought BAMBU might take in the community.

'And what type of stands will your organization be taking?' she asked. 'Will you be pro-violence?' She had already told me that she was a Howard graduate and read everything she could get her hands on. 'I'm referring to groups like the Black Panthers. I wonder if that's really how our young people feel?'

'What do you mean?'

'I mean, do you really feel as though there is nothing else we can do but go out into the streets with guns strapped to our bodies as though we were living in the Old West and shoot everybody in sight?'

'I didn't realize that that was the policy or program of the Panthers.'

'You've seen them, I'm sure. They carry guns and wear berets. And what do they feel themselves capable of? I mean, let's be realistic, Mr Hall. What can several hundred young blacks do with pistols against the United States Army?'

'I think you're missing the point,' I said as lightly as I could. 'The Panthers, to my knowledge, have never attacked the police force or any group of individuals for any reason. They claim they wear their firearms for protection. You know how difficult it is to defend yourself sometimes in the ghetto.'

'*You* are being very idealistic,' she said. 'Of course that's what the Panthers *say* they are wearing the guns for. But in the meantime, they are constantly baiting the policemen and obstructing their duties.'

'The policemen in most cities and towns are not the servants of black people. If you will remember the reason for the riots in 1964 in Harlem and the riot in Watts, they were because a black youth had died at the hands of a white policeman. Beg pardon, that was here. In Watts a man was taking his wife to the hospital for the deliverance of their child, and the policeman claimed his gun accidentally went off. The police force in this country is only an extension of the government.'

'Let me ask you this,' Mrs Walker began. 'What chance do you think the Negroes in America would have in all-out war?'

'The census says that we are outnumbered ten to one.'

'You know that that does not answer my question,' she said. 'But you can still follow the train of thought . . . What do you feel are the best answers in the racial situation? Is the best method violence or nonviolence?'

'Idealistically, I would say nonviolence, but black people are becoming very impatient as far as that is concerned. Black people have lived the lives of second-class human beings in the past and are simply getting fed up.'

'Is this the way you feel? You know, it's very disheartening to see young people without hopes and dreams for better days ahead.'

I was very relieved to see Natalie step into the room.

'By any means necessary,' I said, quoting Malcolm.

Mrs Walker stood and smiled a bit. In spite of the cross-examination, I felt myself starting to admire her a bit. Most people her age leaned on the crutch they call the 'generation gap' and would not confront young people for their opinions. Many times I felt this was because they thought they might come up short in the knowledge department. She walked with Natalie and me to the door.

'What time may I expect you home, Nat?'

'About two.'

'All right. Have a good time. It was nice to have met you,

Tom.' I turned when I heard her use my first name, but the door was closing. Natalie was smiling.

'She likes you,' was her comment.

'Maybe,' I admitted. 'But that wasn't what you wanted me to do. I was supposed to try to get her to wear a natural and blow up Wall Street, wasn't I?'

'No. I don't even think Martin Luther King could have done that.' We both had a laugh as the elevator opened in front of us.

'You sure you won't come to the party with me?' she asked.

'Positive,' I said.

'What are you going to do?'

'Go home and read, maybe watch a little TV.'

Natalie turned to me and kissed me. I put my arms around her for a second and then put her down gently. She turned away as we landed on the first floor.

'I'm sorry,' she said. 'I act like a fool sometimes. It's a very romantic thing, though. Being saved from the tower by a prince. That's almost what it reminds me of.'

The two of us walked outside and started toward I didn't know what.

'Where are we going?' Nat asked.

'I thought we might go down to the Cobra and have a drink and talk about ogres and princesses and night queens and all that.'

'You think I'm kind of silly, don't you? I mean, you think the kind of things that I do are silly.'

'Yep. I do. But in a way they're beautiful, because they seem very real. I can see a whole lot of beauty in you.' I paused. 'Do you drink?'

'Not a lot,' she said. 'I get drunk kinda quick.'

'Well, then, my dear, we'll order you a dragon in milk.'

'What's that?'

'A large Coke with a scoop of ice cream.'

August, 1968

I started seeing Natalie every weekend. There was nothing serious between us. She was good for my ego, and because of me I think she abandoned her plans for going away to school. Her mother and I still had talks from time to time. Once I sat in their apartment and talked until almost four in the morning. The organization became successful, too. The classes that we held for the first week had only about eight students, but by the third week of August our teachers were holding sessions for twenty-five children per night, three nights a week. I had gotten two of the HAR-YOU summer workers to come in during the evenings and work with math and science problems in the tutorial meetings. Sister Mason and her brother covered just about everything else. I was trying to figure out how I could seat eighty students during the school year. I knew that by then I'd have at least three more capable faculty members who were knowledgeable in black history and literature. The men in Harlem sent down an exchange student who attended Colgate to teach Swahili.

N'Bala's was becoming a hot spot. I had put out the word for my friends that I would be expecting to see them come in and buy something. And when the kids in the neighborhood realized that school was sneaking up on them, they started to get their wardrobes together too. That brought the women in, and pretty colors always fascinate women and make them buy more than they had planned on. Many times N'Bala was too crowded and busy to go to lunch. He was as happy as he could be.

Phase Four

There was only one light bulb in the room, and it was placed in such a position that Afro never saw who was talking to him. He could only hear the voice and be sure that the man was black. He had been told to show up at the main office on 132nd Street and Lenox Avenue in Harlem at one a.m. for a high-security meeting within the division leaders of BAMBU. There were three other black men seated around the table when he got there, but he didn't recognize any of them.

'Have a seat, Brother Hall,' the voice from the shadows said. 'I'm glad you were so punctual. I realize that this meeting was probably a great inconvenience for you, but there are some things that we as an organization must realize and deal with. Are you ready?'

'I had a little trouble with the Hawk, but I'm all right.'

'A drink, perhaps, to warm your innards?'

'No, thank you.'

'I will tell you, then,' the voice continued, 'that the purpose of BAMBU is good, but we are still allowing ourselves to be defeated even within our own areas by the devil. He is infiltrating in more and more abundance every day and destroying the foundation we need in order to start a rebuilding of the American black man.'

There was a pause in the narrative as the speaker cleared his throat.

'Just how much of a revolutionary are you, Brother Hall?' the voice asked.

'I don't know what you mean,' he said weakly. He felt intimidated, caught off guard. The other three men were looking at him.

'Are you a fair-weather revolutionary? Be aware of the fact

that Brother Malcolm said that there is no such thing as a *bloodless* revolution. Are you willing to sacrifice your life for the black people in America if it will help to free them?'

'Yes I would,' Afro said.

'Fine!' the voice boomed. 'Fine! It may not be necessary, but it's good to know that the movement is that important to you ... The Man has gotten into our neighborhoods and into the very soul of black people, the very bloodstream, by their use of drugs. I am speaking particularly in terms of our young people. They are the rocks, the foundations upon which all our hopes must be placed. And this must be stopped!'

The voice paused again, and the only sound to be heard whatsoever was the roaring trucks that rolled outside, splashing melted snow and slush against the basement window. Afro sat with his back to the door of the basement room, waiting for the voice to speak to them from the darkness. He was wondering what would happen if he suddenly leaped to his feet and turned on the light switch.

'Already in Harlem BAMBU has started an extensive rehabilitation program for the users of drugs, in hope that their souls may not be lost to us. We have also started a movement to get rid of the pushers and sellers of the various narcotics. It is the sort of thing that had to be done sooner or later to keep our people from the continuous robberies and conning that goes on in the community. We are trying to cleanse ourselves of a disease.' Another pause. 'Brother Hall, you know the geography of the Chelsea area better than any other member of our group. For that reason we are asking you to aid us in our attempt to rid black people for all time from this great plague. I feel it only fair to tell you, however, that once a project like this is begun, your actions will be of interest to the syndicate if they should have any idea that you are behind the events that come to pass. If you feel that you will be taking too much of a personal risk, all you need do is indicate this, and we will think no less of you.'

'I'm prepared,' Afro said quickly.

'Fine, my son. Take a look at this picture,' the voice said. A picture was passed to Afro, and he looked at it for only a second. 'In the Chelsea area this is the largest distributor of heroin, cocaine, marijuana, and pills. It would be a tremendous benefit to your area if he, for some reason, discontinued service.'

'I'm sure this could be arranged. Is it important how it is done?'

'Technique is not important, only results. I am not trying to rush you, Brother Hall, but unless you have more questions, I have some information to pass on to the other brothers here that would only endanger you further if you heard it . . . Pass him the package.'

A small square box was passed to Afro. He took it and put it in his coat pocket.

'That is a .32-caliber automatic pistol and a box of shells. The gun is a hand-load Remington with a range of approximately fifty yards. Six-shell maximum.' The voice rattled off the figures with the same even drone with which he had conducted the entire conversation.

'Thank you,' Afro said, and got up to leave. The men heard his footsteps clicking through the door that led to the basement meeting room. Then his echoes were heard on the stairs leading to the street.

'Do I need give any more instructions to you gentlemen at this time?' the voice asked.

There was no indication from any of the men in the room.

'In that case, when we get the first indications that Brother Hall's mission has been accomplished and the little matter of Mr Valsuena taken care of, I will be in contact with you again. In the meantime, I will tell you only this: we are starting with the smallest possible areas. In this particular case we will handle from 112th Street and Third Avenue to 102nd Street and First Avenue. Our infiltration will begin tomorrow. Our second move will be in the Chelsea area. We are not strong enough to allow any detection of a pattern just yet. That is why I will decide when and where we will take over. Is that understood?'

The other three men in the room nodded.

'Don't worry, gentlemen. With the help of young men like Brother Hall, soon BAMBU will be in control of all drug traffic in New York City.' There was an almost maniacal laugh from the voice in the dark. 'Black Power!'

Afro

I took Natalie home about midnight and started toward the 17th Street park. The weather had been about the same for two weeks. Two days before Christmas it had started snowing, and it hadn't stopped until about eight o'clock Christmas Eve. In the daytime, while the sun was out, the gray-brown slush would melt, but at night the freezing temperatures would harden everything back to ice. I skidded momentarily as I walked by Isidro's house. I had been so busy looking for lights in the building that I hadn't watched where I was going.

There were no lights in the building. On the second floor I knew Isidro's parents lived with younger children. There were six kids in all. Isidro's father was the superintendent of the building. On the third floor Paco, Jessie, and Slothead lived. On the fourth floor Isidro lived by himself. He had been married, but his wife left and took the kid when she found out that he was shooting dope.

I surveyed the scene from the park. Between Eighth and Ninth avenues there is not a lot of cover for anything. On the south side of the street came the park, José's grocery, and then Isidro's. I wanted to get in and out without anyone seeing me, naturally, but the only door that led out emptied into 17th Street. Nervously I fingered the .32 in my pocket. I checked to see if the silencer was in place.

I got through the lobby to the stairs with no trouble. I had taken a look at the door, and it looked as though at one time a buzzer system had been used, but it wasn't there anymore. I walked slowly and carefully, trying not to have the old wood creak beneath my feet. I pulled the coat up around my shoulders. The hallway was cold and damp, like a wine cellar in a castle.

When I got to the top floor, I stopped. There was a melodramatic silence that hung in the air when my hand touched the doorknob. I reached out and started to turn the knob and felt the door give way. The door hadn't even been shut. I pushed in just far enough for me to peek inside, but there was nothing but darkness. The dim bulb from down the hall didn't even penetrate the threshold. I squeezed into the room and closed the door behind me. I was flat against the wall opposite the bed. I took one step forward and heard something swish through the air toward me. I tried to duck, but there was no way to avoid the contact. I felt everything in the room crashing down on me.

I don't know how long I was there. I don't really know if I was knocked out. I could see strange visions creeping past my eyes in slow motion. The sounds of the traffic seemed to play a waltz or something that swung to and fro and swung into my head like a hammer. I expected to see Isidro standing over me with a bat, but the lights were still out. I turned over on my stomach, and the room turned with me. Pain shot through my head, and I wanted to throw up. I moved my hands out in front of me and touched something that felt familiar. I rolled it around in my hand. It was a bullet. I kept feeling in the dark. One, two, three, four, five, six, I counted. I shoved them into my pocket. As I raised to lift myself, my head banged against a foot. Squinting a little, even in the darkness I could see that the foot belonged to a body that was sprawled across the bed.

I jumped for the light switch on the wall, ignoring the pain in my skull. It didn't work. I scrambled through my pockets and came up with a match and lit it. Isidro was lying face up on the bed with a bullethole squarely between his eyes and blood still trickling from the wound. His eyes were open, staring vacantly at the ceiling. I saw that the window that overlooked the back of the park was open and felt the freezing wind rip against my face and chest. I threw the match down and took off for the window. With a slight jump I caught onto the screen that protected the window from foul balls, and I climbed down with as much speed as I could manage. My right glove got caught in the screen halfway down, and I had to take my hand out of it. The wind then took it upon itself to slice my fingers like an ax. I took the last ten feet with a frightened leap and started running down the back alley toward 16th Street. I stopped under the corner light to look at my watch. It was ten minutes until one.

I was walking back uptown on Eighth Avenue when I heard the sirens, screaming and crying. There were more sirens coming from across 18th Street. I heard them answer like some wild animal's mating call. But then I heard something even more clearly. Someone knew that I had been in the room with Isidro! That someone was a killer! That someone had probably done it with my gun! I reached for my gun and found instead only the six bullets. Slowly, as I felt something even more wrong, I pulled out the shells. To my surprise, I saw that there were only five bullets. But I had counted six! The sixth one, I discovered, was a cigarette butt – with a square tip.

March 18, 1969

'Yes, I am glad you remembered,' I said. I was talking to my mother, who was standing over me watching me eat every bite of the dinner she had prepared for me on my birthday.

'You don't look like you had a meal since you left. Look at him, Henry. I don't like you . . .'

'I know, Mom,' I said. 'We've been through this before.

It was time I took a place of my own. I had all of these things to do.'

'And what do you make from it all? Two jobs, and you're losing weight, and you get a hundred and thirty-five dollars a week after taxes!'

'Mildred. Not on the boy's birthday. He's a man today. How does it feel?'

'Just like yesterday, I guess. Only I got some a Mom's fried chicken and potato pie in me,' I said.

'What do you weigh?'

'How is the work coming, son?'

'I bet you lost ten pounds since you left here.'

'Oh, it's coming all right. You know how it is, trying to get something started. But, considering the fact that I had never even taken part in organizing anything before . . .'

'What you need to organize is a wife. How you gonna get married working forty hours a day? I bet you ain't even met no women that looked like wives, with your nose in N'Bala's stocks!'

'Hold it, Mildred!' I knew my father's tone well enough to predict what was coming. 'Tommy is a man. He will make his own decisions from now on. He has a place of his own, and he works. He is in good health, and we have plenty to praise God about. I don't want to hear any more about any of that tonight. Is that clear?'

My mother's reply was to walk back into the kitchen with an armload of dishes and toss them into the sink. My father and I grinned, and he leaned back and lit up his pipe.

'What about this car we were talking about?' he asked.

'I think I'll get it,' I said. 'It's a sixty-four Rambler. The brother wants five hundred dollars for it.'

'Have you seen it?'

'I drove around in it once. I told him I would send a friend to see it.'

'Good. I know that everybody's supposed to be brother this an' that an' the other, but it's one thing to be dealin' with the white man an' quite anothuh when you're dealin' with each other. Have a mechanic look it over real good.'

'I'll do that,' I said.

'Have some more pie,' my mother said, coming out of the kitchen with the pie plate.

'If he's as bad off for food as you say he is, you don't know anything about medicine,' my father said. 'You keep stuffin' him like the fatted calf, an' he'll die of overexposure to good food.'

Everybody had a laugh. 'I'm tryin' to convince him to come an' live with us again,' Dad was told. 'If he eats enough of my cookin', he'll stay . . . I don't care 'bout twenty-one years old. He's still my only child.'

I thought we were going to get into another one of those things about I-remember-the-time-when-you-were-only-so-many-years-old.

'I want two things, Tommy,' she said.

'Yes, ma'am,' I said. 'What can I do for you?'

'They're for you,' she said.

'Now, there's a switch,' my father said. 'Something that's good for both of yawl.'

'I want you to get married.' Pause. 'And I want you to get your hair cut.'

My father and I fell out laughing. 'No bet,' I said.

'I heard you in here with Henry talkin' 'bout a car that's gonna cost you five hundred dollars. That won't leave you any money in the bank,' she said.

'I'll still have enough money in the bank to cover any emergency,' I said.

'I think you need a wife an' family,' she said. 'I think that's an emergency.'

I looked around the living room. My father had done well.

He was a book-store owner. I guess my tendency to learn and read everything had been gotten from him. My mother wasn't much of a reader. She had always been after me to get the education she had wanted to have. My father hadn't been a college graduate either. He had been a partner in the book store from the time he graduated from high school. The man he had shared the ownership with had been dead for nearly ten years now.

'She thinks that if you get a wife and some children you'll want to finish those other two years somewhere,' my father said.

'I wouldn't want to support a family on what I make now,' I admitted.

'I think she has a point, though. Right now, you're very idealistic. That's because you haven't got a lot of responsibility. I'm waitin' to see what happens to you when you get out into the real world. Another mouth to feed. More bills to pay. I wonder if your idealism will support you and your family.'

'I wonder if BAMBU and N'Bala will support you,' my mother said.

'It's hard to say,' I told them. 'I'm doing what I like, though. That's very important. To be able to enjoy your work and watch the young black children reach out for the ideas you're trying to give them.'

'N'Bala is no one's young black child,' my mother said.

'N'Bala is a part of my doing what I believe in,' I said. 'We've been through all of this before.'

'I want more for you than that,' she said.

'Maybe someday *I'll* want more. Maybe someday N'Bala will give me a partnership. Like the one Dad had.'

'This is just a fad. Those African clothes are stylish today and gone tomorrow. I want you to have something stable.'

'Do you mean you want to have something you can brag to the neighbors about?'

'Tommy!'

'I'm sorry, Dad. I'm sorry, Mom.' Pause. 'I love you both. I think I better be going.'

'I was heating coffee. I thought you and your father were going to play a game of chess.'

'Some other time, Dad,' I said. 'I don't think I could stand *another* beating tonight.'

I got my own coat, and instead of stopping downstairs, I went back out into the street. I knew that my mother's questions hadn't been what bothered me. I was still bothered about principles and morals and practicing what you preach. Revolution was on my mind.

There have been no bloodless revolutions. The thirteen states fought off the British Army. From the time of Rome and Greece, and probably further back, man had been fighting and killing for what he believed in. All of the brothers in Africa had had to fight bitter battles against the devil's imperialism. That was the part I had played in doing what I would have done to Isidro.

But killing the white man was different. Shooting the oppressor and killing a man the day before you had called 'Brother.' I wasn't sure. It seemed like the same old thing all over again. CORE against SNCC against Charles Kenyatta's Mau Maus. It still seemed like brother against brother.

The voice in my head was arguing with the voice in my conscience. The voices were raging over my soul. There might never be a winner, I was thinking. They might always fight. There must be a winner!

This is only the first step in the revolution. Cleaning house before you go out to face the Man. This is still the preparatory stage, and there must be men who eliminate the ones who stand in the way of our freedom. When it comes to the Beast and the cleanliness of the community, there is no color. There are oppressors, and there are those who must be free. If the people who are not free are not aware of the way that they must cleanse themselves, then it is up to us who think we have found the solution to help them, whatever the cost. And I had been willing to do that. I had been willing to stain my soul with the blood of another *man* in order to free those who needed freedom most.

I felt good. I felt as though I was right. I felt alive.

April 5, 1969

Dr King was killed a year ago today. He was shot down in Memphis by an assassin. I was watching the reruns on the TV and asking myself when it would all be over. Lindsay was walking around uptown telling the brothers and sisters in Harlem not to be angry. It was the act of one crazed man. But so was the death of Medgar Evers. So was the death of Mrs Liuzzo. So were the deaths of the children of Birmingham and of Cheyney, Goodman, and Schwerner. These were all the acts of crazed men. Slavery itself was the act of madmen. Where would it all end? Be cool? Be calm? Don't riot? Don't tear up? Where would it all end? Every time another Mack Parker story hit the world, it slapped America in the face. Every time there was another bombing or another man like James Meredith was shot at, it was another boisterous round of applause for the United States. One by one the men who stood up for black freedom in this country were being slaughtered, and the only answer was 'Be cool'? It was at times like these when I would say, 'Burn it all down, goddamnit! Burn down every goddamn brick and stick and store! Burn down every piece of concrete and cheap house that the white man ever constructed in this hellhole of a country, and shoot to kill! If we should die today, then what have we lost? Nothing comes from living like dogs. Burn it down!'

May 5, 1969

'I've always wanted you, Tommy. I've always loved you. Since the day I met you.'

'Quiet, Princess. You'll wake up the night.'

'You never believe anything I say, do you?'

'I believe everything you say.'

'Why haven't you ever brought me here before? You've known that I was in love with you.'

'I brought you here because I needed a woman.'

'How did you know I'd come?'

'I didn't know.'

'But that's all there is to it?'

'I care about you.'

'But you don't love me.'

'Why do women always ask so many questions after they've made love?'

'I couldn't ask you this before.'

'Why not?'

'Well . . . I didn't know how you felt.'

'Wasn't it more important to know before you slept with me?'

'I couldn't ask.'

'Because if I had told you this, you weren't supposed to get in bed with me.'

'I don't know.'

'But you wanted to be in bed with me.'

'I loved you.'

'And now . . .'

'Now, I still love you, but I know you don't love me.'

'I care about you.'

'Is that supposed to be the next best thing?'

'Meaning that that's all I have.'

'And you won't ever love me.'

'Ever is a long time.'

Pause.

'Will you ever get married?'

'There's that word "ever" again.'

'Have you ever been in love?' Stop. 'Have you been in love before?'

'When I was eight I loved a girl who was sixteen.'

Giggle. 'Did she love you?'

'She didn't know I was alive. I loved her because she wore pretty dresses and had long pony tails that I would've loved to yank.'

'What happened to her?'

'I don't know. Somehow I knew it wouldn't work out for us. But wow! My hands used to itch sometimes because I wanted to pull her pony tails.'

'For attention?'

'Yes, and because that was the only expression of love that I knew. In school, if my friends ever saw you pull a girl's pony tail, she was immediately your girl.'

'And that was all the love you had?'

'That was *the* crisis. I've had women. We always understood each other. We needed each other, and we made love. That was all there was to it. I really wanted to love some of them. Either because ... It was always gratitude, because they understood the fact that I needed them, and they came with me. Knowing that there would be no wedding bells and knowing everything else about me, I guess.'

'And me?'

'I don't know.'

'Did you think that I would be like that?'

'Like what?'

'Keep coming and coming because I love you, knowing that

all you want to do is sleep with me and then erase me from your mind?'

'I can't erase you from my mind.'

'But, you're not in love with me?'

'I guess I don't really know what love is.'

July 8, 1969

'Good evening, brother,' the voice said. 'So glad you could make it. As you noticed, we were waiting for you.'

I glanced around the room, and the three brothers nodded at me.

'Your work concerning Mr Valsuena was recognized, brother. Believe me, it was a credit to the people of your community and a step forward for black people everywhere in America who are victims of the Beast.'

The voice was coming from the head of the table. I could see that he was seated, but all there was was a silhouette and no more. I wanted to see his face.

'Unfortunately, brother, there was someone else in your area who took up where Mr Valsuena left off, and there must be something done about him. Are you any less willing to help your people now than before?'

'No.'

'Pass the picture to Brother Hall,' the voice commanded. A large blowup the same size as the picture of Isidro was handed to me. The shock on my face must have been plain.

'You know this brother?'

'Yes. I do.' It was John Lee.

'There are two things that we have in mind for you, Brother Hall. One, of course, you have before you. The other is a trip to Detroit. We will discuss the other matter with you later in the week.'

I didn't know if he was through or not. I simply got up and headed for the door.

'I assume, Brother Hall, that everything will be taken care of?'

'Yes,' I said in monotone. 'Everything will be fine.'

I didn't think 'fine' was the word I wanted to use. I climbed the stairs in a hurry. The night air was hot, sweltering, blanketing, smothering me, and choking off the air. I wanted to run. I wanted to run because the air currents go by faster and you feel cooler. I wanted to run because I didn't feel well. I felt like I was going to be sick. I wasn't going to throw up, I was going to be sick in my mind and my heart and my soul. Where are you, other man? Where are you, man who knows all about me? Where are you, man who killed Isidro, because I need you to kill somebody else for me. God knows I don't want to kill John Lee. John Lee! John Lee is a fat boy who lives around my block and used to work at the food market, bringing stuff to my mother on that bicycle with the big tub in front where the food is kept. John Lee is the guy who invited me to his house for a party . . . Why? Why is he so stupid that he has to keep on dealing those goddamn pills and shit? Why is he so crazy? Why can't he just stop?

I think I know all the answers. He's on a merry-go-round, and he can't get off. Now, that's very funny, John, because so am I! Well, in a way I am. The brother asked me if I would do it, but why should anyone else have to do it? You would be just as dead. Well, now that you mention it, I'm not on a merry-go-round at all. I'm out here in this world. That's just about the same thing, because I don't know if this is real. I don't think it is. I think that we are puppets, and someone is pulling the strings on us all. I don't think I can do what I want out here, but I think that there are some things that have to be done. That's what you think? You think that even if you don't see any drugs, let alone sell them, that there will be someone selling them and I'll have to kill anyway. KILL? John, do you know what you just said? You just said the word. Damn! I think I am a dedicated man to the cause of uplifting black people ... I said I *think*, John, because sometimes I just don't know. Like I just don't know right now. I know I don't want to kill you, but I know you have to die.

Then all at once it hit me. John Lee doesn't have to die! I think I can scare John Lee into stopping. Maybe I can just talk to him. And say what? And say that if he doesn't stop, I have to kill him. And he'll laugh and say that I'm his boy. I'm a friend of his. He'll say I couldn't kill him. He'll be right!

July 9, 1969

I went to see a guy that I knew on the block named Game. He was called Game because he was a con man. I knew that he would be able to help me with the problem I was having.

'Look, I need to talk business,' I said. 'Where can we talk?' For the moment we were in the middle of a crowd of crapshooters in the crap corner at the 17th Street park.

'Business?' he asked. 'Brother, you just said the magic word.' He picked up a five-dollar bill from the center of the pile and walked away with me.

'I need a key to put a thing together. Can you help me?'

'What kind of key?'

'Door key. A master for an apartment.'

'Frame-up?'

'Yeah.'

Game smiled a bit and pulled out a pack of Luckies. 'I didn't know I had competition in the neighborhood.' He laughed.

'It's not really comp,' I said. 'Just a small thing.'

'What's it worth to you?'

'A yard.'

'Whew! Can't be that small if it's worth a yard to you. A hundred dollars ain' no small action. Why don't you cut me in?'

'A yard for the key. Your help I don't need.'

'Where's the place? What kinda joint?'

'Brownstone walkup. Three to a floor. Even corners coming off the stairs.'

'A yard?' Game came out of his pocket with a key ring that must have contained at least a hundred keys. He shuffled through them while we strolled to the shade of the park maintenance house. The New York heat was merciless. I was watching the smaller children run through the afternoon spray from the sprinklers and wishing I could do it without looking like an ass.

'In advance, brother,' Game said.

'Half and half,' I told him. 'You take all, I keep the key.'

'What if it wouldn't work an' you paid for it?'

'I know how to find you.'

He wiped his forearm across his face. 'This is it. She gonna work every time out of a million.' I handed him fifty dollars.

'I'll see you tonight in the Cobra. About eleven bells.'

He nodded and walked away.

I headed toward 15th Street. The way I had things set up, John Lee had left his house near noon and was still gone. It was almost two o'clock. I had called N'Bala and told him I wouldn't be working today.

I had found out from Nissy what John's main play was in terms of pills. He told me, for the price of a bottle, that John dealt more Blue Heavens than anything else. Our conversation also pointed out that John's parents had left the day before for Syracuse or Buffalo or somewhere. That was why I went to Game and borrowed the key, or should I say rented the key?

The key slipped perfectly into the lock and brought a

satisfying click from the middle of the door. I opened it and slid inside. I noticed quickly that the apartment had been recently painted and that the Lees lived well. I passed through the living room to the back bedroom, where I saw John's clothes all over the bed. I was searching for almost ten nervous minutes before I found what I wanted.

Inside his closet was a brown paper bag, stuffed under a tall stack of boxes full of old clothes and games and baseball gloves. Inside the bag was an entire cuff, twenty-four packets of pills. I stopped at the four packs labeled: 'Immies. Ivy Hall. July 9.' That was more or less exactly what I wanted. When John delivered the pills and they were no good, he would be threatened, maybe even beaten. The possibility came up that he might be killed. Anything was better than my having to do it.

I took the four packs that were to go to Immies and substituted my own special Blue Heavens. The ones I fixed up, filled with salt. I was very careful to leave things the way I found them. I didn't want John to know.

Phase Five

'Are you Mitchell?' the captain asked the officer seated at his desk.

'Yes, sir,' was the reply.

'I read your name on the report we had last night about previous narcotic arrests in the district. I thought you might be able to help us if we talked and compared some notes.'

'I understand you went to see Paco Valsuena and his brothers,' Mitchell commented.

'We went to see them, but that's about all,' the captain said, leaning backward in the chair. 'If the info we got is correct, the trip was a definite dead end.'

'Why so?'

Lieutenant Thomas sat across from the captain's desk in his usual chair, right in front of the fan. Mitchell, the young Narcotics detective, sat in the guest chair that had been occupied earlier in the day by a man named Watts. Captain O'Malley got busy on the phone.

'Sergeant, give me Manhattan State Hospital, please. . . . Yes, I'll hold on.' The captain started unbuttoning his jacket and tie while he waited for a reply. 'Hello,' he said. 'Yes. This is Captain O'Malley of the Tenth Precinct. I'd like to have your records on a man named Paco Valsuena. Yes. That's P-a-c-o, Paco; V-a-l-s-u-e-n-a, Valsuena . . . Yes, I'll hold on.'

'Did you bring those things that we asked you for, Mitchell?' Lieutenant Thomas asked.

'They're outside at the desk,' Mitchell said, getting up.

'Yes,' the captain said into the phone. 'He was admitted on May 19, 1969, and has been given no definite release date. Thank you.' The captain wrote down all of his information in a notebook.

'Dead end?' Thomas asked.

'Yeah. Paco has been in Manhattan State ever since May 19.'

'What about Jessie and Slothead?'

'I'll call,' O'Malley said.

Mitchell came back into the room carrying a small leather case. He flattened the case on the captain's desk, opened it, and pulled out several pads and other notes.

'Give me TWA at Kennedy International, please,' Captain O'Malley said into the mouthpiece.

Mitchell looked questioningly at the captain.

'Jessie and Slothead left for San Juan on July 4, according to their mother, and haven't been back yet. We're trying to clear them. If they were on the flight they were supposed to be on, they couldn't have been on 17th Street last night.'

'Right,' Mitchell agreed.

'I'd like to have you check your passenger list for July 4. This is the ten-fifty-five flight to San Juan, Puerto Rico. The two names I'm looking for are Jessie Valsuena and Francisco Valsuena. That's V-a-l-s-u-e-n-a.'

Pause.

'They were on the flight?' Pause. 'Thank you ... I will be sending a man named Conroy to your offices at Kennedy later on during the day. He will be checking all of your return flights since then. Is that okay? ... Thank you.'

Captain O'Malley hung up the phone and turned to the two officers.

'They weren't in the States?' Thomas asked.

'Evidently not. I'm going to have to do some tighter checking, of course. I know that it's possible that they came through without using their proper names. The way I understood it, neither of them would move without receiving the word from Paco. He hasn't been available.' The captain turned and spoke into the intercom. 'Sergeant. I want you to send

Lieutenant Conroy in here as soon as he returns from dinner.'

'Yes, sir.'

The three men looked at each other for a second. It was a time of year when no one likes to just sit and think. They were doing a job that always seemed to have too many loose ends and too many details to check.

'What help can you give us?' Thomas asked Mitchell.

'Not too much on this one,' Mitchell admitted with a sigh.

'What about Isidro?'

'Isidro was killed approximately twelve-thirty A.M. on the morning of January 4, 1969. He was shot once with a .32-caliber automatic pistol. There was a silencer on it . . .' Mitchell continued reading. 'There was no sign of a struggle, and his mother testified that to her knowledge nothing was missing from the room to indicate robbery as a motive . . .'

'Clues?' Thomas asked.

'One .32-caliber automatic bullet was found. According to our reports, the gun it belonged to was sold by order to a Robert Miller, 169 West 113th Street. We looked into it. There was no such person at that address, and according to the landlord, never had been.'

'Had this bullet been fired?'

'No. If you care to look at the photographs that were taken at the time the body was discovered, you see where the bullet is in relation to the body.' Mitchell passed the two officers a blown-up photograph with the bullet outlined in chalk.

'If the bullet hadn't been fired, how did you trace the gun?'

'The gun was found the next day in a trashcan on Eighth Avenue,' Mitchell said.

'Fingerprints?'

'Clean as a whistle.'

'We got the word this morning that John Lee and Isidro

were having some hassle because of territory and this kind of thing,' O'Malley told Mitchell. 'What about that?'

'John Lee's name never entered the conversation before,' Mitchell said.

'When you searched the room, did you find any narcotics in quantity?' O'Malley asked. 'Such that would indicate that Isidro was a pusher?'

'No, sir. We found his works rolled up in a sheet in the bureau . . . The one over here.' Mitchell pointed again at the photograph. 'He had the usual needles, eye dropper, syringe, cotton, and alcohol . . . Oh, here's something. There were ashes on the floor, and we took them to the lab to determine whether or not they were from marijuana or what, but they were from regular cigarettes . . . The only reason I mention it was because Mrs Valsuena said that Isidro had developed a light attack of asthma and didn't smoke cigarettes at all. I asked her who had been in the room with him visiting, and she said that Isidro didn't allow his visitors to smoke either.'

'So you think that the killer smoked a cigarette while he shot Isidro?' Thomas asked sarcastically. 'What brand?'

'We didn't find any cigarette butts in the room,' Mitchell said.

'The killer didn't leave his cigarette butt, either?'

'He left the bullet instead,' Mitchell said.

The intercom hummed for a second, and then the sergeant's voice broke through. 'Lieutenant Conroy is here, sir.'

'Send him in,' O'Malley said.

'What do you have on John Lee?' Thomas asked Mitchell. The younger man shuffled through the papers in the valise and came out with a sheet.

'Practically nothing. All of this is information we started running down since this morning. No arrests. No pickups. Nothing.'

'We're going to go and visit Mr Lee after we talk to

Conroy,' the captain told Lieutenant Thomas. 'We'll see what he knew.'

A young plainclothes detective came in. He was about thirty years old, black, and wore horn-rimmed glasses.

'Lieutenant Conroy,' O'Malley said, 'This is Lieutenant Thomas of Homicide and Lieutenant Mitchell of Narcotics.' The three men shook hands.

'What else do you have on Lee?' O'Malley asked.

'Autopsy says that the time of death was approximately eleven-twenty-five. Lee was first hit on the head at the base of the skull, causing unconsciousness and second-degree concussion. He was then shot with ten c.c.'s of pure heroin. The direct result of the injection was a heart reaction, causing his left ventricle to explode under the pressure.'

'Could the lab boys give anything about the murderer?'

'Whoever it was weighed about one hundred and fifty pounds at least. This, of course, is a very rough approximation. The blow was struck at an angle of forty-three degrees, which means the killer was right-handed, or at least used his right arm to strike the blow. The weapon was a piece of clean wood, like a billy stick or a broom handle. There were no chips of wood implanted in the skull from the contact ... When we went through the assumed murder routine, it took us seven minutes to strike the blow, prepare the injection, and then shoot the victim with the solution.'

'A calm bastard,' O'Malley said.

'We think they were trying to make it look like a suicide. There were no prints on the needle that was taken from the arm.'

'What was the cloth that they used for a tourniquet?'

'An undershirt. Been through about thirty washings. It was shredded, and we couldn't uncover any laundry marks.'

'Damn!' Thomas said. 'This is as thorough a thing as I have

ever seen. A dozen possibilities, and we don't know much more than we knew before.'

'Robbery?' O'Malley asked. He was enjoying Mitchell's in-depth, detailed report, and was adding the facts that he did not have to his own report.

'There was $28.42 found in the victim's wallet. Evidently that was all he had. There was a picture of a girl named Debbie Clark. You can check her. Also some *Bambú*, cigarette rolling paper that the block uses for reefers. A library card for the library on 23rd Street and Seventh Avenue. A card that names the food market on 28th Street as his employer. A ticket to see Peter, Paul, and Mary in Central Park ... that's about it on that ... If there was a robbery, it wasn't for money or concert tickets.'

'The brown paper bag,' Thomas said.

'Sounds like a winner,' O'Malley said. 'Probably some dope.'

I.Q. Is Really Ivan Quinn

July 11, 1968

'You were the model for my sketch,' she said.

I took the rough-surfaced art paper she offered and stared at it. And there I was, or so I am to many, sitting on a gray-slate mantel that was formed like a chair, staring out over the small tributary that tumbles from some distant lake within the vast confines of Central Park. Dressed in a dashiki, blue jeans, moccasins, and wire-framed sunglasses – reading *Alcestis*.

'Was I?' I asked. 'You have painted more than me.'

The look she had given me was somehow reminiscent of small children when first they go to the zoo and see the many animals, restless and nervous inside their steel cages. The young mind is alive, and the eyes dart every-where at once, trying to see the fantastic before it disap-pears.

'May I sketch you?' I asked.

'Do you sketch?'

'Not nearly so well, nor with charcoal,' I admitted. 'I consider myself a painter with words. Another mere poet. I really think I'm a romanticist. I would have liked to have been around with Tennyson and Byron, but those were the days when black men were mindless vegetables, if you believe the authorities, capable of nothing more than having a plow strapped to their backs like some pointed-eared jackass, and weaving and stumbling, digging a crooked furrow in the earth.'

'You may "sketch" me if you like,' she said.

I took a good look at her. She was blushing, making

a great to-do about brushing the golden hair from across her eyes. This was more than anything else to keep from looking at me.

She was dressed in a billowing cotton blouse that I disliked. The wind had taken hold of it and blown it away from her breasts. The shorts she wore had once been jeans and came nearly to her knees. I was more interested in her face and skin. The face was soft, so much so that for a moment I thought it only an image of her true face. I felt almost as though I must write quickly in order to capture the impression before the breeze swept it away. Eyes, blue and set wide apart. Nose, thin and well formed, like a sculpture of some ancient Greek goddess. Mouth, sensual and tender, with just a trace of rose lipstick.

It seemed that we looked down together at her feet. They were covered with sand and mud from the bottom of the stream she had crossed to deliver my likeness.

'I like to go without shoes,' she said.

'A true form of freedom,' I said.

She stopped blushing, and her eyes read 'danger.'

'You're making fun of me!' she snapped.

'Be not affronted at a joke. If one throw salt at thee, thou wilt receive no harm, unless thou art raw.'

'A quote from whom?'

'Junius.'

'I ... see the point,' she said.

She sat very still while I wandered over her face and limbs, discovering with my eyes what I would convey with my pen. I picked out a sheet of paper and started to taste her secrets, as she looked first at me and then quickly away when our eyes met.

'Please remember that poets have a license to lie ... Pliny the Younger,' I said.

'And will you lie?' she asked.

'What purpose of a lie except to fool those who come with importance?

   Sweet soft something that must be only now, where were you when I was straight and cast up on the shore for God's inspection? were you only in my mind, or truly in my eyes? with lips like fresh rosebuds, eyes like fountains of mystery, and all of life in your smile that I no longer can see, where were you when my mind was smashed like a rag doll atop a sphere of this concrete hell? . . . and
                              where will you be in the morning?

'Did I make you think of this?'
   'You bring a lot of things to mind . . . What's your name?'
   'Margie Davidson.'
   'I'm Ivan Quinn. Some people call me I.Q.'
   'Hi.' She gave me *that* smile again. 'I thought I was the only one in the world who knew of this spot. It's covered on all sides by the bushes.'
   'I only found it today. Perhaps for you it's an unlucky day.'
   'Why?'
   'Thursday the thirteenth.'
   'But isn't it only on Friday . . . ?'
   'The general root of superstition is that people observe when things hit, and not when they miss; and commit to memory the one, and forget the other . . . Francis Bacon.'
   'Are you superstitious?'
   'No,' I said. 'But I sometimes like to know things like that. I read astrology to find out if the sign is right for whatever I have in mind.'
   'And if the sign isn't right?'
   'It's according to how badly I want to do it.'
   She smiled again.

'Do you smoke?' I asked, offering a cigarette.

'Thank you.'

I lit both cigarettes and took another look. She was about eighteen or nineteen. I noticed a high-school graduation ring on her finger that said 1966. Beneath us and across the stream, I saw her large painting pad, pocketbook, sunglasses, and sandals. She was watching me closely.

'Did you get anything from Euripides?' she asked.

'Only that without gods walking the streets like cops, there would have been nothing for him to write about.'

I reached into the shirt pocket of my dashiki and pulled out a joint. Without looking her way, I lit it, inhaled deeply, and passed it to her. She took it and pulled hard on it once and handed it back.

'I seldom like to read what dead people have written. I don't mean only people who have been buried, but people who were only walking death when they lived ... There was nothing there in the beginning, I suppose. Their lives were only struggles for the merest existence, not a battle for the difference between fantasy and reality. Where is the reality in Euripides and Aeschylus and Homer? They ...'

'They related what the people believed at that time,' she said.

'Then where was the reality within the age they lived in?'

'... Where do you go to school?' she asked.

I paused for a second. Without answering, I took a drag on the reefer and leaned against the back of my throne.

'I'll be entering Columbia as a sophomore,' I said.

'*Entering* as a sophomore?'

'It's really all very funny,' I said. 'Because I will go on being a hypocrite there as I was in high school and everywhere else. It's a funny thing about hypocrisy. You see ... it's contagious. You come to a point in your life where you see the inadequacies and even the stupidity of what you are doing, but you are forced by society to do things that cut against your soul. I would rather be dead sometimes than relating to James Joyce and Norman Mailer, but there is actually nothing else that you can do.' I passed her the stick and lit another. Our pedestal was caught in a fog of perfume.

'You could be a hippie,' she said, giggling.

'Yes. I suppose I could. But even the unorthodox has become a sign of conformity. First there were beatniks, and now hippies, and tomorrow whatever ... They say that they're living life the way they please, but watch them. They get high and cry. They get straight and cry. Where is the reality there?'

'What do you want to do?'

'What the hell do *you* want to do? ... I mean, it's your world. Why do white people always ask so many questions?'

'You were the one asking the questions!'

'Rhetoric. Not to be applied personally, I don't guess.'

I passed her another stick. I was almost certain she was going to get up and go. I didn't really want her to. The sun was setting, starting to drift to another quarter of the flatisphere. God's one great jaundiced eye peering into the insanity of our tabletop world.

'I.Q., who quotes quotes,' she said, giggling. I giggled myself.

'And what were you doing here on a Thursday?' I asked.

She laughed even harder.

'I was stood up,' she said.

'By a doubtless fool. Never see him again. One strike and you're out. Imagine the audacity of the ass to leave you stranded within the boundaries of this mini-wilderness with nothing to save you but a piece of charcoal.' We both laughed. 'I think the swine should be hunted down like a mad dog and shot!'

'And who will be the hunter?'

'I will! It was I who first realized his asininity and made my disapproval a matter of public record. I think that at the next board meeting he'll be castrated and his family jewels set in bronze as a lesson to all those who would dare desecrate the privilege of an afternoon alone with you, disconnected from all the mores and folkways that bind us.'

There was more laughter. The marijuana was affecting us both. We watched, near hysterics, as the poem I had written was caught in a breeze and went floating over our jutting station down into the stream.

'I'm really not amused,' she said. 'I've just – oh – lost – haha – a precious gift. I think I shall have to take my painting back.'

'I'll be damned!' I yelled, still laughing. 'I'll write a thousand more, and all of them will come together only halfway between my ineptitude and the glory of your beauty . . . I mean that.'

'Do you?'

'There was a time when a girl as beautiful as you couldn't stay near me for such a time without being kissed. . . . But I keep thinking that perhaps you are an illusion, something that my fading hope has conjured up to keep me sane.'

'And . . .' I didn't let her say anything at all. I reached for her and gently pulled her to me, until I could crush her cotton blouse beneath my palm and feel her pressing her lips to mine.

Her mouth was wet against my neck, and her tongue darted in and out of my ear, flashing a signal to my loins that sent swift shivers up and down my spine. Still, somewhere my mind was outside, cruising objectively along, snickering and taking notes at the funny-looking black-power advocate and skywriting the word h-y-p-o-c-r-i-t-e across my glasses with indelible foam. Where is the reality here, I wondered. What new games will I play now? I knew all along what she had in mind when she came trotting up here with her silly-assed interpretation of a giant penis charcoaled across that goddamn sandpaper. Here was another blow against the establishment. In the arms of a black man equals running through Central Park without shoes equals wearing cut-off blue jeans instead of Wanamaker's Queen Wardrobe at only a million dollars down and a million a month for the rest of your life. I was all caught up in the whole trip. And the winner of the Miss I-had-a-better-nigger-than-you-did contest that will be held in the girls' dormitory at Miss White America University on the day that school opens. And the reason is because my nigger not only had a tremendous dick, but quoted Junius and other famous people that I had not even heard of.

Here we have, ladeez and gentlemen, the main attraction of the ages. The dainty flower of the Western Hemisphere and crowning feat of world femininity – Miss White Woman! Applause. Whistles. And in this corner, wearing only an XL prophylactic – BIG BLACK BUCK! Boos from the white men in the audience. Right before your very eyes, this beauty, pale as snow, will be ripped to shreds by that incredible instrument that you women are feasting your eyes on between our specimen's legs. He will place it right at the mouth of our fair maiden's sexual opening and plunge it into her very bowels. She will at that time scream. Oh, my God! I'm coming! I'm coming!

In my mind I had to deal with the fact that my discovering a flaw in this new relationship, another ulterior motive that made our frantic involvement still synthetic, was nothing new. I had often related to the ideas of Sartre and Genet as to the basically banal nature of women and my lack of realism when near them. After all, the true nature of existence was one of pure independence, if you believe the Bible. There was no Mrs God, who shared all of her husband's problems, trials, and tribulations. There was no Mrs Jesus to wear black when her man was nailed to a cross. Even without my relating myself to the deity, I could see where men of certain natures would not be able to resolve themselves to sharing all of their innermost thoughts with a woman. The basic nature of a woman is emotional, so how could she possibly be able to relate to an intellectual dilemma? This was a part of the reason for my sneering at women in professional positions. If for no other reason than for the fact that once a month they *had* to deal with these internal issues that would make them sick to their stomachs.

On the block I was constantly engaging in the hypocrisy of daily living, simply trying to find an object or a theory that I could say was something I shared with others. The little girls I knew were incredible. They stared at me as though I were a freak, and when I got high I wondered if subconsciously I didn't perpetuate their images, because I couldn't understand them either.

'Let's go down there,' Margie said.

'Right.' I was talking to her and getting up and walking with her, and mad at myself.

Perhaps, I thought, sex is the link between men and women. It's possible that Western civilization has created a monster by giving women the same rights that men have. This way, they relate to each other in all phases of existence, and this exterminates the mystery that was once involved with romance and the word 'love' itself. If this is the case, then American society has prostituted everything by building up artificial sexual boundaries between black and white. The grass is always greener on the other side of the fence. White women wanted black men because they saw them treated like animals and responding like animals. Chained and beaten, living in a shack without even the vaguest of sanitary props. They wanted the black man because they saw no tenderness and gentleness, and their masochistic tendencies were brought vividly in their own minds. The white man had brought civilization into the bedroom, and black men could not afford the luxury of an inhibition.

Margie and I lay out next to each other in the high grass. I lit a reefer, and we smoked in silence, watching the rainbow colors attack each other as the sun sank and the leaves on the trees swayed gently in the wind. The only signs of the life we wanted to leave behind us were the blaring of car horns out in the street and the laughter and chatter of other people that reminded us that we did not exist alone.

I kissed her gently on her lips, and she smiled shyly.

White women must have a patent on shy smiles, I thought. I wonder how thoroughly it hides their desires in their own minds?

I disguised myself among the thousands of souls that clutter the Lower West Side of Manhattan. I was turning myself into a multiple schizophrenic with such clarity that at times I could even swear that I had seen my other selves. I could see the guy who wore my body and spoke in monosyllables in order to get into bed with an empty-headed, full-bosomed bore. I could see the other Mr Quinn who sat at a card table in the middle of midnight and filled the air with profanity. All for the privilege of sitting inside a circle of subintellects and drinking Thunderbird wine.

I found my hands beneath Margie's blouse fondling and squeezing her breasts. Her face was buried in my neck, sucking, biting, and kissing. I looked up, and the sky was covered with stars that only the darkness could truly expose. They were dim and faded in the twilight.

She bit me hard and started to nip at my Adam's apple. I squeezed her knee and parted her thighs to my hand. The fleshy thigh near the juncture between her legs was hot and damp. I pulled away the protective panties and teased her opening with my fingertips.

'Please, Ivan,' she gasped. 'Please, take me.'

I almost laughed out loud. That seemed like a direct quote from every piece of cheap pornography I had ever read. White women with fantastic builds slid in and out of bed with the ease of a mouse running through the Lincoln Tunnel. They would be tossed across a bed by our hero of inordinate staying power, and then yield to him at least through four thousand orgasms in the next six pages.

Where is the reality here? I asked myself.

I pulled my pants off with my right hand while I continued to tease her and scratch her with my left. When my job of manipulation was done with her underthings, I reached under to spread her legs, and started to enter her, slowly and with as much patience as I thought the situation warranted.

'Ohhhhh . . . Ivan! Ivan!' she gasped. 'Please, Ivan.'

Wow! I thought abstractly. This is the thing that black women are aspiring to when they paint their faces and dye their hair? This is what black women are trying to be when they get nose jobs, faces lifted, padded bras, and wigs? . . . Our people are too much impressed by the media. The white man has done a job on our women's minds. You can't tell the whites from the light-brights without a scorecard.

The things that were going through my mind were just what Afro was telling everybody in the neighborhood when he talked about BAMBU. He said that the only way we could retrieve our people's minds was to take them away from believing that each and every thing they saw on TV would make them more equal.

Afro is really a guy named Tommy Hall. He had been trying to start a chapter of this organization he belonged to in the Chelsea area. I had heard him talk at a P.T.A. meeting in the school on 17th Street. After his speech I acquired some reading material on the group and approached him at a party given by another guy on the block named John Lee.

I had decided to join because I had been fascinated by the idea of revolution, and all of the material spoke of cultural revolutions, and the intimation was that eventually revolution on a grand scale would be inevitable if the demands of black people were not met.

The whole idea of blackness sent your mind through a fantastic tunnel. When I was young, the biggest insult you could throw at an enemy was 'You black bastard' or 'You black something else,' and now there was a stigma about the word 'Negro' that meant you weren't hip to what was happening. But the word 'black' and the theory about white frigidity and negativity took away the word 'individual' from your vocabulary. Anyone who had made a favorable impression on you who was not black had to somehow be made to look as though he or she was something other than white. There was no room within the movement for the search for yourself, because the theory of black unity takes away all of the unique qualities to be discovered within the individual. That was aside from the fact that total autonomy was completely impossible anyway. But what about the countertheories to that? What about the fact that the whole is only equal to the sum of its parts? What about the fact that a chain is only as strong as its weakest link? Without a black man or woman finding out whether or not they were completely compatible with life itself, what was the point of lending total support to the security of a nation? How could a greater cause be supported when first of all the need that we all have to discover our own separate peace was without fulfillment?

The worth of the state, in the long run, is the worth of the individuals within it ... John Stuart Mill, I thought. And we will have a worthless state *and* nation when we find our own insecurity unfolded after there are no more bridges to cross.

I even wrote a poem once to convey my dissatisfaction with a total commitment to the movement.

> i, the finger on the hand,
> refuse to roll up with the fist,
> until someone answers this:
> How long will this anxiety
> persist in my mind? Who am I?

'. . . And my number is EN 6–0897,' Margie said.

'Good night, good night! Parting is such sweet sorrow, that I shall say good night until tomorrow.'

Margie blushed a bit, and I kissed her lips. Then she was trotting away through the clearing, looking back occasionally, perhaps to see if I was real. I waved back, and finally she was gone. The only true reminders of her were the charcoal sketch of me tucked in my pocket and the floating relic of a poem, hung up on a rock in the middle of the stream like a paper ship caught on a sand bar.

I looked up while lying flat on my back, and heard the wind whisper to me and the concert of the animals, unleashed and feeling free to sing now that most of the intruders had vanished into yet another wilderness. The stars lit up the sky like so many fireflies dashed upon a black canvas. The moon watched without so much as a glance at earth's confusion, cold and removed.

I had promised to meet Margie the next day on 59th Street. We would go to a motel and spend the night. Now I was wondering if that hadn't been a too spontaneous move, something brought on by the delirium that follows making love, when you swear about love that is not there and whisper sweet thoughts that truly have no direction.

July 12, 1968

It was nearing midnight, and I had gotten Margie to let me out where we met. The entire situation about entering the motel with her and listening to her moan out her pleasure had not been a pleasant experience for me. I felt ill at ease about the surroundings and the whole atmosphere. I felt myself doggedly going through the motions of a man ecstatic with sexual pleasure, but it would have taken little more than an amateur to realize the truth.

Just as I was about to get into the car, a drunk stumbled into me. I turned, and his face was appalling, something that I felt disgusted by. There were scabs along his forehead, and he stank of wine and urine.

'Looky 'ere, Buddy,' he choked. 'I rilly ain' gon' han' you no line, cauz you know sometimes I jus' ain' got the energy to git all hooked up wit' no tale about all this wil' shit. I'm tryin' a git me a bo'tl an' I sho' wisha God you'a gimme some money. You know what I mean 'bout gittin' all tied to a goddam' lie so like you livin' one? You eveh felt you wuz jus' livin' a lie, man? . . . My goddam' stahs in heaven know I useda be livin' a lie, but I rilly like to git drunk. . . . Thass why I ain' got nuthin' again' a young hippie anna no motherfuckin' else cauz why inna hell cain' a man git good an' fucked up, right? I mean, thass on him. What you rilly care . . . Have yah got annythin' I can help git my bo'tl wit'?'

'Yeah,' I said. 'Can life itself be not at some times intoxicating to such a point that you are a drunk no matter what?'

The drunk smiled, perhaps realizing what I said and perhaps not.

'You know, I'm glad you ainna a goddam' Chrishun, you know? I mean, the onny thing I got agains' God iz Chrishuns.

*BE*cause they is lushes onna one day an' a Chrishun on anothuh. I would give a goddam' dollah to the man who can criticize from the pulpit an' sympathize fromma bar stool. You know what I mean?'

'There is very little near us, save hypocrisy.'

'Nigh lemme tell you somethin',' he stammered. 'Nigh you a colored fella an' you done gimme this quarter. I done been askin' white folks to gimme somethin', an' they look at me like I got some kinda somethin' thass gon' kill they chil'ren. I mean thass gonna kill they chil'ren. You know?'

If he had ever been white, he could not now be truly so classified. The dirt from the floor of bars and the scars of living the life of a man with nothing was ingrained in him and as much a part of what I saw as his ragged clothes.

'Thanx, buddy,' he said, staggering away.

'Think nothing of it,' I called.

I got into my car and took off across 59th Street, turning on Second Avenue and mixing with the light midnight traffic that drifted toward lower Manhattan. The drunk and the things that he had to say were still on my mind.

Who, if there is no God, decides who is righteous and who is not? I wondered. Where is the special reward for the high and mighty here on earth who sneer at their fellow beings because of his or her particular station in life? Imagine the confusion that is caused by people aspiring only to be better than someone else so that they can base their successes only on the lack of accomplishment by others. Regardless of all the talk about milk and honey in heaven, you are still dead. Even the Pope, the man closest to God on earth, will one day be dead. Has he really gone on to a greater reward, or is he in the ground? Are you on the right hand of Jesus walking up and down through golden streets, or are your bones turning to ash and maggots and worms chewing at your flesh?

People rap about reaping the harvest of the earth by gaining friendship, and set out as best they can so that they may count up their friends like S & H green stamps at the end of the day. In the meantime, you can never count on friends the way you can count on yourself. When you are pulled from the womb, dripping and bawling, you are all by yourself. And when they throw dirt on top of the box that contains what once represented you, you are all by yourself. Your friends will not be in there with you. Oh, they may reminisce for a week or so, and your name will come up in the conversation now and again, and your woman will wear a black dress. But after a while your friends will forget you, and the neighbors will stop peering around corners to see what your woman is into, and she will start going to bed with other men. The same gap that first you fulfilled with friends will be covered with dirt and disappear while weeds and grass come to cover the tombstone that carries your epitaph. The same warm thighs that you caressed and the same love funnel that you entered in your woman's bed will be caressed by others and enjoyed by the living.

And what will you have to show for your kind heart and good will? A stone marker saying 'Here lies a man with a kind heart and a good will.' Soon even the greatest of things that stood for you on earth are gone. All the nice comments that were whispered about you as you walked down the street were as worthless as the air that transported them from mouth to ear.

The only true definition that a man can put on death would have to be in relationship to his definition of life. The true philosophical questions must primarily be left out of the ghetto. A man is too overcrowded in Harlem to spend the first sixteen or so years of life establishing the proper moral codes that will guide him when he moves to live next door to a white man. There will be no thoughts of clean, wholesome

America as long as sex, dope, and discord are your next-door neighbors.

These are the thoughts that had first given me my inclination toward joining BAMBU. This and the thought and adventure that the word 'revolution' seemed to intimate.

I remembered my establishing a desire to become a part of it when I listened and commented during a discussion with Afro at a party given by John Lee. It just happened to be after I had written a poem about Harlem and poverty.

HARLEM: THE GUIDED TOUR

Claude Brown has made it out!
Let the world stand up and shout!
Forty nights and forty days
Shall we sing the zebra's praise.
                        coming outside and reintroducing
myself to the cold that was inside,
smoking a cigarette on 125th Street.
On this block I see six liquor stores.
White man set a black dummy behind
the counter and wound him up. He
responds much like Galton's dog must have.
You come in and it pulls a string:
'May I help you, sir?' sort of like
digging on one of the white man's talking dolls that
blew your daughter's mind
and blew your fifteen food bucks for Christmas.
You pay him and it pulls a string:
'Will that be all, sir?'
                    ... and you swear because
that pint is all you *couldn't* afford ...
take about five swigs and the Hawk ignores
you ...

next block you encounter the
get-white-quick man selling numbers,
and you laugh 'cause some fool said
that the problem with Harlem is that there
ain't no factories for black people
to work in. . . . hell! They got a misery factory
manufacturing hardship and busted dreams.
                              . . . put a dollar down on 444 an'
cross your eyes for good luck.

                              . . . bye-bye dollar and
dollar's worth of food and
dollar's worth of heat and
dollar's worth of hope.

                              . . . bye-bye dollar and
dollar's worth of clothes and
dollar's worth of unpaid bills and dollar's worth of love
                              . . . cause your wife is gonna
close her legs and open her mouth when she sees
that bottle in *your* pocket.
Hello! to a junky in the next block
standing on the corner scratching the corners
of his mouth and imitating the leaning tower of Pisa.
Hello! to 400,000 New Yorkers who loved
reality so much that they never want to see it again.
Runaways, hideaways, and getaways from one hell to
        another.

                              . . . climb the stairs and listen:
to the joyful noises your neighbors are making and
say hello to the rats that have so long been a part of your
life that they all have names.
                              . . . climb the stairs to:
soul music and soul food and lost souls in Harlem—
no longer even singing about heaven.
                              . . . get a good night's sleep because

you're on the air again tomorrow morning
at six a.m.

June 28, 1968 / The Party

'All the world's a stage.' William Shakespeare.

'May you live all the days of your life.' Jonathan Swift.

John's party was a typical thing. You dance, you smoke, you drink, and you take advantage of everything that is happening in your favor. If the chick you're with is drunk, try to get between her legs. If she's not drunk, try to talk your way between her legs.

I realized what was actually happening after I had come in and sat down for a while, merely watching the things that were going on in the room. White people *and* black people are really psychological disaster areas. The whites, because they have never had any feeling for warmth and rhythm and are basically, sexually, frigid. Black people are becoming lost because they strive to imitate the white man's symbols of coolness and by so doing lose contact with their own emotions.

The truly interesting aspect of the set was Afro and the discussion that came up about riots and their causes and effects. I felt, for some reason, that Afro had convictions and was truly doing what he wanted to and living life for what it really stood for in his mind. I knew that I hung out, not because it was intellectually satisfying, but because I was searching, looking for something to relate to. After I heard Afro talk, I decided that perhaps through helping others to gain perspective about the things around us and the nature of the society we live in, I might gain new insight to what I really wanted to do.

Afro told me how I could become a member of the volunteer

faculty that he would be needing when BAMBU opened a center in our area.

Being as objective as I possibly could, Afro was real. He didn't seem to be trying to impress anybody with the amount of knowledge he had about the movement and the topics that we covered concerning it. I was almost a bit thrown off balance when he asked me whether or not all I did was quote people. There was an undercurrent of the question 'Where are *you?*' in the middle of his inquiry.

I felt even more unreal and false when later in the evening I made a play for this chick from down south and caught myself pretending to be drunk and filling my mouth with all the hip phrases and colloquialisms that I knew of. She was impressed right away with the whole setting, the New York thing, and the city slicker who had fallen head over heels for her.

'Look here, baby,' I said. 'You ain' rilly gon' git into no "Goin'-back-down-South-thing" only a few days after I have discovered you, are you?'

'Well, that's where I live. I have to go back home.'

'But, you don' seem to be relating to how well we could do if you were here an' I could be with you.'

'I understand what you're saying, but you know what is.'

'Iz that really the way the world is? Give a man a taste of a good thing and then snatch it from him. How cruel are you?'

She turned to me in the dim light and placed the palms of her hands on my cheeks. The look in her eyes was all concern and apparent sympathy for the pain she was bringing me.

'I'm sorry,' she said.

'Then let's be together for tonight. Let me take you out an' show you New York. Jus' to have you with me for as long as I can.'

I.Q. Is Really Ivan Quinn | 203

'All right,' she said after a brief hesitation.

I rambled all through our trip down the elevator about how many things I would show her and how many things I would like to show her if only we had more time.

'I have always dug women from the South. Square bizness!' I told her.

'Why?'

'I don' know. I guess I always thought that they knew more about taking care of a man an' tryin' to understand him ... Women up here cain' cook, cain' sew, an' the only reason I can fin' for callin' 'um women is because they have the babies.'

She laughed. 'You probably just haven't met the right one,' she said.

'I met you.'

We walked down through the Village. It was a Friday night, and all of the hippies and other weirdos were out there doing their thing. Ruth Ann was amazed by all of the wild clothes and the ramshackle buildings that decorated Bleecker Street and West 4th Street. I could only imagine that her idea of what the Village would be like had been closer to the Taj Mahal. She filled the air with a million questions that always related to the semipuritanical curtain that black women are veiled with in the South.

'How can people live like that?' she kept asking.

We saw all the long hair and serapes and sunglasses that she would need to see for years to come. I showed her a reefer, and I thought she might literally die. There was no chance of her putting it to her lips and becoming a junky. We ate at one of the many corner hot-dog stands and simply watched the people go by, mainly young whiteys out for a night of excitement.

When it was time to take her home, for some reason I was very sad that the evening was over. I had enjoyed being with her. The thoughts that I had had earlier in the evening about getting in bed with her inside some Bleecker Street flophouse had somehow disappeared when I first saw her in the light. I felt even more like a fool, because she had her reality, but I was still a long away from mine. I kissed her good night passionately. It was passionate, for me, because I hoped to continue the masquerade she had become attached to. I believed at that time that the thoughts of what had been on my mind were revealed to her. She took my spending an evening with her without a hint of sex as a sign of true love. I told her that I would call her the next day and take her somewhere, but I didn't.

July 27, 1968

I finally received my letter from BAMBU. It rejected my application for a position as teacher.

> Dear Mr Quinn,
> We received your letter of application for position on the faculty at our Chelsea branch. Unfortunately, we are unable to grant you a position at this time. Please feel free, however, to apply again at a later date. Also enclosed are free pamphlets about the program of BAMBU in the greater New York area.
>
> Thank you,
> Brother Domingo

I had never expected anything at all like that, but my little affair with Margie Davidson had taught me that I wasn't really ready to dedicate myself entirely to blackness. I felt it necessary that I talk with Afro though and tell him that I had really tried to join, but that things hadn't worked out.

In the back of my mind was a glimmer of possibility that he might want to hire me anyway. I caught up with him after a speech that he made at the Chelsea center and showed him my rejection notice. He said in so many words that it was too bad, but that there was nothing he intended to do about it. I simply left it at that.

July 15, 1968

On the Monday following my trip with Margie to the motel, she had told me to be sure and call her. She told me that we would be able to get a lot straight at that time. I stayed up late the night before and watched television. It was amazing how much you could see about the lives people led and about the truth that they seemed to be attempting to escape from in their everyday lives. Television was the current that turned America on, because the whole country is strangled by routine and tight schedules and the anonymity that comes along with becoming a number and relating to the life of an automaton, programmed only to exist.

I had had the pleasure or discomfort of seeing an adventure flick with spies and bombs and gadgets that brought me back to the view I had been taking of the existence the country has succumbed to. Black people with sunglasses on at three a.m. in the subway. White people by relating to the lives of Ozzie and Harriet. Black people by aspiring to the level of Ozzie and Harriet, when the whole situation was really ten steps backwards. For a minute I wanted to look outside in the middle of the flick and see if I could catch a glimpse of Judy Garland and L. Frank Baum skipping down a yellow-brick replica of Ninth Avenue with singing junkies instead of Munchkins.

It was at that time that I decided that black people were

never going to get together with enough authority to cause a major revolution in America. Their whole thought pattern in terms of what the revolt would consist of was hazy and vague. They didn't know if freedom meant working alongside a white man with the same pay, therefore necessitating a 'white' education, or if they wanted a separate state of all black people, such as Texas or Mississippi. They didn't know if they wanted integration or separation, war or peace, life or death. They didn't know if they wanted to kill the whiteys or save a few. There was not even a clear definition of liberal. Malcolm said that there was no such thing as a liberal, but the Black Panthers worked hand in hand with the white SDS. There were too many goddamn groups doing too little.

I wished at that point for a return to the humanity and the reality that black people must have once represented.

Perhaps I was wasting my time even worrying about the movement. What was I into? In the movement or out of the movement, or out of the question, I didn't know.

I dialed Margie's number.

'Hello.'

'Excuse me, I'd like to speak to Miss Margie Davidson, please.'

'I'm sorry. Miss Davidson isn't in.'

'Do you know when she'll be back?' I asked.

'She'll be back on August 11,' came the reply. 'She's gone for her vacation in Paris.'

'Thank you.'

And I'll just be a monkey's uncle or an ass's ass! I almost laughed about the whole situation. I should start some sort of interracial Hertz Rent-A-Dick, giving privileges for any strung out ofay bitches to get their ashes hauled anytime of the day or night. No wonder she had said we would get things straight!

December 10, 1968

Of all the months that there are, December is the worst one to be alone, out on the corner with the Hawk, drinking wine and thinking prose. The people in the city are frozen under ordinary circumstances. Too busy to pay much attention to a faggot strutting down 42nd Street dressed in a G-string. Too preoccupied to feel sorry for a wino or lush strewn in the gutter on the Lower East Side. Much too dead inside to see the pain around them and inside them.

Life whistles by us. We sit in iron castles and scream an occasional 'Slow down!' realizing only that before we are alive there is someone standing over us whispering in Latin. We know that there should be some way to bring existence under our command, so that we might savor the good things and speed the intolerable sadnesses that blanket us far too often on their way to memory banks without keys. The only true disaster is that the thought of death has become so frightening that the reality of life escapes us.

December came, and many of the things that I had seen as life rafts on a stormy sea had gone hurtling by me. Margie was gone, and though she had played only a small role in relation to my total existence, a big part of my mind had been dedicated to the enigma of her presence. I had severed my position with her from the rest of my mind, and set thoughts of her aside as though my head contained volumes and volumes, each covering a separate subject. My attempt at joining BAMBU had been liquidated, and now only came up when I saw Afro or the Swahili teacher they had employed from Colgate.

There was still one person left in the neighborhood that I felt at ease with, however. His name was Ricky Manning. Ricky was almost two years younger than I, but we stayed with each other much the way wallflowers cluster at a party. Neither of us quite fit in anywhere. The only real problem with Ricky was his overwhelming preoccupation with death and the purposelessness of life.

'What are we going to do when we can't get high anymore?' he asked one night.

I looked down at the empty capsule packets between my feet: Darvon Compound-65/ propoxyphene hydrochloride, aspirin, phenacetin, and caffeine. xs3751 amx.

'The human capacity for being bored, rather than man's social or natural needs, lies at the root of man's cultural advances. Ralph Linton. *The Study of Man*,' I quoted.

'And we will advance when we get bored again? To what?'

'To nirvana.' I laughed.

'Will nirvana get us down there?' Ricky pointed at the street below us. We were standing in the loft of the warehouse E. W. Cook abandoned on Eleventh Avenue when the rats moved in.

'That's really the problem, isn't it? Whether or not we want to be down there? What's stopping us from going down there or going into the Cobra or anywhere else?'

'Are we free down there?' Ricky asked.

'Man is free anywhere his mind is free,' I quoted.

Ricky sighed disgustedly. His breath was making steam in the darkness. The steam bumped the windows like stray clouds and blurred my view of the streetlight that illuminated our position.

'Eastern philosophy?' he asked.

I looked at him severely. This is the problem with the whole world. A boy, seventeen, mentally superior to his playmates, and lost. Not lost because his parents didn't love him or for any other trite sociological reason, but lost because a world full of people still make up an empty world.

'It may be the answer,' I said.

'Will you stop it?'

I was acting again, and I could feel it. I thought for a second that Ricky could sense it too. He was always so critical of everything that I got into, trying to save myself. Maybe that was why I always found myself hanging out in places like this, talking about things with more enthusiasm than I really felt.

'You can really understand this,' I said. 'Stretch your mind a little. Why do you think Americans always shake their heads in stupefaction when they look at movies and things that take a close look at the kamikaze pilots? They simply can't imagine a man being willing to commit suicide for his beliefs. They can envision heroism, but not the giving of life. They can see the risking of a life, but not the deliberate dismissal. They see life as an end.'

'But that's brainwashing. There were no free kamikazes.'

'But it displays the point I'm trying to make. The total commitment to a way of life!'

'So you now suggest that we go out and shoot up Times Square so that we can get killed, but knowing that we have taken a few more idiots out of their misery.' Ricky's sarcasm was thick in the air, as thick as his breath against the window. I clenched and unclenched my hands in my pockets.

'It shows the importance . . .' I began.

'Just knock it,' he said. 'I don't need it! If you're committed to the idea of the mind being the controller of everything, go see one of the whitey hippies an' get yourself some LSD. Take a trip after every meal. What do I care?'

'I may do that,' I said.

'And when you come back with your copies of the *Vatsayana* and the *Kama Sutra*, make sure they have epitaphs somewhere in the back that you can read over my body . . . I think I'll come back as a wine bottle.' He laughed derisively. I headed for the ladder that would take me to the roof and back outside. I was very puzzled by Ricky's whole bag. He would find me to laugh at me and my ideas, and I stood for it, when I could blow his whole bag away with ease and show him just where we were. I never quite knew why I didn't do it. There was a ton of confusion involved with the whole scene. I would stay away, come, go. Ricky would come by my house, laugh, sing, and write epitaphs for himself in my notebooks.

Maybe the answer was the 'cats.' There were certain downs that we took every once in a while, called 'cats' colloquially, and I noticed that Ricky was at his lowest when we took them. What I needed to do was check with the man on the block who was giving out with all the dope. I went to see John Lee.

'Look, John, I ain't askin' you to quit dealing altogether,' I told Lee.

'Shhh! Keep it down. You want my old man to hear you?'

'I just want . . .'

'Okay! Okay! But go see Seedy. I ain't the only cat around here with a deal. I ain' sold Ricky no catnip in a long time, anyway. Most of them go to the whiteys in Chelsea and up near 19th Street.'

'So you think he's been getting them from Seedy?'

'What the hell I know? I jus' wanna make sure you don't hold me responsible if Seedy turns out wrong.'

'Where does Seedy live?' I asked.

'Up on 17th Street, next door to José's. The top floor. You won't catch him now. It's too early. He gets in about twelve onna weekdays. Eleven on Saturdays and Sundays.'

'You know a lot about him,' I commented.

'It pays for number one to keep up with number two,' he said, laughing a little.

'Yeah.'

I left John's, making a mental note to catch up with Isidro and tell him what I told John. I was going to protect Ricky, whether he wanted me to or not.

January, 1969

I had been toying with the idea of taking LSD for some time
before Ricky sarcastically suggested it. When our school took
its midyear break, I decided that the time was right for me to
take the plunge. I had a free weekend with nothing to tie me
down in the way of homework, so I took off downtown to a
spot on Astor Place where a white classmate of mine told me
they were always 'making that scene.'

The room was dark and musty; dust seemed to rise from the
rotten floorboards with every step I took. A small, apprehensive
whitey with big, bloodshot eyes had asked me for a reference at
the door, and I told him my classmate's name.

'Anybody know Allan Rosen?' he called.

'Yeah!' I heard. 'Let him in!'

The door was unlocked with a snap and the chain unhooked.

'It's not him. It's a friend.' The doorman turned back to
me. 'You never can tell what kind of package the Man will
dress up in.'

He led me back through the narrow, dim corridor to a larger
living room where all of the furniture had been discarded and
crammed into corners. The floor was used for sitting, sleeping,
or whatever the people on it happened to be into. There were
about ten teenagers and early-twenty-year-olds lying all over
in various stages of dress. The only light was supplied by two
giant candles. I peered through the shadows uneasily, and the
curious peered back.

'You a friend uv Alley's, huh?'

'Yeah. He told me to come down and check you out.'

'Yeah? Why don't he come down and check me out?'

'Are you Barbara?'

'That's right.'

'Well, he said . . .'

'Save it,' she said, cutting me off. 'Sit here. All this yakkin' will blow everybody's high. Me an' you can converse softly.'

I sat next to her in front of the candles, looking around the room now and again. She immediately lost interest in me and started to toy with the melted wax that dripped along the candle vase, forming thin and thick red stalactites. Somewhere behind me there was incense burning, and the aroma twisted its way through the smell of sweat and funk to my nostrils.

'You come to get high or write an article for TV?' Barbara was laughing and twisting the ends of her dark hair through the wax on her fingers. 'That's what some people want to do, you know. I think I coulda been on TV ten times. Dum-De-Dum-Dum.' She started humming the 'Dragnet' theme. 'I mean, like on TV programs about freak-outs and all that . . . I didn't do it, 'cauz I want my parents to think I'm dead.'

She took her hands out of the wax and started waving them over the candles like one of those strippers from the Far East in an Ali Baba movie. I was caught up in watching the patterns formed on the walls and listening to her voice. She giggled.

'This guy from *Life* magazine comes in, an' he wants to have my picture in the magazine along with my philosophy about everybody gettin' high an' doin' their own thing. He comes in here with his camera and a checkbook, the whole bit . . . So we're sittin' here rapping about this an' that, an' this chick Susie I had in here comes outta the john freaked out of her mind on speed . . . Like, she's havin' a bad time, an' she goes through her thing, an' I'll be damned if Mr *Life* magazine doesn't get the hell up an' run outta here!' Her laughing became so wild that she gave up her hand patterns for a second to put her hand over her mouth. 'I mean, like, imagine a big company like that sendin' a square to dig on life . . . *Life* can't dig life!' The laughter started all over again.

'I came to get high,' I said.

'Goddamn magazines anyway!' Barbara coughed. 'D'you have a cigarette? I need to go out an' buy a whole lotta shit, but I don't feel like it.'

I tapped the bottom of the cigarette pack until the filter of a smoke stood out, and Barbara grabbed it. I lit it for her, and she nodded. The guy who had let me in came over to us.

'Barb, if I'm goin' to the store, I better go now.'

'So go! You know where the money is! Did I tell you what to get?'

'Yeah.'

'So what now?'

'I wondered what this cat wanted,' he said, indicating me.

'LSD,' I said.

'Seventeen hours'll cost you four bucks,' Barbara said.

'Okay.'

'Get it, Jimmy,' Barbara ordered. Jimmy disappeared into another back room. 'My doorman. A good strong wind come through this dump, an' I'll need another one.' Jimmy came back with a small round tab.

'I guess you gonna take it here,' he said.

I nodded. Barbara took the tab and dumped ice cubes into a glass of water. Jimmy zipped his coat and went through the corridor toward the front door.

'You ever trip before?' Barbara asked.

'No.'

'I didn't think so. It's wild, man, really wild.'

I was lying flat on my back in an open clearing with no one around for miles and watching clouds play leapfrog. The scene reminded me of Coney Island and the bump cars that you get into and try to knock each other to hell. The tall wires that connect your car with the mesh-wire ceiling zoom to and fro like tight barbed steel as you laugh hysterically in the middle of the chaos.

There was nothing near me save a few strands of haggard corn and wheat stalks. The whole countryside was yellow and pale, with few splotches of green about. The trees were naked against the sky, barren and shivering, branches doing their best to conceal the trunk's privates. Birds flocked on limbs and dotted the scenery, chirping uncontrollably. The whole connection seemed to shake loose in my mind. Corn, wheat, birds, but no leaves. What season is this? The grass seemed to be growing under me, pushing me up toward the clouds that were really only bump-'um cars. I looked down at my rising carpet. Blue grass. I was in Kentucky with a banjo on my knee. I looked at my knee. No banjo.

The word that was tugging at my head for attention was 'photosynthesis.' The grass was germinating, copulating, procreating, multiplying under my eyes. I had a microscope inside my head, or a magnifying glass in my hand. Maybe it was only a monocle. But there was the grass reproducing more grass that spread all over the countryside, six feet high. It covered the scrawny corn and wheat stalks and seemed to rise like a sea of blue grass up around the waists of the wading trees. Inside the hollow sprigs of grass were tiny people, tossing buckets of water into one tunnel while buckets of sunlight were being mixed in the next compartment. These were grass follicles; like hair on a human head, they were hollow, and there were things going on inside. I wondered quickly if I had landed on top of some giant's head. A poor giant with blue hair and tiny men living inside the follicles as slaves. *Slaves!* Tiny men and bigger men, and me not being either. I was not a giant or a lilliputian. I was still outside, watching and reporting to myself. There was no one else around to listen. I think I will call out to see if there are any other people near here like myself.

'Hello!' I called. Echo. Echo. Echo. Echo. No reply.

'I'm Ivan Quinn. Is there anyone else here like me?' Echo. No reply. 'I am a human being from the planet Earth. I don't know how I got here, but I am in no particular hurry to get away. My intentions are friendly . . . Take me to your leader.' I laughed at that last part, because it was obvious that I was still on earth. All of the things I saw were totally recognizable. The little men were shaped like humans. The hair on the giant's head had follicles, and I could relate that back to biology. The fact that there were trees on his head being rapidly covered up by the hair was no concern of mine. Or was it? The trees were up to their necks in blue sea hair. The expressions on their faces were sad but resolute, as though they were only succumbing to the inevitable. Oh, no! I thought. Don't tell me that this is a dream with a hidden message about conservation. The only fact that was disturbing me now was the question of what I would breathe once the trees had been killed. This would eliminate the oxygen and the rest of that silly-assed cycle that's supposed to be going on all the time. Unless, of course, this was really just exceptionally speedy grass. In that case, where were all of the people? I would really just like to see someone and ask them what the hell they thought of all this madness. The birds were definitely not in favor of it. They had flown and taken up new perches on the wires that connected the electric mesh with the bump-'um clouds. They were pointing accusing wings at me.

'Birds!' I screamed. 'Get the hell away from that goddamn electric stuff. Don't you know that as soon as someone pays another quarter to ride, you're going to be electrocuted?' The birds didn't seem to be as interested in their preservation as they went about chirping back and forth and pointing at me.

216 | The Vulture

'Then stay the hell there!' I said, still rising. 'At least one problem will be solved. When I see someone get into one of those clouds, I'll be able to find out what gives around here.'

I came to a theory at that time that I had died and gone to hell. I was very disappointed in the fact that hell was a lot like earth. The real exception so far was that there was no sun. Was it day? It was light. I came to the conclusion that the sun had been only a giant electric bulb that God had at last decided to turn out. In that case, what was I doing here? Maybe I was in hell, after all. According to the Norse legends, the center of the earth was ruled by a giant demon named Satyr, who had been banished to that internal oblivion by Odin for attempting a revolution that would have taken power away from Odin and Thor. But where was the heat? Giant demon? Satyr was rising to the surface. Did he have hair? Evidently. I was caught on top of Satyr's head, and there would soon be another conflict with Odin and Thor. I was going to a battle with a front-row seat.

No sooner had I come to my conclusion when I stopped rising. The trees had only their faces above the surface. The birds flew back to their stations at the trees' topmost branches. Their singing had ceased, along with their gestures toward me. I was surrounded by a wall of silence.

PLASTIC PATTERN PEOPLE

(preface to a poem) like, will you come back to the real?
black people – oh – walking cool – oh – silly woman
crying over AS THE WORLD TURNS – like, can't you
dig that you have no tears to spare/like, can't you see that
the chains that bound your limbs now bind your mind?
making you relate to silly, make-believe, fairy-tale-type

shit! like, will you come back to the real and see that
Snow White was just that, and a thousand shades later
won't get it.

THE POEM

glad to get high and see the slow-motion world,
just to reach and touch the half-notes floating.
world spinning (orbit) quicker than 9/8 Dave Brubeck, we
   come now frantically searching for Thomas More
rainbow villages.
   up on suddenly Charlie Mingus and Ahmed Abdul-Malik
to add bass to a bottomless pit of insecurity, you
   may be plastic because
you never meditate about the bottom of glasses,
the third side of your universe.
                           Add on
Alice Coltrane and her cosmic strains, still no vocal
on blue-black horizons/your plasticity is tested
by a formless assault: *THE SUN* can answer questions
in tune to sacrificial silence/but why will our
new jazz age give us no more expanding puzzles?
(Enter John) blow from under always and never so that
the morning (*THE SUN*) may shout of brain-bending
   saxophones.
   the third world arrives with Yusef Lateef and
Pharaoh Sanders with oboes straining to touch the
core of your unknown soul. Ravi Shankar comes
   with strings attached/prepared to stabilize
   your seventh sense (Black Rhythm!)
up and down a silly ladder run the notes without
the words. words are important for the mind/the
notes are for the soul.
                          Miles Davis? SO WHAT?

Cannonball/Fiddler/Mercy
Dexter Gordon/ONE flight UP
Donald Byrd/Cristo
                            but what about words?
would you like to survive on sadness/call on
  Ella and José Happiness/

                                              drift with

Smoky/Bill Medley/Bobby Taylor/
Otis/soul music where frustrations are
washed by drums – come, Nina and Miriam—
congo/mongo beat me senseless
bongo/tonto – flash through dream worlds of
                    STP and LSD. SpEeD kIllLs and some/times
music's call to the Black is confused. our
speed is our life pace/not safe/not good.
i beg you to escape
  and live
    and hear all of the real. to survive in a
                            sincere second of self-self
until a call comes for you to try elsewhere.
                        we
    must all cry, but must the tears be white?

My assignment, that is, my task for the coming spring was
to connect myself more closely with the interpretation of the
insight I possessed so that I might be able to turn others
on to the inequalities and hypocrisy involved with everyday
survival. I resigned myself to carry a pen with me everywhere
I went in order to paint these word pictures during moments
of inspiration. Sometimes the thoughts that I wanted to bring
out were pages long and often took on the form of essays,
but even more often than this I was attacked by little blasts
of feeling and sensitivity that I decided to describe as mind
messages, for lack of a better name.

MIND MESSAGE #1 I.Q.

Poet am I seeking a separate peace. (John Knowles)
Knowing no boundaries west or east.
Taking the pulse
        of a dying world

MIND MESSAGE #2 I.Q.

minds, like beds, hard to make up in the morning.
so many things to decide for a new day.
so many things went on between the sheets.

I was so concerned with the compact nature of the poems that I even decided to abbreviate my name during these intervals. The tragedy was that I still felt a bit like a hoax, an almost everything and a not-quite-anything. I told myself that someday when I had compiled these notes and gotten a concrete theory from the loose ends that I now saw, I would start a sort of cult to rescue people from deadening of the emotions – a disease I enjoyed comparing to hardening of the arteries, because the structure of the syllables was so similar. The results being equal in my mind, fatality.

School was tolerated. Not because I was hung up about becoming a status symbol for my folks, but because it was so easy to do acceptably while still not devoting a lot of time and energy to it. Half the time the school was in an uproar anyway, with all the young SDS hippies and Village 'anarchists' helping to stage a quasi-revolution. The purpose was to allow a college student to do his thing while still maintaining this student facade. There were hassles, with heads being beaten in by the City Man while chicks and cats ran around up and down 116th Street with signs about Columbia tearing down the buildings in the community and ruining people's lives and so much wild stuff that I never got involved. My stand was that whiteys didn't need any help getting their heads kicked in, when, in fact, they were the target of my revolution and eventual cult. I was going to intellectualize on the redevelopment of the emotions while they were running around succumbing to a mob-type stimulus that made them emotionally weak.

In the neighborhood things rolled along as before. I was into a rap-when-necessary thing with the women that allowed me to woo them when I felt like it was physically necessary that I recharge my battery. I would get drunk and get into a beg-and-plead, prayers-and-entreaties type of groveling, when we should have been begging each other, praying for a union of the soul also. The last of this was idealistic, but it expressed my sentiments on what type of hypnotic, puritanical veil the American black woman had become destroyed by. There was always an overtone of 'I'm doing you a favor,' until you were both between the sheets.

The only real problem that did not concern the path I was choosing concerned Ricky. He was more of an enigma than ever. He was warm and then cold. He was laughing and then sobbing. I wasn't sure if it was autonomous schizophrenia or drug-induced depression. As far as I could tell, he was still strung out on 'downs.' His attitudes intimated smoke, Darvons, liquor, and cats.

It was the cats that I was most concerned about, because he went through the thing about death. It was at a time like that when I felt closest to him and farthest away. Close because I knew I had an answer, and far away because he didn't really listen to me anymore. He came around when he was lonely and just couldn't express what was on his mind within his clique. There had been a time when John Lee first started dealing when he would come to me and ask about highs he should try and for suggestions about combinations that would give him a good ride. Now, there was just an occasional glimpse at what was going on.

July 3, 1969

At the end of the school year I went through a hell of a thing with my parents. During the year I had assured myself of a job as counselor at Camp Cheyenne for boys near Syracuse. At first it was a nice deal for my parents. I would be in the great outdoors soaking up a lot of sunshine, getting a lot of exercise, and all the other garbage that parents like to read into the comics of your life. But, as the year progressed and I finally broke down to them that I was into drugs, not heavily, but experimenting, they became paranoid about not seeing me for two months. By the end of June, when school was out, we had regressed to the 'We'll think about it' stage, and they offered me a trip to Boston for the Fourth of July weekend as a peace offering in case their decision went against me. I was already wondering what form my retaliation against the bureaucracy would take, and I thought seriously about leaving home, which I'm sure was a factor which delayed my parents' decision.

I wasn't very sure that as a writer I shouldn't be away from home anyway. Out from under the umbrella and away from the maternal umbilical cord and the paternal strap. There were many things that I was unable to experience while living with my folks. Things that would be essential in terms of human relations and depicting reality. There was much more involved with introducing yourself to life than a few excursions into drugs. Upon realizing this, I realized how many things there were to do before a man could say he had lived and had nothing more to live for. The problem had been that I experienced too much, too soon, thereby eliminating much of the adventure that comes along with legal, chronological maturity.

I did decide that leaving home would be a poor move, regardless of how my trial turned out. Being able to live at home had given me a taste of both worlds through my first year of college. I decided that to try to make it on my own would involve a job and college and interfere with my further discoveries within my soul through my writing.

I left for Boston resolute on playing pensive if I could not go to the camp, but remaining at home for a while longer anyway. The plane took off, and I was touched with the reality of *real* flying; how unimaginative it was, and how unlike what flying high was. Being high was a floating, cruising, microscopic drifting through all manmade stops. It was a slowdown for the showdown with your mind. This was nearly nothing after the takeoffs, except a tugging force that kept you erect. I vowed to fly back high.

July 6, 1969 / 7:00 P.M.

'That's all there is to tell,' my mother said. 'Evidently he jumped from the top of the warehouse and killed himself. Lord knows that that's probably the only thing that could have gotten him up there . . . But the poor thing. Ivan. Hating everything so much that he would have to do that! His mother almost died too. Can you imagine? Seventeen years old . . . But you know, Ricky did always seem like an old man. He never knew when to be young and when to be mature. He was always old.'

'Was there an autopsy?' I asked.

'Yes. I think she said there would be an autopsy, but no funeral. Ivan, that woman couldn't stand it! I tell you, it was the most pitiful thing I had ever seen in my life . . . They're going to have the body cremated.'

Sunday night. Went to Boston on Thursday. Said good-bye to Ricky before I left. Said I had some very important developments to tell him about when I got back. I had had in mind a purpose for both of us. The purpose of life being to experience all that you can along the specter of emotions and senses. Then to leave pictures and phrases depicting more beauty in the world than could be noticed when you were born. Death being not an end to life, but another experience, the final one, that you could not relate to people. Death being *the* experience, and the one that Fate would not let you describe to your fellow man.

Sadness overtakes the man who runs after it. Death overtakes the man who pursues him. Yama and Charon are alive and well in New York City! Ricky Manning jumped from a building, and there would be an autopsy and then a cremation. Where is the reality here?

8:00 P.M.

'Yes,' Mrs Manning sniffed. 'Ricky was taking drugs. I knew this. He got mad at me and started talking about being down all the time, and I was the reason . . . I never even dreamed that this was what he meant. I just thought it was angry talk. He swore at me about cocaine and all sorts of pills . . .'

'I know,' I interrupted. 'You know, you really shouldn't be out here talking about all this now. You've gone through quite a thing.'

'But I had to talk to you. You were very important in my son's life. All he ever talked about was I.Q. this and what you and he had discussed. I had to talk to you, knowing what a big part you played in my son's life.'

I wanted to say, 'But not a big enough part in his life. And maybe a part in his death.' Because if what Mrs Manning said was true, Ricky had not been looking forward to me leaving for the summer. But that was absurd. Naturally I had mentioned it. Maybe Ricky was jealous of my having found my answer, an answer which he was afraid he might not be able to relate to.

'Thank you, Mrs Manning,' I said. 'Remember, if there's anything in the world I could do for you, just feel free to call on me. I'll do all that I can.'

'Thank you, son.' She smiled through her tears that nearly made me cry. God! There's your reality! In that woman's eyes was a real piece of life and sadness that I had never experienced. Piece by piece, I saw the picture forming again at the top of my mind.

Fuck you, God! my brain was crying. Fuck all that you stand for, because you never even gave him a chance! I was so close! I was close enough to helping him to see my hopes in his eyes. I needed one more day to get back here and talk to him, and you fixed everything! Fuck you, God! And fuck death, because it's real, and there are certain realities that I know exist now. But I'm not ready for them.

'One more thing, Mrs Manning?' I asked. 'Were you told what kind of drugs Ricky was using?'

'I was given some long chemical term,' she said. 'But the police told me that they were called cats. Ricky had taken at least three of them.'

July 10, 1969

'Look,' John said, 'I ain't had no cats in months. I didn't sell Ricky no cats, an' I didn't see him on the night he died.'

John and I were sitting in my bedroom. I had called him after the ceremonies for Ricky were held on Tuesday and told him to come by my place.

'Look, man,' he continued. 'You keep giving me a hard way to go. I wanna know why! Am I the only man in the world who can spell cat?'

'All right,' I said. 'You want a beer?'

'Yeah,' John barked.

I went out into the kitchen and probed the refrigerator for two beers. I opened them and plucked coasters from the rack and took all the equipment back to my room.

'Where else could he get the stuff?' I asked after John took a big gulp from the can.

'What the hell I know?'

There was a thick wall growing between John and me. With every question that I asked and with each minute he spent in the room with me, the wall was growing. I didn't sense that he was afraid of the questions; I believed him. But nonetheless he was annoyed and irritated and a bit shook up. I could see the dark circles under his eyes. The thing that he was doing to the Junior Jones boys took on new meaning. It was no longer only supplying kicks, but quick deaths.

'What about . . .' I began.

'Cut it, Q. Cut it! I don't know nothing. I ain't seen nothing. And I don't want you talking to me about it anymore.'

I made another analysis. He seemed too uptight. Maybe guilt. Maybe personal guilt, and maybe guilt by association, but John Lee was uptight. His face was a sneer. His eyes were on fire. He gulped the last half of the beer in the can and stumbled to his feet, off balance in his hurry to leave. I heard the door slam out in the hall. He was gone.

July 11, 1969

'Hello?'

'Yeah, Q. This is Lee.' I heard the voice coming over slowly and with a hint of danger. 'Where were you on about the night of January 3 and the morning of January 4?' he asked.

'When? How the hell would I know?'

'Think hard. That was the night Isidro was killed.'

'I don't remember,' I said after a pause.

226 | The Vulture

'Well, suppose I told you that while you were getting the beer last night I was looking around your room a little. And what if I said I found the .32-caliber piece you used to carry on the corner when the times was hot?'

'I'd say "So what?"'

'And what if I told you that out of curiosity I took it to the man who made it. A man from your block named Game; and he ran it through a check or two and told me that it was definitely the gun that was used to kill Isidro. Where would you say you were on the night Isidro was killed?'

I heard John's voice, rolling toward me like a giant boulder that I couldn't get out of the way of. His breath was rasping, heavy in my telephone, as though he had been running. I felt the sweat materialize on my top lip.

'I was downtown in the Village. Lower East Side. Hanging out with a few friends of mine. No, my friends didn't show. I was just sort of wandering around looking for them, because I lost the address. Uh. I was going in and out of dives and clubs, trying to find some tail. You know, uh . . .'

'What do you think the Man would say if he knew what I knew and had what I have?'

'I get the message,' I said. 'What do you want for me to get the gun back?'

'You know what I didn't like about the thing?' John breathed. 'I didn't like the fact that you set me up for a lot of people when you killed him. I didn't give a damn about Seedy. I didn't care if he lived or died. The people who dealt with him when he got shot never came to me. But you set me up.'

'What do you want?'

'I want seven hundred and fifty dollars in cash. I want it by tomorrow night. If I don't see you before midnight, I'm taking the gun to the cops, or I'll see that they get it anonymously.'

'What if I say that. I'll see that they get you?' I asked.

'So what if they get me if I ain't got nothing and my house

is clean? They may watch me, even close down my business, but I will survive ... You won't. Murder is a very serious thing. I remember when we didn't think so. We know better now ... You shouldn't have kept the gun, I.Q. A man of your intelligence should know better.'

'Where will I see you tomorrow night?' I asked.

'I'll be around. I won't give you a particular place to meet me. There's too much risk involved. But I'll be watching you. Be in the streets by eight o'clock with the money. I'll be watching you.'

'Where do you expect me to get that kind of money so quickly?' I yelled into the receiver.

'I don't care.'

The phone clicked shut. I was standing there with my ears burning, my ears stung by sweat, my whole shirt wringing wet. I could see the look on John's face. Seven hundred and fifty dollars for the gun. It was really too late to do anything but hope. I picked up the phone again. Many people can play at blackmail. I was all hung up with the adventure of pitting my mind against other people, while the reality of it all gave me a tight feeling in the pit of my stomach that made me think I might piss on myself.

'Hello, Margie?' I asked.

'Yes. Who is it?'

'This is Ivan Quinn, from the Festival Motor Inn,' I said.

'Who? ... Oh!'

'You didn't pay your bill when you left,' I sneered. 'Not all of it. The fact that I know you have an appendix scar and a birthmark on your right inner thigh was tabulated along with the bill. You owe us seven hundred and fifty dollars. Payable tomorrow afternoon.'

Phase Six

'Yes, sir. I'm Captain O'Malley, an' this is Lieutenant Thomas.'

The two policemen were ushered into a neat living room, where their host offered them seats. They sat next to each other on the sofa, and Thomas took out his black note pad.

'Now, Mr Lee, I know you've been through quite a bit today, but we have a few more questions for both you and your wife.'

'My wife is in bed now,' Hamilton Lee said. 'The doctor was in and gave her a shot. She has a bad heart condition. I think the shock almost killed her.'

'Then we'll come back and talk to her,' O'Malley said.

'Are you sure I can't answer everything?'

'Well, how long had your son been dealing drugs?'

'I didn't know anything about it until this morning,' Mr Lee said. 'We were out of town until this morning ... I thought that I had spoken with every cop in town.'

'Then you're saying that you were informed of the drug situation by the men from the Narcotics Department.'

'That's right,' came the reply. 'A short man, Ramirez, and Sergeant Holder.'

'Did they search John's room?'

'They searched the whole house. Everything was in an uproar. The lady next door was kind enough to come over and straighten up.'

'They must not have found anything,' Thomas commented to the captain.

'What about enemies? Did John have any personal enemies he might have mentioned to you?'

'No. John was never involved too much in the gangs. He's only been out around in the last year and a half or so. . . . He got himself a job at the food market and made himself a few friends.'

'You made no notice of the fact that John was out a lot at night?' O'Malley asked.

Hamilton Lee was very uncomfortable. He was searching the walls of his apartment for something to look at.

'John was eighteen years old. The first sixteen years of his life or so were miserable. He was far overweight. He weighed almost 230 pounds, and then the doctor gave him some medicine for losing all this fat. He started going outside, playing a little ball. He got himself a girl friend. Sure, we noticed that he was out a lot, but we thought it was because he had been embarrassed about his weight for so long that he was just making up for lost time ... My wife and I were so happy to ...'

'Yes, sir,' Thomas cut in. 'You mentioned a girl.' The lieutenant searched back through his notes. 'Would her name be Debbie Clark?'

'That's right.'

'Do you happen to know her address?'

'Well, yes, but she and John weren't together ... They had a little fight of some kind. John said he wasn't seeing her anymore.'

'When was this?'

'In April.'

O'Malley and Thomas looked at each other. 'We'll take the address anyway,' Thomas said. Mr Lee recited it.

'What about close friends? People who might have known what John was doing?'

Mr Lee seemed to be lost in thought.

'Spade,' he said. 'That's a boy who lives in the projects. His name is Eddie Shannon. Junior Jones, who lives on 19th Street.'

'Do you know Shannon's address?'

'No.'

'And Jones?'

'His real name is Theodore. They just call him Junior.'

Thomas wrote hurriedly.

'And Ivan Quinn.'

'Who?'

'Ivan Quinn. He's a student at Columbia.'

O'Malley cut in, 'These three know about ...'

'I don't know if they knew!' Mr Lee said. 'They were friends of my son.'

Tears were streaking Mr Lee's face. He had tried to wipe them away with his hand, and was now simply crying unashamedly.

'I don't know what to say,' he began softly. 'I knew that John was doing something wrong. He was buying clothes I knew that his job couldn't be paying for. He was buying presents for his girl ... The things he bought for me and Cassie for Christmas cost almost fifty dollars ... But what could I say? I told him if there was anything he wanted to talk to me about to come and sit down and we'd discuss it ... Money. A car. Anything. But he said everything was fine. I thought maybe he was stealing money from his job. Drugs? I never even detected John's being drunk. And now this ...' The big man sniffed and rubbed his eyes. 'Miss Carter, the woman across the hall, told me when she was here this morning that she had had a dream about John. You know how old people have these visions? John was a nice boy. Everybody told me he was always courteous and ran errands for them. And you want me to tell you something – Lord knows, I wish somebody would tell me – Cassie's heart is broken. When we had John, the doctor told us that she couldn't have any more. You know what that does to a woman who's been plannin' on a big fam'ly? Her only son. Her only son.'

July 5, 1969

'Yeah,' Junior Jones said. 'I been waitin' t'git high an' jus' be high alla time. Ya know?'

'Yeah.'

'I been wantin' t'git high wit' you cauz I wanned t'show you som'thin' that Afro gave me today.' Junior reached into his pocket and pulled out a cigarette with a squared tip. 'Ya know where Afro said he got this? He said he found it in Seedy's room. He said he went to talk t'Seedy, an' somebody flattened the back a hiz head. When he came to, whoever killed Seedy wuz gone, but he left this cigarette . . . You the only one 'roun' here square off the butts like this. Right?'

'Afro came to shoot somebody. He had a gun.'

'Yeah. You took it. But my seein' this butt here made me know everything real perfect. The night Seedy wuz killed, you saved me from Pedro. You came up behind us an' tol' him I had been wit' you smokin' reefers. You said that t'give yourself a alibi. The only thing that bothered me was why Pedro believed you . . . That wuz 'cauz Seedy had tol' all the P.R.'s that you could be trusted 'cauz you tol' him when I wuz gittin' ready t'rob him . . . You damn near got me killed twice. Once when Seedy found out I wuz gonna rob 'im an' started carryin' a gun, an' the other when you shot Seedy an' all the P.R.'s thought it wuz either me or John Lee.'

Ricky Manning smiled sourly.

'Does Afro know that I called to tell him about I.Q. an' that white bitch?' Ricky asked.

'I wuz gittin' t'that. I figgered it when me an' Afro started talkin' 'bout how somebody inna neighborhood wuz a dime dropper. When he tol' me 'bout what happened ta I.Q., I started tryin' t'figger out who me an' Q had in common. The answer wuz you. An' to top it all, you had a motive wit' me, but I thought you an' Q wuz tight.'

'I.Q. fell in love with a white bitch!' Ricky said bitterly. 'He met her at a motel an' screwed her. It wuzn't right!'

'Why not?'

'Ha! You simple bastard. You couldn't understand. I.Q. was mine! . . . How would you know what we had? We related on all levels. But there was no way for us to stay with each other. I.Q. is supposed to have a girl. Junior, did you ever love something that you knew you couldn't have?'

'Yeah. I guess.' Junior spoke through a cloud of cigarette smoke.

'Then you know what I mean. I came lookin' for you that night to tell you that Seedy was dead and to be looking out for Pedro. I knew he would probably try to get you. He hates your guts. I had to do something. I was getting all my cats from Seedy. I.Q. told Lee not to sell me any more. I went to Seedy and told him that I could give him some valuable information if he would keep me supplied with cats. I told him that you were going to make a hit on him and take all of his stuff . . . For a while things went on fine. He supplied me. Then John Lee told I.Q. I was getting my pills from Seedy, and I.Q. told Seedy to stop selling me anything. He thought I was going to commit suicide. Seedy got scared because everyone told him that I.Q. was crazy. When I showed up for my cats, he told me to get lost. He said that if I ever bothered him again he'd tell you how he found out about the attack you planned. I had to kill him.'

'Where'd you get a gun?' Junior asked.

'I took I.Q.'s gun. The .32 he has with the silencer. I killed Seedy, and then I put the gun back in I.Q.'s room. He never missed it.' Junior watched carefully as Ricky seemed caught up with a sudden wild sense of humor. 'I.Q.'ll go to jail for me if the Man ever finds that gun!'

'An' you tol' I.Q.'s secret love life to Afro because he stopped you from getting pills?'

'No. No. No. I told Afro long before that. It was about two weeks after I told Seedy about you. I.Q. wanted to join BAMBU, but I couldn't let him do anything that would keep him from seeing me every day. So I told.'

'So you told,' Junior repeated.

'Ha! Ha! You don't know what it's like to have to admit to yourself that you're a freak. To say to yourself that society does not accept what you want. You do a lot to hold on to what little you have. I knew I.Q. would never love me, but I had to keep him near me if I could.'

'And one thing led to another?'

'I told on you to get cats, Junior. Seedy gave me cats for nothing. They have to be the most beautiful high in the world. I told on I.Q. because I love him. You have to try to get the ones you love. Don't you? . . . And I killed Seedy to keep everything quiet. He was scared of I.Q. He was scared I.Q. would kill him if I got another cat from him. He was going to tell you that I was the traitor you were looking for. I couldn't let him do that to me.'

Junior looked away from Ricky. Tears had been welling up in Ricky's eyes as he confessed the things that he had done. It was all quite a coincidence. A light discussion with Afro about Uncle Toms had put them on the subject of brothers who informed on brothers. Junior had not told I.Q. when it dawned on him that the square-tipped cigarette butt made Ricky Manning the missing link. Junior had called Ricky and told him to join him on the roof of the warehouse where they often got high. Ricky agreed to come and get high, but now that everything was clear and tears were rolling down Ricky's face, Junior realized he still had no total answer. He looked across the New York skyline, a thousand twinkling lights, as though he would receive a coded message from the neon jungle. That was why he didn't see Ricky Manning jump eight flights to his death.

July 12, 1969 / 11:46 P.M.

'It's too bad you had to kill him, but I told him night before last that tonight was the deadline. Nobody can hit me for seven hundred and fifty dollars and then tell me to wait ... How much did you get?'

'he had about a hundred and ten in them blue heaven pills. i ain' riff 'im fo' cash.'

'Wednesday night he call me an' tol' me that he had two hundred and fifty dollars' worth of bad pills in the load I sent him. Anything wrong with the pills?'

'not nuthin' i can see.'

'What else?'

'he had a .32 inna paper bag wit' de pills. he gotta be a stupid cat runnin' aroun' wit' a unloaded gun inna paper bag.'

'But, so far as the five hundred dollars he took Monday and the rest, there were no signs, right?'

''ass right.'

'Yeah ... Well, c'mon in then, Smoky. I guess the party'll start in an hour or so. Did you reach Spade?'

'yeah. i caught 'im onna job.'

'That's a good boy. Look, I got this amazon go-go girl for you.'

'right. i need t'go-go fo' a while.' Smoky laughed. 'twenny minits i be there.'

Behind the twenty-five-story apartment building that faces 17th Street between Ninth and Tenth avenues, the crowd of onlookers stared with eyes wide at the bespectacled photographer who fired flashbulbs at the prone body. They did not notice the vulture flying overhead.

THE NIGGER FACTORY

this book is dedicated to:

Sister Jackie Brown
Brother Victor Brown
Brother David Barnes
Brother Brian Jackson
Brother Eddie Knowles
and
Brother Charlie Saunders
whom I met on the assembly line

Contents

Author's Note

Black colleges and universities have been both a blessing and a curse on Black people. The institutions have educated thousands of our people who would have never had the opportunity to get an education otherwise. They have supplied for many a new sense of dignity and integrity. They have never, however, made anybody equal. This is a reality for Black educators everywhere as students all over America demonstrate for change.

It has been said time and time again that the media makes the world we live in a much smaller place. It is no longer possible to attend Obscure University and be completely out of touch with the racist system that continues to oppress our brothers and sisters all over the country. Black institutions of higher learning can no longer be considered as wombs of security when all occupants realize that we are locked in the jaws of a beast.

Change is overdue. Fantasies about the American Dream are now recognized by Black people as hoaxes and people are tired of trying to become a part of something that deprives them of the necessities of life even after years of bogus study in preparation for this union. A college diploma is *not* a ticket on the Freedom Train. It is, at best, an opportunity to learn more about the systems that control life and destroy life: an opportunity to cut through the hypocrisy and illusion that America represents.

New educational aspects must be discovered. Our educators must sit down and really evaluate the grading system that perpetuates academic dishonesty. The center of our intellectual attention must be thrust away from Greek, Western thought toward Eastern and Third World thought. Our examples in the arts must be Black and not white. Our natural creativity must be cultivated.

The main trouble in higher education lies in the fact that while the times have changed radically, educators and administrators have continued to plod along through the bureaucratic red tape that stalls so much American progress. We have once again been caught short while imitating the white boy. While knowledge accumulates at a startling pace our institutions are content to produce quasi-white folks and semithinkers whose total response is trained rather than felt.

Black students in the 1970s will not be satisfied with Bullshit Degrees or Nigger Educations. They are aware of the hypocrisy and indoctrination and are searching for other alternatives. With the help of those educators who are intelligent enough to recognize the need for drastic reconstruction there will be a new era of Black thought and Black thinkers who enter the working world from colleges aware of the real problems that will face them and not believing that a piece of paper will claim a niche for them in the society-at-large. The education process will not whitewash them into thinking that their troubles are over. They will come out as Black people.

Wednesday Night

1

Seven p.m. Phone Call

Earl Thomas was wiping shaving cream from under his chin when the telephone rang. He waited, thinking that his neighbor Zeke might answer, but when he heard a second shrill jingling he opened the bathroom door and released the receiver from its holster.

'Earl Thomas,' he announced.

'Thomas?' A bass voice boomed. 'This is Ben King. I called cuz I wanned t'tell you 'bout this meetin' we had dis afternoon wit' the studen's.'

'Meetin'? What meetin'?' Earl asked. He was afraid that he already knew the answer to the question.

'MJUMBE had a meetin' wit' the studen's this afternoon 'bout fo' thutty. We had drew up some deman's fo' Head Nigger Calhoun an' we had t'fin' out 'bout hi the people felt 'bout things . . . I called you befo' but I got a bizzy signal.'

'Zeke,' Earl muttered.

'What?'

'Nuthin'.'

'Anyway,' King continued, 'I wuz callin' befo' cuz we were gonna like confer wit'choo befo' we handed the shit to the Man, but when I couldn' get'choo we cut out over t'the Plantation,' King laughed. 'Calhoun wudn' home so I called agin.'

'Yeah . . .'

'We figgered you might wanna be in-volved,' King added.

The sarcasm that dripped through the receiver as King slowly drawled his way through the monologue was beginning to grate on Earl's nerves. Something very screwy was going on; something that Earl felt an immediate need to pinpoint. But too many ideas were dashing through his head. There was no real way to slow down the thoughts that were turning him into a huge knot. What were the demands? Why hadn't he heard anything from anyone? Faster and faster the questions came, obscuring the words King breathed slowly through the telephone.

'What did you say?' Earl asked. 'I missed that last part.'

'I ast you hi long it's gon' take you to git down here.'

'Down where?'

'Well, we in the frat house on the third flo'.' King said.

'I guess I can be there in 'bout twenny minnits,' Earl calculated.

'Right on!' King laughed. 'We'll be waitin'!'

The call was terminated. Earl felt for the first time the beads of sweat that had been sprung loose from wells at his hairline. Blood was circulating again in his left ear now that the phone had been unclamped. A very sick smile was spread over his face.

There was nothing he really felt capable of doing or saying at that moment. It was sixth grade all over and he was watching his girl being walked home from school by someone else. Everyone in the world was waiting, watching to see what he would do. There was nothing that could be done. Odds had warned him. Lawman had warned him. The pulse of the campus had told him. 'MJUMBE is up to something!' the messages read. But Earl Thomas was not a hasty young man. He had been drawing up a list of demands and researching every item carefully with the Board of Trustees and members of the administration. When he went after Calhoun he was going to be damn sure that everything was perfect. Now the whole thing was shot to hell.

'Where the hell is Victor Johnson?' he asked out loud.

Victor Johnson was the editor-in-chief of the Sutton University *Statesman*, the campus's weekly newspaper. Earl often referred to Vic as the editor-in-everything because the bespectacled senior seemed to be the only one who ever did any newspaper work on campus. Wasn't a coup newsworthy any more? Wasn't the story of the president of the Student Government Association being shot down worth the print? They printed shit like the ZBZ sorority's news.

Earl slumped heavily on the side of the bathtub. See! See! he heard stumbling through his head. Here you sit inna damn bathrobe splashin' aftershave on yo' mug while some two-faced muthas run 'roun' an' pour freezin' damn water down yo' goddamn back! An' you can' rilly even ac' su'prized cuz evybody tol' you . . .

Earl started counting backward. He was trying hard to remember the various dates he had marked on his political calendar; still searching for that one elusive idea that felt so important but could not be captured. Today was October 8th. School had opened on September 9th. He had been elected the previous May and had taken office on June 1st. He had promised the students then that by the end of the coming September he would have a list of their prime grievances drawn up and ready for their approval. It had taken longer than he had thought it would. The old bylaws and old Student Government constitution hampered everything that he wanted to do. He found himself struggling like a man in quicksand; the harder he fought the deeper he sank. It had been as bad as Lawman had predicted: 'It's impossible to move faster within the system than a turtle with two busted legs.'

The truth was that it was his inability to make any headway that was really upsetting Earl about King's call. The message meant that MJUMBE was running head on into Ogden Calhoun, the university president, with nothing to back it up. MJUMBE's act might have been courageous, but it was definitely unwise politically. Calhoun hadn't lasted at Sutton for nine years for no reason. He knew what could and could not be allowed. He had kicked more student reformers out of school than the presidents of any other five schools combined.

Earl switched off the bathroom light and flip-flopped in his shower shoes down the second-floor hall to his room. He strode past the room of Zeke, the handyman, with the record player playing Mongo Santamaria full-blast, and past Old Man Hunt's room, where absolutely nothing was ever going on.

'So the great Sutton revolution has finally begun,' he muttered sarcastically, flinging his door open. 'And Earl Thomas has been kicked the hell out.'

At that point another real question arose. Why had he been called? To hell with why Lawman and Odds, his best friends, had *not* called. Why had Baker let Ben King call? Earl Thomas and Ralph Baker, the MJUMBE leader, were political enemies. Earl had defeated Baker for the post of SGA president. What was going on?

The chain of events that had wired Earl for the phone call were at that very moment wiring others to the fuse slowly smoldering on the campus of Sutton University. The meeting. Phone call. Busy signal. Calhoun not home. Second call. Earl speaking. A million possible combinations were spiraling across a background of human skin; dominoes that stretched out and were nudged, forced to collapse into one another until a whole line of white dots drilled into black rectangles stumbled jointlessly through a massive collision and lay silent.

Earl pulled his pants on hurriedly. He wasn't sure how much he could do. Maybe nothing. There would be little sense in his asking MJUMBE to halt plans that were off the ground. No one would wait. There would be little point in his explaining to the MJUMBE leadership how much work he had done to get things together. No one would wait. At least he was involved. That was something that would allow him a little say-so. It was much better to be invited in than to have to control the situation from outside. The students would be watching very carefully to see what happened between him and MJUMBE. MJUMBE would doubtlessly be watching to make sure he didn't get away with anything. Everyone would be watching him.

'Ice. Ice. Ice.' He muttered to himself. 'I got to be very cool.'

The train was moving, gaining speed as it left the comparative safety of the yards. The first stop would be a funky frat room on Sutton's campus. Earl knew that if he wasn't cool the train might go no further. He wondered if he could take it. Baker and King laying down the rules. Earl Thomas caught in the middle. He definitely did not dig the plot. But he realized that he had no real choice. He was not the train's engineer. He was a passenger.

2
MJUMBE

Mjumbe is the Swahili word meaning messenger. On the campus of Sutton University, Sutton, Virginia, it was also the identifying name for the Members of Justice United for Meaningful Black Education. MJUMBE.

The name was chosen by Ralph Baker, a six-foot two-hundred-pound football player who had organized the group and served as its spokesman. Baker sat in the third-floor meeting room of the Omega Psi Phi fraternity house waiting for the results of Ben King's phone call to Earl Thomas. He was also reliving the day.

The day had really started for Baker at four o'clock that afternoon. He had left a note in the frat house lounge after breakfast notifying the four other MJUMBE chieftains of a four o'clock meeting. When he came into the lounge at four the others were waiting.

'Brothers,' he had said, 'the time has come.'

'Right on!' Ben King had said, sitting up.

Baker placed a stack of one thousand mimeographed sheets on the battered card table. Each man took one.

'We been layin' an' bullshittin' too long,' Baker commented as the men read the paper.

'Fo' hundred years,' Speedy Cotton mumbled.

'Thomas said when he was elected that by the enda September he wuz gonna have everything laid out like a train set ... I don' need ta tell nobody that iz October eighth an' we ain' heard from the nigger yet. He ain' nowhere near organized an' ...'

'He a damn Tom!' King said. 'I tol' yawl he wuz a Tom!'

The members of MJUMBE all nodded. Baker glared down at them as though they were to blame. Ben King and Speedy

Cotton sat on the same side of the table as usual, a set of diagrammed football formations in front of them. Fred Jones, Jonesy, tapped a deck of cards on the side of the table. Abul Menka, the only MJUMBE member who was not a football player, sat in the corner of the room with his feet propped on the window ledge.

'So na',' Baker went on, 'it's pretty clear t'me that if anything gon' get done, we gon' do it!'

'Right on!'

'I wanna know what yawl think 'bout the stuff,' Baker said gesturing to the paper. 'We gotta have it t'gether 'cuz we gon' be meetin' wit' ev'y man, woman, an' chile on this campus in 'bout fifteen minnits.'

'That wuz the meetin' we heard bein' announced?' Speedy Cotton asked.

'That wuz it!'

'Then this las' deman' means Calhoun gon' get these deman's t'night?'

Baker smiled. 'I think you catchin' on.' Baker, King, and Cotton shared a loud laugh.

'What 'bout practice?' Jonesy interrupted. 'We s'pose t'be at practice at fo' thutty.'

'No practice today.' King snorted. 'We gon' be bizzy.' He laughed.

'Why today?' Jonesy asked. All four men knew that Jonesy was the worrier. He was never comfortable until he was on a football field where all he had to do was knock hell out of anything that moved.

Baker ran a big black hand over his bald-shaved head. 'I figger we got a surprize fo' Calhoun. He been in Norfolk for two days an' he ain' gittin' back 'til 'bout six t'night. By then we be done had our meetin', ate, come back an' wrapped everything tight . . .'

'What 'bout Thomas?' King asked.

Baker frowned. 'I'm gittin' to that . . . if Thomas ain' at the meetin', an' he may not be . . .'

'Why wouldn' he be there?'

'Look. Lemme say the shit. All right? . . . Thomas ain' got no classes on Wednesday so he don' be here. All right? So if Thomas ain' at the meetin', after we come back an' git our shit right, we gon' call 'im an' tell 'im to come over here an' do somethin' fo' us.'

'We gon' blow his min' this time,' Cotton laughed.

'Him an' Head Nigger if shit work out.' Baker laughed louder.

'We gon' have him take Head Nigger this list?' King asked waving the demands.

'I wanned to s'prize Thomas.'

'It'll s'prize a lotta folks,' Cotton remarked.

King, Baker, and Cotton enjoyed another good laugh. Jonesy simply frowned and Abul Menka, as usual, did nothing.

'What if Thomas don' dig bein' out the driver's seat?' Cotton asked, getting serious.

'Either secon' or nothin',' Baker said setting his jaw. 'From now on we runnin' shit!'

Baker continued to go over the afternoon in his mind. The four o'clock prompting for the MJUMBE team had set the stage for the four-thirty rally with the students. The five of MJUMBE had left the meeting room together. They had strode across the Sutton Oval that was set in the middle of the campus to the Student Union Building. They crushed the dead grass beneath their feet and quickly scaled the thirteen steps that led to a balcony overlooking the crowd of students that had already begun to gather. All five were dressed in black dashikis. All except Abul Menka were heavily muscled athletes who had shaved their heads when the coach complained about bushy heads not allowing helmets to fit tightly enough. All five were intent and stern-faced, silhouetted by a fading red disc that had darkened their bodies during an early-autumn heat wave. All bad. All Black.

The student response to Baker's demands had been greater

than even he expected. He had thought there might be some question as to his authority. Nobody had even mentioned Earl Thomas. The students seemed very unconcerned as to who actually became the leader for the change the campus needed so badly. All they wanted was action.

Baker had been in his world. He bathed in the light of the handclapping, whistling, and shouted support heaped upon him and his comrades. It seemed that with the reading of each demand the support grew. He had said everything he could think of about Ogden Calhoun, the Head Nigger, and the members of the administration. When he finished, the five men marched through the crowd that still stood chattering like monkeys. All Baker could hear was:

'Do it, Brother!' and 'Right on with power!'

There was little they could do now but wait. Wait and think. Baker knew that the support had been good, but he also knew that Ogden Calhoun had a reputation as a destroyer of student dissent. The Sutton president had been asked recently how Sutton had escaped the student disruptions that had rocked other Black campuses. Calhoun had replied to the interviewer: 'I have a saying for students on my campus. It says: "My way or the highway!" In other words: "If we can' git along, *you* goin' home!"'

So the lines were drawn. Calhoun had no room in his plans for student disruption. MJUMBE had no plans for going home.

Baker's mind drifted. After the afternoon meeting his plan had started to become shaky. Just at the point when his name was on the lips of every Sutton student, he was knifing himself in the back by having Earl Thomas notified. He hated to think of turning the least credit over to a man he considered an enemy, but there was really no way out of it. While running for Student Government president he had preached Black collectivity; all political factions putting their heads together. And there was no denying that Earl Thomas was a smart politician. The election had proven that. Then too, if Earl endorsed Baker, another bloc of students would fall easily into line.

In late August when Jonesy had arrived for summer football training Baker had started talk about MJUMBE. 'If you ain' out fo' nuthin' but revenge on Thomas fo' beatin' you,' Jonesy had said, 'forget it.'

'I ain' lookin' fo' nothin' but progress,' Baker had sworn. 'I think MJUMBE can serve a two-way purpose. First, Thomas gon' move if he know somebody lookin' over his shoulder. Second, all the athletes would be down to back Thomas up if we wuz organized an' spoke fo' him.'

The possibility that MJUMBE might give Earl its backing was what had sold Jonesy. And now that the time had come Jonesy had not objected to any of Baker's arguments about why MJUMBE should cast the first stone. But Baker knew well enough that Jonesy would pull out if he felt as though the group spokesman had lied about his intentions. Earl had been called.

That's when things started fuckin' up, Baker thought.

Earl's line had been busy. Baker decided on a second's notice that since Earl couldn't be reached MJUMBE would deliver its own mail.

'It's six thutty,' he said when King notified him of the busy line. 'Calhoun was s'pose to git home 'bout six. He prob'ly got wind a the deman's already. We can' give 'im too much time to pull no fas' stuff on us.'

They had started out. Five men in black dashikis crunching through the dead leaves across the quadrangle behind the fraternity house, across the football field to the big white house Sutton students called 'the Plantation.' Calhoun wasn't home.

Calhoun's absence implied several things to Baker. It indicated that Calhoun knew nothing of the demands. God knew he would have been setting up some counterattack had he heard. It also meant that MJUMBE might have *peaked* too soon.

As a football player Baker knew a lot about peaking. A team

is built up by a good coach to reach its emotional and competitive *peak* just before the charge down the shadowed runway; when the only sound to be heard is the thunderous clacking of forty pairs of cleats grating against the rough-grained concrete. The team tears down the ramp ready to tackle a moving van. Every inch of your body would be choking with the smell of forty men, practice jerseys, wintergreen, urine, and the sweaty jocks that lay in a corner hamper. Your heart strait-jacketed in your chest, climbing up bony columns of your throat, tightening you into a gigantic ball.

Baker had been a bad coach. He knew now that he should have called the Plantation before he and his cohorts started out. There had been an emotional letdown when there was no one at the Calhoun residence to accept their papers. They had stood on the threshold with hearts the size of a football, ready to slap all authoritative danger in the face. The silly old maid seemed to mock them, though she knew nothing. The air had been let out of them.

Now they sat. Thinking and waiting.

'Thomas will be here in twenny minnits,' King said barging through the partially open door.

'Good,' Baker said without conviction. He took a look at his watch. In twenty minutes it would be seven thirty. It was getting late.

The MJUMBE spokesman reread the sheet he had handwritten and practically memorized. He would take everyone through their parts again before Thomas arrived.

He looked at his comrades closely; looking for signs of panic or fear; looking for things that he might feel if they were indicated anywhere in the room.

Baker started with the man he knew best. He had grown up in nearby Shelton Township, Virginia, with Fred Jones. Jonesy was a plodder, a man of few words who checked things out very carefully before getting involved. Since their elementary school days Baker had always been the outspoken, active leader and Jonesy the quiet, steady henchman who did his leg work and faithfully stuck by him. Everything about the smaller man signified concentration and determination. Baker knew that as long as he, Baker, kept his word there would be no problems.

Baker had met Speedy Cotton during their freshman year at Sutton. Speedy was a coal-black, West Virginia miner's son who had been a second-string high school All-American at halfback. They had spent quite a few nights together going over football plays in Baker's room when they started playing football together and had become even faster friends when they pledged for the fraternity. College was not really of primary interest to Cotton. He wanted to play football and perhaps go on to play professionally. Baker supposed that his political involvement was based solely on their friendship, but the wiry six-foot-two speedster wasn't afraid of anything and Baker knew that he wouldn't back down.

The MJUMBE spokesman shifted his attention to Ben King. When it came to courage there were few legends that he could recall that did Ben justice. During their junior year at halftime in the last game Ben had come limping off the field. Pain had been chiseled into the deep creases around the young giant's mouth and eyes. Baker had watched King conscientiously avoid Coach Mallory and the trainer as he grimaced in the corner of the locker room during the intermission speech. Twice he asked King if someone shouldn't be notified, but was put off with a frown. Only after the game did the huge tackle permit himself to collapse from the pain. X rays taken that night showed that King's right ankle had been fractured, but somehow he had played on, had virtually held up the left side of the Sutton line, and insured the hard-fought victory.

The question in Baker's mind was whether or not Ben could or would keep his mouth shut. The big tackle had a notoriously bad temper and had been expelled from the track team for tearing up the training room during a fit of rage. It had been all Baker could do to avoid a fight between King and Thomas when Thomas, speaking the day before the election, said that 'certain bullies would not be able to threaten anyone into voting against their wishes.'

Baker knew that there was also a great deal of hatred and animosity between King and the university president. Calhoun had been the one to put King on the carpet after the training-room explosion. Baker nodded thoughtfully, thinking that he would have to watch King as closely as he watched Thomas.

In the dim light of the meeting room a flare ignited in the darkest corner where Abul Menka lit still another cigarette and attracted Baker's attention. If ever there was a man who puzzled the MJUMBE leader, Abul was that man.

When Baker arrived at the first pledgee meeting of Omega Psi Phi during the spring of his freshman year, the only man present he did not know was introduced by the Dean of Pledgees as Jonathan Wise. Baker had seen Jonathan Wise (who later began calling himself Abul Menka) driving around campus in a new Thunderbird with women hanging all over him, and he could not have imagined the man as fraternity material because the style-conscious New Yorker from the Bronx already had everything. And the perplexing thing was that during the two-month pledge period Abul had done nothing to indicate why he was there. Even during 'Hell Week,' the last week of the indoctrination schedule, when their line, 'The Jive Five Plus One' was not allowed to sleep, Abul never complained, never reacted even in private to the paddlings they were receiving or confided in the others during their restless nights in the 'Dog House' when they waited nervously for Big Brothers to come in and deal with them.

Baker had asked Abul to join MJUMBE as a matter of course because of their common interest in the fraternity, but he had been a little surprised when he accepted. Baker had seen him frequently in the frat lounge with a Black history book or reading material relating to the Black struggle, but the man had never expressed an inkling of political consciousness in the way he spoke. But there was little question of Abul's dedication to the organization. He was on time for every meeting and faithfully carried out every duty assigned to him.

'He ain' got a nerve in his body,' Baker decided. 'He'll go with us all the way.'

The roundup had given Baker a little more confidence in his co-workers, but his personal confidence was slipping. The thought of working with Earl Thomas did not appeal to him. Even if everything looked good. He compared himself to Thomas critically. Earl was six-two, perhaps one hundred and eighty pounds. He had a broad chest and wide shoulders like a boxer. Next to him Baker looked like a powerful Black barrel. Football had developed Baker's arms, neck, and chest until he resembled a tree trunk. Baker's eyes were deep set and his nose was African flat. Earl was a bushy-browed Indian-looking man with a wide mouth and two inches of kinky hair. The MJUMBE leader rubbed his bald head thoughtfully. When football ended he would grow it again.

Sitting in the half-light of the MJUMBE meeting room, the massive strategist was slowly turning new facts over in his mind. He had been so let down by Calhoun's disappearance that some aspects of MJUMBE's move had slipped by unseen. Now, with time to think, new evidence was focusing on his mental screen.

First of all, Earl Thomas was going to be his pawn. He felt very good about the position the SGA president was in. It didn't matter if the students saw Earl puttering around in connection with MJUMBE demands. They knew who the real leader was. But second and best, Calhoun didn't know who was in charge. He would identify Earl as the leader of the detested militant faction on campus because Earl would present the demands. Earl couldn't do anything to stop MJUMBE. The students would construe any negative move as jealousy. The deposed SGA leader would be a *Mjumbe* for MJUMBE. Pleasure at his own play on words almost capsized the chair in which Baker sat, back-tilted.

Gone was the animosity he had felt the previous April when

told that some skinny, ostrich-looking nigger from Georgia had defeated him for the SGA post. Gone was the bitter gall he tasted when told forty minutes before: 'Mr and Mrs Calhoun returned from Norfolk, but they are attending the theater this evening. They are expected to return about ten o'clock.' The small, wigged maid who delivered those lines had stood in the Calhoun door-way like a reject from a Steppin' Fetchit movie wiping her greasy hands on a napkin and trying to sound like a fancy British bitch.

Baker laughed out loud. He could imagine Thomas sitting helplessly in front of him like a jackass with an Afro.

'Did'joo, did'joo hear that bitch?' Baker asked when he realized everyone was watching him. 'Did'joo hear that funky-ass maid callin' the Sutton moviehouse wit' wall-to-wall rats a thee-ate-uh?' He told them that because he knew what Jonesy would say if he told them why he was really laughing.

Evidently everyone had heard because a faint smile choked through their clamped mouths. They smiled because they needed to. No one really thought that it was very funny. The crooked grins bounced off the dimly pulsating light bulb and skipped nervously out through the window. The room then returned to its tomblike silence.

Baker felt grimy. Sweat had stuck his underwear to his crotch.

Jonesy was visibly worried.

Speedy Cotton and Ben King were tired and nervous. They sat directly beneath the bald, waxy wattage that illuminated itself and little else. They tried to convince themselves that the tightness in their groins came from too much beer, too much football, and too little sleep. Their eyes wandered about the room but they saw very little.

Abul Menka remained cool. It was impossible to conclude exactly what was on the man's mind. Baker called him 'Captain Cool.' He sat in the corner, feet propped, smoking a cigarette. In truth, Abul Menka was very seriously thinking about cutting out. He would have been gone had he not known that his motives would be misinterpreted. The MJUMBE men would have thought he was leaving because he was afraid of Calhoun.

'Fuck Calhoun,' he thought sullenly. Abul did not care if Sutton's Head Nigger had *eight* strokes and *ten* heart attacks, outdoing all of the other university presidents who were cracking up as a result of student demands. No, Calhoun was no problem. But Abul Menka was not anxious to see Earl Thomas.

3

Earl

There were only three tenants at Mrs Gilliam's boarding house on Pine Street. The three men lived on the second floor of the white three-story structure. It was not for lack of applicants that the third floor was empty, but because Mrs Gilliam was very particular about her roomers.

Earl had always considered himself highly fortunate when he thought about how quickly Mrs Gilliam had taken him in. At the end of the previous school year he had decided not to leave Sutton, but to take a job as a mechanic at the nearby computer factory. All at once the dormitories were closing for the summer and he was without a place to stay. It was then that he remembered Zeke, the Black handyman, who had often mentioned his room at Mrs Gilliam's, where he also took his meals. With three days remaining before school closed Earl had gone to see her. The two of them had hit it off immediately.

Mrs Gilliam was sixty years old. A short, gray-haired, thickly built matron of a woman who had lived in Sutton for thirty years. Her husband had been a conductor on the ICC railroad, making runs from Miami to Chicago on the Seminole, when she met him. She was a waitress at a coffee shop in Kankakee, Illinois, and after having seen the big, raw-boned Black man twice a week over a six-month period, they married. The railroad rerouted Charles Gilliam soon after, and his route carried him through Sutton and other parts of southern Appomattox County in Virginia. He bought an impressive three-story frame home on Pine Street and started his family. He had been working for the line nearly twenty-six years when he died of a heart attack.

His wife, Dora, thrived on company. She was a cornerstone

at Mt. Moriah A.M.E. Church and the head of her sewing circle. Soon after her husband's death she began to take in tenants, mostly for the companionship it provided.

Earl had made Mrs Gilliam break one of her cardinal rules. She had vowed never to rent rooms to college students. For the most part she considered them to be impolite, disrespectful young men with no idea of the meaning of the word responsibility. Earl was somewhat different. In the first place he was working his way through school and intended to add his summer's earnings to a partial scholarship. Secondly, he was as polite and mannerly a young man as Mrs Gilliam had ever met. And he had looked so let down when she told him, quite gruffly, that she didn't rent to college students, that she had had no choice but to invite him in for a cup of coffee to better explain her position. Somehow over coffee the word 'college' came to mean more to her than it had meant before. It took on the meaning of her dead husband's unfulfilled dreams. She found it very easy to overlook the fact that Earl was a student. She even rationalized her decision by pointing out the fact that he wouldn't be a student during the summer, but when September rolled around there was no mention of Earl moving out.

As Earl combed his head of thick hair his mind ran through the maze of emotions that gripped him, identifying first one and then the other. Jealousy? Fear? Anger? Anger was the most predominant. He felt as though he had been betrayed. Not betrayed by friends, but by that insidious 'Brother' term. MJUMBE subjugated the entire campus into one giant malignancy and classified all constituents under the heading of 'Brother.' The word seemed to have less meaning every day. Long ago he had decided that he would not be a part of the group that criticized the hypocrisy without an alternative. Who was sure how it felt to be Black? Maybe running your tongue over the word 'Brother' a thousand times a day was a step in the right direction.

Earl felt the muscles at the hinges of his mouth tightening

to form knots of energy. He looked like a cracker ballplayer on the Baseball Game of the Week with a quarter package of Bull O' the Woods chewing tobacco poking his mouth out a foot and nowhere to spit.

He knew he must not allow himself the luxury of rage. He knew he could never accomplish anything that way; barging into the MJUMBE meeting room and screaming, 'Just what the fuck is everybody tryin' to pull?' He decided to play it New York-style. Be cool. They had him by the balls. Everybody knew that. But if he acted as though he didn't know it or didn't care he might be able to jive them into a mistake. Then what? He didn't even know if he wanted them to make a mistake. He couldn't decide which side of the fence he was on.

He thought about the election that had taken place the previous spring. When March rolled around and the first signs about nomination procedures were pinned on dormitory bulletin boards he had thought little of it. He had never run for a school office and often thought that the only reason he had been a high school basketball captain was because he was the only returning letterman his senior year. But one afternoon after a heated argument between him and his Political Science teacher he had been halted in the hall by a classmate he knew only by sight.

'Excuse me, brother,' the other had said. 'My name is Roy Dean, but people here call me Lawman. I was wondering if I could talk to you for a minute.'

'Sure,' Earl had replied, caught off guard. 'I'm Earl Thomas.'

'I know,' Lawman said as they started walking. 'I couldn't help but know you after all the hell you raise in Poli Sci.'

'The man bugs me.'

'Me, too . . . where were you goin'? You got a class? . . . how 'bout a cup of coffee in the SUB on me?'

'All right,' Earl said a bit hesitantly.

'Poli Sci is my major,' Lawman said, going on. 'Everybody calls me Lawman because I'm thinking seriously of going into law . . . we used to have a thing called 'The Courtroom' when we were freshmen. If somebody on our wing of the dorm did something questionable, like trying to steal another cat's woman or something like that, we would have a mock trial. I was a laywer for the defense.'

'You win a lot of cases?'

'It was just a joke, but I pulled a lot of fast ones on the jury. Most of law is just semantics anyway. You can say a thing one way and make it sound entirely different from the way it appears if you rearrange a few words.'

'I guess so,' Earl agreed.

'But what I wanted to talk to you about was your political thing,' Lawman continued.

'My political thing?' Earl laughed. 'I don't really guess I have one. Just trying to be Black, I guess.'

The two of them walked on toward the Student Union Building, leaving Washington Hall where liberal arts classes were taught, Carver Hall, the science building, Adler Annex, and the mini-square referred to by students as the 'quadrangle,' where students sat and studied and talked on the benches.

'Sutton is fucked up,' Lawman began as they entered the crowded Student Union Building. 'A lotta in quotes Black schools are fucked up, but they seem to be gettin' something done about their problems. If Sutton is doing anythin' it's digressin', you know what I mean?'

Earl nodded.

'This school was founded in eighteen eighty-three and for all intents and purposes it's still eighteen eighty-three here, because there hasn't been much progress.'

'What about the things the Student Government president, Peabody, planned to do?' Earl asked as they left the service area with their coffee.

'Peabody ain' nuthin' but a lot of mouth,' Lawman snorted. 'What I mean is that the man is disorganized. He's spent the whole year havin' Calhoun twist his mind around like a rubber band . . . he goes to Calhoun and sez: "The students want this and that." Calhoun laughs and sez: "So what?" You dig?'

Earl nodded for Lawman to continue.

'So next month *ther's* gonna be another Student Government election and something needs to be done . . .'

'What are *you* planning to do?' Earl cut in.

Lawman laughed uneasily. He wasn't sure how to handle Earl, how to handle the question he was fed.

'I personally can't do very much. I can't dedicate the kind of time you need to give to the Student Government job to run for office 'cause I have an outside job that pays for my schooling. The point of this conversation is to find whether or not you'd like to run.'

'What?'

'You care, don'choo?'

'Yeah. I do, but . . .'

'But what?'

'But I'm a transfer student. This is just my second semester here. I don't think I know enough about the place to . . .'

'You mean,' Lawman cut in, 'that until I mentioned it you hadn't had one thought about the kinda things that might be happ'ning if you had anything to do with it?'

'I suppose I had some thoughts . . .'

'What did you decide you would do?'

'It didn't matter since I wasn't the president,' Earl said.

'Give it some thought,' Lawman suggested. 'You've got a good political mind. Anybody who can hold his own with old man Mills has to have a good political mind.'

'What about the two guys I've seen listed as candidates already?'

'Worthless,' Lawman spat out. 'Hall is a "egghead" dude from Boston or somewhere. He spends about thirty hours a day in the library reading Emily Dickinson and shit like that. He's a brown-nosed jackass as far as I'm concerned. I go to the SGA meetings sometimes and see him rapping. He's a junior class senator. Calls himself filibusterin' when he gets up with a little Robert's rule book on parliamentary procedure and starts hangin' everything up with points of order . . . thass what democracy has done for niggers. They lay in that idealistic crap all day and smell like shit all night.'

'What about Baker, the football player? He's runnin'.'

'Yeah. So what? He's a maniac as far as I'm concerned, although he'll prob'bly win unless you or someone like you goes against him. I never heard a sound political thought come from his direction. Him and King go through political issues like they're runnin' an off-tackle play. Everything that they don't like is wrong. I can't . . .'

'I understand,' Earl said thoughtfully.

'Good!' Lawman said as he got up. 'You give it some thought, brother, and I'll be talkin' to you.'

That was the beginning. Earl and Lawman talked about it again the next day. Earl admitted that he had often thought about things that would be done differently if he were president. Somehow it had never gone any further than that. Together, the two men constructed a platform for Earl to run on. Odds, Earl's best friend, was drafted as a campaign manager. They were on their way.

The memory of all the things he had been through with Odds and Lawman brought still another question to the surface. Why hadn't either one of them called to say anything about the meeting with MJUMBE and the students?

Earl came out of his bedroom and locked the door behind him. He checked his pocket for the keys he needed. Door key and car keys were there. It was then that his light sweater and slacks almost collided with Zeke's khakis and T-shirt.

'You got troubles?' Zeke asked.

'No,' Earl lied. 'Why?'

'You in such a durn hurry yo' leavin' shavin' cream stuck behin' yo' ear,' Zeke pointed out.

Earl wiped at the spot and Zeke nodded.

'Dumplin's t'night?' Earl asked mischievously.

'Naw, but we'da had'um if I'da wanned 'um.'

'Yeah. You an' Miz G. runnin' a game on me an' Ol' Hunt.'

'Shit!' Zeke waved. 'Mosatime you ain' here an' Hunt could be eatin' cobras an' drinkin' elephant piss fo' all he know. May as well have chicken an' dumplin's since I lak 'um.'

'Naw,' Earl laughed. 'That ain' it. Tell me, man, whuss happ'nin' wit'yo' kitchen thing?'

Zeke played the game. He looked both ways down the narrow hall and then lowered his voice in a conspiratorial tone. 'I shouldn' be tellin',' he admitted, 'but since you an' me s'pose to be boys . . . I, uh, sneaks down to the galley wit' Miz G. every other day o' so an' we gits high on Barracuda wine. Then I starts talkin' 'bout hi' I been all over the worl' an' still ain' dug nothin that tastes as good t'me as her chicken an' dumplin's. Jus' lak that they out there on the table. Same as when you talk 'bout banana puddin'.'

'Without the Barracuda wine.'

'Wit'out that.'

Earl laughed aloud. Zeke maintained a straight face somehow, but the thought of Mrs Gilliam drinking anything stronger than iced tea was too much for him. Zeke was notorious for drinking anything that could be classified as liquid and Earl had often met the handyman at O'Jay's, a local bar, but Mrs Gilliam? A pillar of Mt Moriah? Sacrilege!

'We love dem grapes!' Zeke said as Earl scurried down the stairs.

'Right!'

Zeke was a good man as far as Earl was concerned. The older man had never had a family or a real home until Mrs Gilliam had started renting rooms. There was nothing that could be described as his real profession either. He mowed lawns or shoveled snow or worked on cars at Ike's garage and come the first of every month he always had his rent money and he rarely missed a night at O'Jay's. At forty-five he was a slightly built, balding man with a coffee complexion and a contagious sense of humor.

Mrs Gilliam was stirring the evening stew when Earl rushed

through the kitchen with a quick 'Good evening.' He was halfway to the back door when she stopped him.

'Where might you think you goin' this evenin' befo' you eat yo' dinner?' she asked indignantly.

'I got a meetin' to go to,' he said. 'It jus' came up.'

Mrs Gilliam looked at him fondly for a second. With purpose she clamped the lid down on the stew pot and wiped her hands on the red trim apron. She took Earl by the arm and led him to the kitchen table where she sat him down.

'Let me tell you something,' she began. 'I've been in Sutton a long time. A long time to realize certain things. When I got here Sutton University was sittin' right where it is today. My husban' went to Sutton fo' a year at night . . . why you runnin' yo'sef into a fit fo' them? They ain' never been organized. Why you think you got to do so much to organize 'um? Why you got to be there every blessed minnit? No, I take that back. You ain' over there half as much as my daughter was. Laurie was there all day an' wuzn' no studen' . . . how she got away wit'out havin' one a them men's babies is still beyon' me. Go on, chile, do what you think you got to do.'

Earl nodded constantly during her monologue as though he understood all of the things that she was trying to say. But as he reached the porch he was more sure than ever that he didn't understand her and he wanted to go back and tell her to talk, say everything that was on her mind.

'Earl,' she called, 'I don' wanna hear you ramblin' 'roun' in my kitchen at no thousan' o'clock like las' night. I know you gon' be wantin' some a this somethin' t'eat, but you can' have it so if you don' git it na you won' have it.'

'Yes ma'am, I hear you,' he said.

Zeke heard Earl leaving as he came down to the kitchen. Mrs Gilliam still sat resting her elbows on the kitchen table as though she was tired. It was always a strain for her to deal with her youngest tenant. He never seemed to think twice before agreeing to skip a meal to attend something on campus. She personally didn't understand why so many meetings demanded his presence.

'Earl ain' eatin' again,' Zeke surmised.

'That boy gonna run hisself to death,' the landlady commented getting up and walking back over to the stew pot.

Outside, Sutton was just feeling the first kisses of autumn. The wind was a baby chick wiggling inside an egg beneath its mother. Evening came gliding down early to chase the sun and bring in Father Night with a blanket of black air to cloak the dying leaves. Though not a moment had passed since Earl's hasty exit, both Zeke and Mrs Gilliam heard the footsteps on the back porch. Earl reentered the room allowing the screen door to slam behind him.

'Uh, it's not too cold now, but I think I'm gonna need my coat later,' he announced looking around. 'Uh, where is it?'

Zeke smiled and Mrs Gilliam put on her sternest face.

'Iss hangin' in the hall closet, but I oughta not let'choo have it 'cause it was layin' 'cross the kitchen table when I got up this mornin'. You mussa lef' it here when you sneaked in las' night tryin' t'git somethin' t'eat ... I'm tellin' you Zeke, ain' he somethin'?' They exchanged glances. Earl smiled.

Earl grabbed his jacket off the hook in the hall closet and went back outside. His car was parked and the motor hummed a throaty tune. The night held a tingle of expectation. When Earl thought about the things that lay ahead for him there was a feathery tickle in his stomach. The sidewalk yawned up at him. The lawn was speckled with leaves of a thousand shades, dead or dying. At the side of the house Earl spotted Old Man Hunt pawing the ground with a toothless yard rake. They exchanged waves.

Earl's car was a '64 Oldsmobile; a gift from his father two summers past. It had been just the sort of thing he had come to expect from his father. The car had been in an accident and the left side had been caved in near the driver's door. The owner had been asking three hundred dollars for it, but after a brief conversation with John Arthur Thomas he had been willing to let it go for half that price. The elder Thomas said nothing about the purchase to his son, but kept the car parked in a garage and presented it to his son as a going-away present after Earl's graduation from the two-year Community College.

'It ain' but a small thing,' John Arthur Thomas declared struggling for words. 'It ain' like what I really want you to have, but I knew you wuz gon' need a car to git around in.'

There was a stiff handshake and a rugged smile from the older man. Everything had been warm but awkward, sincere and yet limited. Earl had wanted to ask if his father had talked to his mother or seen her but had been afraid. The subject was a sore point; a constantly aching tooth that one became used to after awhile.

When he had been fifteen and his mother and father had been apart for almost a year, Earl had asked his father outright why the couple didn't live together any more.

'Yo' mama's a good woman,' John Thomas had said softly. 'She a independent woman by nature, but I convinced her when we wuz seein' each other that she could depend on me an' be a woman for a while. I knew that wuz what she wanned to be. But I wasn't a good provider for her. Everything wuz workin' out bad for me an' her. We wuz damn near at razor's edge when we found out you wuz comin' ... I guess that saved our marriage if you can call what we ended up havin' somethin' worth bein' saved. We said we wuzn't gon' bring you out without some people lookin' after you. So we tried to keep things together, but we stopped talkin' to one another an' really stopped havin' anything for one another exceptin' the fact that you were a link b'tween us.'

'I'm s'pose to be grown now?' the fifteen-year-old Earl had asked.

'Grown enough to understand, I reckon,' his father had replied.

'I really don't,' Earl had confessed.

'Whoa!' John Thomas said laughing a bit. 'Neither do yo' mama an' me. Folks don't never really understand themselves,

274 | The Nigger Factory

but they always rely on havin' someone that they love understand. Thass what we wuz doin'.'

Earl pulled away from the curb thinking about his father. He
would have to write the man a letter and admit that he had
received some valuable information. Things were happening
in his life that he didn't understand. Yet he was the only one
who could be held responsible for them.

In the rear-view mirror Earl caught sight of a black Ford
that seemed to be trailing him. He was brought back to the
present, hoping that the car was the Ford supplied by the
school to members of the Sutton newspaper staff who had to
travel to get their stories. Just as he was about to pull over and
allow the Ford to draw abreast of him, the trailing car pulled
off down a side street.

But now Victor Johnson was on his mind again. Somewhere
at that moment he knew Vic was working on a backbreaking
story against him. The move by MJUMBE would probably
be built up as a great blow against the Sutton establishment,
which included the SGA. It didn't matter that Earl hated the
establishment as much as any of the rest of them or even
more since he knew exactly how it sucked in Black students
and warped their minds. It only mattered that during the
course of the election none of Earl's speeches had made
reference to faculty members as 'racist bastards' and that
he hadn't filled students' ears with militant denunciations
of Calhoun or the administrators. To many narrow-minded
students anyone who didn't carry out the flimsy, outraged
rhetoric of a television revolutionary was a Tom. It was
just circumstance blown up out of proportion to truth. Earl
could already picture the front-page story in the student
paper asserting that his inactivity had spurred MJUMBE's
movement.

'Shit!' he swore loudly.

Earl's mind was busy trying to organize strategy. It was too
late for any of the moves that came readily to mind. He was

now *under* the eight ball. The only thing that he could do was wait.

'One more week,' he grumbled again without conviction. 'Johnson would have had the story of his life. There would be no way for any demands to be turned down!'

MJUMBE COUP D'ETAT! the headline would scream.

'Goddamn hick bastard Johnson,' Earl breathed. 'Goddamn hick bastards! I need a damn drink!'

4

Lawman and Odds

When Earl Thomas arrived on Sutton University's campus for the very first time he had in his pocket a letter that he had received over the summer from a junior named Kenny Smith. The letter was actually a mimeographed note from the Dean of Admissions office designating Kenny as a student orientation assistant who should be looked up when the newcomer arrived; he was the person who would help the incoming student find his way around campus.

Kenny Smith had been easy to locate. Earl found him sitting in the Admissions Office reading a copy of the special *Statesman* that welcomed freshmen and transfer students. The thing that immediately warmed Earl to his orientation assistant was the young man's dress. Kenny was wearing a pair of low-cut sneakers, no socks, cut-off blue jean shorts, and a Sutton sweat shirt. He was a world apart from the other orientators lining the walls dressed in slacks, shirts with collars; even a suit and tie or two could be seen.

'My whole wardrobe is odds and ends,' Kenny told Earl when the transfer student pointed out the contrast.

It had become understood between the two young men, who hit it off immediately, that Kenny could not be held to tradition and conformity of any description. Kenny did not seem to care in the least what any other students did, thought, wore, or acted like. He was his own man and described himself as the odd one even in his family circle. The nickname 'Odds' became quite natural between them.

At approximately the time that Earl was leaving Mrs Gilliam's boarding house for his meeting with MJUMBE, Odds was just learning of the day's political activities. Earl's campaign manager had been in bed all day with a cold and had managed to sleep through the afternoon MJUMBE announcements in his room. Only a trip to the bathroom and an open dormitory door gave him any inkling of the ingredients that were bubbling in the political cauldron.

'Wonder why Thomas let Baker take over?' someone was asking as Odds passed the open door.

'Aw, bruh, c'mon,' was the reply. 'Thomas ain' lettin' Baker do nothin'. Thomas ain' never been nowhere. Baker just dug that we was gittin' ready to have another bullshit year an' did his thing. The bullshit intellectuals voted for Egghead Hall, the brothers voted for Baker, and the bitches put Thomas in office from the col' ass jump.'

Odds tried to place the voices and couldn't. He wanted to hear more about the 'takeover' they were discussing and he didn't particularly like being referred to as a bitch. He had voted for Earl.

'Ya gotta be tough to deal wit' Calhoun, man. You know what happened to Peabody las' year,' the voice went on. 'He bullshitted an' Tommed jus' like Thomas an' in the end didn' nuthin' git done.'

'As usual,' someone added.

'An' Baker's gonna mess with Calhoun?' Odds asked entering the room.

'Whuss happ'nin'? ... Fuckin' right!' The speaker went on. He was a tall, bearded boy wearing sunglasses. 'Baker'll git over.'

'Kin I git a match?' Odds asked.

'Yo, bruh. I got one,' a second student with sunglasses offered.

'Did'joo see the thing today when MJUMBE got it together? They came out on that platform bad wit' capital letters!'

'I didn' dig it, man,' Odds admitted. 'What happened?'

'Man,' came the enthusiastic reply. 'You missed a helluva thing. Lemme tell you. All day long they was announcin' this meetin' for fo' o'clock in fronta the SUB, right? Nobody knows who's callin' it or what it's about. So at four bells damn near the whole school is millin' 'roun' in front a the platform steps leadin' t'the SUB, but the only thing there is a mike. No people. Up through the crowd comes Baker and King an' them. They all dressed in black dashikis with gold trim. All five of 'um got bald heads except my man from New York, whuss his name? Abul. Abul Menka. You know that dude wit' the big 'fro an' the T-bird? . . . well, they read out this list a deman's, grievances that they got t'gether for the Head Nigger an' they say they gonna lay the shit on 'im t'night. That mean this muthafuckuh gonna be jumpin' in the mornin,' Jim.'

'Or not,' Odds said. 'What did Earl Thomas have to say?'

'Nuthin', man. I didn' even see him. What could he say? Iss all true. Most a the shit is stuff he been sayin' he wuz gittin' t'gether, but he ain' done nuthin'.'

Odds already knew where Earl had been. Chances were that Baker had known too. Earl seldom came on campus on Wednesday since he didn't have a class. For a second Odds was tempted to point this out to the students in the room, but he decided that there would be little reason. He wanted to tell them that Earl *had* been trying to get things together too, but his association with Earl would have made everything sound like a mere cop out.

'Later,' he said, sliding back out into the hall. Echoes of the discussion followed Odds back into his room, but his mind was far away. What should he do? Call Earl? No. Earl probably wouldn't be at home by now. What time was it? Just past seven his watch told him. The best thing would be to try and find Earl and get something started. Started? Ended? Stopped?

It was at that moment that Odds thought of Lawman. Lawman was a good friend. He was surprised, as he thought about it, that Lawman had not called him. If ever there was a guy who could sort out a political mess it was the ever-serious pre-law major.

Odds grabbed a dime from the top of his desk and padded back out into the darkened hall. Quickly he uncradled the receiver and dropped a dime into the pay phone. He turned the dial seven times and waited. The phone rang twice.

'Hullo?'

'Hello. Lawman?'

'Yeah.'

'Look, brother. This is Odds. We got problems. Have you heard?'

''Bout what?'

'As near as I can tell Baker an' his knuckleheads took over Earl's program this afternoon an' s'pose to be goin' to Calhoun's t'night.'

'Goddamn!' Lawman breathed. '*When* did this happen?'

'This afternoon. Were you on campus?'

'I had a one o'clock class. I went to it an' then I split.'

'You didn' hear?'

'Nuthin, man. I met this bitch over here at two. She was talkin' 'bout calculus, but you know better than that.'

'Yeah. I know 'bout what got calculated . . .'

'Where were you?'

'In bed. Man, I had me a ass-kickin' chest cold all week.'

'You sound like it. Where's Earl?'

'You got me. Out makin' like a hero I guess.'

'Tryin' to carry it by himself too. He didn't call me.' Lawman was thoughtful. 'Whew! Man, this is too much. I can hardly get this shit together.'

'I know.'

'Where you at?' Lawman asked.

'In the dorm.'

'Let's get together an' talk this over. I was jus' sittin' down to eat when you buzzed. You want to come over here and have a bite to eat?'

'No grit, man. I figger with a half-gallon of Esso Extra or something I might be able to deal . . . why don' you meet me at O'Jay's 'bout eight o'clock?'

'All right,' Lawman agreed. They hung up.

Odds scuffled back down the hall to his room and prepared to wash up and brush his teeth. He was no longer concerned with the nagging cough and chest cold that had kept him in bed.

The Lawman turned back to a small pot of soup and the slices of ham that rimmed his plate. His small one-room apartment was a mess. Records were scattered all over the floor near his record player. The books he had been attempting to deal with when the young woman arrived earlier in the afternoon were still open and loose-leaf notes from his notebook had blown onto the floor. His small army cot in the corner was a disarranged mess with the stained sheets from three hours of love-making tangled up at the foot of the bed. He stepped over to the sink next to the hot plate and rinsed his mouth out and splashed his face with a double handful of cold water.

'Rraugh!' he snorted as the water shocked his circled, reddened eyes. He felt around the wall for the wrinkled towel and rubbed his face roughly when he ripped it from the rack.

'Fuck!' he cursed out loud. Then he sat down to eat.

5

Confrontation

Earl's green Oldsmobile wheeled through the open gates at the mouth of the university. The arch stretching between two twenty-foot-high stone pillars announced: SUTTON UNIVERSITY. A small wooden plaque nailed into one of the columns noted that the arch had been donated by the class of 1939.

Fifty feet from the gate was a huge oval flower bed, containing now, in autumn, only dead reminders of the blazing color that had decorated the front of Sutton's administration building from early spring until late summer. An arrow in front of the flower bed pointed all traffic to the right, around the famous circle that emptied into a large parking lot.

Earl drove slowly past the Ad Building, Washington Hall, the remodeled Student Union Building, Adler Annex, Paul Lawrence Dunbar Library, and Simmons Hall which housed almost six hundred men. To his left, the old science building, Carver Hall, Garvey Plaza for freshmen women, Mallory Hall for upperclass women, and the three-story fraternity house which had once been for home economics (before Adler Annex) completed the other half of the oval.

Earl parked in the ample lot, took a look at himself in the rear-view mirror, lit a cigarette, and got out. The newborn wind whistled at him. Smoke came from the chimney atop the small wooden hut that housed the security guard in the corner of the area. He saw through the naked branches of trees a pale-eyed, unblinking moon that hovered low in the sky like an oval of cold, shadowy clay.

Jonesy was standing on the steps of the frat building. The stocky MJUMBE chieftain, who played linebacker on the football team, was dressed in a black, short-sleeved dashiki and dark trousers.

'Niggers always rather be hip than warm,' Earl thought as he contemplated how strongly the wind was whipping against the short-sleeved African shirt.

Jonesy looked as though he wanted to say something, but noting the cold indifference on Earl's face he merely nodded. He led the way into the building.

The first floor was in total darkness. Earl could hear couples positioning themselves in the dark. It was against school regulations for women to be in the frat houses unless there was a chaperoned dance or some other university-sanctioned function going on. The frat men gave little attention to what school regulations stipulated. They unscrewed the first floor lightbulbs and did as they damn well pleased.

'Upstairs,' Jonesy mumbled.

The two men took the stairs quickly and entered the thirdfloor meeting room where Baker, King, and Cotton sat around a square card table. Abul Menka sat in the corner staring intently out of the window. Earl took the chair directly opposite Baker. Jonesy stood by the door and folded his arms, looking over his shoulder out into the hall from time to time.

'Happ'nin', Earl?' Baker asked.

'Nothin' much,' Earl replied lightly. He hated bullshit like this, but he had expected a great deal of it. 'I could use a run-down on the score.'

'Yeah,' Baker said as though bored. 'We got a lista shit t'gether fo' the Head Nigger.' He grinned and continued to look through a pile of papers in front of him. 'We figgered maybe you could take 'um over there if you wanned to.'

Here we go, Earl thought as he took the list from Baker. If I wanted to.

There was a tight feeling in the pit of the SGA president's stomach. He could feel his pulse vibrating and drumming an uptempo solo next door to his brain. He lit a cigarette and left the pack on the table. He could feel the pairs of eyes drilling holes into his forehead. Though he noticed that Abul Menka

Confrontation | 283

had not looked up when he entered, he felt that even the notorious Captain Cool was tense, watching and waiting.

'Yeah,' was all that Earl said when he had completed his reading of the list.

Ben King snorted like a bull. Earl cast a glance in the black giant's direction and the returned stare blazed dislike. He met the look head-on. He was by no means intimidated by the huge football hero, though he had no eagerness to test the myths that had been built up pertaining to the larger man's strength and ferocity.

'So, uh, this is the score,' Baker stammered uneasily. 'We decided that perhaps, uh, things might be working out a little slowly for your office. We know how hard it is to get organized since we're always tryin' to organize things in the frat ... we thought maybe you could, uh, use a little help to get the ball rollin' an' get people behind you.' Baker was choosing his words very carefully. 'Uh, it was shapin' up like another one a them years like las' year.' The tension in the room could be felt as Baker dragged on. Earl did nothing to ease the pressure. He did not move or frown.

'So we got things off the ground!' King said suddenly.

Earl chose to ignore King and did not even look to his left in the challenger's direction. He wondered how much more he would be told about the things that were lying beneath the surface. He didn't buy what Baker was saying for a second and the lie was infuriating him more than the overall maneuver. Everything was too hazy, but Baker was waiting for Earl to start the name-calling. Earl would have to force any direct split that became visible between the two groups. Baker could then go back and report that he had tried to work with the SGA leader without success. Ice. Ice. Ice.

'Everybody knows the problems around here,' the MJUMBE spokesman said slowly.

Earl almost laughed. He could see that he was rattling Baker instead of the other way around. Baker had wanted to see him squirming, nervous, and uneasy in the unfamiliar position of follower. Earl's deadpan composure was reversing the pressure and anxiety was crawling deeper and deeper into Baker's eyes.

'We got the same pains in the ass that they had here forty years ago if you read back issues of *The Statesman*. But whenever it comes time for a direct confrontation the students shy away. They so concerned wit' a fuckin' piece a bullshit paper that they refuse to pull their heads outta the fuckin' groun'. Who cares if they spent four years in hell and lived like pigs in a sty? Thass why I sed: "if you wanted to get involved." I don't know how concerned you are about graduatin' on time.' Baker leaned back.

'You may git in trubble,' Ben King baby-talked. 'We wudn't wan' anything like that.'

'Look aroun',' Baker injected. 'We all seniors. Fo' uv us are on football grants that they could snatch in a minnit, but ain' no *man* s'pose to sit fo' alla this shit! We cain' live with a pipe up our assholes, can we?'

He was talking to keep Ben King quiet. Ben was spoiling for an argument with Thomas. He had been told to lay cool. They had everything on their side. Earl had nothing. But the SGA leader's apparent calm was unnerving.

'What do you expec' Calhoun t'say 'bout these?' Earl said, fingering the demands.

'He has 'til tomorrow noon. We don' expec' him t'say anything in particular t'night. When you take him a copy a the things, you need not even ask what he thinks. We'll wait 'til tomorrow when the new copy a *The Statesman* hits. We boun' t'git some readin' out befo' he does. Then we'll be in good shape wit' trustees, faculty, all the resta the bullshit artists . . . what we want 'um to see is some laid-out thought 'bout whuss happ'nin'.'

'That's short notice,' Earl commented. Baker's last lines about *The Statesman* had let him know that Victor Johnson was lined up with MJUMBE.

'Shit! We too damn late!' Speedy Cotton snorted.

There was a pause and the only sound that could be heard was the tap-tap-tapping of Jonesy's foot on the hollow floor.

Earl was glad that shadows cloaked most of the room. He knew that a smile was creeping into his face. If he stayed there much longer he was a cinch to blow everything.

'Waddaya think?' Baker asked suddenly.

Earl almost laughed. If anyone had ever told him that Ralph Baker would ever ask his opinion on anything he would have called them absolutely insane.

'I couldn't say,' Earl breathed. 'Like I sed: thass pretty short notice.'

The room stirred. Something was going on in the doorway behind Earl. He didn't bother to turn around.

'What, man?' Baker asked someone.

'Dude name Johnson downstairs t'see you.'

Baker watched Earl. No reaction.

'Tell 'im ta wait. I be there.' Baker snorted.

'What time is Calhoun comin' home?' Earl asked.

''Bout ten,' Cotton said. 'From the thee-ate-uh.'

'Ol' bag bitch!' King cursed, recalling the maid.

'Does he know about these?'

'I doubt it,' King said. 'The firs' thing you do when people start plottin' on you' shit ain' goin' to the movie.'

Earl got up. 'I'll be goin' over there 'bout ten.' He turned toward the door. He could feel that heat rising to his head. Somehow he could feel that Abul Menka was looking at him for the first time since he entered the room. He turned and caught the stare head on. Yeah, he thought. I got alla these muthafuckuhs shook . . . thass good. But it's not time fo' you yet, Captain Cool. Or you, unfriendly Giant, as he thought of King. Time *will* come though.

'You can wait here!' King exclaimed on the verge of rage. Earl confidently estimated that he had upset King more than any of the others.

'No. I missed dinna, man. I'm goin' to O'Jay's for a bite befo' I go to the Plantation.'

'Yeah,' Baker mumbled.

'Later,' Earl said, leaving.

When Baker next looked up Earl had gone and the only reminder of his presence was the echo of Ben King hammering the already battered card table time and time again.

6
The Plan

'Jonesy? Do me a favor and go down ta git Johnson.'

'He in the lobby?'

'Somewhere down there.'

Jonesy exited. The four remaining young men in black dashikis sat in silence. Baker ran his hand over his hairless head. Speedy Cotton, the lithe, coal-complexioned halfback, yawned broadly. Ben King sat frozen in his chair. Abul Menka looked out of the window.

Jonesy came back in, followed closely by a short young man of medium build who wore thick glasses and a blue business suit. He carried a pad and a pen under his arm.

'Hi, brothers,' he said emitting a smile that looked like a cracking mirror. He was extremely nervous and uncomfortable with the five MJUMBE chieftains and they were all aware of it.

The three seated members vaguely acknowledged his presence. Abul Menka remained silent. Johnson didn't notice. He fidgeted with the pad, looking through it for notes that obviously did not exist. He wished he hadn't allowed Baker to talk him into this situation. He had wanted the details for his story over the phone, but he had been bribed. Baker had promised him an inside seat and the real detailed story Victor wanted in return for two promises. One, that Earl Thomas not be interviewed until after Calhoun had been served with the papers. That demand had not bothered Johnson. He didn't like Earl and had never received any real cooperation from his office. But the second point was a sore spot with him. Baker was asking to see the story before it was printed. That went against a lot of things. It went against professional ethics, objective standards, and everything else. Baker sounded intent on having his way however. So what could Victor Johnson really do? Nothing. He sat there, knees rattling.

'Did'ja bring them numbers I ast for?' Baker questioned, breaking the silence.

'I, uh, already knew those numbers,' Johnson smiled weakly. Naturally he wanted to be cool.

Ben King was already on edge. He was tempted to reach across the table and slap the sniveling muthafuckuh! Those goddamn glasses and that bitch's voice. Shit!

'I'll take 'um down. What are they?' Cotton asked.

Johnson handed Cotton the pad and pen.

'Uh, *Portsmouth Bulletin* – TU 6–3090. Uh, *Roanoke Tribune* – UL 9–6200. What were the others? I forget?'

'The *Norfolk News* and AP and UPI county offices.' Baker snapped.

'Yeah. Uh, *Norfolk News* – LO 2–0000. AP and UPI news services can, uh, be called through the *Norfolk News*. Extension six-nine-nine for AP. Extension eight-two-two-three for UPI. Uh, I donno what county this would be for.'

'You got 'um?' Baker asked Cotton.

'Uh-huh.'

Baker hoisted himself upright. He never talked to the group sitting down. He needed his hands and arms to gesture.

'Everybody know what to do?' he asked.

No one commented.

'All right then. One more time: Speedy, you an' me go wit' Johnson. While we gittin' the paper t'gether you gonna be callin' them people tellin' Calhoun been served wit' deman's on Sutton University's campus. Tell 'um tomorrow we expectin' a answer. At that time we gonna respon' to his responses.'

'Right on.'

'Ben? You ready?'

'You know that,' King said.

'What you gon' do?'

'When Calhoun come out tuhmaruh, if he don' say we gittin'

what we want, me an' the guys gon' start closin' shit down fa' the boycott.'

Johnson's eyes popped. 'Boycott?'

Baker laughed. For a minute the tension was knifed, stabbed, and floating melodramatically to the floor. Everyone except Abul smiled at the grotesque look of horror that masked the editor's face and the awkward, choked question that had slid from between his tightly closed teeth.

'Yeah,' King growled. He was especially dramatic for the benefit of their visitor. 'Tuhmaruh if shit don' go right we callin' off classes an' we stop eatin' inna cafeteria an' alla resta that shit. People who don' dig it can come see me. I'm gon' be the complaint department.'

'Jonesy? You ready?' Baker asked.

'Yeah. I got it done . . . the statements you want released to the press and whatnot been typed up by some sistuhs in the dorm. I kin git 'um anytime I need 'um.'

Baker smiled. He felt better. 'We'll want 'um t'night, okay?'

Everybody laughed.

'Abul?'

Abul Menka swiveled away from the window with exaggerated slowness. The eternal question was in his eyes. Baker laughed again.

'Captain? Captain, why you *so* damn cool?' Baker almost choked on the words. 'Johnson, why is this man so muthafuckin' cool? Goddamn! This is the iceman an' what have you.' He turned to King. 'Benny? Why?'

'I donno, brother.'

'I swear. Captain Zero! Ha! Tell me, captain, hahahahaha, iz you or iz you not ready?'

'I iz, suh,' Menka drawled *slowly*. 'Tuh-ma-ruh afternoon iz in my con-trol. When I heard you needed a bit a my help I immediately stole the white boys' quickes' steed an' hopped nimber-ly into the saddle. I iz gonna pass out copies a yo' statements to the faculty hopin' alla while ta pull a few insomnia cure-ahs ovuh to our way a thinkin'.'

Johnson's mouth fell completely open.

'You the cooles',' Baker said.

'Ultra cool,' Jonesy chimed. Baker almost collapsed. Whoever heard of Fred Jones saying something without being asked?

'Uh, what 'bout my story?' Johnson asked, trying to capitalize on the upsurge of good spirits.

'Ha! Baker, did this cat ast you somethin' or am I gone completely outta my head?'

'Vic, my main man an' campus Waltuh Cronkite, I'm gonna give you a story to take the salt outta the shaker. After this muthafuckuh thay givin' me a gig writin' fo' the *Secret Storm*. Ha!'

Everyone was thinking the same way. 'To hell with Thomas! To hell with Head Nigger Calhoun! We gonna step out there with a program God hisself cain' do nuthing with. We bad! We Black! We MJUMBE!'

7
O'Jay's

Earl found Odds and Lawman engrossed in conversation when he joined them at a back booth in O'Jay's, the most popular off-campus hangout. He slid into the booth casually.

'Earl!' Lawman exclaimed. 'What in hell's happ'nin'?'

'A whole lotta bullshit,' Earl said disgustedly. 'Lemme get a beer an' I'll fill you in ... where the hell yawl been?'

'Nowhere. That's the point,' Odds grumbled, picking up his glass.

A waitress came over with a pad and pencil.

'Black Label,' Earl said.

'I'll take one mo',' Lawman told her. She didn't bother to write the orders down.

'C'mon, man. Whuss up?'

'MJUMBE iz up. My gig iz up. The jig iz up.' Earl replied smiling wryly.

'Start at the beginnin',' Odds said impatiently.

'That iz the damn beginnin'!' Earl said raising his voice irritably. 'The beginnin', the middle, the ... Look, uh,' he paused to light a cigarette, 'I jus' hit campus a l'il while ago, right? I don' know shit.'

The waitress arrived with two bottles of beer and one glass. Odds put a dollar on the tray. The waitress pulled thirty cents out of her apron pocket and laid it on the table.

'I got a call 'bout seven,' Earl continued. 'It wuz King from MJUMBE. He sed they wuz havin' some kind a meetin' an' they wanned me t'come over to the frat house.'

'Thass where you were? We jus' called an' Zeke sed you wuz gone.'

'Well, I wuz.'

'What happened?'

Earl was making patterns from the circles left on the rough-grained surface of the table by his beer glass.

'This,' he said sourly, 'is what happened.' He pulled a mimeographed sheet of paper from his pocket and placed it before Odds and Lawman.

We, the student body of Sutton University, request that:

(1) The Pride of Virginia Food Services, Inc., be dismissed.

(2) Gaines Harper, present Financial Aid Officer, be dismissed.

(3) The head of the Chemistry Dept. be dismissed.

(4) The head of the Language Dept. be dismissed.

(5) The men of the present Security Service be forced to leave all weapons (clubs, guns, etc.) inside the guardhouse while making their rounds.

(6) The supervision of the Student Union Building be placed under the auspices of the Student Government.

(7) The book store be placed under student control.

(8) The Music and Art Fund for Visiting Artists be placed under the auspices of the Student Government.

(9) A Faculty Review Committee be established consisting of students and the heads of the remaining departments (exceptions being Chemistry and Languages) to review the performances of the present faculty. This committee's findings would be honored by the university and all decisions forthcoming would depend on their decision.

(a) A Faculty Interview Committee be established in order to carry out whatever necessary changes be recommended by the members of the aforementioned Faculty Review Committee.

(10) A Black Studies Institute be formed at Sutton including courses in Racism, Black Literature, Black History, and Negro Politics. The head of this Institute would be hired by the committee mentioned in request 9a.

(11) The Comptroller, Financial Aid Officer, Treasurer, Music and Art Department Head (of funds), Maintenance Staff Coordinator, and Student Union Director be forced

to open their books to an auditor hired by the Student Government Association with Student Government funds.

(12) The present medical staff be reorganized and made larger in order to facilitate the Black people within the Sutton University Community.

(13) These demands be responded to no later than noon tomorrow.

Lawman whistled and turned the paper over after reading the demands through. Odds slapped himself.

'Noon tomorrow?' Odds asked aloud.

'In black and white.'

'Thirteen demands,' Lawman said to no one in particular.

'How many of these things had you done research on?' Odds asked Earl.

'All of them and more. These are practically my words. I had a few more things jotted down with notes, but the whole damn thing is like a muthafuckin' gypsy turned them on to my shit.'

'A gypsy?'

'Hi 'bout a gypped-up bitch?'

Odds's question smacked Earl in the face. 'I donno,' he coughed.

'D'you think whut I think?' Lawman asked, swallowing half a glass of beer.

'I donno what in hell you think,' Odds squirmed, 'but I think that lazy bitch in Earl's office turned Baker on to all the shit we had been tryin' ta get together. I think that!'

Odds's voice was carrying like unleashed thunder. All three of the men seated in the booth turned to see who was watching and perhaps listening to their conversation. There was no one in the black half of the bar with them except the waitress who appeared to care less what happened.

'Yes – it must have been Sheila,' Earl said softly.

'What'choo doin' when you leave here?' Odds asked nervously.

'I'm s'pose t'be goin' ta Calhoun's wit' these,' Earl said shaking the paper.

'I think it might be hip if you . . . look, when wuz the las' time you wuz in yo' office?'

'Monday night,' Earl said.

'Did you check the papers we had written out?'

'No.'

'When wuz the las' time you took a look to see if everything wuz in order?'

'What?' Earl lit another cigarette irritably. 'Man, I don' check on no goddamn papers every day. I ain' got time fo' that kinda shit! I'm runnin' aroun' this deserted muthafuckuh like a chicken wit' no goddamn head already . . . I saw the papers las' week. They wuz all there.'

'Las' week when?'

'Las' Thursday or so. Yeah, las' Thursday.'

'So, fah all you know Baker an' MJUMBE could a had yo' work since las' Thursday? Right?'

'For all *I* damn know, longer than that. They coulda been makin' copies a all the shit fo' a month.'

The friends fell silent. Questions were appearing from nowhere and going nowhere. If Baker and MJUMBE had gotten to Earl's notes inside the SGA office there was no telling how much of the information they had. Earl, Odds, and Lawman had been placing pieces of information in a filing cabinet in the SGA office since the beginning of September. There were five keys to that office that Earl knew of. Odds had one. Lawman had one. Earl had one. The maintenance staff had a fourth. The fifth key belonged to Sheila Reed, the SGA secretary. The demands listed by MJUMBE resembled so closely the things that the three men had been working on that they could not help but suspect that they had somehow been betrayed.

'What about MacArthur?' Odds asked.

'Naw, man. Not Mac. He couldn' let nobody in. That job iz all he got.'

'So if Mac didn' do it, it wuz Sheila.'

'We're jumpin' to conclusions,' Lawman said. 'We seem to be assuming that MJUMBE got inta our files.'

'Listen to Mr Law Major,' Odds said, pointing a crooked finger at Lawman. 'Whatta hell it look like ta you?'

'Fuck whut it looks like,' Lawman exclaimed. 'How do we know that they been in the files?'

'Go check?' Odds asked.

'What good would that do?' Earl asked. 'If they got in to take the stuff, they could git in to put it back.'

'Somehow we got to know whether or not they been in there,' Lawman realized. 'We gotta know whether or not they got all our info or what.'

Earl got up stiffly. 'I gotta make a call,' he said. 'I came in here ta eat, but I don' feel like I could take a bite without throwin' up all over this joint. Matter of fact,' he added, 'when I dug this list I almost upchucked then.'

'I bet'choo did,' Odds laughed.

'Get another round a beer,' Earl said dropping a dollar on the table. 'I'll be right back.'

O'Jay came by. He was a big man with a charcoal tan. His face was battered by the six years of professional fighting he had endured. O'Jay had been the fighter's fighter. In thirty-nine fights he had never been knocked out. He had lost sixteen, but all of them had been by decision. He was very proud of that. Though he had never been ranked or made anything that resembled a main event, he had been in demand because he came to fight. He was never one for much cute, tricky punching. It was all or nothing for him. When he had acquired enough money and enough beatings to feel that his call was elsewhere he gave up the ring and bought himself a tavern.

'Hi iz it, brothuhs?' he drawled as he made his way toward the oval bar in the front of the tavern. He was hassling with an apron string that was frayed at the end and difficult to make stretch around his rather imposing stomach.

'Better for us than you, Orange Juice,' Odds laughed. 'Na it ain' but so much you kin ask of a damn apron.'

'Iss gon' fit,' O'Jay chuckled.

'Look like a rhino inna bikini,' Odds retaliated.

The four men all howled. O'Jay, at length, tied the apron around himself.

'Gonna have a good weeken'?' Lawman asked.

'Wuz goin' fishin' tuhmaruh,' O'Jay said scratching his head, 'but the way I hear it, alla yawl may be livin' wit' me come the weeken'. I heard people tryin' ta git some things done 'roun' here.'

'Tryin' to.'

'That means who ever doin' the tryin' bes' be packed. Calhoun ain' noted fo' playin' that young man revolution shit. HAHA!'

'We'll see.'

'Yeah. Lemme run up here an' help out at the bah.'

'Right on!' Earl said as O'Jay made his way between the rows of tables.

'Hey!' Earl called, 'when you gonna git some new furniture. I'm back here gittin' splinters.'

'Where at? In ya elbows?'

The three students laughed again.

'Lemme make this call,' Earl said.

'Hello?'

'Shorty? This iz Earl.'

'Shorty? I like your nerve.' The tone became softer. 'How are you? I heard you've had some trouble.'

'No real trouble. Not yet.'

'You comin' to see me?'

'Thass what I called 'bout. I got a few things to do. I'm, uh, s'pose t'be the one who lays the deman's on Calhoun. I'm goin' over there in 'bout an hour or two. Hey! You still there?'

'Ummm. Uh-huh. I was asleep when you called.'

'Were you? I'm sorry.'

'No. I need to be up. The place iz a wreck. Bobby had Peanut over here playin' cowboys an' Indians . . .'

'What time iz it?'

'Must be close to nine.'

'Well, I'm goin' over to Calhoun's at ten,' Earl said. 'Can you have me somethin' t'eat when I git by there?'

'By where?'

'By yo' house, baby. Wake up now.'

''Bout ten thirty?'

'Uh-huh.'

'I imagine I can do that. But you cain' keep me up all night like you did las' night.'

'Okay.'

'You promise?'

'No.'

'Good . . . Earl, I love you.'

'You mus' still be sleep. Bye, baby.'

'Bye.'

The beers were arriving at the booth when Earl got back.

'S'cuse me, Miss Pretty Legs,' Earl said. 'Will you tell Ellen to come back here, please?'

'Ellen, the waitress?' Earl nodded.

'Sure,' the booth waitress replied, smiling.

The three men sat in silence sipping beer. Ellen, the waitress from the front of the bar, came back. She was a student at Sutton as were most of the young women who worked at O'Jay's. The owner seemed to realize where his interests were. His clients were students. His employees were students.

'Can I help anyone?' she asked the trio.

'I jus' wanned a better look at that smile,' Earl said. 'An' perhaps . . .'

'I knew you wuz lyin',' Ellen said, mocking irritation.

'. . . a bit of information.'

'About who?' Ellen said. She took a furtive look up front and then slid into the booth next to Odds.

'About SGA's secretary, Sheila Reed,' Earl said.

'You mean you cain' get it?'

'Well . . .'

'You better start winkin' at some a these wimmin,' Ellen smiled.

'Who is Sheila's boyfriend or man or whatever?' Earl asked. Lawman and Odds leaned forward. All at once they knew what Earl was getting at. Sheila would definitely give the key to the office to her boyfriend.

'Oh really?' Ellen asked. 'Lawd, Sheila's been goin' wit Che Guevara. You better get busy.'

'Che who?' Lawman asked.

'The Revolutionaries!' Ellen giggled. 'She been goin' wit' Ralph Baker from MJUMBE.'

The three men looked at each other. Truth is light.

8

The Head Nigger

Earl pulled up in front of Ogden Calhoun's huge white home at exactly ten o'clock. The house had been built for the president of Sutton College in 1937. Since then it had changed hands eight times, had been destroyed almost entirely by fire in 1940, was remodeled twice, but remained a landmark in the area. Two years before it had been remodeled for Mrs Calhoun, and now it stood like a sentinel of southern history, a replica of the label the students applied to it – the Plantation.

The lights burning on the first and second floors told Earl that the Calhoun household was not completely asleep. He had been here on other occasions as representative of the SGA for various meetings. He realized at a glance that the first-floor lights were shining in the living room and Calhoun's den and home office.

He was surprised when Mrs Calhoun met him at the door.

'Good evening, Mr Thomas,' the president's wife said, smiling politely. 'How are you?'

'I'm fine, ma'am. How have you been?'

'Just a bit run-down,' Gloria Calhoun said with a hand at her forehead. 'Won't you come in? I'm sure you're here to see Ogden. Is he expecting you?'

'No, ma'am,' Earl replied smiling. He commented to himself that he certainly hoped that Calhoun was not expecting him.

'I'll run back and see what he's doing,' Mrs Calhoun said. 'We haven't been here for the past couple of days and our maid was very busy. When I came home from the theater this evening I told her to go right to bed.'

Earl smiled lightly and Mrs Calhoun made her way across the spacious living room toward the den. There was no question in the young SGA leader's mind but that Gloria

Calhoun was indeed tired. As far as he could see she was always on the run; speaking on a Woman's Day program at somebody's church, helping to raise money for a drive of some description, or just appearing with her husband at a university function.

Earl admired her. Not only because she had been married to Ogden Calhoun for almost twenty years, which put her in line for sainthood, but because throughout all their brief encounters she had impressed him with her sincere interest in community problems and genuine concern about the issues confronting Sutton students.

She emerged from the den having given Earl just enough time to light a cigarette.

'My husband will see you now,' she said with a pleasant smile. It seemed to Earl that Gloria Calhoun was always smiling. He considered it quite a tribute to her that she could continue to do so after living with the grouchy, grumbling Calhoun for so long a time. 'By the way, how is Dora Gilliam? You do have a room with her, don't you?'

'Yes, ma'am,' Earl replied. 'She's fine.'

'I must have a chat with her soon. She's such a fine woman. I've been thinking about having her return a favor and speak at my church's Woman's Day next month.'

'I'm sure she'd enjoy that,' Earl said.

'Good ... well, do give her my regards. I've got to run along now.'

'Good night.'

'Good night.'

The president of Sutton University sat in a leather swivel chair behind his desk, smoking a pipe, with a pair of bifocals perched on his nose. Ogden Calhoun was fifty-seven but didn't look a day over forty-five. He was dressed in a silk bath robe with a pair of maroon silk pajamas peeping from beneath the robe. As Earl entered the room Calhoun put down the sheets of paper that he had been studying. He stood and shook hands with Earl rather stiffly and then sat back again. He ran a hand through his thick, silver head of hair.

'How are you, son?' he asked Earl.

'I'm fine. Yourself?'

'Good,' Calhoun boomed.

Earl looked around. The working den was well decorated. An oaken bookcase against the wall to his right was stacked with thick volumes on law, a multi-volume encyclopedia, textbooks, and pamphlets that proselytized for Sutton University. Behind Calhoun was a sliding door that led out onto a glass-encased patio where sat yet another desk, plus a round patio-table with an umbrella, a glider, and a couch with plastic cover. In the corner directly to Calhoun's left was a lamp that seemed to grow out of an expensive-looking jade vase. The illumination was detoured by a rose-patterned lampshade. The thick green carpet was wall-to-wall here in the office. There were several chairs in the room: a captain's chair, a reclining easy chair that resembled a leather throne, and another plastic-covered couch.

'Sit down!' Calhoun boomed, sucking on the pipe. 'An' tell me what I can do for you.'

Earl offered the mimeographed sheet of paper. 'I have a list of requests here from the students,' Earl said choosing his words very carefully. 'They're for you ta take a look at.'

Calhoun adjusted the glasses across his nose and took the copy of the demands. He read them, lost deeply in thought for a moment. Then his head snapped up. There was a crooked grin on his face.

'Requests?' he asked. 'There's nothing here that I'm requested to do. These seem to me like threats! It says here that I'm to respond to these by noon tomorrow. Is that right?'

'Thass right,' Earl agreed.

'What's requested then? These are intimidating. This is an intimidating document . . . never mind,' Calhoun tried to lower his voice, 'it sez by noon tomorrow. What if I don't reply by then?' There seemed to be real amusement in the president's voice at this time.

'I suppose I'll jus' have to wait until then,' Earl dodged.

'For what?'

'To see what the studen's have to say.' Earl replied evenly meeting Calhoun's eyes.

'Meaning that *I'll* have to wait until then too?'

'Thass right.'

Calhoun backed down a bit at that point. He took another look at the paper. Earl had half-expected to get kicked out.

'This is a short-time thing you have here,' Earl was told.

Earl said nothing.

'I doubt seriously,' Calhoun went on, 'that I kin do anything excep' reread these damn things before tomorrow noon.'

'Do what you can,' Earl said icily.

Calhoun blazed at that remark. 'Look!' he said almost shouting, 'I have asked students over an' over again to talk 'bout whatever the hell it is they want in them various meetings that students are a part of. If this isn't enough for them I will not be intimidated by a piece of paper tellin' me what *I* have to do by tomorrow noon or no time soon! I will make a call or two. I'm gonna have a meeting to ask the people on them various committees what they have been doing if and when these suggestions came up. Chances are none of *these* things have been brought up. Students generally don't appear at the meetings even when they have elected positions to serve on various functioning committees that we have. Now you come in here with a piece a paper telling me to put students in charge of damn near all the money that this institution spends within a year! Telling me that I will allow students to check books behind the people that I have appointed to take charge of various funds. And telling me that I, meaning the university, will pay for it? I think that you think I must be outta my mind! I don't respond to this sort of thing. Ha!' Calhoun sat back in the chair and puffed the pipe forming a cloud of the sticky-sweet cherry blend tobacco over his head. 'I will call this meeting! I will tell the students when these issues will be open for student-faculty-administrative discussion. That is all I will do.'

'All right,' Earl said. Calhoun appeared not at all prepared for that response. He regained his composure very quickly.

'Then I'll see you tuhmaruh?' Earl asked.

Calhoun cautiously fielded the question. 'I'll try an' call a meeting in the morning,' he said, getting up to see Earl to the door.

'I can make it out,' Earl said holding up his palm as a restraining gesture. 'I'll see you.'

Ogden Calhoun had not allowed the sound of the closing front door to die entirely before he picked up the phone on top of his cluttered desk. He dialed seven hasty numbers. Calhoun sucked at his pipe, but the flame was dead. He didn't like the tone of voice or the sarcastic glint in Earl's eyes. He didn't like the way Earl had gotten up to leave.

'Hello. Gaines? This is Ogden. I jus' had a visit from that boy Thomas. Uh-huh. The transfer that the students elected. Uh-huh. He brought over a list of *requests* from the students.'

Calhoun listened for a minute. 'You weren't there, but you heard about it? What?' The president sat bolt upright in the chair. He reached for a lighter and set his cherry blend on fire. 'Can you come over here tonight? Good. I'm going to call Miss Felch and a few others and see if I can't get to the bottom of this thing right away ... I said Miss Felch, my secretary ... One more thing. I suppose you must not have heard everything because request number two is that Gaines Harper be dismissed. ... What am I going to do? I don't know.'

9

Wheels in Motion

Ogden Calhoun came down the carpeted, spiraling staircase from his bedroom wearing a blue suit, white shirt, and tie. The tie was a bit loose at the collar and the jacket was a touch wrinkled, but the president had a stern policy of never holding any official university business when not dressed for the part. Consequently when he heard the bell ring he knew that Miss Felch had arrived and he came quickly down the stairs to meet her.

The maid, up and around at Calhoun's request, showed Miss Felch in. She was a tall, willowy, white, matronly-looking woman with pinched features and thin rectangular glasses squatting on a razor-sharp nose. She was dressed in a navy blue, two-piece suit and carried a matching handbag plus a corduroy zippered satchel with papers and note pads. The expression on her face was one of severe annoyance. She had been upset when the call interrupted her movie, when the cab driver tried to take a long route to increase the fare (thinking perhaps she didn't know the Black section of Sutton), and when she got out of the taxi realizing that she had forgotten her lipstick in the rush and looked like absolute hell. She pushed a lock of dirty-blond hair away from her eyes.

Calhoun stepped on the first-floor carpet like a man walking on eggs. He glided up to Miss Felch with his most gracious smile intact.

'I'm terribly sorry, Miss Felch. I've had a real emergency situation arise in the last hour and I've had to call a rather hasty meeting. I thought it would be appropriate if you were here to take notes and keep things in some sort of order ... As only you can.' The compliment bounced off Miss Felch's unpainted face. 'Louise, could you get Miss Felch coffee. Cream, no sugar. Right?'

Miss Felch attempted a smile and nodded. Louise began her exit.

'And Louise, I'm going to be in my den. I'll need a few of the light folded chairs from the back. Use the big coffee pot because I've invited quite a few men and we'll probably be keeping late hours. I hope you don't mind. This emergency, y'know.' Louise made her exit. Calhoun and Miss Felch entered the den.

'What makes you think this iz so much different from the las' time when Peabody woke everybody up in the middle of the night?' Vice-President Fenton Mercer was asking Calhoun in a corner of the den while the others who had been called were gathering. 'I saw the meeting, but I didn't even go out to investigate.

'Maybe you should have,' Calhoun told him. 'There should have been a note on my desk when I got here.'

'Most of the faculty members and administrators were gone. I was talkin' to the man from that Kentucky Graduate Program an' happened to look out the window . . . I thought it might've been a prep rally for the game on Saturday.'

'It wasn't,' Calhoun said, keeping his voice lowered. 'And I *don't* know if it's any different from Peabody.'

'Then why are we here?'

'I just didn't like Thomas's attitude when I questioned him about certain things. He looked . . . smug. That's the way he looked.'

'Like he had it in hand, huh?' Mercer chuckled.

'Yes. Like that.' Calhoun walked away from Mercer and stood next to his desk. It seemed that everyone who had been called was present. Calhoun made a quick head count. Yes, eight people.

'Harrummph. Uh, I'd like to get this over with as quickly as possible,' he said. 'If everyone will be seated I'll, uh, get things going. Most of you have some idea as to why this

306 | The Nigger Factory

meeting was called. I had a visit tonight from the president of the Student Government Association, Mr Earl Thomas. He presented me with a list of what he chose to describe as "requests." Miss Felch?' Calhoun turned to the secretary, who nodded. 'Miss Felch has made everyone a copy.' Miss Felch passed the stack of papers around and handed Calhoun the original folded print.

There was a slight buzzing and mumbling as everyone read the list. Calhoun sought out particular facial reactions from various individuals.

Mercer, the chuckling vice-president, wasn't chuckling any more. Gaines Harper, the sallow-faced, flour-colored whale of a Financial Aid Officer was catsup-red and coughing. Cathryn Pruitt, the Dean of Women, was biting her right index fingernail. Edmund C. Mallory, the stocky, mustached football coach frowned and continued to sip his coffee. Arnold McNeil, head of the History Department and chairman of the Student-Faculty Alliance was nervously smoking his cigar and rubbing his balding head.

'As you can see,' Calhoun continued drily, 'there are several issues covered in the document here, but I wanted to ask for a few comments from the people present here before continuing.'

'You have your mind made up?' Mallory asked, fingering his mustache.

'Not entirely,' Calhoun hedged. 'Every president at every university has a different way of dealing with lists of in quotes requests. I have my particular way of dealing with them and may well do what I generally do ... tone is important, Ed. I've been doin' quite a bit of running here and there trying to align things for Sutton. I wondered what the tone was; what the feeling was that the group of you had gotten and then I would, quite naturally, proceed from there.'

'I don't think it's good,' Mrs Pruitt chirped. She never thought anything was good. 'The girls have been coming to me talking constantly about things.'

'*These* things?' Calhoun asked surprised.

'Many things. Primarily social things like curfews and late time and visiting time . . .'

'These issues are not listed,' someone reminded her before she went into one of her tirades about being handicapped at her job. They had all heard it before.

'But it's an indication,' she continued. 'It indicates the unrest.'

'We live in an era of unrest,' Calhoun said flatly. 'Mallory?'

'Yes, well, I would say that there are some things here worth investigating. I went to a meeting last week that Arnold was having and . . .'

'Right,' McNeil said rising. 'Ed was at last week's meeting of the Student-Faculty Alliance. Right in the middle of one of our discussions a student came in and started shouting loudly about our committee being the, pardon me ladies, "Bullshit Squad". He went on about us never handling the *real* issues at Sutton. Who was that Ed?'

'I didn't know him. The students called him "Captain Cool" or something,' Mallory laughed.

Calhoun leaned back against the desk. He struck an imposing figure. He was over six feet tall and his complexion was burnished leather. The silver hair gave him an air of importance and command.

'And "Captain Cool" disrupted your meeting,' Calhoun said, with the proper exaggeration applied to the use of the nickname.

'In a sense,' McNeil stated. 'But then he left. Just like that.'

'And this was not . . .'

'No. I didn't report it.' McNeil rubbed his balding head again. He was, along with Mallory, the only under-thirty-five-year-old present. 'I didn't report it because I wasn't sure what the complaint was.'

Calhoun was shocked. 'You didn't . . .'

'Allow me to finish,' McNeil said, waving a calming hand.

'The implication was that our committee wasn't really doing anything . . . it isn't.'

Gaines Harper looked up. He and McNeil were the only two white men there. McNeil was turning red. 'I mean,' he continued, 'I became the head of the Student-Faculty Alliance because I thought it would give me a chance to more closely associate myself with the students and become a part of some of the meaningful change that my classes are always speaking of as necessary . . . we have hassled over the price of a new score-board for the football field. We have handled a few minor disciplinary problems about curfews and violations of visitation, but we haven't *really* done anything.' He sat down.

'Are you suggesting that we go along with these?'

'I'm not suggesting anything!' McNeil said, raising his voice. 'I said that I didn't report the man who interrupted my meeting because he was absolutely right! The damn committee *has not* done a damn thing! The things that are listed on this paper are the things that students come into the meetings to hear discussed. Instead the agenda is full of crap like the allowance for decorations at various dances and allowances for the Homecoming Committee to prepare for the Homecoming Dance!'

There was absolute silence in the room. Everyone, except Miss Felch who continued to jot things down in shorthand, was looking at Arnold McNeil who was self-consciously trying to pretend that he was unaware of their scrutiny.

'Then I can gather that there is a mood of dissent,' Calhoun said through a cloud of smoke from his pipe.

'I think so,' Mrs Pruitt chirped.

'Looking at this list I would say that there are several alternatives left open for us as administrators and faculty members.' Calhoun was fingering the paper carefully. 'We can tell the students that this is a list of things that we will look into . . .' There was a dramatic pause. 'Or we can tell them that this is a document of intimidation and that the university will continue to work on the problems which face the institution as a whole as we have done in the past.'

'What about the remark about noon tomorrow?'

'That's when we'll tell them.'

'I think we should hold a meeting in the morning and discuss this with the whole faculty and everybody else on the nonstudent level,' Mercer said.

'Why?' Harper asked.

'Because there are going to be faculty members who do not want to be associated with the administration,' Mercer replied.

'Thank you,' McNeil commented, head down.

'We've all been grouped together by the students,' Calhoun boomed. 'They all realize full well that within this paper is a question of faculty solidarity. There is a deep professional question here for faculty members. It is a question of professional allegiance.'

'It's a question of whether or not a man is doing his job too,' Coach Mallory stated.

'I think there should be a meeting too,' Mrs Pruitt said thoughtfully.

Heads started to nod all around the room. Calhoun squirmed. He knew that he could take charge and pull the rug out from under all of them and make it appear that he was just doing his job as he saw fit. That was not what he wanted to do however. This was an opportunity for him to take a good look at the people he had working around him and find out exactly where everyone stood. No matter what happened in the meeting he could always take over and say what he felt should be said.

'Take this down please, Miss Felch,' Calhoun said, striking a thoughtful pose as he leaned against the mahogany desk. '"To all faculty members and administrators. There will be a general meeting in the small auditorium tomorrow morning at ten o'clock. There will be a meeting of all department heads directly after this meeting." Put a copy of that in every mail box in the morning. Post in the Student Union

Building and cafeteria that there will be no classes in the morning.'

'Ten did you say?' Mrs Pruitt asked in her singsong.

'Ten,' said Calhoun.

10

Angie

Angie Rodgers had been dealt most of the blows people have in store for them in life by the time she was twenty years old. Her mother had died when she was born. Her father's death had occurred when she was eighteen. The young man who had spoken to her of marriage had run off when she became pregnant, leaving her to raise her son alone. Now, at twenty-three, she lived alone in the home that had been her father's one achievement in life aside from his daughter. She had been lonely in the little red brick house with only her son Bobby as company. She had even gone so far as to invite her father's unmarried sister to share the three-bedroom house with her, but she learned that her relatives felt that her unmarried pregnancy had contributed to her father's death. In a bitter scene on the steps of Angie's home her aunt had called her the Sutton whore and university tramp, unworthy of the love her father had given her.

Earl Thomas was the nicest thing that had ever happened to Angie. She trembled when she realized how she had nearly never met him, and even after their meeting had almost turned him away with her bitterness and icy reserve. He was so good to her. She felt so safe with him. And best of all, he got along well with Bobby.

Her relationship with Earl had not started off well. She had considered him just another application for a summer job when he applied for work at Sutton Computers, where she worked as the employment secretary. Her son's father had been a Sutton student and nothing in the world meant more to her after her father died than saving enough money to leave Sutton and the rest of Virginia far behind.

But it hadn't been that simple. Though her father had paid

for the house, after the funeral expenses and lawyer fees to close out all responsibilities to the hospital and the doctor, what little insurance there had been was exhausted, and what with car payments on her second-hand Volkswagen, and living expenses for herself and Bobby, there was no money to move and no time to do extra work to save any money.

She had been approached several times by the younger Black men at the factory, but she always felt she could detect a sneer behind their eyes because she was the mother of an illegitimate child and would supposedly have hot pants. At times she felt herself near tears because she was lonely but so far she had not found sincerity in any of the eyes that coolly surveyed her across her desk or over a cup of coffee in the lounge.

Once or twice when tossing restlessly, unable to sleep, she had even considered giving in to some of those inquiries, even though she knew it would only mean a fleeting chance to hold a man in her arms and later facing up to the bitter humiliation. She never tried to convince herself that she was a strong woman. She had missed Don, Bobby's father, terribly, and even when she sat up late at night trying to balance her small budget, she never claimed that anything other than love for her son was making her so firm.

But Earl had surprised her. The first time he stepped into the front office she had been there. She gave him a cool 'How are you?' and handed him an application, pointing to various lines where specific information was required. When he had finished she took the form from him and said very formally, 'Mr Egson will see you now, Mr Thomas.' Earl passed through the gate, into the secretarial area, and on into the back of the office where Mr Egson waited.

She had thought about him only briefly. She considered him handsome. He was tall, well muscled across the shoulders and chest. He had a thick head of hair, but it was trimmed and neat as was his mustache. He had been dressed in a short-sleeved sports shirt, open at the throat, and a pair of slacks. His eyes were serious, almost sad, but he had a strong chin and his nose was just right for the soft, but firm lips. The only point that she readily did not approve was the fact that he smoked and his index and middle fingers on each hand were stained yellow, clashing with the smooth amber of his hands, arms, and face. She had been tempted to ask him if he was Indian or of Indian descent, but that would have been definitely out of character.

She nearly forgot about him. Her position in the front office rarely brought her into contact with the mechanics who worked on the assembly line. It was almost three weeks later when she next saw him. He had come into the air-conditioned personnel department mopping a handkerchief across his forehead, dressed in a faded sweatshirt and work jeans with an oil-stained mechanic's apron tied around his neck and waist. He had marched straight over to her desk.

'I'd like to take you out this evening,' he said quite suddenly.

'I'm sorry,' she stammered trying to recover from his matter-of-fact approach. 'I go directly home from work . . . I don't even believe I know your name.'

'Then you haven't been nearly as interested in me as I have been in you,' he replied quietly.

'Really?'

'Really.'

'Well, I'm sorry, but I can't go out with you.'

'What about a movie sometime?'

Angie had looked furtively around the front office. The other secretaries and workers didn't seem to be paying the least bit of attention to her. Earl propped himself on the corner of her desk and lit a cigarette.

'Mr Thomas,' Angie had exclaimed. 'I'm . . .'

'". . . a liar,"' Earl cut in. '"Because I said I didn't know your name, but I do and though I can't have dinner with you this evening I would love to have you drive me home after work because I didn't bring my car in today."'

'How did you know I didn't bring my car in?'

'We mechanics get here early,' Earl said, brightly smiling for the first time. 'And if we saw a good-looking woman taking her car in to LeRoy's the night before and happen to wonder whether or not she got it fixed, we look out the next morning to find out how she arrives. Never can tell when you might get a chance to drive somebody home.'

Angie was unable to control a smile. It had felt good smiling at him and with him that first time. She still felt warm when she remembered the way he sat on her desk in front of everybody as though he didn't have a care in the world about being spotted by the boss and fired or reprimanded.

'I'll meet you by the punch-out clock at four-oh-five and if you work late I'll wait.' Earl had smiled a bit shyly then and left her sitting with her mouth open at the desk.

They had been dating now for almost five months. They stopped going out so often when he started back at Sutton, but Angie didn't mind. She was a good cook and loved to cook for him. He always acted as though he were starving and as if she were the best cook on earth. And she loved the feel of his arms around her. He was strong and masculine. She liked to rub her hands over his shoulder blades and feel the muscles rippling under his skin. She loved to have him crush her and then revive her with a kiss when she was almost breathless. She loved Earl Thomas.

She was sitting alone in the kitchen at nearly eleven o'clock having a second cup of coffee when she heard a car pull up outside her house. Seconds later she heard a car door slam and steps trotting up the brick path that led from the curb to her front door. Then there was a knock.

'If it's not the late Mr Thomas,' she said smiling at the door.

Earl kissed her on the forehead and stepped into the living room. 'If it's not the lovely Miss Rodgers,' he said. She took his coat and hung it on a hanger in the closet next to the front door. Earl was looking out through the curtains at the darkness of Maple Street. She bent over his shoulder and pecked him on the cheek. He turned to her and embraced her and kissed her mouth.

'You've just got to tell me everything,' she exclaimed, remembering the day's activities. 'Louise called me an' told me just enough to drive me out of my mind. She said that nobody knows the full story but you and Baker and Calhoun. The rest of the campus is in a frenzy, I suppose.'

'Everything's fucked up,' he said gruffly. 'Where's the eats? I think I jus' may starve.' He wrapped a long arm around her waist and walked side by side with her to the kitchen.

In the kitchen he sat in the corner and leaned back sighing. She watched him close his eyes as though he would go to sleep. He yawned a big yawn and stretched his long frame, finally exhaling while pounding his chest.

Angie took pride in her kitchen. It was, as was the rest of the house, spotless. Earl often marveled at how she managed to keep the place so clean, especially in the wake of the 'Black Hurricane,' which was his nickname for Bobby. Bobby had a tendency to lose baseballs and guns under beds and sofas and there were times when he had the entire Santa Fe railroad in miniature lined up to make stops all over the house.

She took a minute now to set the table with dishes that had been arranged across the drainboard. The pot was on the stove atop a low flame. When the lid was removed the kitchen was filled with the aroma of tomato sauce and Angie appeared to have a halo of steam around her head.

'We had spaghetti for dinner and I added some for you and some meatballs,' Angie commented without turning around.

'Good,' Earl said.

'Uhl! Uhl, I knew you wuz here!' Bobby's head had appeared at the door and he was taking a flying leap into Earl's arms. Earl caught him with a big laugh and placed the youngster down between his legs and held his giggling captive a prisoner between his knees while he tickled the boy lightly under the arms.

'Bobby Rodgers if you don't get back in that bed,' Angie said, coming to the table and reaching for her son with mock anger. 'Earl, don't tickle him. You know he won't go back to bed.'

'Bobby? Will you go back to bed?' Earl asked continuing to tickle him while holding the lad away from his mother's reach.

'Can I have a soda?' Bobby wondered. 'I'll go back to bed.'

'No soda,' Angie stated firmly. 'You know he almost drank a whole thing full of Kool-Aid by himself.'

'You can have some of my beer,' Earl said. 'Get me a beer out of the refrigerator.' He let Bobby go and the youngster bounded away. 'They gotta be makin' four-year-old giants nowadays. I was seventeen befo' I was as big as he is now.'

'Earl, you oughta stop,' Angie said going back to the spaghetti.

'Here go,' Bobby said climbing into Earl's lap. Earl gave out with a muffled 'Oof!' as the boy plopped a slippered foot into his stomach.

'Bobby, Earl may not want you climbing all over him. Earl has been busy today and he's tired.'

'You tired, Uhl?' Bobby asked unbelieving.

'Little bit, my man,' Earl said. He had poured a couple of ounces of the beer into a glass and handed it to Bobby.

'Cheers!' Bobby said, imitating what Earl said when they drank anything together. Angie laughed.

'Cheers!'

Bobby downed his beer thirstily in one gulp.

'Good man!' Earl said. 'Now off to bed.'

'Do I . . .'

'You promised me,' Earl reminded him. 'But tell me something. Where you get them pretty eyes?' he asked the boy, pretending to reach for Bobby's eyes.

'From my momma.'

'And where'd you get that big ol' smile?'

'From my momma.'

'And where you get them plump cheeks?' Earl pinched a cheek. Bobby started laughing again.

'From my momma.'

'And where you gonna get a spankin' if you don't head for the sack?'

'From you!' Bobby cried wrenching away. He ran to Angie who stood laughing. She appreciated the routine that Earl and Bobby had worked out during his late visits.

'G'night, Momma,' Bobby said, holding her over for a kiss. She kissed him and he returned to Earl. 'G'night, Uhl.'

'G'night, my man,' Earl said allowing himself to be smacked soundly on the jaw.

Bobby ran out of the kitchen and the couple heard his muffled footfalls on the stairs leading to the bedroom upstairs.

'This spaghetti seems to be good,' Angie said heaping Earl's plate. 'Bobby ate two plates full.'

'Doesn't have to be too good for Bob,' Earl laughed. 'Thass a big-eatin' rascal.'

Earl dug into the large pile of spaghetti that was overflowing with steaming sauce and chunks of ground beef. Angie busied herself washing the utensils and pans she had used for cooking.

'You're not going to tell me, are you?' she asked after Earl had finished and lit up a cigarette.

'Baker took over,' Earl said through a stream of smoke.

'I know that. I mean . . .'

'They had some grievances that the students approved. They called me 'bout seven an' tol' me they wanted me to carry the things to Old Nigger Calhoun. I went over there an' took 'im the papers and did some other stuff.'

'Other stuff relating to this?'

'I checked my own papers relating to the things in the deman's because me an' Odds and Lawman all noticed how similar they were to the things we had been workin' on.'

'Were they your papers?'

'Not exactly. Not there. I don't know how much of my stuff they have. I figure they must have copied it all or Xeroxed it, but they put it back in the same order they found it.'

'All your work is down the drain?'

'I don't know yet. It depen's on what happens.'

'How did Calhoun look when you went there?'

''Bout as happy as a man walkin' through hell wit' gasoline drawers on.'

'Oh, Earl. What did he say?'

'Jus' what I thought he would say,' Earl admitted, lighting another cigarette. 'That the list was intimidating and that he would see what he could do, but that that wouldn' be much done. Hell! They asked for a reply by noon tomorrow.'

'Noon tomorrow?'

'High noon,' Earl said shaking his head.

The phone in the living room rang and Angie got up to answer it. 'I wonder who that could be,' she said.

Earl smoked and waited, listening to Angie answer the phone, but not overhearing the muffled conversation that followed.

'It's for you, Earl,' Angie called. 'It's Odds and Lawman.'

Earl went through the open door that separated the kitchen from the living room.

'Earl the Pearl,' he said, taking the receiver from her.

'Look, Pearl,' Lawman said in his ever-serious tone. 'Do you know what's happening over at Calhoun's right now?'

'Midnight. Jus' like everywhere else in Virginia,' Earl cracked.

'Yeah. Well, midnight an' Gaines Harper and Fenton Mercer and a few other personifications just landed on our president's runway.'

'Ah so,' Earl said. 'Not to watch the Late Show, I bet.' Earl took note of the fact that he had not amused Lawman again.

'Doubtlessly not. What did you find out?'

'I'm damn sure MJUMBE got our notes,' Earl admitted.

'You gonna talk to Sheila?'

'Not if I can help it. I'm pissed off at her already. She's prob'bly hip to the fact that I'm onto her.'

'And . . . ?'

'And nothing. Too late to do anything now.'

'How'd Calhoun take the paper?'

'In his hand, man. It got over like a lead balloon.'

'You swallow some funny pills?'

'No, brother,' Earl said sighing and turning serious. 'I guess I just got hung up in that ol' axiom about makin' the best of a bad situation, you know?'

'Yeah. I know. What gives in the mornin'?'

'Yo' guess is as good as mine.'

'Ummm . . . well, I guess I'll au revoir.'

'Okay.'

'I'll see you in the morning. Me and Odds tapped out. Nothin' more to report.'

'All right.'

'G'night.'

'G'night.' Earl cradled the receiver.

'Bad news?' Angie asked when he reentered the kitchen.

'No news is bad news at this stage,' Earl replied.

He lit a cigarette.

'You smoke too much,' Angie said softly.

'Thass right,' Earl admitted.

'There's goin' to be trouble, isn't there?'

'I don't know . . .'

'You're going to get in trouble, aren't you?'

'I don't know about . . .'

'You're the one who took Calhoun the papers and you know how he is about those things.'

'There's always trouble,' Earl said.

'Not like this . . .'

'Trouble is the same. When you got them they're all just big problems, and when they're gone you don' remember why you had such a hard time.'

'Calhoun is going to be your hard time.'

'Just as long as I have you for my good time,' Earl laughed gently. 'I'll just try to deal with one time at a time.'

11

Calhoun's Assessment

Gaines Harper was the last administrator to leave the Calhoun home after the president's impromptu meeting. The fat, red-faced Financial Aid Officer had dawdled, scanning stacks of periodicals in the president's bookcase until after even Miss Felch had gathered her notes and departed.

Ogden Calhoun returned to his den from seeing Miss Felch into a cab. His face was drawn and tired. He was irritated by the whole affair.

'What do you think?' Harper asked the president breathlessly. He was always breathless; grossly overweight, he was a victim of too much beer.

'Please don't ask me what I think, Harper,' Calhoun snorted as he stripped off his jacket. 'You heard everything I heard.'

'I heard it all right. And I didn't like it too much.'

'It wasn't for you to like or dislike,' Calhoun said irritatedly.

'McNeil acted as though he even wanted those things to be,' Harper continued, as though he hadn't heard. 'I wonder what Mr Ostrayer would say about that. He recommended McNeil just like he recommended me.'

'What could he say?' Calhoun asked.

'He'd have plenty to say,' Harper assured the president. 'You know how trustees think. He wouldn't like McNeil taking the students' side against you.'

'Is that what you think McNeil is doing?'

'It was plain. He told you he wasn't even angry when that student came in and disrupted his meeting!'

'Yes. But I think it's quite another thing to imply that he was in favor of these demands.'

'It's all the same to me. They'll be after him next and all

of the other white workers here. I wonder what he'll have to say then.'

'I don't see where color has anything to do with it,' Calhoun said coldly.

'Why do you think they want me fired?' Harper blazed.

'They don't say.'

'Naturally it's because I'm white. The ones in charge of that meeting today were militants. They are against everything white . . . Yeah, they'll be after McNeil soon. Mark my words. He won't be so quick to agree that the faculty shouldn't only answer to the administrators then. He wouldn't want the students looking over his shoulder, checking his books, doing things like that . . . it's only because he's on the other side of the fence now that he can afford to be so liberal.'

Calhoun shot Harper a quizzical look. 'Is that what it is?' he asked sarcastically.

'Yes. That's it,' Harper said breathlessly, hurrying on. 'You can afford to be high and mighty and in favor of student reform when you've got tenure and a Ph.D. He wouldn't be like that if it was his second year on the job like me, just trying to find his way around.'

'We'll see,' Calhoun said.

'Well . . .'

'Well what?' Calhoun asked standing up. 'Your point is that you want to know whether or not I'm going to give in to the students, isn't that it? I'd rather you have asked. But it's an indication that you've only been here for a year because then you'd know that I never respond to papers like this one. Thomas should know better too.'

'Maybe he does,' Harper said thoughtfully.

Calhoun was struck by the idea. Harper was pulling on his huge raincoat and hat.

'I'll see you at ten o'clock,' he said. 'Don't bother to see me out.'

'Good night,' Calhoun said.

Calhoun remained in the den long enough to turn off the

lights and straighten up his desk. He then made his way up the spiral stairs to the bedroom where, much to his surprise, his wife was still sitting up, reading.

'Surprised to find you up,' he said wearily.

'You're the one who needs the rest,' she said. 'I know how Norfolk tired you out. You were looking forward to coming right home from the theater and going to bed, weren't you?'

'I really was,' Calhoun said, sitting on the edge of the bed and taking off his shoes, socks, and pants. 'I'm afraid I'll have an early day tomorrow too.'

'The students are being unreasonable again?' Gloria Calhoun asked. Her husband wondered if he detected a note of sarcasm in his wife's voice.

'Damn right!' he said gruffly. 'Imagine asking me to fire Royce, Beaker, and Harper and wanting to audit all the school books and have me turn everything in the Student Union over to them plus funds so that they can invite the performers and speakers on campus. I imagine we'd have James Brown every night. Not even asking me,' Calhoun went on. 'Telling me.'

'What reason do they give?'

'None. Just a piece of paper pointing out how to do my job.' Calhoun was properly disgusted at the thought. 'And what difference does it make what reason they give? It's still an intimidating paper. They're still telling me how to do my job. I've been president here for nine years, Gloria. You know that that's not the way we get things done here.'

'Maybe the students are just trying to be dramatic,' Mrs Calhoun suggested.

'Dramatic? This is a threat!' Calhoun asserted. 'Thomas must not be any older than twenty-two. I'm damn near three times that. We're trying to teach the boys and girls at Sutton how to be men and women and cope with their lives outside. You can't take your boss a note saying do this and that by tomorrow noon or else.'

'But this is different,' Gloria said. 'You're not their b . . .'

'It's the same principles. Channels have been established!' Calhoun was raising his voice.

The last thing Gloria wanted was an argument. 'You should come to bed, dear,' she said. 'It's almost twelve thirty.'

'I know,' Calhoun grumbled. 'As soon as I wash my teeth and try to refresh myself a bit.' He got up and carried his pajamas with him into the bathroom next to their bedroom.

Gloria Calhoun listened for a second to the running water that alone disturbed the silence of the house. She was amazed at how easy it had been for her to avoid the argument that would have come and how natural it seemed for her not to challenge her husband. She remembered how, when they were courting, they had stayed up until all hours of the night arguing points about world politics or the movement or even about a movie they had seen.

The water stopped running in the bathroom and Calhoun returned to the bedroom, turning out the light from the wall switch as he came.

Thursday

12

Preparation

Ralph Baker sat brooding over an early cup of black coffee at a corner table in the Sutton cafeteria. His roommate and closest friend, Jonesy, had just left to have more copies of MJUMBE's demands mimeographed, and the big MJUMBE spokesman was alone for the first time in what seemed like days. He didn't particularly like the feeling.

Calhoun was on Baker's mind. Calhoun and Thomas and Sheila and a lot of other things, but Calhoun was a special worry. He couldn't help feeling that he had made a big mistake by not accompanying Earl Thomas to the Plantation the night before. He wanted to know what was on the university president's mind. He wondered what the reaction to the demands had been. Not necessarily what had been said, but what had flashed across the old fox's eyes. Eyes were a good sign of what was going on inside the mind. Discussing the situation earlier with Jonesy, he had spoken confidently about the bind in which MJUMBE had put the Sutton administration. Now, alone, he wasn't quite as sure. There were too many loose ends; things that he needed to know and had no way of finding out. Signs would have certainly been in Calhoun's eyes, even if he played it cagey and diplomatically. Baker felt like a blind man, lost without knowing those signs; like a blind man who would stumble, either into the light or out onto the highway with a bus ticket clenched in his huge hand.

But Calhoun was not the only problem. Just when he hadn't needed anything else to upset him, his relationship with Sheila had disintegrated. He didn't know exactly what had gone wrong. As a matter of fact he had never really intended for anything to happen between them.

He had known Sheila for almost six years. They had met

when he was an All-State candidate from their high school in Shelton Township, Virginia. Sheila was a cheerleader with a crush on him, but he had been going steady with another girl and hardly had time for the short, baby-faced freshman who followed him halfway home every day after practice. He had laughed at the thought of her and at one of the victory dances even made a joke of her crush on him. That had seemed to cool things down. During his senior year Sheila was no longer a cheerleader and Baker rarely saw her. Then he had won a scholarship to play football at Sutton.

The next time he saw Sheila was when she arrived on Sutton's campus as a freshman. He had been cordial as he would have been to any new student from his home town. But they moved in different social spheres. He was a fraternity man and a football player. She was just one of the many coeds on the predominantly female campus.

Baker had met Sheila at a party given by a mutual friend. They chatted about school and Greek organizations and football. She expressed an interest in Delta Sigma Theta, the sister organization of Omega Psi Phi, Baker's fraternity. He found himself not only interested in the conversation, but in Sheila. They began dating off and on. The young woman who had once been so much a part of Baker's life had gotten married during his freshman year and already had a child.

Upon their return to school in the fall Baker had been surprised to learn that Sheila was working as Earl Thomas's secretary. She had told him that she was going to try to get a job, but even when she landed the secretarial post Baker paid it little attention. Football had started again. The fraternity had another line of pledgees to indoctrinate. Plans for MJUMBE were only vague shadows forming in the back of his mind. The organization had been formed by Baker as a safeguard against another year of political apathy. Baker had been willing to admit that Earl Thomas was a fast talker and a man who could think politically while on his feet, but he had never felt that Earl's administration stood for radical change, which was what he felt that Sutton needed. He felt that between Earl and 'Lawman' Dean a few small problems might be alleviated, but it was a question of timing. If the students were allowed to slip into the middle of another non-productive year it would be difficult to shake them up and ignite a fire under them once they settled into a pattern or an attitude of acceptance.

But Earl had waited too long. Virginia institutions of higher education come up for their accreditation markings during the third week of October. Baker knew that the ideal time to hit the school with a list of demands would be just as the accreditation service began looking into the mechanisms of the school. This move by students would bring about more pressure on the administrators to force a quick halt to the disturbances. With these things in mind Baker moved.

He found himself seeing more and more of Sheila. Talk about her work and the SGA let Baker know what Thomas was doing and exactly what information was on hand in the SGA office. He wanted very badly to see the information that Earl and his team had gathered, but there was no way he could legitimately go into the office and ask Thomas for permission. He started an Uncle Tom campaign against Earl with Sheila.

'I shoulda known better than to think that nigga was doin' somethin',' he had said in Sheila's room one night near the end of September.

'Who you mean?' Sheila asked, looking up from her homework.

'Thomas. He said when he got elected he was gonna have somethin' goin' by October an' tomorrow's October an' ain' nobody heard hide nor hair a' him.'

'He mus' be doin' somethin',' Sheila sighed. 'Wit' all them different things he has me typin' all day.'

'I wish they'd open up them records for everybody,' Baker snorted. 'I bet I'd get something together.'

'They don't open everything up for . . .'

'No. SGA's a special thing. Thass why I was runnin'. You get a chance to look in everybody's closet. There's no tellin' jus' what Thomas knows, but we'll never find out. Lucky for Head Nigger Calhoun that some Tom always gets elected.'

'This whole political thing is very important to you, huh?'

'Damn right! Look at alla the things you have to put up with when you're here. The damn dorms are crumbling. The food tastes like warmed over garbage. The teachers don't know their asses from a hole in the ground. Somethin' oughta be done.'

'You think the records Earl has tell about how to fix these things?' Sheila wondered.

'That's what he was s'pose to be workin' on,' Baker pointed out.

'Why would he work on them if he wasn' gonna do anything?'

'Because he prob'bly knows that people like me are gonna ask him what the hell he been doin'. Then he can haul out this big pile a papers an' show us how bizzy he's been even though nuthin' came outta it.'

'But what could anybody do who's not in an office? Even if they had the papers?'

'Sheila,' Baker said seriously, 'all studen's want 'roun' here is for somebody to have guts enough to stand up to Calhoun. They don't really care who it is. It could be Thomas or me or Mickey Mouse.'

Sheila had been thoughtful and quiet for a moment. Then she got up from her desk and reached into her purse. When her hand emerged from the bag there was a short, round key in her grasp dangling from a rabbit's foot key chain.

'Take this key,' she told Baker handing him the chain. 'This is the key to the SGA office. The papers are in the filing cabinet in the back, listed under G. Everything that has been done this year is there.'

The rest had been easy. Baker had been back to the office on two other occasions to tighten up information and copy things that he thought would be needed. Aside from Sheila nobody, not even Jonesy, knew anything about Baker's access to the office. He had taken the notes and worked on them by himself, forming the list of demands from the papers he had seen and from information that he had collected before his campaign.

The entire plan had gone exceptionally smoothly. He had been very pleased with himself until the night before, when he and Sheila had argued and he had left her in tears.

He had gone into her room tense and angry. The confrontation with Thomas had been upsetting. Thomas had looked as if he wouldn't give a damn if MJUMBE took over the United States Government. He had listened to Baker and the others in the MJUMBE group talk briefly about their actions and then he had taken the list of demands and departed. That was the last that any member of MJUMBE had seen of Thomas, and no one had seen Calhoun. Baker felt as if he were somehow being manipulated instead of himself manipulating what was happening. When he got to Sheila's room in Garney Plaza, she had noticed that something was bothering him.

'You were good today,' she had remarked quietly when he sat at the desk instead of coming to sit on the edge of the bed with her as he usually did. 'I mean, your speech was good. Everybody said so.'

'Thanks.'

'Are you all right?'

'I'm okay. It's raining.'

'I was listening to it. It put me to sleep.'

'Yeah? Well, I got me some work to do, you know. I got a lotta things I got to tighten up befo' tuhmaruh.'

'Can I make you some coffee or something?' Sheila asked getting up. She slipped into her robe and lifted the arm of the record player that sat next to her bed. She lifted the stack of records that had played through and started them over again.

'Where's Bucky Beaver?' Baker asked, referring to Sheila's two-hundred-pound roommate who was a dead ringer for the animated character of the Ipana commercials in the fifties.

'She moved,' Sheila said absently.

'She moved?'

'Monday. She took her things an' changed her room down the hall.' The Temptations came on doing 'Psychedelic Shack,' and Sheila turned the record player down. She pulled a hot plate from under her bed and then went out into the hall. When she came back she had a coffee pot full of water in her hands. She filled up the top with coffee from a two-pound canister and lit the hot plate, putting the pot over one of the burners. Baker sat hunched over a pile of papers with his back to her. She started to speak and then stopped, busying herself with coffee cups and saucers from her dresser.

'She couldn' dig me, huh?' Baker asked disconnectedly.

'Huh? . . . oh, I guess not. She and I didn' really get along. She's got problems.'

'Yeah. About three or fo' hundred of 'um.'

'Ralph,' Sheila giggled, warming a bit. 'She's not that fat.'

Baker lapsed into silence. He was thinking about Victor Johnson, the skinny, bespectacled editor from *The Statesman*. He had left the MJUMBE meeting and gone directly to *The Statesman* office. Along with Johnson he had put together the issue that would greet the community when the sun rose. He had felt that he had done a good job in pointing out the things that had to be done at Sutton. He had even tempered his words to appeal to the lackeys and eggheads that he despised. He didn't particularly care for political diplomacy, but he knew that he had lost the election because there were so many soft-hearted Toms on Sutton's campus who daily sold their asses for a diploma and that he didn't dare do otherwise. Now, in Sheila's room, with copies of the paper being run off in the basement of the Trade Building, he wondered if he had done the right thing. Maybe Speedy Cotton had been right when he pointed out what kind of spot Baker's article was going to put MJUMBE in. Baker had snorted that it was time for some people to get on the spot. Now he wasn't sure if a Victor Johnson editorial and the pictures of Thomas in one corner and the MJUMBE meeting in the other wouldn't have been enough.

Sheila interrupted his thoughts by coming up behind him and wrapping her arms around his neck.

'Look! I'm bizzy. All right?' Baker snapped.

Sheila looked as if she had been kicked. She was turned off.

'Look, I didn't mean it like that ... I'm uptight. Okay?'

'That's what I thought I was for ... I mean, when things were bothering you and like that.'

'There ain' nothin' an' nobody who can do anything 'bout this. It'll all be taken care of tuhmaruh.'

'Will it?'

'Yeah.'

Sheila turned the flame down under the coffee and poured two steaming cups from the pot. She poured a little milk and sugar in her cup and handed Baker his black. They drank for a second in silence.

'What's going to happen?' Sheila asked suddenly.

'I wish I knew,' Baker said rubbing his bald head. 'Things went all right today except for a few things.'

'Like what?'

'Well, we called Thomas to take the things to Calhoun, but his line was busy. So we decided to carry the ball ourselves and Calhoun wasn't home. Then we got ahold of Thomas and he took the things over there.'

'That's bad?'

'Not really bad,' Baker admitted. 'Things just weren' clickin' like I thought they would. There was too much confusion. Everybody was restless. It's a whole different thing when you ain' in fronta the crowd no mo'. They come to the meetin's an' clap an' carry on, but it's just a different set when you're by yo'self.'

'You worried?'

Baker laughed. 'I been waitin' fo' this fo' three years. I'm jus' impatient to git it on.'

'You hate Calhoun?'

'Naw. I hate bullshit. Sutton could be a beautiful place fo' Black studen's to come an' get their minds together, but what happens? Fo' years a bullshit an' then ill-equipped people go back home an' ill-prepare another set to continue to merry-go-round. It's gotta stop.'

Sheila laughed a little. 'You'll never change. You always want to be the one . . .'

'Somebody has to be the one,' Baker said.

'Well, I hope it's over soon, because I'm not use to you bein' uptight.'

Baker put down his coffee cup and went to sit next to Sheila on the bed.

'I thought you were goin' to work,' Sheila smiled as he reached for her.

'I was,' Baker admitted.

'And now?'

'Well,' Baker said untying his shoes, 'I had this idea that I was gonna sit at the desk an' jot down notes an' stuff and the nex' thing I knew it would be mornin'.'

'An' now?' Sheila persisted.

Baker held her around her waist and turned her until they were both flat out on the bed facing each other. His hand was in her hair and their mouths were pressed tightly to each other, tongues sucking deeply. Baker's huge hands were fondling and squeezing, running down her side and between her heavy thighs. Sheila was gasping, scratching the small of his back with her nails and running her tongue in and out of his ear sending shivers down his spine.

He could feel her wetness, the sticky fluid of her womanhood moistening her pubic hair. He bit her on her neck and felt her jump and squeeze his hand between her legs. She tightened her hold around his neck even as he twisted her slightly to remove her robe and pajama top.

As Baker bent to kiss her breasts Sheila shivered and felt for the rising lump between his legs. She squeezed him hard and he wriggled away. She reached for his belt and unlocked it, breaking the button that secured his trousers. With impatience she unzipped the front of his trousers and lowered them so that she could gain a sure hold on his swelling manhood.

Baker groaned and teased her breast with his teeth. He could feel the pressure mounting in his loins as she stroked him up and down and sighed and moaned in his ear. Sweat was beading at his hairline and dripping onto her face. Sheila was tossing and turning under him; rising to meet him as he strained to move away from the grip of her hands. He scooted down and away from her and kissed her stomach, kicking his pants off as he moved. He pushed his tongue inside her navel and she squirmed and wiggled more frantically beneath him. Her hands left his organ for a second to grasp his testicles and tickle the hair of his lower stomach.

Baker straightened up in a kneeling position between her thighs. She was breathing heavily, eyes closed, thighs spread apart waiting for him. He teased her opening gently, allowing only a small portion of himself to lodge between her legs. She groaned and sobbed a small cry and reached for him, digging her fingernails into his buttocks, pulling him forward. With a crushing certainty he entered her. He felt a lightning flash of pain-pleasure as he eased inside her. She called his name, and wrapped her thighs around his waist; thrusting herself up to him, impaling herself totally. Baker felt a rush coming from his thighs as he moved within her. He crushed her to him and heard her groan. Their rhythm and speed increased as he strained to hold off against the surging flow of his orgasm. She screamed as she shared his liquid fire until she was left spent and exhausted.

She clung to him tightly, wanting to lie there with him and allow the heat of their bodies to smother them and shelter them. Baker withdrew slowly and pressed his head to her bosom. She squirmed closer to him, kissing his heavily muscled arm. Their heavy breathing subsided. The sweat was cooling them as it traced crooked paths down the lengths of their bodies. Sheila hooked a leg across Baker's flat stomach and fondled him between his legs, pressing it to her thigh. Baker inched away.

'Ralph,' she began tentatively.

'Yes?' he replied, sitting up on the side of the bed and looking around for his shoes.

'Ralph? Are you leaving?' Sheila asked as though frightened.

'Yeah,' the reply came hardly above a whisper.

Sheila rolled away from Baker's side of the bed. She felt hurt again. She had known what he was going to say somehow. She had known all the time that things weren't right. She had sensed it. But there was no way to stay away from him when he held her in his arms like a doll and crushed her to him.

Baker was struggling for something to say. He knew that she was hurt. He knew why. He was berating himself for feeling that he had to leave. All through the act of love he had heard the words from the Last Poets' album banging into his mind: 'All over America bitches with big 'fros and big asses were turning would-be revolutionaries into Gash men ... Gash needs man. No experience necessary ... Gash man. Gash man ... Come on, daddy. And he came. Every day he came ...' Baker shook his head. He wasn't thinking straight. That was why he was leaving. He needed some sleep. If he stayed Sheila would crawl all over him all night long and he would respond; grabbing her pillow-soft breasts, running his hand between her thighs, squeezing her firm ass. All night long. All night long. He would fuck as though he were inventing pussy and the next day he would be useless, drained, out on his feet. He knew he had to be sharp when the sun came up. That was why he was leaving. He watched Sheila out of the corner of his eye as he put his shoes on.

She was lying on her back searching the corners of the ceiling, acid tears springing from salty wells in her mind, a sick emptiness jerking at her stomach.

'Why won't you stay?' she called. 'I know I shouldn't be

raising my voice an' gettin' upset an' cryin' or anything, but I shouldn't be doing a lot of things like laying in bed with you or waitin' up all night for you. I wait an' wait sometimes Ralph and you don't come or call. I feel like Ralph Baker's private whore.'

'You're wrong, baby,' Baker said in monotone. 'You're wrong again.'

'Am I?'

'Yeah. You wrong. Tomorrow night I be by an' we'll talk about it.'

'Tomorrow night? I'm sick an' tired of waitin' for tomorrow nights that aren't comin'. You don't have to say nuthin' special. A woman can tell, Ralph. I knew all the time, but I thought I was gonna make you love me. Well, I give the hell up. You don't give a damn 'bout nothin' an' nobody but Ralph Baker. It's always been that way. You have to be the head of everything; the king of everything, the leader. When you can't get it one way, you get it the other. All I was was the key to the damn office! An' now that you have all the papers an' things I hope you're quite through with me.'

'You're wrong, Sheila,' Baker said sadly.

'Get out! Get out of here and leave me alone!'

Baker had wanted to say something special then, but the words he needed were nowhere to be found. He finished dressing quickly and left. The last sight he had of Sheila was a sad picture. She was lying in a heap on the bed, her bathrobe open exposing the glossy brown texture of her breasts, jerking as she sobbed and cried.

It hadn't done much good to go back to the room. Jonesy had been in bed fast asleep. Baker showered and fell heavily into his bed, but sleep was a stranger far into the night. He found himself turning over the day's events and the events of his life with Sheila as far back as he could remember. He had really come to like her. He had come to appreciate her and enjoy her company. He had come to love her. No. That was a lie. He didn't love her. But it wasn't the sort of plot that she thought it was. That had been a coincidence. An unhappy one at that. No. He didn't love her. But he missed her. He missed having her change the records and fix coffee.

Ben King came through the door to the cafeteria. Baker waved and King came over to the table and set his tray down.

'Git me another coffee, brother?' Baker said.

King nodded and went back to the line where the coffee was being handed out. He turned with two cups and sat down opposite the MJUMBE spokesman.

'So whuss happ'nin'?' King asked.

'Everything, man. You seen anybody?'

'Man, I'm so ready it don' even make no muthafuckin' sense. You git a look at Thomas?'

'No. Did'joo?'

'No. I seen Abul. His shit is togethuh too.'

'I figgered that.'

'He got his shit on!' King laughed.

'The gol' dashiki?'

'The brother is layin' tough.'

Both Baker and King were wearing black dashikis with gold trim.

'Hi many dudes you got lined up if we haveta boycott?' Baker asked.

'Shit! I got the whole football squad an' half the players on every othuh team near here.'

'You git any static?'

'You kiddin'?' King asked as he gulped down the scrambled eggs. 'I heard a lotta "you goin' 'bout this the wrong way" type shit, But I thought I wuz gon' hear that shit.'

'You listened?'

''Course I listened. I din' tell no punks 'bout the plan. I jus' don' wanna hear no shit when the real deal go down.'

'Right.'

King ate in silence for a moment. Baker drank his coffee

thoughtfully. The cafeteria was filling up again. A glance at his watch told Baker that it was almost eight thirty.

'I got to go,' he announced standing up.

'Fo' you do,' King said, 'tell me somethin'.'

'What?'

'What'choo rilly think gon' happen?'

Baker looked down at his big backfield mate and friend.

'I think we gonna haveta close this mutha down fo' a helluva good while.'

'Good,' King said. 'Thass jus' what I wanna do.'

13

Evaluation

'Did'joo dig whut wuz happ'nin' outside?' Odds asked, as he blasted into the SGA office on the first floor of Carver Hall.

'You mean wit' there not bein' any classes an' all?' Lawman asked.

'Yeah!'

'Somethin's cookin'. Where's Earl?'

The question was no sooner out of Odds's mouth than Earl came into the front from the file room in back with a handful of papers in one hand and a cup of coffee in the other. The SGA president took a seat at his desk while Odds hung up his raincoat in the closet.

'What'choo think's happ'nin'?' Odds asked through his nose.

'Me an' Lawman wuz gettin' ready t'take a look at the deman's again an' see what kinda changes everybody is gonna go through. They havin' a faculty meetin' at ten o'clock. I tried ta see 'bout gittin' in there, but they ain' lettin' nobody in but faculty an' administrators.'

'Where the papers at?' Odds asked sitting down.

Earl pulled a folded copy of the demands out of his desk drawer. He handed the sheet to Lawman and sat back with his coffee. He looked tired and felt the same way. He had not slept well. From the looks of things neither had Odds or Lawman.

'Numero uno,' Lawman began. 'The Pride of Virginia Food Services be dismissed.'

'Relevant, man. I had a stomach ache for fo' damn years. I'll be glad to graduate jus' to git away from this grit.'

'I had taken a long look at that,' Earl said. 'The company's workin' on the third year of a three-year contrac'. When they had the boycott at the beginnin' a las' year the SGA secretary took notes at the confrontation meetin'. They said mos'ly a whole lotta bullshit. Their real source of income comes from the canteen at night. The percentage of profit from the meals iz only 'bout two per cent ... y'know it wuz the same ol' bullshit. You cain' please everybody an' ya can only prepare certain types of food for a lot of people an' ya cain' season food to suit everybody.'

'But the question is ... what is Calhoun gonna say?' Lawman asked.

'He's gonna quote from the same damn thing I been readin' an say the same shit.'

'No new food services,' Lawman deduced and put a check mark.

'Right.'

'Number two is that Gaines Harper be dismissed,' Lawman said.

'Thass tricky,' Odds said. 'Why they wanna git rid of him? 'Cuz he's a whitey or what?'

'I guess.'

'Thass prob'bly why Calhoun will turn it down. The primary student complaint against the man is that he's a drunken devil.' Earl laughed out loud. 'They tired of goin' over there an' havin' him puff cigar smoke in their face an' treatin' what they consider a serious problem as though it didn' mean shit.'

'Whuss the real charge?'

'It can't be incompetency,' Earl admitted. 'I guess it'll have to be that the man doesn't relate to the students in terms of the job that he's doin' which is s'pose to be a personal student service.'

'No new Financial Aid Officer?' Odds asked, looking over Lawman's shoulder.

'No,' Earl said.

'Three and four are new heads of the Chemistry and Language Departments respectively.'

'Accreditation,' Earl sighed. 'Everybody knows that Beaker and Ol' Royce shoulda been gone. Calhoun iz gonna rap 'bout not bein' able t'git anybody wit' the proper credentials to take their places. You have to have a Ph.D. in those departments.'

'What 'bout Phillips in Chemistry? He's a Ph.D. Why can't he take Beaker's place?'

'Thass the student argument,' Earl said. 'An' Connoly in French has at least a leg on his Ph.D. He'll have it by the time school convenes again in September . . . I mean, the people they got in here gonna haveta finish this year anyway. They may as well be plannin' on gettin' somebody for when all these oldies fall the hell out an' die.'

'The students can get numbers three an' four?' Odds asked.

'Uh-huh. Not without Calhoun rappin' a lotta shit 'bout tenure an' alla that action, but maybe.'

'Number five. The thing about the Security Service leavin' their guns an' shit in the guardhouse.'

'Yeah. Thass in the bag,' Earl said confidently.

'I'm glad somethin's in the bag,' Odds sighed.

'You thought we wuz gonna get shut out?' Earl asked laughing.

'It wuz lookin' that way.'

'Each and every one of these things coulda been worked out in time,' was Earl's comment. 'I been over damn near alla them. If we, and I mean the formal SGA, had been given time to present workable plans in terms of alla these things . . . I mean like an alternative an' a formal plan for alla these things, everything woulda been all right. Keep readin' an' I'll show you what I mean.'

'Well, six, seven, and eight would give the SGA supervision over the Student Union Building, the book store, and the Music and Art Fund.'

'Dig it. If we had drawn up statements that documented how much better for students things would have been if we controlled these things and sent copies to the alumni an' the Board of Trustees . . .'

'An' na it's too late?' Odds asked.

'Look, brother,' Earl said. 'If you can spring a sudden thing on Calhoun an' hit him where he's weak, you can git over. But every time you go after the man an' don' make it, it gives him a chance to shore up whatever spot it was you wuz after. Then you haveta try somethin' else.'

'An' by the time we git somethin' else t'gether he will have gone through changes with the alumni an' everybody to show them how wrong we are. It's jus like I tell people when they ask who'll win if we have about a week-long nuclear war with Russia: I tell 'um ain' gon' be no war like that 'cuz whoever slides a bomb on the othuh one first is gonna win. Thass all.'

There was a minute of silence while each of the three young men became involved with himself. Lawman and Odds had been at Sutton for four years and had seen demonstrations throughout their college careers. The real difference in this one was their involvement. In past years they had been just interested students hoping that something would get accomplished. This time they sat in the SGA office trying desperately to think of something that would make the dark picture of possible success shine a little brighter. Earl Thomas was in his second year at Sutton. He was a transfer student who had turned the entire Sutton political world around when he ran for SGA office and won. He had never seen much done at any of the schools he had attended. He too was searching for a clue. But aside from all that he was searching for his own particular position. He had been thoroughly fouled up by MJUMBE and still had the power to stop the train in its tracks. He didn't know what he wanted to do.

'Number nine is about the Faculty Review Committee and Interview Committee,' Lawman snorted. 'Not a chance. The faculty wouldn' give the studen's any kinda say over their jobs.'

'Shit!' Odds exclaimed. 'All this shit is dead end!'

'Whuss number ten again?' Earl asked.

'Ten is the establishing of a Black Studies Program.'

'Maybe,' Earl hedged. 'Calhoun sent Parker from the History Department to Atlanta in August for the Black Studies

Conference that they held. I don' figger the firs' year would have alla this shit in it even if we *got* some kinda phony Black Studies thing.'

'The school would have a wider appeal if we had the program,' Lawman added. 'More students would come here and we'd get more money.'

'Yeah, that's true. But you gotta find some way to git it accredited first. You also gotta have some professors who know what the hell is goin' on. Sutton ain' got but 'bout three a them.'

'What 'bout eleven?' Odds asked impatiently. 'Thass 'bout havin' everybody open their books for an auditor.'

Earl mouthed a curse. 'Man, lemme tell you. Calhoun is gonna kill this shit dead. He's gonna rap that when they had the annual report there were only about forty students there. He's gonna say if we had been there we would know where our money went. He's gonna swear up an' down that there's nothin' wrong wit' the books (which I myself believe), an' thass gonna be all. He's gonna rap 'bout professionalism an' shit like that. Then he's gonna say that the SGA has many more things to worry about an' spen' their money on.'

'Twelve is the thing about the Medical Service,' Lawman said disconsolately.

'Thass okay,' Earl said. 'All they gotta do is move some beds an' open up those two rooms in the back. They'll do that.'

'In othuh words all they're gonna do is the shit that don' make any real difference in Sutton University whether they do it or not,' Odds managed lighting a cigarette.

'Thass the point,' Earl admitted.

'An' good ol' number thirteen says: ANSWER ME BY NOON!' Lawman said with all the theatrics he could manage.

'Thass next,' Odds breathed.

'I wishta hell I could git in the faculty meetin',' Earl said.

'I wishta hell I wuz runnin' that bastard!' Lawman said.

'I wishta hell it wuz over!' Odds contributed.

'I wishta hell I wuz dreamin',' Earl said. 'All that fuckin' work down the drain.' He laughed. 'There mus' not be no God.'

14

Ten O'Clock Meeting

It was apparent to Ogden Calhoun that every member of the Sutton faculty and administrative staff had come to the scheduled meeting early. The small auditorium where lectures and forums were held in the rear of the Paul Lawrence Dunbar Library was filled at ten minutes before ten when he entered carrying the black attaché case that held all of his papers.

There had been whispered speculation all morning as to exactly what the meeting would consider. Many of the older faculty members and administrators looked on it as perhaps the close of an era; the end of the iron hand of Ogden Calhoun. Their thoughts were centered about the fact that in their memories student protest had never detoured the regular academic duties of the institution. Therefore it was quite obvious to them that Calhoun was weakening.

Calhoun himself looked upon the meeting in quite another light. In many institutions where he had visited for various conferences and meetings he had been told by the presidents that student dissent had not only polarized the administration and students, but the administrators and faculty as well. The net result in these instances had been mergers between all three groups. The faculties on many campuses did not want to be identified with the students, but neither did they want to be considered a part of the administration. The real truth was that most college professors wanted the right to choose whatever side they wanted and make no statement at all on behalf of 'the faculty.'

Calhoun did not need another wedge driven between the administrative position and anyone else. The purpose of this meeting was to enable him to identify any members of the faculty who might be easily drawn to the students' side of the fence and make damaging remarks about whatever stand he took. He had seen the first glimmer of this sort of conflict during the outburst by Arnold McNeil at his home on the night before. In Calhoun's eyes McNeil was not a man from whom he needed any particular trouble. Not only was the man a leading American historian, but he had considerable influence among the younger members of the Sutton faculty, both Black and white.

Calhoun waved and nodded as he passed down the right-hand aisle to the small platform at the head of the meeting room. Miss Felch, looking a bit more herself, smiled as he stepped up and informed him that she had coffee coming.

Fenton Mercer walked up to the platform. His pudgy face was a mask of worry that even his thirty-two teeth could not destroy. He was perspiring freely and batting his eyes furiously as sweat seeped into the corners of his eyes beneath the thick-framed glasses. Calhoun was sitting on a cushioned seat trying to light his pipe.

'How are you?' Calhoun greeted the vice-president cheerfully.

'I'm, uh, fine,' Mercer smiled. 'Is, uh, everything in order?'

'Everything's always in order 'roun' here, isn't it, Miss Felch?'

'Yes, sir,' Miss Felch said as though she had not even heard the question.

'Is everything in order with you?' Calhoun asked, laughing perhaps a bit too loudly.

'I've, uh, just been receiving quite a few calls is all,' Mercer said. 'Y'know, mos'ly from parents here in Sutton whose sons an' daughters came to school t'day an' found out there were no classes.'

'Well, classes will resume right after our meeting,' Calhoun assured his right-hand executive. 'I would've waited until tonight to call the meeting but everyone was so insistent that their voice be heard last night ... well, I mean it wouldn't have been fair for me to come out with an administrative decision if all of the administrators weren't up-to-date on the issues.'

'There will be classes this afternoon?' Mercer asked.

'Certainly. The "*re-quests*" asked for a reply by noon. I'm sure this meeting will be over by then and I can respond to the paper ... Miss Felch, did you get copies of this form passed out?'

'They were run off first thing this morning,' Miss Felch said. 'Mr McNeil was passing them out ... oh, here's your coffee.' A student set two cups of coffee down on the desk in front of Miss Felch. Calhoun scanned the room. He saw McNeil in the rear of the auditorium smiling at Miss Anderson from the Women's Phys. Ed. department and handing her a copy of the student requests.

'Did you put those security guards in front of the door?' Mercer asked Calhoun.

'Yes. I put them there,' Calhoun said, lowering his voice as Mercer had. 'Why?'

'You know that that was a part of the student ...'

'I know,' Calhoun said with a smirk. 'But there are things that are going to be discussed in here pertaining to that question. It hasn't been decided yet what will be done about the security force. This is not an *open* faculty-administration meeting. Some of them are and this one isn't.'

'There have been students out there trying to get in,' Mercer said worriedly.

'That's why the damn guard is out there! I knew there would be some there trying to get in.'

Calhoun straightened his tie and cleared his throat. He pulled a corner of the gray kerchief in his breast pocket up a bit higher. The pipe had gone out again so he pulled out a silver lighter to set fire to the cherry tobacco. The teachers and administrators were finding their way to their seats.

'Before I begin to deal with the reason this meeting has been called,' Calhoun began, 'I'd like to apologize to the members of the faculty who were asking questions about why we were having the meeting during their class time and not tonight. The reason has been passed out to you and I speak directly now to the thirteenth point on this paper. It is very clear that some of our more impatient students sought an answer to these questions immediately and therefore a general meeting was in order. I was tempted last night when Mr Earl Thomas brought these demands to my home – and make no mistake about the fact that they are *demands* – to give an immediate answer to all of them by folding them up and tossing them in the garbage can. I am not a man who likes to be threatened. I'm sure we all feel that way. And there's a certain air of contempt involved when a student comes to you and *demands this* or *demands that* ... I put down my first impulse. I tried to talk to Mr Thomas about these issues on a man-to-man basis, but he seemed to be in quite a hurry at the time. The only thing I could do at that time was to try and call in a few of you and speak quite frankly about the issues that are raised here. During our midnight meeting last night – which might be why so many of us look like we can't open our eyes this morning – we decided that it would be best to call a meeting among all of us and discuss these things and come up with an answer on each and every one of them for the students.' Calhoun paused to sip some of the steaming coffee.

'What I would briefly like to do is go over these questions one by one and give you the administrative point of view in some sort of detail so that all of *our* cards will be on the table. If there are any questions that come up, please hold them until later after everything has been done ... just write them down and we'll have plenty of time for questions.'

Calhoun paused to finish his coffee. 'Now, under number one, if everyone will read along, they have: "the Pride of Virginia Food Services be dismissed." This is by no means the first complaint that we have had against the Food Services and each and every time we have heard a complaint we have called in Mr Morgan from the service to have certain things clarified. The last time this happened, if you will recall, was during Homecoming last year when students started throwing their trays in the cafeteria. I, uh, sent out a piece of literature on that to all the parents. It said, in effect, that for the money the students are paying here they are receiving the best, most professional food service possible. I have no further information regarding just why this issue has been raised again. When I speak with Mr Thomas at noon I will ask him if the established Student Government Food Committee would not like to have another meeting with Mr Morgan about the food.

'Numbers two, three, and four should all be handled in the same light as far as I'm concerned. There are several things that have directly to do with students, such as the food. The hiring and firing of members of the faculty and administrators is strictly *not* a student matter. If enough complaints are launched against a particular faculty member as was the case two years ago when we had to let Mr Carruthers go, then naturally the institution has to do something. But until we are given further information . . .' Calhoun paused. 'I hope you understand that the main point of irritation that I feel about *all* of these demands is that there is obviously a breakdown in communication somewhere. The students are not giving us any of the real information that we need to deal with these things. Uh, yes, so in reference to two, three, and four nothing will be done until students have given us more to work with than this statement here.'

Gaines Harper was sitting in the last row. When Calhoun stated flatly that he would not be dismissed, the Financial Aid Officer wiped his sweating face with a damp handkerchief and managed to light a cigarette.

Harper was his usual disheveled self. The dark blue suit was hanging at an angle from his neck and looked as though it had been slept in. He smelled like a brewery and was sitting in the last row in the hope that the heavy beer odor would not be noticed by any of the others present.

Professor Beaker and Professor Royce said nothing. They

had been friends of Calhoun's throughout his tenure as university president. Royce started taking notes when Calhoun had concluded points two, three, and four. He had something important that he wanted to say.

'Now, point five is another thing that has just been thrown in front of me.' Calhoun accentuated the word 'thrown' by tossing his list of demands onto the desk in front of himself. 'I wasn't really aware of all the ins and outs of the security routine if you understand me. When I received this note I made sure to set up a talk with Captain Jones this morning and we discussed things. I think that both of us had pretty much the same thing in mind. All of our guards are Black men and the students are all involved in this Blackness program. We felt that considering this it would be clear that a guard making his rounds is looking for thieves and people who are doing things to endanger university property or university people. However, it was agreed that the guards will leave their weapons inside the guardhouse from now on. It seems like splitting hairs to me,' the president added a bit sarcastically.

'Have you got everything, Miss Felch?' Calhoun asked. 'Good ... for points six, seven, and eight it should be clear that these particular problems would take a lot of legislating and reapportioning of funds. I spoke with Mr Calder, the Comptroller, this morning and we agreed that at this time it is very hard to imagine the Student Government taking on these new responsibilities which call for the proper handling of thousands of dollars when the SGA meetings are scarcely attended and the entire burden is being carried by a very few.

'Number nine is a reasonable idea,' Calhoun said as though reading it for the first time and talking to himself. He was peering a bit quizzically over the top of his glasses at his audience. The atmosphere of the room was hushed and was becoming more so with the reading and response to each point. 'Number nine is the suggestion for a Faculty Review Committee and Faculty Interview Committee. The one thing that is quite obviously in need of restating is the part that excludes Professor Beaker and Professor Royce from this committee. I would suggest that this committee consist of the heads of departments, a student representative from each class, and an administrator who could be named at a later date. I would further suggest that the committee meetings start in December so that we can have some idea of its finding by the end of the first semester.'

Calhoun stopped his monologue at that time to try and light his pipe. Miss Felch used the time to erase notes and catch up with the points that had been handled. Those attending the meeting used the time to whisper back and forth to one another. Gaines Harper got up and left, heading for the Mine, a bar that he frequently visited. He had heard enough. He was going to have a drink and go home. He felt slimy; in spite of the brisk October day his clothes were soaked with nervous perspiration.

'All of us know about the things that were covered in reference to a Black Studies Institute. True, schools are adopting a program of this nature all over the country, but we at Sutton will not be ready until we can have all of the classes accredited. I will suggest a series of lectures to start later on in this semester by visiting lecturers in this field. This can be done on a twice-a-week basis and enter our files as a course. However, it will not in any way fulfill the requirements for graduation under any heading. There will be a report in November about the progress that has been made in establishing a Black Studies Institute here next year. I mean, uh, next September.' Calhoun turned several sheets that he had placed in front of himself. He placed his pipe down in an ashtray.

'Point eleven goes back to points two, three, and four as far as I'm concerned,' he said as though he were bored. 'I would *never*, and I do mean *never*, ask any of these people to do the things requested on this page. I'm quite sure that performing their duties is job enough and that the state auditors who come in here check on things quite sufficiently.

'As far as point twelve is concerned, both Dr Maxwell and

Dr Caldwell agree that if we clear out the two back rooms and realign our stock with a couple of larger cabinets we will be equipped to treat members of the community. I would like to remind everyone that our medical staff has never refused to serve anyone in this area and that most of the community people with the exception of those people who work here at Sutton, all go to the Community General Hospital.

'Are there any questions?' Calhoun asked. He pulled a tan leather pouch from his inside pocket and started to refill his pipe.

'I'd like to know why there was a deadline on these papers,' Professor Ingram of Psychology asked. He was a small, balding man in a gray suit.

'From my talk with Mr Thomas last night I must admit that I don't have the vaguest idea what will be done when I respond . . .'

Calhoun was interrupted by Gaines Harper who reentered the small auditorium practically on the run and came down the middle aisle to the platform waving his hand.

'S'cuse me,' Calhoun said quickly and got up.

'Uh, there's a reporter outside from the *Norfolk News*,' Harper whispered breathlessly. 'He was wondering what time the statement was going to be made to the press. I didn't know anything about it but he said there's reporters here from everywhere.'

Calhoun looked out through the partially open entrance to the meeting hall, but he could see nothing except the back of the uniformed security guard on duty. The faculty and others in the room were buzzing noisily.

'Are there any more questions?' Calhoun asked in a voice to discourage questions. 'If not,' he hurried on, 'I will be interested in meeting all department heads in my office in about fifteen minutes. I have something to check on.'

No one said anything, but no one made any real effort to leave.

'I want you to be in my office too, Miss Felch,' Calhoun said.

There was still no movement from the crowd in the pews. Calhoun picked up his coat and marched through them with a breathless Gaines Harper hurrying behind him.

15

Captain Cool

The young man coming down the stairs from the main lobby of the Student Union Building was in a hurry. He was dressed in black trousers, gold corduroy dashiki, and gold-framed sunglasses. His hair was bushy and natural with a part on the left side. He was almost six feet tall and weighed about one hundred seventy pounds. He had a smooth, caramel complexion and unlike his counterparts from MJUMBE wore no beard or mustache. He was called Captain Cool, but his name was Abul Menka.

When Abul Menka had first joined the Sutton University community he had gone through a great many changes. The majority of the students at Sutton were from the South and had very little to do with New Yorkers; especially New Yorkers who were so firmly aloof from the things that went on at Sutton. The majority of Abul's time had been spent drinking Mother Vineyard's Scuppernong and smoking reefers that he brought back from his frequent trips to New York.

As a freshman Abul had had absolutely no ties to anything, political or otherwise. He had a girl at Howard in Washington and a girl at Morgan State in Baltimore. On weekends he was to be found on either one of those campuses or back in New York. But as a sophomore he decided to pledge for the Omega Psi Phi fraternity. He made the move for several reasons. The first was that his uncle, who was financing his college career, was a 'Q.' The second was that on Sutton's campus and every campus Abul visited the women were 'Q crazy.'

The pledge period lasted a little over two months. During that time Abul was not allowed to use his car for anything other than errands run for his fraternity brothers. This eliminated his runs to Morgan and Howard. It also brought him into some standing within the Sutton community. He had never warmed up to anyone except for a few girls he had tried to take to bed. But after he became a member of the fraternity his coolness was attributed to being a 'cool Q' rather than a cold individual.

Six others were on the line with him when he 'went over' and became a member of the fraternity. Five of them were members of the present campus organization called MJUMBE. The other had graduated.

The reason for Abul's hurry at the moment was related to his involvement with MJUMBE. He had just finished running off fifteen hundred copies of a proclamation from MJUMBE. He was rushing to the fraternity meeting room where he had an eleven o'clock appointment with the group.

There was no doubt about the things that were happening to him because of MJUMBE's coup. People had spoken to him in the past twelve hours or so who hadn't seemed to even look in his direction before. He was thinking materialistically that the political thing he was doing would be another stepping stone for his rap.

There was nothing wrong with Abul's ability to hold a conversation with women. His major concern at the moment was the progress that had been made by the other members of the five-man committee. As he walked around the oval he saw several things that made him believe that the day before had not been wasted. One was a car that was parked in front of the Paul Lawrence Dunbar Library with the words *NORFOLK NEWS* stenciled across the left-hand door. A weasely looking whitey sat in the front seat eating a ham sandwich. There was also the sight of Ogden Calhoun and Gaines Harper turning into Sutton Hall, the administration building, damn near on the run. There was also the campus-wide news that no classes had been scheduled for the morning hours.

'Glad ta see da massuh up an' movin' 'bout so early dis mawnin',' Abul mimicked, chuckling.

A bit of nervous tension was growing at the base of his

spine. He supposed that everyone involved felt the same way now. For Abul the feeling was very new. He was a master at picking spots where he felt most comfortable and uninvolved, but the political situation intrigued him. He was a student of Black history and was fascinated by the way in which power continually shifted from one pole to another and from one party to another, Democratic or Republican, and yet people who were the victims of one administration managed to gain absolutely nothing from the installation of a new regime. The same sort of political showdown which could be viewed nationally at election time was emerging at Sutton. Nothing had ever been gained from the use of student power because the wishes of the students were rarely followed. The requests were an indication that the student form of protest was about to take another road just as the protests of minority and disadvantaged groups were taking a different form everywhere. On some campuses, such as Berkeley, Abul could understand a comparison with New York City where there always seemed to be a strike or some kind of disorder. Students on these campuses had damn near over-demonstrated and the real reason for attending a college in the first place was lost. That was not the feeling on Sutton's campus. Everyone felt the mounting tension. Abul and the members of MJUMBE felt it more so, Abul decided, because they knew what the next step would be if Calhoun and his bunch of black and white flunkies didn't have their stuff together by noon. Most of the students were uneasy because they didn't know what to expect either from MJUMBE or Calhoun, but many had the feeling that Baker and his group were headed for the highway.

'We'll see who's headed where,' Abul muttered.

Under his arm the tall MJUMBE chieftain was carrying mimeographed sheets. He only hoped that the ink had dried sufficiently so as not to blur or stain the printed words. Abul was particularly proud of this paper because he had written it himself before Baker showed up. All Ralph had done was take a look at it and okay it.

As he neared the fraternity house he thought about Earl Thomas and MJUMBE's move to take over the functions of the SGA. He had been waiting to see what Earl Thomas was going to do the night before in the meeting room. Earl had done and said nothing. Maybe they had had Earl in more of a bind than was apparent. Abul knew that anything Earl might have said to discredit him, Abul, could have been denied, but the point was that he hadn't had to deny anything.

His thoughts returned to the paper he had under his arm:

TO ALL FACULTY MEMBERS AND ADMINISTRATORS

The thirteen demands that were submitted to President Calhoun by the Sutton student body were pleas for necessities long overdue. Sutton University, once a leading Black institution, has fallen far behind in every respect. The reason has been the administration's unbending, inflexible position in terms of the needs of the students who must, for nine months out of each year, call Sutton University their *home*. It has been the understanding of the students that college was a place where one learned to deal with life as a man or a woman must upon leaving the institution for the last time. Sutton students are now prepared when they leave to accomplish the same things their parents were able to do – or less. The reason is the fast pace that one is forced to live with inside this rapidly changing society.

For years Sutton students have been good niggers, waiting and hoping that the bare essentials they have requested would be granted them by the administrative powers that be. They have, for the betterment of the community, chosen all except disruptive patterns of revealing their needs by working through the system. All of this has been to no avail. Sutton University continues to sink 'grain by grain.'

The demands that have been submitted may appear at first glance to be dramatic and hasty, thoughtless proposals. On second glance and a look at the Sutton history of students' requests, however, one will realize that these are the same types of things that students have been after for twelve years here.

Students on Sutton's campus have been asking for three years that the Pride of Virginia Food Services, Inc. use a meal ticket system that will give students an option over whether or not they pay for the slop that is served each and every day. The Food Service has refused because they know that a majority of students would not touch that poison a majority of the time.

Gaines Harper is a man whose professional qualifications are questionable. We feel him to be absolutely incapable of sharing the personal confidences finance-wise of the Black students on these premises.

Professors Beaker and Royce are both past retirement age. They are fine individuals for whom students have high respect. The problem is that their methods of conveying the subject matter are archaic and in this modern world students cannot plunge into society ill-equipped to face the challenge of competition that awaits them.

The Security Service guards have been known to drink while on duty and there is a student committee investigating the relevance of their role at Sutton. In the interim period we cannot allow a man without all of his wits about him to walk among us with a gun on his hip.

The Student Union Building, book store, and Music and Art Fund all need to be under the auspices of the SGA. The monies from these departments go now into the pockets of Pride of Virginia (for the canteen), Educational Assistance (books), and the Music and Art Fund, which seems to be tossing its student monies down into a bottomless pit for the amount of pleasure students receive from the artists they hire. The need within the student body for more jobs which could be supplied in the canteen and book store, and for better entertainment due to our geographic location, is obvious. The need is also immediate.

The Faculty Review Committee and Faculty Interview Committee were originally proposed by Mr McNeil of the history department. They were not intended to frighten members of the faculty. The saying goes, 'The guilty fleeth when no man pursueth,' and it is true here. The question was raised often about student academic apathy. The answer can only be discovered in more and better communication between students and faculty members. Too often faculty members get the guided tour of Sutton, seeing only what the administration wants them to see, and then sign a contract that becomes an unpleasant situation for both faculty member and student. The Faculty Interview Committee would attempt to avoid this and the Review Committee would keep those who become sluggish and lackadaisical about their duties on their toes. The ideal situation in both cases would liven Sutton professionally and academically.

A Black Studies Institute is essential. This is a time in this country where a Black man or woman cannot afford to bypass the quantities of information that are suddenly available about themselves. Too long now Black people have been forced to carve an image out of rock in order to survive and lead a successful life. Too often also Black people have been forced to copy the white man's life style and this both frustrates and kills the Blackness and beauty within him. Black Studies would teach us about ourselves and give us a direction that we have never had before.

Seniors have been graduating for years from Sutton having spent over ten thousand dollars during their college careers with very little idea of what happened to the money. The administration has been playing too many word games when asked serious questions about the whereabouts of X amount of dollars. The word games consist of things like 'general fund' and 'student activity fund' and 'community fund.' People have not asked for a cent of their money back. They have asked to see where in hell it went. This should entail a dollar-by-dollar description if necessary because it is *their* money. Once again we say: 'The guilty fleeth when no man pursueth.' There are state *legislators* and *Congressmen* who are required to give detailed accounts of their monies. This is what we want. Proof that our money is being put toward the best possible end.

The community surrounding Sutton's campus is Black. The people there are poor people who need medical services that at times they cannot afford. We ask that our services be available to them and that this point be publicized so that the Black people will never be in doubt as to whether or not medicine and aid are available to them.

Abul had to curb a smile of pleasure when he thought about the diplomatic job he had done in the statement. There was very little fault to be found. Even the last lines had been written in good taste:

We are not here to protest or demonstrate or discontinue the academic routine of the university, but there comes a time when men must be men and women must be women. We feel that if we cannot receive the respect that we believe men and women deserve, then we must take this respect 'by any means necessary.'

*　　*　　*

Abul took the fraternity steps two at a time. MJUMBE had a scheduled meeting at eleven. He did not intend to be late.

16

Executive Conference

Ogden Calhoun was raging into the receiver. 'Well, why in hell didn't you call me, Miller, if you were so goddamn hard up for something t'print in that rag sheet? Why didn't you call me an' ask for a story? . . . huh? I don't care if you weren't there last night. The man didn't leave 'til this morning an' you were there then!'

The harried president of Sutton had never gotten as far as taking off his coat before he was on the phone speaking to the editor of the Norfolk newspaper. Gaines Harper sat in the chair across from Calhoun with sweat pouring off his face and his breath shouting up from his lungs in fiery gasps. The fat Financial Aid Officer was in no shape to chase Calhoun around.

'Well, when he calls in you be sure that he gets up here to get my side of the story before you print. You hear me? . . . all right! Yeah. Well . . . I wasn't having any trouble until somebody saw your man. I still don't have much. I just don't want or need any of my people panicking an' shooting off their mouths. I'd have trustees down here going through their bullshit . . . well, I'll talk to you!' Calhoun slammed the phone down.

'He said he was going to call me, but the night editor sent a man down here last night because everybody else was sending somebody down here. You know them newspaper guys. Nobody wants to do any real work, but nobody wants to get scooped either.'

'You mean there's more down here?' Harper asked in a gasp.

'He said AP an' UPI and some more . . .' Calhoun pressed his intercom button down. 'Miss Felch?' There was no answer.

'She probably didn't get over here yet,' Harper choked.

'Right.' Calhoun dialed a three-digit number. 'Miss Charles?' he said in a syrupy voice. 'Miss Felch hasn't come in yet and I am in desperate need of a cup of coffee and the morning paper. Do you ... Thank you.'

Calhoun took off his coat and gloves. He hung the coat in the corner closet and sat down again in the leather high-back chair leaning against a large window overlooking the oval.

'I don't have any idea what Thomas is doing,' he admitted. 'I know he'll be in trouble once I find out.'

'This doesn't change anything, does it?' Harper asked.

'Not for me,' Calhoun grunted. 'Not until I get some more information about exactly what's going on.'

Miss Charles, a young honey-blonde from Fenton Mercer's office, came in with a copy of the morning paper. She gave both Calhoun and Harper a dazzling smile.

'The coffee'll be ready in a moment,' she said in a soft Southern drawl.

'Good!'

'Here's the paper. How're you Mr Harpuh? I so seldom get to see you.'

'I'm fine,' Harper lied.

'Back in a minute,' she said, starting to leave.

Fenton Mercer almost ran her down coming in as she was exiting.

'Excuse me, Miss Charles,' Mercer said. 'I was just looking for you.'

'I was gettin' coffee for Mr Calhoun.'

'Good. Would you get me a cup too? Good and strong,' he grinned his business grin.

Miss Charles managed to get out at last.

'I see ...'

'We saw,' Calhoun muttered drily. 'I s'pose each an' every one here has seen by now.'

'Well, everybody saw them parked there when they came out of the meeting,' Mercer supplied.

'Where's Miss Felch?'

'She's comin',' Mercer said. 'There's some more information coming from the meeting you left. I think it would be best if I let the department heads tell you.'

'All right. Where are they?'

'Coming.' Mercer began thumbing his way through the morning paper.

'We'll need some more chairs,' Calhoun observed. 'Gaines . . .'

'I'll get them.'

'They're in the closet out front.'

The various department heads came in at that moment. Beaker agreed to help Harper get the chairs while the others stood around. Calhoun was nervous about what he might hear from the faculty, but he said nothing.

Before everyone was seated Miss Felch came in with her pad and pen. Miss Charles also returned with two cups of black, steaming coffee.

When everyone was seated Calhoun cleared his throat to begin. He stopped himself:

'Where's McNeil?' he asked.

'He's not coming,' Marcus from Political Science said quietly.

'Not coming! I asked all department heads to be here!'

'We took a sort of quorum in the auditorium,' Nash from the Music Department said finally. 'I suggested that since we all knew the issues that we make things simpler by not really having a meeting here. I suggested that we simply give you our approval.'

'That was when McNeil said he was leaving,' Marcus said, barely above a whisper.

'I'll be damn!' Calhoun muttered. The meeting was over.

17

High Noon

Isaac Spurryman of the *Norfolk News* was the first reporter in the crowd to see Ogden Calhoun appear at the front door of Sutton Hall. He broke away from the small huddle of reporters who were comparing notes near the steps and tried to enter the building. He was cut off by the president's secretary, Irene Felch, who opened the door and squeezed her narrow frame through.

With the secretary's appearance the group of photographers and reporters scrambled closer and the buzzing from the group of gathering students subsided.

'The president will be out momentarily,' Miss Felch said as loudly as she could. 'We're waiting for a microphone to be brought over from the Music Department.'

'May be waitin' all day,' a student snorted.

'Will the president be holding a question-and-answer session?' reporter Spurryman asked.

'I have no idea,' Miss Felch said. 'I don't really know what he'll be saying ... I would imagine that if he held one it wouldn't be here.' She tossed an expression of disdain toward the milling students.

Spurryman nodded and walked away with his head buried in his note pad. There were students at the base of the walk carrying three wooden platforms that they sat on top of each other. A small, sturdy-looking podium sat in the middle of the make-shift platform. The students nodded at each other and then moved off.

'Ike?' Spurryman heard his name called and looked up to see Arnold McNeil wading through the crowd toward him.

'How are you, Neil?' Spurryman asked as they shook hands. 'You look like you've had it.'

'Hot,' McNeil said, consulting his watch and attempting a smile. 'How have you been?'

'Fine. Everybody's fine,' the reporter said. 'How's Millie?'

'Good. She's expecting!'

'I'll be goddamned!' Spurryman said. He looked around for a second before continuing. 'You old sonuvabitch! I'll tell ya. Drinks on me after I knock this off.' He nodded toward the still-closed door.

'Nothin' said so far?'

'Naw. Calhoun's secretary came out an' said he'll make a statement when a mike gets here.'

'What're *you* doin' out here?' McNeil asked. 'You're a front-page man most of the time.'

'Well, I'll tell ya. We had a policy of either ignorin' these student things or sendin' cubs out to cover them. I guess we went through that for nearly three years. We got burnt a couple of times though. We got burnt bad at Virginia Union. They had tipped us off about a thing an' we didn't check it. When the damn place had to close we weren't even informed enough to do anything for ten hours.'

'So now you check everything?' McNeil asked smiling tightly.

'Well, the desk got a call las' night. Emple called UPI and AP an' they said they were sending people ... what's it all about?'

'The students supplied a list of demands an' turned them over to Calhoun ...'

'What were the demands?' Spurryman asked poising his pen.

'Haven't any students been over to talk to you all?'

'Not a soul. Well, maybe I jus' didn't see them. They here?'

'I don't see ... Wait! You see the tall one next to the tree over there?' McNeil pointed through a cluster of students to a six-footer with a thick head of hair who was talking confidentially to two companions.

'Uh-huh.'

'His name is Earl Thomas,' McNeil confided. 'He's the head of the SGA. You could ask him. He's the one who gave the demands to Calhoun.'

'O.K.' the reporter agreed. 'Where will you be? I'm serious about that drink.'

'Good, I'll need it. I'll be right here afterward.'

Spurryman waved and drifted away through the crowd. He found himself approaching Earl at the same time as a number of others. Two of them were reporters. The others were students.

'Mr Thomas,' he began, 'I'm Ike Spurryman of the *Norfolk News*. I was wondering if I could ask a few questions.'

Earl looked up curiously. 'I don' really have anything t'say right now.'

'I'd just like to ask you about what your demands were an' what you are expecting from President Calhoun.'

'There are thirteen deman's an' we are expecting Mr Calhoun to comply.'

'What are the thirteen demands?' a reporter asked.

'I don't have a copy with me,' Earl said. 'I hadn't planned to deal with the press. I'm sure Mr Calhoun will give everyone a copy.'

'Do you have any idea who called the press if it wasn't a representative from your office?' Spurryman asked still writing.

'The student body was informed of the deman's yesterday afternoon so it could've been any student or faculty member.' Earl knew who had notified the press.

'What time yesterday?'

'About four thirty.'

'And when were the demands served on the president?'

'About ten last night.'

'Did the demands call for a statement today?'

'It called for a statement today at noon.'

'Any particular reason?' someone quizzed.

'I suppose noon is the best time because mosta the studen's are not in class as you can see. We knew everyone would be anxious to hear for themselves.'

'Testing. Testing. One-two-three-four-five. Testing,' a voice cut through. A white youngster with long, dirty hair was speaking into a round, mesh microphone that had been set up next to the podium.

The microphone testing attracted the attention of the crowd. It also brought Ogden Calhoun into view. The president strode purposefully through the reporters and students who stood between the administration door and the makeshift platform. His glasses were in place and he held several sheaves of notes in his hands. Several reporters attempted to stop him for comment, but he only shook his head 'no' and kept right on going. Flash-bulbs were fired at him. Miss Felch and Fenton Mercer walked right alongside him.

The crowd continued its murmuring even after the president stepped up onto the stand. The reporters who had been clustered around Earl edged closer to the hastily prepared stage. Students who had been laughing and talking among themselves from the sidewalk across the street ignored the possibility that they might be hit by cars driving around the oval. They left the opposite sidewalk that circled the huge Sutton flower bed and walked into the road blocking off traffic.

Calhoun had imagined that there would be quite a few students present, but the gathering before him seemed to simply go on and on. He wondered for a second if he shouldn't have called the meeting in the large auditorium. Clearly every member of the student body and faculty was there.

'Members of the community,' Calhoun began, 'I was asked by what I shall refer to as a list of "intimidating *requests*" to respond to these *requests* by noon today and here I am. I want to speak directly to the issues, but before I do I want to say a few words to the students in the community and particularly to those students who find themselves in leadership positions.

There are certain channels of communication established on Sutton's campus through which problems that bother students can be handily dealt with. I refer now to the committees on which both students and faculty are members. I refer now to the Board of Trustees and members of the administrative staff. These channels are present because everyone realizes that within all institutions there are needs that must be met. They are there because we all realize that neither students nor faculty members nor administrators have all the answers. May I also add here that none of these groups has all of the problems. A problem of one member of the community is a problem of all. If one is to deal with a problem one must be made aware of its existence. There are certain ways to make others aware of an existing problem. This particular way *can* be used but at times it serves to cause another problem if not considered carefully. I refer now to the fact that these particular *demands* (not requests) were given me last evening at ten o'clock. The last point on the page was that I respond by noon.

'This can be construed as little other than a threat. My first reaction was to throw the entire list into the garbage can. Let it suffice to say that there are proper channels that are available to us all. Let us use them . . .' Calhoun paused and looked around. There could be little doubt that the atmosphere had changed during the president's opening remarks. An unmistakable tension was becoming evident.

For the first time Earl noticed the gold-trimmed black dashikis circulating through the crowd. Fred Jones walked directly in front of him and handed a card to reporter Isaac Spurryman. Other members of the press were being handed these cards by Speedy Cotton and Ben King.

'Somethin's up,' Odds whispered.

'Git a look at one a' those cards,' Earl said.

'Better let me,' Lawman said. He moved over until he was directly behind the Norfolk reporter.

Calhoun's voice could be heard as he continued discussing the students' demands.

'Point number one relates to having the Pride of Virginia Food Services dismissed. We are directing Mr Morgan of the Food Services to make himself available for another meeting with the established Student Government Association Food Services Committee.

'Number two is a demand that Gaines Harper, present Financial Aid Officer, be dismissed. The administration is responsible for the hiring and firing of its staff. That includes administrative personnel and faculty members. When evidence is presented that indicates a necessary change, we make it. No such evidence has been placed at our disposal. Mr Harper will not be dismissed.

'Numbers three and four require that the heads of our Chemistry and Language Departments be dismissed. I, uh, will remind everyone present of an organization called the Southeast Accreditation Association which is in charge of accrediting all colleges so that degrees received from these institutions will be valid. This in itself is enough to make it impossible for us to dismiss Dr Beaker and Dr Royce. In addition, the issue about a lack of formal complaints holds true here also.

'Number five demands that the Security Service be forced to leave all weapons – clubs, guns, and so forth – inside the guardhouse while making their rounds. We consider it regrettable that our own community members do not realize the importance of our guards, who carry arms to protect our people and property, but we have talked to Captain Jones and he agrees to have his men leave their arms in the guardhouse.'

'Did'joo git a look at the card?' Earl asked Lawman.

'Yeah. I tol' this cat I was a member of *The Statesman*'s staff who had obviously been overlooked. The card sez that there's gonna be a student meeting in the large auditorium right after this one.'

'Izzat all it sez?'

'What else?'

'Does it say why or anything?'

'No. It doesn't.' Lawman turned away toward the droning Calhoun who continued to read from his notes. He was turning down the suggestions that the various Sutton departments – Student Union Building, book store, and Art Fund – be placed under student control.

'Whatta y' think?' Lawman mumbled.

'Can't say,' Earl admitted, looking around. 'I haven't seen Baker or Abul.'

'Thass a dangerous bastard,' Odds said. 'Abul Menka, I mean ... Baker too, but ...'

'I feel the same way,' Lawman said, reaching across Earl to shake Odds's hand in agreement.

'Number nine,' Calhoun was saying, 'indicates that we should establish a Faculty Review Committee and a Faculty Interview Committee. I have suggested that these committees be established and that they consist of the heads of the departments, or a faculty member from each department, a student representative from each class, and an administrator. The specific people can be named when we hold our next faculty meeting.'

There was a murmur rippling through the crowd at this announcement. Even Earl and Odds had to exchange pleasantly surprised glances that turned into weak smiles.

'That wudn't the whole deal,' Lawman reminded them.

'It's more'n I expected,' Odds said.

Calhoun completed his speech by mentioning the series of lectures he was establishing in order to supplement the curriculum until a meaningful Black Studies program could be instituted. He raised his voice in dismay when commenting on the request that certain administrators' books be audited by students, and he concluded the session by reporting that he had conferred with the Sutton medical staff and that the suggested changes would be instituted.

'As for this morning's missed classes,' Calhoun said, handing Miss Felch his notes, 'there was nothing that could be done to avoid it. This afternoon's classes will be held . . . I would stop at this time for questions and answers, but since it is almost time for classes to resume I will schedule a university assembly for later in the week when I can handle these questions and answers from the community. I will meet the press in my office directly after this for their questions. They will be given duplicate copies of the demands.'

There were a few raised hands, but Calhoun turned quickly from his audience and followed closely by Miss Felch and Fenton Mercer he strode back down the walkway and into Sutton Hall.

The whitey with the long, dirty hair started to take the microphone down. As he did the students who had assembled the makeshift platform gathered to take it down.

It was then that Ben King stepped onto the impromptu stage and facing the far corner of the oval raised both fists. The next instant brought the echoing ring of the auditorium bell. This was the traditional signal for a university assembly. Before Earl and his two comrades were able to comment on Calhoun's hasty departure, King, Cotton, and Jonesy were double-timing across the path that split the oval.

'MJUMBE is at least a *little* organized,' Odds said drily.

'They run good,' Lawman said laughing.

The auditorium bell continued to hammer away. The student body was drifting toward the meeting. Faculty members could be seen gathering in small apprehensive clusters. Reporters were comparing notes and asking one another which way they should go. Earl Thomas was asking himself that same question.

18

MJUMBE Mandate

It was a typical early autumn day for southern Virginia. The temperature was in the mid-fifties. A breeze kicked the colored leaves closer to the curb and across the oval. The residents were dressed in sweaters and light jackets. The sun watched from a sky decorated with whipped-cream clouds that floated south with the wind.

The weather was not the reason Earl Thomas was fastening the top button on his light safari jacket. He was chilled with the prospect of being put on the spot at the meeting ahead of him. Each thump of the hollow bell in the auditorium chapel seemed to bang equally hard at the pit of his stomach.

He paused at the auditorium entrance and lit a cigarette. Ben King handed him a copy of a statement from MJUMBE and a copy of *The Sutton Statesman* which this afternoon was a one-page special that carried a picture of the five MJUMBE chieftains as they had appeared the day before. There was a larger picture of Earl himself. The two articles on the page were both editorials of a sort. One had been written by Ralph Baker. The other was signed by Victor Johnson.

The three entrances to the auditorium were being manned by King, Jonesy, and Cotton. As students or faculty entered they were handed the MJUMBE statement and *The Statesman* special edition.

'Let's skip to the john,' Earl said, nudging Odds.

The three men entered the lobby and cut right, crossing in front of congregating students until they reached the southern corner where they turned downstairs to the lounge area and rest rooms.

'Bone up,' Earl muttered once inside the lavatory. He banged the pages across the palm of his hand.

'Gittin' tighter,' Odds noted, making a choking gesture. 'Ya know what this indicates, don'choo? This sez right here, this picture, that you are down wit' MJUMBE.'

'Iss almos' too hip to be anywhere near Ben King,' Lawman said. 'I have dug the whole damn thing an' there's not one word about you. The whole implication stems from the picture.'

'I wasn't even thinkin' las' night when I saw Johnson. I wuz damn sure the paper wuz gonna knock me an' give me a free opportunity to say anything that I wanted.'

'You still can,' Odds snapped. 'Shit! You didn' call this meetin' or the one yesterday. This ain' rilly got nuthin' to do wit' you or your office.'

'I know . . .'

'But nuthin'. All you gotta do is say what you feel, man. You won the election. You still in a helluva good position.'

'Say what I feel where? Here? I didn' call this meetin', you say? Then what gives me a right to speak?'

'You the Man! You the Head Man! If you see the studen's headed in the wrong direction you haveta speak up!'

'What direction do you think they're goin' in?'

'No direction yet.'

'Right. But Baker's gonna play on emotions. If he directs them through this emotion they will not be ready to hear from me.'

There was a loud feedback screech from the level directly above the three men. Another man entered the washroom. Lawman signaled his companions to exit. Out in the hall at the bottom of the stairs Earl's former campaign manager grabbed the back of his safari jacket.

'Play it by ear,' he advised. 'Whatever goes down you gotta be cool. Right?'

'Right.'

On the upper level the three men took seats along the side near the middle of the student body. Ralph Baker and Abul Menka were onstage huddling. Meanwhile, two microphones were being set up and hooked into the public address system.

Victor Johnson was seated behind the two MJUMBE leaders scribbling away at a pad on his lap.

When at last the microphones were set up and the MJUMBE men were ready, Baker approached the podium with his papers. The three MJUMBE members who had been passing out the MJUMBE statement and *The Statesman* climbed the steps to the stage and took seats.

'We are trying to give everyone time to read the paper we issued and *The Statesman* before we begin ... Uh, for those of you just coming in there are copies of the MJUMBE paper on the tables to your right. Take one and a copy of *The Sutton Statesman*. The essence of these two pieces will be our text.' Baker moved back into another huddle with his associates. The audience buzzed again. Earl lit a cigarette.

'First of all I'd like to thank everyone for comin',' Baker said after a moment. 'I had thought we'd lose some people to the lunch line an' some to the dispensary who were sick to their stomachs after the things they had just heard.' There was a muffled laughter.

'We would like to come right to the point this afternoon. We did not like the answers that we heard from President Ogden Calhoun. His reply to our requests displayed a portion of the same tired, bullshit replies that Sutton students have been receiving from administrators for as long as there has been a Sutton. Some of these buildings that we're in lead us to believe that there has always been a Sutton.' More laughter.

'The question becomes, however, what we plan to do about it. Do we plan to merely laugh at our situation an' go on pretendin' that it doesn' exist? Do we plan to go back through the same clogged channels of communication an' watch our hard-earned money go down the drain? ... These are questions that I want answers for. Will we allow Ogden Calhoun and his band of legal pirates to continue to rob us? I'm asking you?'

'No!' came a voice from about the fourth row. Then a chorus of 'no's' rang out.

'Will we continue to sit around daily wondering what

happened to our money when the only thing that keeps us from findin' out is Ogden Calhoun?'

'NO!'

'Will we continue to eat the slop dished out in the cafeteria like garbage piled into a pig's trough?'

'NO!'

'Will we continue to cooperate with Sutton under the present conditions with only token response from Sutton Hall's shirt an' tie renegades?'

'NO!'

'The members of MJUMBE are proposing a students' strike against Sutton University until such time as all of these basic needs that we have requested receive a positive response.'

There was an initial smattering of applause that grew and grew until it seemed to Earl that the building's foundations had been loosened. Students were whistling, clapping, and stomping their feet.

'This student strike,' Baker continued, 'will call for the boycott of all classes, all conferences, lectures, coed-visitation rules, and all other university functions.

'The end of this strike can only be caused by an administrative 'yes' to each an' every demand that we submitted . . .' There was more applause. 'The student strike will go into effect as of now.'

One of the sisters in the first row was raising her hand. Baker nodded to her.

'How will the students be kept informed of what happens?'

'A Strike Communication Center will be established in the MJUMBE office on the third floor of the fraternity house. All information will be available there. We will also have brothers going from dorm to dorm distributing information at night.'

A male student asked a second question. 'It was my impression that student body had a SGA president who was in charge of all of these types of activities. I'd like to know why he's not on the stage an' how he feels.'

Baker flashed a quick look at Abul Menka and then scanned

the thousand people in the auditorium. 'Earl? You wanna say somethin'?'

Earl got up stiffly, feeling the weight of the two thousand eyes that were on him. Lawman flashed him a grimace. He found himself still questioning exactly what he would say when he fully faced the audience, so he trotted down the side aisle to the stage. Baker moved away from the microphone hesitantly.

'Salaam,' Earl said greeting the students. 'Brother, you are absolutely right when you refer to the SGA. I think you might be overlooking one fact however. It was pointed out yesterday, I understand, that *I* would be giving the petition to President Calhoun. *I* was the one who served the, pardon me, proposals, on the president. I was aware of the possibilities when I served the papers. Calhoun has made his move. It is now time for us to make ours ... it's not so much a question of who leads. No one can lead without a following. Do we all agree that something is necessary?'

'Yes!'

'Do we all agree that a student strike is necessary?'

'Yes!'

Earl nodded to Baker and trotted back down the stairs and walked quickly back through the audience to his seat, sweat forming at the edge of his face, itchy patches seeming to appear all over his body.

Just as Earl found his seat the audience erupted. Focusing on the stage Earl saw Vice-President Fenton Mercer waddling toward the microphone. The sweating, obviously upset vice-president said something to Baker who spoke into the mike.

'Brothers and sisters, I have been asked if our vice-president, who came over since the president couldn't make it, uh, I've been asked if Mr Mercer could say a few words ... I'm gonna leave it up to you, but I say now that the man is not here wit' anything new to say. He is here to rationalize and philosophize, an' bullshit. MJUMBE IS LEAVING!'

For one breathtaking instant the entire auditorium was

silent. The silence lasted long enough for Baker and the MJUMBE leaders to take two steps toward the stairs. Then, as though on signal, the huge meeting hall was turned into an echo chamber of screaming, applauding students and chairs being pulled back. The noise was so loud that no one could hear Fenton Mercer's plea for attention. The entire aggregation turned toward the exits, leaving the disturbed administrator on stage.

19

A Three-pronged Spear

'Iz everybody in place?' Baker asked Ben King, when the largest MJUMBE member entered the new Strike Communications Center.

'Everythin's good,' King said dramatically. 'All of our enforcers is on their posts makin' sure don' nobody go to class. I sent a few men ovuh to the women's dorm to break the coedvisitation rule . . .'

'I'm sure they were disappointed at their jobs,' Baker laughed.

'Ha! Yeh. They wuz real disappointed . . .'

'What the faculty doin'?' Speedy Cotton asked.

'Ain' nobody messin' wit' them. It seem like they went on ovuh to their posts an' waited fo' alla the knowledge seekers to show up.'

'Do they know who the enforcers are and exactly what they're there for?'

'Hell, yeah! Wuzn't no real way to keep them from knowin' that. We gittin' bettuh cooperation from the studen's than I thought though.'

'Because of the enforcers or because of the studen's?' Baker asked.

'A little bit a both,' King admitted.

'Today means nuthin',' Abul Menka said suddenly. The entire group turned to him where he sat in his favorite corner looking out over the campus. 'Today people have a small dose a strike fever. They're all anxious t'be activists an' radicals. Niggers always go in for fads like this to show everybody how goddamn militant they are. Tuhmaruh iz gonna be a better indication a whuss happ'nin'.'

'I'm onna try it one day at a time,' King laughed. 'The point iz we got the thing offa the groun'!' King reached over with a huge grin on his coal-black face and Baker and he exchanged the African handshake.

'An',' Speedy Cotton mused, 'wit' Thomas's help.'

That was a point that Abul Menka had been mulling over in his mind but had not brought up. There were some very puzzling things going on with Earl Thomas. Abul had agreed that a picture of Thomas in the issue of *The Statesman* might serve as an intimidating factor and keep the deposed SGA leader quiet. The indication in the meeting had not been one of intimidation. But neither had Earl appeared anxious to jump on the emotional MJUMBE bandwagon and share any of the credit for the campus political mobility.

Abul had been watching Earl all through the meeting. He had not liked what he had seen. The reason for his distaste was the lack of responses coming from a man who had been, all through his campaign for SGA office, decisively emotional, never giving an indication that in the thick of a political confrontation he would sit like the proverbial Iceman and do nothing. Abul hated niggers he couldn't figure out.

'Abul? . . . Abul?' Baker was calling. 'Where you at, brother?'

'Right here.'

'Yeah. In the flesh you there. Where you at in the head?'

'Right here.'

'You got them notes ready to be typed?'

'Guard notes?'

'Yeah. We cleared the office down the hall an' imported a typewriter you can use 'til we rustle up a secretary for you.'

'What happened to . . .' Abul's question was cut off.

'She said she couldn' make it,' Baker remarked.

Abul picked up his folder and left the meeting room. He was followed closely by Ben King.

The room adjacent to the regular MJUMBE headquarters was being prepared for business by Fred Jones who was standing with a broom in his hand in the middle of the floor when the other two associates entered. Jonesy waved at them and continued his clean-up job.

'What were we using this room fo' anyway?' King asked.

'Lamps,' Abul mumbled, referring to the Omega Psi Phi pledges.

'Huh? Oh ... Look, here's my list. We gotta have at least eight copies. One for each of us an' one to be posted in group commander rooms. We forgot that shit 'bout postin' anything on the bulletin boards cause some ass would take them ... or some administrator would.'

'Some ass,' Abul agreed. The MJUMBE man in the black and gold dashiki sat down at the large portable typewriter and rolled in a sheet of typing paper. King lounged in a near corner watching Jonesy sweep.

'I wanna ask you somethin',' he admitted finally to Abul. 'What'choo think come over that bastard Thomas?'

'When?'

'T'day. I wuz jus' linin' him in my sights for a good right han' when he up an' agreed wit' us.' King shook his head in wonder.

'Y'know,' Abul confided, 'that might jus' be the reason he agreed.'

King thought that over for a moment. He looked down for some sort of sign that Abul had been pulling his leg. But the man in the sunglasses continued his typing and said nothing.

The office door was locked and the shades were drawn on the first floor of Carver Hall. There were three men inside the SGA office, but none of them made any move toward answering either knocks on the door or the constantly ringing telephone.

'Y'know in all likelihood that phone has been ringin' fo' good reason,' Lawman pointed out.

'Reason bein' that someone somewhere was callin' here,' Odds quipped drily.

'I'm talkin' 'bout important calls,' Lawman said.

'That may be why I ain' answerin',' Earl sighed, running long fingers through his bushy head.

'Ha long we gonna stay here?' Odds asked. ''Til the coast iz clear? I think the coast is gittin' more an' more unclear wit' each passin' minnit.'

'Point,' Lawman agreed looking quizzically at Earl.

The harried SGA president got up from the swivel chair behind his desk and poured himself a cup of the mud he had made as the result of an inexperienced attempt at instant coffee.

'Yeah, I know. I'm s'pose to be makin' all sortsa brilliant political moves, but everything I think of is a trap of some sort. Dig all this. If I call Calhoun an' try to establish some sort of communication, I'm trapped. Either I confess that things are outta my hands an' tell him who's runnin' shit ... that's one. Or I reenforce the deman's an' bring an open confrontation that I can't afford. Or ...'

'Stop!' Lawman ordered. 'How can't you afford a confrontation? Personally or politically?'

'Neither way! Politically he has the power. I mean, you can rap all you want 'bout student power an' alla that shit, but until the Board gits organized an' places a clamp on that automatic boot of his ... Wait! The Board! The Trustees!'

'What about 'um?'

'They can do jus' what I wuz talkin' about – put a clamp on that automatic boot!' Earl reached for the telephone.

'Wait a minute!' Lawman said. 'Let's have everything together in our heads befo' we make any moves. We been in here damn near twenny minnits. I think we agree that however much time it takes, our first move had bes' be a good one.' Odds nodded. 'Now. What you gonna say to the Board? I mean, let's face it. They ain' jus' sittin' 'roun' waitin' for a call from you. They got specific times when they meet. Somethin' like two big meetin's a year an' small cluster meetin's the resta the time. What action can you get from a phone call? The Trustees are spaced all over the U.S. map ... first, who you callin'?'

'I'll call Miz Stoneman.'

'Okay. Where is she?'

'She's in D.C.'

'All right. How long you think it'll take her to get anything together?'

'I see yo' point,' Earl said a bit crestfallen. 'It'll take hours. But it won' take hours for her to call Calhoun!'

'Thass exactly what you don't want her doin'! If she calls Calhoun he's gonna minimize this shit to a speck an' try an' keep her from doin' anything national. The ol' man don' want no publicity!'

'How long do you think it'll take Calhoun to move?' Earl asked.

'I can't say. For all we know he's already gettin' walkin papers formed for a lot of us.'

'Doubtlessly,' Odds added.

'Then I gotta call Miz Stoneman,' Earl said picking up the receiver. 'I have ta impress upon her the need for her to get in touch wit' some people an' have them *all* call Calhoun unless they're comin' out here in person. Then they can call each other back an' get a conclusion together.'

Earl dialed the operator. Lawman agreed by his silence, but he was shaking his head from side to side as though he believed it to be the wrong move.

'I'd like an outside line,' Earl said. 'This is Earl Thomas.'

'I've been ringin' an' ringin' you,' the switchboard operator said in a whining tone.

'I jus' got in,' Earl lied. There was a momentary pause before he started dialing a number from an address book he located in the top drawer of his desk. There was a long period of silence.

'Hello,' Earl said when the phone was finally answered. There was a clear expression of relief on his face. 'Mrs Stoneman? This is Earl Thomas of the Student Government at Sutton. Yes, ma'am. Well, I have quite a few things to tell you too . . .'

*   *   *

Ogden Calhoun was facing what was doubtlessly his most trying day as president of Sutton University. Not only had the past sixteen hours produced a group of demands that he had seen coming for over six months, but it had also produced a militant student faction called MJUMBE of which he had been totally unaware, a series of conferences that he had detested, and a student strike in the midst of a press conference that had seen him lose almost every ounce of restraint with a Norfolk newspaperman.

The last of the reporters had just left his office and he was leaning back in his upholstered swivel chair when the intercom buzzed.

'Yes?' he replied dimly.

'Still no reply from the Student Government office,' Miss Felch reported. 'No response from the business office either.'

'Keep trying the SGA office,' Calhoun said. 'And please bring me a cup of coffee and send out for a sandwich and some tea when you get a chance.'

'Yes, sir,' came the reply. 'There's a student here to see you from the Inter-Dormitory Assistants. She says it's rather important.'

'Send her in.'

The oaken door to the president's inner office swung noiselessly open and a young coed came in with books under her arm. She was about twenty and dressed in a short plaid skirt and white blouse, red sweater, and knee socks. Her hair was fixed in a pony-tail and wide round sunglasses were propped on her nose. Calhoun rose to greet her.

'How are you?' he asked with extra charm. He grasped her hand lightly and directed her to a seat.

'I'm all right ... I'm Allison Grimes. Do you remember me?'

'From the Inter-Dorm meetings,' Calhoun asserted. 'What can I do for you, Miss Grimes. So much going on.'

'Yes, sir. I know.'

'Seems like everything happens at once,' Calhoun pointed

out, waving his arms in a general gesture. He smiled and reached for his pipe and cherry blend.

'I jus' wanted to ask about how we, as dorm assistants, should be conducting ourselves in terms of the things that are happening,' Miss Grimes asked nervously. She removed her sunglasses and wiped them on a handkerchief. 'I mean, it's understood as how we take care of things under ordinary circumstances, but there are men all over my dorm an' these aren't visiting hours an' all of the girls are upset about their jobs and everything.'

'I understand exactly what you mean, Miss Grimes. It's unfortunate that the students are so insistent on their points that they place other students in jeopardy. I haven't gotten all of the facts, but in military terms this would be referred to as "smoke-screen" tactics or "distracting" tactics. I think that the whole point is to place every student in some sort of trouble with the administration so that no students can be punished for their actions.'

'But the other girl assistants and I . . .'

'Have a job to do. But under the circumstances it would be unreasonable of me or anyone else to expect the assistants to keep up with every male and female involved in these types of activities. All I can really ask is that you try and maintain as much order as you can and wait for other instructions from Mr Bass or Miss Freeman. Is that all right? . . . just understand that we know how hard everyone is trying to do their jobs. That might also be considered on the other side of the fence in relation to administrators trying to do their jobs too.' Calhoun finished with his best political smile.

'All right,' Miss Grimes said for lack of anything better to say.

'How're the grades and schoolwork coming?' Calhoun asked.

'Oh fine,' the student replied rising. 'I'm on the list.'

'Good!' the president boomed. 'I have a lot of room on that list! Ha! Ha!'

Calhoun showed the student to the door. He was no sooner seated than the intercom was buzzing again.

'Yes?'

'There are just an awful lot of things going on!' Miss Felch said, irritated past any previous standards. 'The Student Government line was busy, but now I can't get an answer. Mr Mercer wants to talk to you in private. Mr Harper wants to talk to you. Your wife has called. She'd like to have you call back. Victor Johnson wants a statement for *The Statesman*. He says he's running another special . . .'

'Did you tell him what I . . .'

'Yes. He said this issue would be getting your side of everything. He said he had to go to press and you weren't here for comment. All he could print was the student side.'

'Where is Mercer?' Calhoun asked.

'He's in his office,' Miss Felch replied.

'Tell him to come up. When the food arrives please don't hesitate to bring it in.'

'Fine.'

Calhoun was left alone then for a moment. He had been on the go constantly since sunup and he was just beginning to realize how little food and rest he had had. At the same time he thought to himself also of how quickly and authoritatively he would once have dealt with this current crisis. He had ruled the school with an iron hand. But in more ways than one the heat was being applied by the Sutton students, and the question was whether or not Ogden Calhoun's iron hand would melt.

The thought that he had already exhibited too much concern for student opinion shot the silver-haired president straight up in his chair. He was jotting down the outline for an ultimatum that he would issue when Fenton Mercer scurried breathlessly into the office.

20

Self-help Programs

'Mrs Stoneman sez she'll do what she can,' Earl spat out
mockingly. He pushed the telephone to the far corner of the
scarred desk.

'How hip!' Odds offered. 'I could tell from yo' expression an'
the things you were sayin' that you wudn' gettin' too far.'

'Jus' what did she say?' Lawman asked.

'Shit! Yo' guess is as good as mine,' Earl admitted, lighting a
cigarette. 'She wuz a pure politician. "We'll have ta investigate
this thoroughly," an "Why wudn' it be wize fo' me to call
Brother Calhoun if I'm to get to the heart of the matter?" . . .
Brother Calhoun! Can you dig that shit? I'd sooner call Lester
Maddox a damn brother.'

'Jus' shows that it don' take much to qualify in some circles,'
Odds sighed.

'Well, *Sister* Stoneman got a long way to go,' Earl confided.

The wheels were turning inside Lawman's head. He had not
thought it to be a good idea to call the present Head Trustee,
but he hadn't been able to suggest anything better. Now, with
time slipping through their fingers and one trump card already
nullified, it was apparent that another course of action had to
be taken.

'You gonna have ta see Calhoun one a these days,' Earl was
reminded.

'I think I'm gonna have ta do mo' 'bout seein' that it ain't
today,' the SGA leader laughed.

'What can he do to you?' Odds asked. 'Crucify you?'

'It's not a matter of that,' Earl said. 'I just would rather have
him make a move now. The lines are drawn.'

'But you ain' entirely satisfied wit' the lines that have been drawn,' Odds supplied. 'You think that by lettin' that phone ring and ring you turnin' the fire up under Calhoun?'

'Not necessarily. But if I go to see him an' try to bail out, all I can do iz cause further division among the student body. The question wuz put to them in the auditorium an' they made their decisions.'

'An' you got up there an' agreed,' Lawman said wearily.

'That wuz the right move!' Earl exclaimed. 'It's time to do *something*! Shit! You know that as well as I do. Sutton people have sat an' waited an' sat an' waited until every drop of blood in their bodies has gathered in the asses. Jus' like Black people everywhere. We waited long enough.'

'But whenever you decide to move agains' the man you gotta be prepared.'

'I can't say how prepared MJUMBE wuz. All I've been doin' for the past month is gettin' ready to try an' organize somethin' along the same lines. Che said nobody would be ready when the revolution came. I wasn't ready, but I wasn't gonna try an' stop people from standin' on their feet jus' because Earl Thomas wasn't at the head a the damn thing ... thass the problem! Too many chiefs an' no fuckin' Indians!'

'So now Calhoun's on the spot?' Odds asked.

'I din' say that. I said it was his move.'

'An' what if he moves on you an' MJUMBE an' goes through his "My way or the highway" routine?'

'Then we'll find out jus' how committed people were to all that shoutin' they were doin' over in the auditorium. If people are committed there won' be no leavin' campus for one group without the others. What I don' need to do is show any signs of weakness. That's what I would be doin' if I got into any extended dialogue with the man. He knows what we want. He knows how to stop the strike.'

'He knows several ways to stop it,' Lawman interjected.

'I wonder how I can rationalize my sudden arrival at home,' Odds said to no one in particular.

'The eternal optimist,' Lawman commented drily.

'Look for the silver lining, my mama said.'

Earl wasn't particularly concerned about the reactions that his mother and grandmother would have. There was no question about how disappointed they would be. They had been disappointed when he decided not to go back to Southern University in Baton Rouge. They had known that he would lose credit and spend more money to attend the Virginia university, but they had said very little. They took pride in watching the man of the Thomas family making his own decisions and doing what he thought was best. And if he was sent home from school, after the inevitable questions, they would still be proud of him.

Earl was berating himself for being so thoroughly unprepared. To him the politics of the university were as complicated as national and international politics. In order to organize a campus one first had to organize the organizations: the fraternities, sororities, clubs, classes, and foreign students. One had to appeal to the best interests of all cliques and still apply himself to the whole picture of campus improvement. Money was a problem. Most of the things that were needed simply could not be handled by a small, predominantly black school's endowment. Funds were not available to attract the best professors. The rush was on for Black professors with the proper qualifications and the great cry for Black instructors was falling on deaf ears because Black teachers were being lured away from their communities by the smell of fresh greenbacks. As for equipment, it was the same story. Sutton was capable of doing but so much. You had to spend the money for the purposes it was donated. The money was being donated so that you would name a building after your great (white) benefactor. It was not there to purchase a 16 millimeter camera or film for photographic experimentation. It was not for badly needed instruments or uniforms for the marching band. It was not meant for buying a new bus for the teams to travel in. It was not for a new burner in the cafeteria. It was for a new gymnasium or dormitory which gave Sutton the capacity to expand in one direction, but not the ability to facilitate the present enrollment in other areas.

The job of distributing the student activities and organization funds fell to the Student Government. Organizations submitted a budget for the following year in May. It was the first order of business for the new SGA president. Earl arrived in office just in time to discover that a congressional filibuster was holding up appropriations of institutional funds and that at best he would have to make appropriations in September. Enter September and less funds for student activities than in the previous eight years when the institution was three-quarters its present size. There was a great deal of grumbling: 'How do you expect us to present a program on this much money?' The noises came from everywhere. The Homecoming Committee was up in arms. The Greek organizations were furious. The object of their anger was not the U.S. Congress, however, but Earl Thomas. The women were outraged. Proportionately the women on Sutton's campus outnumbered the men almost two-to-one, but the Women's Association budget only allowed them half the money they requested after Earl's budget cut. The president of the Women's Association had vowed even after Earl's explanation that though he was eligible for another year as SGA leader, he would not receive the support of her organization as he had during his first campaign.

Earl was recalling the campaign and all of the preparation he had gone through to get elected. He wondered now why winning the election had been so important to him. All he had gained from his victory was a series of migraine headaches. He didn't know now if he had been unprepared for the true responsibility his position required, or if he had never really stopped to consider how many moves it would be necessary for him to make once he had gotten background and prepared his statement for Calhoun.

The paper that he had given the university president was a list of essentially the same things he himself had listed as priorities, plus a few points that he had not deemed as important. Thus, he was politically clear on the issues. The issues were vital. Somehow at that moment he was feeling naïve because he had no plan. Had he expected Ogden Calhoun to drop dead at the sight of the demands? Of course not. Had he expected the president to agree with him if he also submitted a supplementary document to prove that he had done his political homework? Another no. Then why was he totally unprepared to do anything at this moment while his political followers sat around their dorms waiting for words of wisdom?

He decided that the answer lay in his political idealism. He had long ago silently decided that when the people in charge of the system were given proof positive of the negative effects that the system was having, they would move for change. The U.S. Government had wrecked his national ideal, but he had never thought of Ogden Calhoun in terms of analogies with the U.S.A. Maybe that was another oversight. What did they always say in political science? 'It doesn't boil down to a question of race. It boils down to *haves* and *have nots*.' Earl was a have not and Calhoun was a have. All of the recommendations meant extra work and extra effort on Calhoun's part. Therefore the students weren't getting anything for the asking. They were placed in a position where they had to take what they wanted. But how long could they enforce any position like that? There would definitely be a confrontation in Calhoun's back yard, so to speak. Using the proper channels was just another way of trying to beat a man at his own game.

'I blew this one,' Earl muttered aloud.

'Not yet,' Lawman hedged. He took a quick glance out of the side window. 'We were not truly prepared, I admit. I don' know how many times we'd have to say that before I'd figure I realized it. But we're still in a better position than we could be.'

'Howzat?' Odds asked.

'We could be by ourselves,' Lawman pointed out. 'If we had

waited until Earl got alla them surveys together an' all that other information, we could've gone to Calhoun an' been flat on our asses. Doubtlessly, since the students knew what we were workin' on, there would have been no need to approach them before we made our first appeal. Then when we received a flat no and went back to get the students, Calhoun would've been over-ready for us.'

'An' we would've gotten another no,' Odds said solemnly.

'But at least this is not an indefensible position,' Lawman went on. 'We've made an offensive move so we can afford to retreat. There could be no retreat if our backs were up against the wall.'

'Exploratory surgery,' Odds said.

'What?'

'Takin' a look to see how sick somebody is. You cut into the patient and peep aroun'. If there's anything wrong you try to isolate it.'

'Isolate it?' Earl asked. 'Isolate it!' The second time he repeated the phrase it was as though he had come across a new meaning for the two words. 'Odds, my man. I think yo' pointless conversation might've had a point anyway.'

Odds put his index finger to his temple and pulled the trigger, indicating to Lawman that he thought Earl was insane.

'Suppose we call a faculty meeting without Calhoun,' Earl suggested, barely concealing his excitement. 'And try an' put a wedge between our Head Nigger and his hirelings?'

'What can we base the meeting on?' Lawman asked. He too thought that Earl might have a point.

'We can say that we're ready to publicize our position nationally an' wouldn' want to say that we were striking against the faculty an' administration if we were only striking against the administration. We can say that all we want to know is where they stand.'

'I know right away we can pull a few faculty members,' Odds said. 'We can get McNeil an' Coach Mallory an' . . .'

'It's not important how many we get,' Earl said. 'All we want the faculty members to say is that they don't share Calhoun's viewpoint. Once they say that we ask them to strike with us or hand us an alternative position.'

'Naturally they'll give us an alternative that has something to do wit' formin' committees an' shit like that.'

'Fine!' Earl said. 'That then will become our safety valve. We wait until Calhoun goes through his thing about acting to keep from being intimidated or threatened an' we call this meetin' to his attention.'

'An' then what?' Odds asked, still not fully understanding.

'An' then *we* decide who'll be on the committees. Don't you see? The faculty pulls away from Calhoun. Calhoun can't dictate who goes on our committees. The committees are split evenly between the students an' faculty an' all we need is one faculty member who agrees with us to throw every decision our way ... Then if this committee finds the student view to be correct, Calhoun has no alternative but to abide by it.'

'When do we start?' Lawman asked, catching Earl's enthusiasm.

'Right now,' Earl said. 'We put notices in the faculty boxes and wait.'

21

Reactor

While the three men in the Student Government office prepared notification of the *Faculty Only* meeting for the next
morning, Ogden Calhoun was not inactive. He had eaten
a sandwich for lunch in his office, assured his bumbling
second-in-command that no sudden moves would be made
without him, talked briefly over the phone to a seemingly
inebriated Gaines Harper, and now faced a neurotic Victor
Johnson, editor-in-chief of *The Sutton Statesman*.

'You got my message, sir?' Johnson asked without looking
up.

'I got it,' Calhoun agreed noncommittally. 'I don't necessarily swallow it, but I got it.'

'You were unavailable for . . .'

'I know what you said,' Calhoun said, trying to light his
pipe. 'But you place yourself in a very dangerous position
when you do things like this issue.' Calhoun raised a copy
of the day's *Statesman*. 'All right. You have the position, and
I gave you the authority to print specials, but you have to do
this sort of thing with a discriminating eye. Especially when
you're playing politics . . . from the role of pure objectivism
you become a participant by reporting a slanted story.'

'Yes, sir,' Johnson swallowed.

'What can be done is this,' Calhoun suggested. 'Take a copy
of the demands, a copy of my reply, which you can get from
Miss Felch, and a copy of this interview. Go to press again
tonight. I want the usual number available for the student
body and copies sent to the alumni an' trustees. Plus all the
major newspapers. Is that clear?'

'Yes, sir.'

'I assume that as in the past you did not send a copy

of today's special to alumni and trustees.' Johnson nodded.
'Right. Now along with the issue you send to the newspapers
send the public relations photograph. Not that picture you
took today. The one upstairs.'

'Right. Well, when I asked for this interview I had no
idea 'bout a studen' strike. I guess that this will change the
whole slant of the story.' Johnson had known full well about
the strike.

'Not necessarily. You can print the story and say that there
had been rumors of a coming demonstration to protest my
decision.'

'But once again, sir,' Johnson said, 'I would be leaving my
role as objective reporter and giving a slanted account.'

Calhoun turned away from the chore of lighting his pipe and
faced Victor Johnson squarely. The small reporter nervously
took his glasses off and wiped them with a handkerchief that
dangled from the breast pocket of his suit.

'I think that you should know I hold you partially responsible for the things that happened today,' Calhoun said acidly.

'Me?' the editor squeaked.

'From my reports this paper of yours was an ingredient in
the emotional concoction that served to bring a strike here.'

'I'm sorry, but I still have my job to do.'

'Print what you want to about the strike,' Calhoun warned,
'but choose your *objective* terms carefully. There are certain
things about government I suppose I should tell you. The
first is that any government is subject to criticism. You can
see every day in the papers and on television examples of this
sort of criticism. But a government does not pay to support this
criticism. . . . Now hear me out. I'm not saying that because I
allocated money for the newspaper that it should be slanted in
my direction, but I do say that I would be foolish to allocate
money to an organization that is directly responsible for a
certain amount of my administrative trouble. Are you clear?'

'I believe so,' Johnson replied. He was bristling from the
threat implied in Calhoun's speech.

'About the demands I have this to say. They called for a total realigning of a great deal of the Sutton financial system. At this time it is inconceivable that the students maturely handle the sort of responsibility *demanded* in this document. Many of the matters brought up in the paper had never come to our attention in this manner before. I have referred certain issues to the Student-Faculty Alliance and I will look into others myself. Under no circumstances do I intend to crawl on my belly before the students, however. I think that my record indicates an intense concern for Sutton University and a proficiency in my position as president. I will do my best in the future as I have in the past. I am willing to work with students, but I will not be dictated to by them.' Calhoun finally succeeded in lighting his pipe.

Victor Johnson, head down, made a few final notations on his crowded note pad and then looked up.

'Is that all?' he asked.

'That's all unless you have questions,' Calhoun said, looking out of the window. The president's concern about the activities outside his window kept him from seeing the middle finger on Victor Johnson's right hand being raised in his direction, indicating the editor's heartfelt opinion of the whole thing.

The intercom came on.

'Yes?' Calhoun waved unconvincingly at the editor's retreating back.

'Coach Mallory is on the line,' Miss Felch reported.

'Good.' Calhoun switched lines. 'Lo, Coach . . . right . . .'

'They didn' come in,' Coach Mallory reported. He had read the note from the president's office instructing him to send in the four members of MJUMBE who played football.

'None of them?'

'Baker, Jones, Cotton, and King. Those right?'

'Those are the four. I wanted to talk to them because they seem to have as much to do with this whole mess as Thomas does. I can't locate Thomas either.'

'Oh.' The coach wasn't paying a great deal of attention.

Thirty of his men were on the field doing calisthenics. He thought he would be able to deal with the missing four when he found them.

'Tell me, coach,' Calhoun was saying, 'are those four boys on some sort of athletic scholarship?'

'Yes,' Mallory said guardedly. 'They are.'

'I see,' was Calhoun's comment. The way the two words were said raised the hair on the back of the young Black coach's neck. 'Well, have a nice practice. I'll be at the game on Saturday looking for a victory.'

The phone was returned to its cradle. Mallory stood behind his desk for minutes staring down at the instrument. He was dressed in a sweat suit and baseball cap. He had yet to trot out onto the baked Virginia soil and take the three laps with which he generally started his practices, but there was a line of perspiration reaching his thick eyebrows and sweat stains stood out against his armpits and crotch. In the dead silence of the empty locker room, Mallory decided to break his long-standing rule about practice. He stepped quickly into the corridor and trotted out to the door that led to the practice field. He immediately caught the eye of his assistant coach and beckoned him.

'Run them through everything, Bob,' Mallory said hurriedly. 'Double on the running an' the calisthenics. I've got an emergency.'

The Sutton senior physical education major who served as assistant coach frowned and was tempted to ask what was happening, but he knew better. He nodded, walked toward the players, and the last thing Mallory heard before the wooden door slammed shut was the shrill whistle splitting the early autumn calm.

Edmund C. Mallory was a Sutton graduate. He was a short, stocky man with a fierce, driving determination that he instilled in his athletes. It was not uncommon for Sutton to walk onto a football field as heavy underdogs and walk away as winners. For even though the university did not give out as many scholarships as they needed to compete athletically, Mallory teams were well trained physically, psychologically, and strategically. Mallory loved to tell his team: 'There are no underdogs as far as we're concerned. When you go on the field the score is zero-zero. Your action from that point on decides who the underdog is.'

The sort of relationship that Mallory sought with his athletes went beyond the coach-player relationship. Most of the time Mallory got to know the men who played under him rather well. Mallory thought he knew Ralph Baker, Ben King, Speedy Cotton, and Fred Jones very well. The four seniors had all advanced from the freshman team together. Cotton, King, and Baker were at starting positions for their third consecutive year, and though they had never gone into any great amount of detail about their campus-political involvement, the coach was reasonably sure that their college careers were now on the line because of their political commitments.

The thought of Ogden Calhoun's sly but pointed inquiry into the financial situation of the four men made Mallory positive that the political move dictated by MJUMBE was pushing Ogden Calhoun in the direction of repression.

As he showered it occurred to Mallory that he had not yet decided exactly where he was going and what he was going to do. Then he thought of Arnold McNeil and vowed that some preventative moves would be made. Standing there under the steaming water, he could not resolve completely what direction he would take, but he knew something had to be done to stop Calhoun.

22

Counterthreat

The members of MJUMBE had been busy. The members of their 'enforcer' program had met and been informed of what to do in practically all possible situations. These were the men, primarily athletes and members of Greek fraternities, who guarded the entrances to class buildings and informed students who were thinking of going to class that Sutton was on strike. There had been no physical restraint used during the first two hours of the strike. None had been necessary.

Baker had written another newsletter. His article referred to Ogden Calhoun's noon declaration and called it 'extremely unsatisfactory' and vowed that Sutton students should be prepared for a long wait. It stressed the fact that under no circumstances should the members of the student body be willing to accept less than the requests called for since the list had only mentioned 'the bare essentials.'

Abul Menka had typed up lists of needed equipment for the Music Department student who had asked if any microphones or sound machines would be needed. MJUMBE proposed to invite in a series of lecturers for a seminar program if the strike stretched into the next week. A second list was sent to the Fine Arts Building requesting majors to contact MJUMBE for possible lecture assignments. There was a great apprehension about the students moving to break the strike out of sheer boredom.

'We'll be all right this weekend,' Baker asserted. 'The Alphas are havin' some kinda dance. As long as the niggers can dance they'll be all right.'

'If we wuz to knock the dance they'd turn on us,' Cotton quipped.

'In a minnit.'

'If we get to the weekend,' Abul said, coming into the main meeting room. 'I expect Calhoun to move on us before then.'

'He'd be movin' on the whole community,' Cotton said.

'Idealistically,' Abul admitted, 'but if we had that much faith in any type of ideal unity we wouldn'a needed to have the brothers on the doors blockin' classes.'

'But . . .'

'But nothin',' Abul stepped in. 'That meetin' in the auditorium means zero. If Calhoun moves before we get the necessary power nobody leaves here but MJUMBE an' Thomas.'

'What necessary power?' Cotton asked. 'What mo' can we git?'

'Thass the problem. We gotta make Calhoun think we got more goin' for us than we do.'

It was at that instant that Fred Jones came through the door with a tray of sandwiches and plastic cups filled with Coke.

'We're bein' paged in the student union,' he said quietly.

'We who?'

'We all of us,' Jonesy replied. 'Ben King, Ralph Baker, Everett Cotton, Fred Jones, and Jonathan Wise.'

Baker laughed. 'I had forgot yawl's names,' he said, turning to Speedy Cotton and Abul Menka. No one on campus could have pointed out Everett Cotton or Jonathan Wise. 'Jonathan, my boy,' Baker said to Abul, 'we gotta educate people 'bout you.'

'What were we bein' paged for?' Abul asked Jonesy.

'We're wanted in the Administration Building.'

The sandwiches and Cokes were distributed and the men ate in silence. When the phone rang Jonesy answered and told the person on the other end to call back later.

'Maybe we should go,' Abul said suddenly.

'Where?'

'To see old Assbucket,' came the reply.

'What good would it do?' Ben King asked. 'He knows where we stand.'

'Does he?' Abul quizzed. 'He knows one thing. He got a

buncha deman's an' a strike. There's two ways of lookin' at a meetin' wit' him. One way is the way you lookin', Ben. A sign of weakness. The other way of seen' it is as a chance to find out what the ol' bastard's into.'

'Is he gonna tell us?'

'Sure. He'll tell us by the type of questions that he asks. He'll tell us by the way he approaches the whole set. If we don' go he can look at that as a sign of fear. If we show up an' freeze him, he won't know what to do.'

'Freeze 'im how?'

'Freeze, baby, freeze! You can dig that! He's gonna throw out a lotta stimulators aimed at makin' us blow our cool an' goin' through an' emotional thing. You're right when you say he knows what we want, but he doesn't know what our limits are; what we're willin' to do to get what we're after.'

'He don' care,' King said.

'Maybe not,' Abul admitted, 'but you gotta remember he ain' never really been put to the test. No one student movement on this campus ever had total support. Las' year Peabody had the frats an' the sororities. The year before Coombs had the block-heads. This is a thing that has everybody pullin' an' Calhoun may be walkin' on eggs.'

Baker made the decision. 'Let's go! If he had everything under control he wouldn'a been pagin' us. Maybe if we show a little more unity he'll be even more shook up . . . Lemme do the talkin'.'

Jonesy was about to suggest that they let Abul do the talking. He had never heard Abul say as many things as he had heard today. The strange thing was that he found himself agreeing with all of the things that he heard. He said nothing.

23

Choosing Sides

Edmund C. Mallory, Sutton football coach, found out from Mrs Millie McNeil that her husband had telephoned from a Sutton bar called the Mine where he was having drinks with an old reporter friend. She admitted that the call had been placed at one thirty and though it was already three she assumed that her mate was still there.

Her assumption turned out to be a valid one because Mallory spotted McNeil and a man he did not recognize sitting in a booth just inside the air-conditioned bar and grill.

'Ed Mallory,' McNeil said, doing the introductions. 'This is Ike Spurryman, an old college friend of mine. Ike, this is Ed Mallory, our highly productive football coach.'

They were approached by a waitress who appeared startled when the coach ordered a 7-Up. She quickly regained her composure however and departed.

'Knowing that you're not a drinking man,' McNeil began, 'I suppose I must have something to do with your visit to this little hideaway.'

It appeared to Coach Mallory that his proposed ally was a little drunk.

'You have everything to do with it,' Mallory admitted, getting right to the point. 'I'm quite sure that you and I didn't agree with all of the methods that Calhoun or the student group have been using.'

'Indeed,' McNeil smiled. 'Both parties are wrong. Stop! You're both wrong! ... Pardon me, but I'm a product of the television age.'

'The question is what we propose to do ... can I talk in front of you without fear of jeopardy, Mr Spurryman?'

'Of course. And call me Ike,' the reporter replied.

'Well, I don't like the idea of the student strike,' the coach admitted. 'But I don't like the way Calhoun is going about dealing with the student leaders either.'

'How's he dealing with them?' McNeil asked, sobering up a bit.

'Intimidation as far as I can see. He called me a little while ago and asked me if the MJUMBE members were on scholarship.'

'Whew! Trouble. What can I say? The people knocked me last night for admitting that I was a member of the Bullshit Squad.' The history professor chuckled again.

'We can't just sit around. Who else is with us?'

'Mrs Pruitt. Most of the younger people, I suppose.'

'Why can't we set ourselves up as sort of mediators?'

'The main reason is because the people who suggest this, namely you and I, are known student sympathizers. If we could talk Royce and Mercer and people like them into taking some kind of stand, we'd be all right.'

'Why them?'

'Because most of the young faculty members who are on our side are white. That's giving the students a way out. They are naturally suspicious of the white faculty members, or they overreact to them to show their militancy. It would just be better to have some solid Black figures for them to ally themselves with.'

'And any mediation tactics we tried to implement would be put off by whom?' Mallory asked.

'Initially by both sides,' McNeil asserted. 'We'd be more clearly in the middle than ever before.'

'Then at least this would give us an opportunity to break away from being constantly identified with Calhoun. I'm tired of political discussions with students about what needs to be done at Sutton starting off with, 'You people.' The students clearly mean the administrators but they don't see the faculty as other than the administration.'

'How can they?' McNeil asked. 'You have to look at political things on a college campus as a conflict on many levels. It is youth against the Establishment. It's youth against age. It's freedom against repression. It's both real and symbolic. We are not of their generation.'

'I can't talk that generation gap theme. I think it's fairly well played out.'

'You don't have to talk it, man. You're living it! You have kids, don't you? What do you think they're going to throw at you when they're old enough to start wanting special privileges? They'll say: "You don't understand. You don't realize what I mean." Mark my words. It will take a lot of serious time and energy for you to even begin to remember when you were in the same situation aside from vague generalities. I mean, aside from major events. Feelings. That's what you won't be able to remember.'

The 7-Up came along with another draft beer for the reporter who sat in the corner of the booth smoking a cigarette and saying nothing. The arrival of the waitress took on the appearance of a signaled time-out. Mallory sipped from the glass, watching the bubbles and clinking the two small ice cubes together. McNeil pulled on his drink and tamped his cigar against the side of an overloaded ashtray.

'Then what do we do?' Mallory asked, 'if we can't set ourselves up as mediaries or a liaison sort of body. Do I sit by and watch four of my men railroaded onto the highway?'

'I'm not saying we can't set ourselves up that way, but if we did we would be doing it for the students, right?'

Mallory nodded.

'Who says they want us?' McNeil asked. 'They won't completely trust us. They might reject us publicly and alienate all but a very few of us ... I propose that we find out first of all whether or not they believe we can do anything positive. Then if they do, we can move. I don't think we should try to do anything at all before that.'

'And how do we find out if we can do any good?'

'Contact them,' McNeil said, finishing his drink in a gulp.

'Where would we find Thomas at this hour. It's nearly three thirty.'

'I suggest we try and find your football players,' McNeil said. 'They are the ones who seem to be most directly under the gun. And the young man who has allied himself with them was very impressive.'

'Who?'

'This one.' McNeil proffered a copy of *The Statesman* and poked a yellow finger at the only MJUMBE man who was not a football player. 'Captain Cool?' McNeil asked.

'Abul Menka,' Mallory said. 'Where could we ... wait! I know. They'd probably be at the fraternity house. We can go there.'

'I don't know how wise that would be,' McNeil balked. 'That could be misconstrued in several directions.'

'Man, I ain' got time fo' no who construed what!' Mallory said, raising his voice for the first time. 'If we gonna be concerned about what we might construe, we can stop now. Somebody's always gonna get the wrong idea from what's done.'

'All I'm suggesting is that we call and let them know we're coming,' McNeil said. 'That way they'll know why we're coming and that might break down a little of the suspicion that would lead them to believe that we're administrative spies or some such nonsense.'

'Call if you want to.'

McNeil left the table. It was then that Spurryman voiced his personal opinion.

'Just my luck,' he said finishing his beer. 'Seems like damn near every *real* story I get I'm bound by some kind of personal thing not to print.'

'If you weren't a friend of McNeil's you wouldn't have been in any position to hear what you just heard,' Mallory pointed out.

'Yeah. But nevertheless ...'

'May just turn out to be talk,' the coach said, slowly turning back to his glass of soda.

'A damn chess game!' Spurryman exclaimed. 'If there had been no student strike I could've been back in Norfolk with my wife. Tomorrow's her birthday.'

'I could've been gettin' ready for my Saturday game.'

'You play A & T on Saturday, don't you?'

'Right here.'

'At least I'll get to see a good football game if the damn thing's still on an' they tell me to stay.'

McNeil came back to the booth and slid in opposite the reporter and the coach.

'The entire MJUMBE team has left the fraternity house. The information center could not inform me as to where they were. I told the man on the phone that I would call back.'

'I guess that's all you could do,' Mallory admitted nervously.

McNeil reached for his drink and realized that it was empty. Anyone who knew the history teacher would have easily been able to tell that he, too, was more nervous than he was letting on. They would point out the fact that he rarely drank as proof positive that something was troubling him. They might have been able to narrow it down to the student strike if they had the background. No one could safely say any more than that, however. Arnold McNeil himself couldn't safely talk about more than that. There was something eating away at the corners of his consciousness, something he could not put his finger on for the life of him. It caused him to raise his hand and order another drink.

24

On the Spot

Miss Felch's ironclad composure was so severely punctured when the five young Black men entered her office that she almost poured the steaming coffee from the pot in her hand down the front of her suit.

'MJUMBE here to see Mr Calhoun.' Baker spoke as if he had not noticed the nervous juggling act.

Miss Felch pushed down the far button on her telephone and spoke into the receiver. 'MJUMBE here to see you, sir,' she reported.

'Send them in!' was Calhoun's audible reply. Miss Felch gestured toward the door to the inner office.

Calhoun was on his feet when the five men entered. The four football players all wore black center-pocketed dashikis. Their heads were shaved and hardened muscles were revealed below the short sleeves of the shirts. Abul Menka wore a gold dashiki with black trim. He had a thick head of bushy hair with a part on the left side; sunglasses concealed his eyes.

'Sit down, please,' Calhoun said, gesturing to a sofa and chairs in the corner of the room closest to the outer office. The men sat down. Abul produced a package of cigarettes and lit one. He looked around for an ashtray and found one on the desk behind him. He had never been in the president's office before and to him its most apparent aspect was a sickly odor of cherry tobacco.

'I understand from this copy of *The Statesman* that your organization is known as MJUMBE,' Calhoun said, holding a copy of the paper. 'You have to excuse me, but the only organizations that I'm aware of on campus are the organizations that have university charters.'

'We're a newly formed organization,' Baker said. 'I don't

necessarily see the need of political organizations to form any kind of communications with the charter anyway. We don't need money from the Student Government or the university proper either.'

'That's not the purpose of the SGA charter entirely. There are quite a few groups listed who don't come under any university funds. I suppose the primary purpose is in a social vein. If your organization wanted to hold a function on campus and needed permission you would need to be included in the charter. Especially if you wanted to charge an admission fee.'

'It would allow the administrators to keep tabs on us,' Ben King suggested.

Calhoun smiled thinly. 'You can look at it that way if you choose to,' the president admitted. 'I'm sure that Mr Baker, having been a candidate for Student Government office can give other reasons. It seems particularly appropriate if you intend to organize yourselves as another political party or even as political spokesmen since I had no knowledge of your group or of how to get in touch with you.'

'We heard that you were pagin' us,' Baker said. 'We'll be glad to leave our number with your secretary.'

'Frankly,' Calhoun said, looking away momentarily, 'I had an idea of talking to you men along with Earl Thomas of the SGA. I wouldn't want to give one side of the issue any information that was not available to the other team. Maybe I should have Miss Felch try the SGA number again.' Calhoun left his guests where they sat and talked to his secretary on the intercom.

'Mr Thomas was seen in the building not long ago,' Miss Felch said. 'I sent a messenger over to his office.'

'What was he doing in the building?' Calhoun asked.

'He was in the lobby when the messenger saw him.'

'Thank you.'

Baker had taken Calhoun's absence as an opportunity to make sure that Ben King muzzled all side remarks such as the one about administrative tabs being kept on organizations.

'I'd really like to have Thomas here,' Calhoun said regretfully, 'since he brought the demands to my house last evening.'

'We don't represent diff'rent points of view,' Baker said.

'I have to feel that there is some sort of dichotomy,' Calhoun said diplomatically. 'Otherwise there would be no real need for two representative bodies.'

'We are a group of concerned students who were not appointed to any Student Government posts through election. We didn't feel that that was any reason for us to abandon our political feelings. We work with the SGA and Brother Thomas has been workin' with us.'

Ogden Calhoun's eyes hardened considerably. 'Then I will say this to you with the assurance that it will get back to Thomas,' he said. 'I have not appreciated the tactics used; the attempt to *force* me to make decisions contrary to my belief and my experience as president of this university. I have prepared a statement for the press when they reconvene at four thirty. Here are copies for all of you.

'Follow along please: The call for a student strike against Sutton University by the members of a political organization (unchartered and unrecognized) along with the Student Government Association is an obvious attempt to continue the intimidating and provocative means that were initiated by the set of demands placed before me last evening. I remind the community that these demands were issued with an ultimatum included, namely that I reply by noon of the following day. The SGA leader who visited my home gave no indication that the SGA would be available for the type of constructive dialogue that has always marked progress at Sutton. Neither did he indicate as much as one reason why any of the demands should be agreed to. The idea of a student strike was never mentioned. The number of demands that I should answer positively was not set as a condition for averting a student strike. Therefore, with a clear conscience, I state that if the student leaders responsible for the student action do not reconsider their immature decisions and offer other more democratic channels for administrative consideration, I will be forced to take action to restore order to the university. This includes probable action against the student leaders and against all students who participate in the student strike.'

Calhoun looked up upon concluding his press statement. The faces that he saw aside from the face of Ben King were absolutely emotionless. The expression on Ben King's face read: Danger.

Baker tapped his copy of the statement against his nose. 'I hope you are as prepared to deal with the situation as this statement indicates,' Baker said, getting to his feet.

'I prepared this statement when it appeared that all of the "student leaders" had gone on vacation,' Calhoun said, trying hard for a smile that he could not get. 'You must understand, gentlemen, that it is now three thirty and I haven't been able to contact a soul about negotiating these demands.'

'That's because the demands are not for negotiating,' Baker said. 'I feel obligated to tell you that *those* demands are only a few of the students' most pressin' needs. There are a hundred other things that will need negotiating that we didn't include because they are things that can be dealt with later.'

'Such as?'

'I just said that those other things shouldn't be approached now ... You have to remember, Mr Calhoun, that for you Sutton may only be a job as it is to a number of administrators, but for the students it is home. The workers *go home* after a day's work. We are here all day every day for nine months. We can't take our home situation too lightly.'

'But the things on this paper can be worked on,' Calhoun said.

'That's where you're wrong. These things *must* be done. They must be done, instituted, before *we* have anything to do with calling off the student strike.'

'Then it is very clear that we both have things to do,' Calhoun said with incalculable coldness. 'I must prepare for the press conference. I am glad, however, that your group is forewarned.'

'We are happy to have had the opportunity to forewarn you,' Baker said with a sour smile touching the corners of his mouth. 'We'll see you.'

Within seconds all five members of MJUMBE had left Calhoun to the solitude of his office. His first thoughts were that he had to see Earl Thomas and find out if there was any division in the student point of view, but the assurance with which Baker had confronted him and the fact that Thomas had been unavailable for almost four hours made him realize that if there was to be a power showdown it was now his time to show.

The intercom buzzed.

'A Mr Isaac Spurryman from the *Norfolk News* here to see you,' Miss Felch informed Calhoun.

'I can't have any private interviews,' Calhoun snapped. 'Tell him that I will make a blanket statement here in half an hour as I had planned. Did you get Thomas?'

'Nothing, sir,' Miss Felch said, contemplating overtime. 'Nothing.'

'Call Mercer and Hague from Admissions,' Calhoun sighed. 'Tell them I said I need them here immediately . . . you may have to stall the press because I'm preparing an alternate statement.'

No sooner had Calhoun put the phone down than the intercom was signaling him once again.

'Yes?'

'Mrs Calhoun wants to talk to you,' Miss Felch reported.

'Put her on . . . Hello, hon.'

'I've heard so many things about what was going on,' Mrs Calhoun said in her small worried voice. 'What has happened and how are you?'

'I'm fine,' Calhoun said gruffly. 'I just talked with some of our responsible student leaders. They are unreachable.'

'How do you mean?'

'I was trying to impress upon them the need for some sort of negotiating proposals. They as much as laughed in my face.'

'Oh, Ogden.'

'I think I'm going to have to be forced to close school down and go through a readmission program.'

'Oh, Ogden!'

'I'm waiting for Hague and Fenton right now.'

As Calhoun spoke Charles Hague and Fenton Mercer entered his office. With very little formality Calhoun cut his wife off. She was still protesting his decision when he hung up.

25

Calhoun Moves

At five o'clock the auditorium bell had summoned virtually all sixteen hundred members of the Sutton community. The dorms had been cleared of their thirteen hundred occupants, eight hundred female residents and five hundred males. The commuting students had been sitting in the lounge area of the Student Union Building waiting for word from Earl or Baker as to what they should do. The administrative staff had been completing a day's work at their posts in Sutton Hall. In the entire community only a few faculty members had already left campus for the day. They would learn of Calhoun's statement at six o'clock when the news was broadcast statewide.

The MJUMBE members sat in the first row talking softly to one another. Baker had already prepared a statement in reply to Calhoun's expected ultimatum. Earl, Odds, and Lawman, caught totally by surprise in the canteen, stood near the rear door with a group of MJUMBE enforcers who planned to hold students inside long enough for them to hear Baker's counter-statement.

The SGA representatives had been working intensely on a statement that they had planned to read at the Friday faculty meeting. The last thing they had wanted was a political reprisal from the president so soon.

When Calhoun stepped up to the microphone conversation and chair scraping ceased. The enforcers blocked the paths of all who were not inside to that point. Flashbulbs popped from directly under the podium.

'There is much about the job of president that one likes,' Calhoun began, 'and then there are those aspects one is not so fond of. I have been at Sutton for nine years and I suppose I have had it easier than most men who have held my position. Nevertheless I am always hurt when situations of today's nature come about. I am hurt because it indicates a lack of communication. It indicates a breakdown between my office and the students who make up Sutton University. It indicates a lack of understanding on both parts.

'Sutton has had a Student Government Association for over seventy years. It has had responsible leadership from members of the student community for over seventy years. It is of the utmost importance that this leadership be chosen with the most critical eye possible. It is important because it indicates a political understanding of the nature of campus government.

'When I received the demands last evening I went to work immediately to do as much as I could on so short a notice. I looked into every demand with thoroughness. I replied to each of the demands as I saw fit. I did, in short, as much as I could. But it seems as though my best was not enough for your student leadership. I offered to sit down and negotiate the demands with them. This too was insufficient.

'Based on this, I have decided to close Sutton University until such time as the university can institute a readmission program to make sure that the community is able to function at one hundred per cent efficiency.

'We will begin to take new admission requests next Tuesday, October fifteenth, and will reopen on November first. Our school year will last until June ninth instead of May twenty-second.' There was a dramatic pause. 'Are there any questions?'

His audience was stunned. More flashbulbs popped. The roar from the assembly erupted as though provoked by electric shock. The members of MJUMBE were on their feet screaming at the president, but no one was able to hear above the noise. It was then that people realized there were armed security guards at almost every exit and standing at both stairways leading to the stage.

Calhoun shouted into the microphone, 'I can't possibly handle the questions that I am sure are on everybody's mind unless there is silence. Mr Baker, you'll get your chance!'

There was a question from a female student: 'As of what time is the university officially closed?'

'As of right now, Miss,' Calhoun replied. 'We are giving students until six o'clock tomorrow evening to leave the dorms.'

'What'll happen then?' Baker shouted.

The security guards looked to Calhoun for instructions, but the president said nothing. The newsmen were scampering for the exits to get their stories in. They turned in shock when the audience screamed and the five MJUMBE men were leaping directly onto the stage. Baker squeezed in front of Calhoun and grabbed the microphone. The crowd was on its feet in a veritable frenzy. The guards were blocked by Ben King and Cotton from one side and Abul Menka and Fred Jones at the other. The guards were shouting to Captain Jones, stationed at the rear of the building, asking what they should do.

'Don't leave!' Baker screamed. 'Whatever you do, don't go home! If we allow him to run us away we'll never git anything for as long as Sutton University stands. We must stand our ground.'

Captain Jones broke through the crowd that was swarming around his men. He led the charge, billy stick in hand, that carried him into the waiting arms of huge Ben King who pinioned the older man's flailing arms until he saw Baker leap back to the floor from the platform.

Calhoun was trying hard to maintain some semblance of order from the stage when Abul Menka ripped the microphone from the wall sockets and wrenched the instrument itself from Calhoun's hands and dropped it roughly to the floor.

Baker had started a chant of 'Hell no! We won't go!' that swept through the entire audience until it was as though one thunderous voice was shouting the words in unison and pointing at the retreating figure of the president. Reporters at the front exit were pushed to the ground and cameras purposefully torn from their shoulders and smashed to the floor.

The security force formed a wall to protect Calhoun's way

through the back exit. The crowd of a thousand students pushed its way out of the auditorium and continued the chant on the sidewalks, in the street, and across the oval.

The three SGA representatives became separated briefly during the surge out of the building, but found themselves staring dumbly at the procession led by Ralph Baker that cut a trail directly across campus to the door of Sutton Hall where the chanting continued.

'The wimmin hangin' tight wit' that SNCC shit, ain' they?' Odds asked. 'Out here leadin' the damn revolution. Need to have they asses kicked so they go the hell inside!'

'They've got to leave. We have to protect them from the cops.' Earl breathed heavily. 'Le's git the car an' put the speaker on it. We can direct dudes to stay if they wanna but we need to git the wimmin outta here.'

'Calhoun gonna call the man?' Odds asked.

'You bet'cho balls he is,' Earl asserted. 'Le's go!'

The three men started off at a trot angling away from the crowd forming at Sutton Hall. They were going to get a small, portable public address system that Earl had used during his campaign to solicit votes. It had been taken from Earl's car and stored over the summer months in a back closet in the Student Government office.

'You think they gonna leave?' Odds asked, wiping a handkerchief across his nose.

'We gotta do a convincin' job,' Earl said. 'Remind people of Jackson State an' Kent State, things like that.'

'I ain' anxious to stay an' get shot either,' Odds admitted.

'Better leave with everybody else, then,' Earl said, pulling up in front of Carver Hall and fishing for his office keys.

'This is gonna be the split,' Lawman said, glancing back over his shouder.

'What split?'

'MJUMBE tellin' everybody to stay. You tellin' people to go.'

'I'm jus' tellin' wimmin to go,' Earl snorted irritably. 'I ain' askin' none a the nigguhs to leave.'

'If you think you can ride aroun' here loudspeakin' about Kent State an' Jackson State an' Orangeburg without niggers flyin' you must be crazy.'

'Malcolm said it wuz a new Negro,' Odds laughed.

'There's some new ones,' Lawman agreed, 'but it's a whole lotta ol' ones too . . . Earl, if you tell people to leave you gonna be cuttin' off yo' own nose,' Lawman pleaded. 'Who in hell you think Calhoun is after? You an' MJUMBE, thass who. If the students leave you as good as finished here.'

Earl managed to get the door open. 'I know,' he said softly, continuing into the back of the office. 'But I gotta do what I think is right. Don't I? How can I ask people to follow me if I'm leadin' 'um to Bull Run jus' to save my own ass?'

'This may not be Bull Run,' Lawman argued.

'But it might be Jackson State revisited,' the SGA president offered.

Odds picked up the connecting wires from the public address system. He took a long look at Lawman and shrugged. Then the two men followed Earl out of the door.

The green Oldsmobile was in the Carver Hall parking lot directly next to the old science hall. Odds scooted in under the wheel and started connecting the sound equipment. Lawman and Earl watched what resembled a congregation of ants standing in front of the Administration Building on the opposite side of the oval. They could still hear many of the students shouting. Others stood in smaller groups watching the windows of Sutton Hall and talking among themselves. Security guards blocked the entrance to the building itself.

'Somebody gon' shoot them fuckin' F Troopers,' Lawman reasoned.

'I wouldn' be surprised,' Earl admitted.

'Ready,' Odds said.

The three men rolled away from the lot, Odds behind the wheel and Lawman in the back seat. When the car made its first turn around the oval in front of the con- gregated demonstrators Earl began: 'This is Earl Thomas, president of the Student Government Association. We are asking that all female students leave Sutton University as has been proposed by the administration. We are making money available from our emergency fund for transportation and for phone calls and telegrams. We ask nothing of the male students, but we ask that all women co-operate. This is not a question of politics. This is a question of safety and I feel that my office has no way to offer protection to the women of the community. Need I remind Black people of what happened at Jackson State when devil policemen fired into a women's dormitory? Need I remind Black people of the slaughter of the four students at Orangeburg? Need I remind Black people of the treatment we have always received from the devil law officers in America? Brothers, our first responsibility is to the women on campus and we must not ask them to risk their lives ... Sisters, please go home.'

The chanting had subsided as students watched the green auto cruise around the oval.

'This is Earl Thomas ...'

MJUMBE continued chanting at the door of Sutton Hall hoping to overcome the damper that Earl had put on its demonstration. As if on cue a police siren was heard wailing in the background. Many of the men stayed to save face with their friends, but women slipped quietly away. Earl continued his broadcast and was not only heard, but listened to. Teachers and administrators nodded silently.

'But baby, there ain' rilly nuthin' like that goin' on, is there?' a tall male student wearing a Sigma sweat shirt was asking a coed.

'Not now,' she admitted, speeding up her exit toward the dorm.

'Thomas is jus' a jive-ass Uncle Tom,' the fraternity man continued. 'I been tellin' you that for the longes' time.'

'Maybe,' the girl admitted walking faster. 'I don' know.'

And so it went all over campus. Men talked freely and loudly about the stands that they would make and complained about their 'Uncle Tom' Student Government president who was chasing their women away. But still coeds made hasty plans to leave Sutton University, Sutton, Va.

26

Lying in Wait

Angela Rodgers sat nervously in front of her television set waiting for the six o'clock news. She had received only enough information from a girlfriend who attended Sutton to set her nerves on end.

When she called Earl's home and got nothing but more questions from Mrs Gilliam, who had not seen Earl since seven thirty that morning, a call to the Student Government office put her in touch with Earl's secretary. Sheila Gibson explained that Odds had gotten her away from her luggage to man the SGA telephones. Earl, she said, had been last seen driving around the oval asking women to go home. That had been an hour ago.

The assurance that Earl had been all right up until five o'clock set Angie's nerves at ease for a moment. Then a radio report informing her that police were conferring with the university president put her on tenterhooks again.

'Good evening. In tonight's WSVA headlines Sutton University is closed until November first. We'll have the details on this and other stories making today's Big Six news in just a moment.' The minute seemed to stretch over a week before the deadpan face of the newscaster reappeared on the small screen.

'At Sutton University this afternoon university president, Ogden Calhoun, stated that he has decided to close the school until a readmission program is instituted on October fifteenth. Calhoun stated that the reason for closing the school was based on thirteen non-negotiable demands placed before him at ten o'clock last evening. He says that it was demanded that he reply by noon today and that his answers brought on a student strike called for by the Student Government Association and an unauthorized campus political organization known as MJUMBE. Earl Thomas, the Student Government president, was unavailable for comment, but Big Six reporter Larry Herman was on hand for Calhoun's five o'clock announcement which brought on a near-riot at the eighty-seven-year-old institution. For that report we switch you to Larry Herman at Sutton University.'

The scene changed to a younger reporter standing in the middle of the oval path with perhaps one hundred or more male students in the background standing in front of Sutton Hall.

'Behind us you see the remaining demonstrators after almost one thousand students congregated to protest the closing of Sutton University by university president Ogden Calhoun who said and I quote: "I have decided to close Sutton University until such time as the university can institute a readmission program to make sure that the community is able to function at one hundred per cent efficiency." The demonstration here at Sutton Hall came after five students in dashikis took over the stage and microphone following Calhoun's announcement. The leader of this group called MJUMBE, Ralph Baker, a senior football player, urged students not to leave the campus saying that students at Sutton would never achieve their goals if they allowed Calhoun to close the school. The students then shouted: "Hell no! We won't go!" and marched on this site you now see in the background. The demonstration continued until a car driven by members of the Student Government Association toured the campus with a public address system urging female students to go home. We are waiting now for a statement from Ogden Calhoun and Police Chief Michael Connors who have been conferring somewhere on campus for over half an hour now. Larry Herman. Big Six News.'

'On other campuses nationally . . .'

Angela turned off the television and sank back into the sofa. She ran long, slim fingers through her short natural hair and started to remove her earrings. She suddenly realized that she hadn't changed her clothes since she had arrived home from the office or even thought of Bobby's dinner. Her thoughts were interrupted by the sound of the four year old's running down the stairs from his bedroom.

'Mommy? When we gonna eat?' the youngster asked.

Angie reached out and pulled his cowboy hat over his eyes.

'Soon. Mommy's had a lot of things on her mind. Why don't you go out an' play with Peanut?'

''Cause Peanut's eatin' his dinner,' Bobby replied. 'Is Uhl comin' to eat dinner?'

'I haven't seen *Uhl* today,' Angie said, starting to slip out of her dress.

'Mommy? You gonna marry Uhl, Mama?'

'I know a certain little cowboy who's gonna get scalped,' Angie said smiling at her son. Bobby ran behind the sofa and laughed heartily. Angie made a gesture as though she would chase him and he scampered to safety up the stairs.

Angie thought seriously about her son's question all through the preparation of dinner. She rarely liked to think about the implications of her relationship with Earl although she was sure that she loved him and that he loved her. She was more than a little bit nervous and afraid to give herself totally. She wondered sometimes if it wasn't an unbreakable wall of suspicion that she had built up around herself. It always seemed as though, real or unreal, someone was taking from her and she wasn't getting anything back. Often she felt empty after she quarreled with Earl. Even when she felt that she had been right during an argument she felt that he walked away with a piece of her inside of him.

She heard the shrill toot of the toy train that Earl had bought Bobby for his birthday. Bobby was a blessing. For a while he had been all that had kept her going. She couldn't imagine facing the house without him; without the echo of his laughter in the yard as he ran and ripped with the young boy from next door; without the big grin on his face when he had been doing something that he had no business doing. He was the spitting image of his father. Round head with curly hair, dark brown eyes planted carefully in a caramel face like the pieces of coal on a snowman, large grin and even teeth. Bobby indeed was a blessing.

Earl was a blessing too. He had completely changed her life. In his own way he had given new shape and strength to her life. She had taken pains to explain her family situation to him over dinner on their first date. She suspected that he wouldn't be interested in her any more and considered that unfortunate because she had such a wonderful, natural time with him, laughing and talking as though they were long-time friends. He had surprised her by approaching her during lunch the following day and asking for a second date, which she had happily arranged.

They met in midtown on the following Saturday. Saturday was always her shopping day and Bobby usually spent the afternoon with Peanut, the youngster next door. Angie picked up the few articles that she had in mind for Bobby before meeting Earl and taking in a movie. After the show he had driven her to the shopping mall and helped her select the groceries and then had taken her home.

Earl and Bobby hit it off like old friends. Earl was up-to-date on Batman, Gunslinger and Mighty Mouse, to name only a few of Bobby's favorites. Angie had commented that apparently Earl spent as much of his Saturday morning in front of a television as the four-year-old.

Earl and Angie began to see each other regularly. She began to feel he was what had been missing in her life during her self-imposed isolation after Bobby's father had left her. She began to realize that all the frustration she had felt during that time was a result of her need for a strong, mature man. Earl Thomas was that type of man.

She also felt that Earl was good for Bobby. She had approached the situation of rearing Bobby with anxiety. As far as she was concerned all boys needed male figures to identify with and the only question in her mind was how much Bobby would be hurt by the absence of a man in the house.

It had seemed as though the summer lasted only a few days because before Angie knew it Earl was back in school. She had been happy that he seemed so pleased with his summer earnings. He told her that he had never made as much before during a summer. He had also been offered a permanent opportunity at the factory, but he had turned it down to concentrate on his schoolwork and his duties as president of the Sutton Student Government Association.

Their lives had slid into a nice groove as far as Angie was concerned. No less than two or three nights a week, many times more often, Earl was at the house when she got home from work. She would cook for him and he would talk to her about the things that he was doing. That was more than important for Angie. It was necessary. Earl had opened her eyes to the fact that she was lost without a man and he had turned out to be the kind of man that she needed. She had come to depend on him to be there when she looked for him. And now there was trouble on Sutton's campus and Earl was neck-high in it. She felt helpless and frightened. She felt alone.

27

The House on Pine Street

In the kitchen of Mrs Gilliam's boarding house on Pine Street two other interested observers had watched the six o'clock news on WSVA, the local channel. Mrs Gilliam and her favorite tenant, Zeke Dempsey, were discussing the news report when Earl Thomas barged directly into the kitchen through the back door from the driveway.

'Well, if it ain't the star of the show,' Zeke said lightly. 'How you doin' stranger? You know Miz Gilliam, I believe.'

'Yeah. Right. How're you, ma'am? Whuss the put-on?' Earl asked, sitting down opposite Zeke at the kitchen table. Mrs Gilliam, as usual, was stirring up a concoction at the stove.

'Well, we see ya so rarely 'roun' here,' Zeke began laughing. 'Thought it might be a good idea to reintraduce ourselves an' start all over.'

'I guess I know what you mean,' Earl apologized. 'I'v been rather brief. I came in late last night an' when I got up Miz Gilliam had already had her breakfast an' gone to the market. I don' know if you was at work or what.'

'I went to rake leaves at the Coles's this mornin',' Zeke admitted. 'I guess that was 'bout eight.'

'I was later than that,' Earl said.

'I'm usually here, but I went out in the country this mornin' to get some fresh veg'tables. Me an Old Hunt,' Mrs Gilliam replied.

'That car runnin'?' Zeke asked laughing. The talk in the boarding house generally was that Old Man Hunt's Dodge wouldn't run downhill.

'Didn't go too fast,' Mrs Gilliam laughed, waddling back over to the table. 'Every time we did above forty or so it start coughin' like a tubercular, but did all right.'

'Fresh veg'tables?' Earl asked picking up the lost thread.

'Had to, child,' Mrs Gilliam mocked. 'Sto' bought veg'tables start to tas' like wax after while. I hate to go to the country 'cause it generally take so long after you talk to them 'bout everything thass happened since you las' saw them, but I had bought this oxtail for some oxtail soup an' I couldn' see the point in havin' it without havin' some good veg'tables.' She took the top off the large pot with a potholder. The warm, tantalizing fragrance of oxtail escaped from what Earl referred to as 'the cauldron.'

'Heard school been closed down,' Zeke said offhand.

'Yeah,' Earl said quietly. 'I was out there all day tryin' to get different things together. We called the head of the Board of Trustees in D.C., but she was so busy talkin about how great "Brother" Calhoun was that I knew I wouldn' get anywhere. Then we printed notices an' put 'um in faculty boxes callin' a Faculty Only meetin' for in the mornin', but I don't know what I'll say if we have it. The things that we had in mind aren't really relevant any more.'

'Calhoun took care of that,' Zeke said.

'I s'pose it was my fault,' Earl said. 'I'm sure that most of the overall picture is my fault, but it seems that I should know better than to think Calhoun will take a long time to move by now. I should've been expectin' him to close school down when I handed him the paper las' night.'

'I don' think you're right this time at all, Earl,' Zeke said quietly. 'Now I know I'm not a college man like yo'self an' I have always regretted that I wasn't, even if I hadn't had any particular use fo' a degree in the kinda work I'm doin' now,' the handyman smiled. 'But many's the person has tol' me that I'm blessed with what I call common sense, good ol' horse sense. I believe that along with the bookin' that you have done God gave you some horse sense also. None of the other school presidents have reacted so quickly to their protests like Calhoun. I don't think there was any way for any person to predict that he would do that ... I think sometimes you try to carry more than your share ...'

'Amen,' said Mrs Gilliam.

Earl was sitting opposite Zeke and looking out of the window. He hadn't looked at his friend and fellow-boarder once, but it was obvious that the words were having their effect.

'You know it's not but so much that one man can do,' Zeke continued. 'It's not but so much that one man should do . . . you know I heard you talkin' las' week 'bout how you had to hurry to get them papers together because the students were expectin' them an' would be on yo' back.'

'That was about keepin' my word,' Earl said, interrupting and lighting a cigarette. 'I was . . .' the young man cut himself off. He began to feel as if he were becoming defensive though he didn't feel a need to be defensive with Mrs Gilliam and/or Zeke.

'You remember what I'm talkin' about?' Zeke asked, lighting a smoke of his own. 'Na mebbe this thing today an' las' night has got somethin' to do with yo' not havin' yo' papers done, but how many a them was helpin' do the work? I mean aside from the two friends who come by here?'

'Nobody really,' Earl admitted.

'An' yet they wuz the ones you *knew* wuz gonna be on yo' back,' the handyman said laughing. 'The firs' complainers an' the las' workers. Thass been a problem wit' Negroes forever an' a day in the United States. The firs' complainers an' the las' workers.'

'I had things I was s'pose to do,' Earl said, refusing to see the point.

'Right!' Zeke agreed. 'But the whole thing is that you would have done yo' work an' been in the same situation. You'd be still the only one doin' any. Martin Luther King did his work. Malcolm X did his work. But when they died the movements that they started died.'

'Oh, man,' Earl exclaimed.

'All I'm sayin' really is that you were workin' for a buncha ingrates who wouldn' appreciate you if this was yo' thing by yourself. That with a li'l help you mighta made it . . . what I mean is that you always blamin' yo'self somehow no matter what happens. You ain' never gonna make it through life that way. It's all right to take yo' responsibilities seriously. It's the bes' thing in the world for a man if he's gonna be a man, but you gonna fin' that yo' responsibilities are gonna be enough without you takin' on what people should be volunteerin' to share since it's for everybody's own good.'

'I agree,' Mrs Gilliam said. 'How're your grades? I bet you don't have a point in none of 'um. When was the las' time you wrote yo' mother? I bet she don't know nothin' 'bout this foolishness. You still ain' been to see Dr Bennett about that tooth I gave you that stuff for . . . you see what I mean? Neglectin' yo' own good for a bunch that won't even help you. I know that Sutton crowd. They always have upper-class students who're too lazy to work.'

'Middle-class niggers,' Zeke said. 'The Deltas an' A.K.A.'s an' Alpha niggers who wouldn' know a job if it bit 'um. Thass the kind you wastin' yo' time on.'

'I don't agree,' Earl said. He lit another cigarette as he got up. 'You know when you get a job what it entails. You know that a great many students don' know anything about the campus politics an' that most of the res' don' care. You take on the job 'cause you have a certain set of ideas that you'd like to implement for the good of the community.'

'An' what if the community won' help you?'

'Thass not the point. They do somethin' when they elect you.'

'Write a X nex' to yo' name on a piece a paper. I think . . .'

'I don't agree,' Earl said cutting in brusquely. He was standing with his back turned to Zeke and Mrs Gilliam watching more of the red and brown leaves being added to a small fire in the middle of the back yard. He always felt he was watching something beautiful when he saw Old Man Hunt putter around in the yard. At that moment the warm glow of the fire illuminating the old man's face seemed to disclose some secret pleasure that was causing a smile to creep across the burnished wrinkles. 'I know that this talk was staged to make me feel better or somethin', but I don't feel the same way.'

'It wasn't meant that way at all,' Zeke said. He met Mrs Gilliam's questioning glance with a quieting gesture indicating that he would handle it. 'I'm quite sure that Miz Gilliam an' I would need a whole lot mo' facts befo' we started to tell you what to do, but we've been watchin' you go through these months of work an' school an' we'd been talkin' about how wrapped up you get in the things you feel need to be done.'

'The people at Sutton elected me to do a job,' Earl reminded them. 'Anything else is a cop-out.'

'It's good to be committed to yo' race,' Zeke said. 'Miz Gilliam will tell you that as ol' as I am I wuz right out there wit 'um in Selma in sixty-four. I was doin' all I could with the NAACP right here . . . an' one a the things that held me back in terms of maybe leadin' in the community was the fact that I didn' have much education. Both of us feel that you can be a great man in terms of helpin' our people an' that the thing you really need is yo' diploma.'

Earl turned around very quickly. Somehow he had been missing the point all through his conversation with the handyman. He was amazed to see why Zeke had been so persistent and had not let the subject drop. Zeke had seen the news. He had heard about the closing and the readmission program. He and Mrs Gilliam would easily see that if this were carried out that he would not be admitted. Zeke was asking him to back down.

'You can't think I'd go to Calhoun,' Earl said.

'No,' Zeke said, taking up the cup of coffee that Mrs Gilliam placed before him. 'I didn't think you would. But you should. I believe you should.'

'Earl's response to that was cut off by the jingling of the phone in the hallway. He waved Mrs Gilliam away and moved through the hall to answer it, discarding his sweater as he went.

'Mrs Gilliam's,' he said. 'Earl Thomas speaking.'

'Earl, this is Sheila,' the SGA secretary announced into the receiver. 'I've got a problem. We've gone into the limit for emergency funds. I've given out almost two hundred and twenty dollars. I'm sure there are more people coming in too. Especially after dinner.'

'Cut into some of those dance allowance funds then. It doesn't matter because all the money has to be paid back. It's jus' for gettin' students home in bad situations. Keep a good record.'

'Okay,' Sheila said. That should have been the end of the conversation but Sheila stayed on the line.

Earl felt embarrassed. He told himself that his conversation with Zeke and his experiences over the past twenty-four hours had made him hypersensitive.

'It doesn't matter now,' he said into the receiver. 'I know what's gone on, but it doesn't matter now.'

'I feel like an ass,' Sheila said. 'I feel like I ruined everything. I could sort've see it when you got up at the meetin' in the auditorium at twelve o'clock when the strike was called.'

'It's all over now,' Earl said.

'Not really. I wanted to tell you something when you came in and asked for me to distribute this emergency money, but I didn't know what to say. I was embarrassed.' There was a long pause. 'Did you know all the time?'

'No.'

'Did you know that that key was probably the only reason he went out with me?'

'No.'

'Earl, what's gonna happen tuhmaruh?'

'You've got me,' Earl breathed heavily. 'You have got me.' The SGA president laughed. 'Who knows? Ask Head Nigger ... Hey! How long you gonna be on campus?'

'Til tomorrow afternoon,' the secretary replied.

'Well, man the station 'til I get there. It's about six thirty? I'll be out there by quarter-to-eight. That letter that I left out on my desk needn't be touched 'cause it's already useless since Calhoun closed school. I'm comin' out to do another one that I'll run off myself. Me an' Odds or somebody'll be out there tuhmaruh also, so leave the checkbook where I can find it.'

'Okay ... what's the new letter gonna say an' to who?'

'It'll be to the faculty at this meetin' if we have it. I have no idea what it's gonna say. Prob'bly: Help!' Earl laughed feebly. 'Later on,' he said.

'Good luck,' she said.

'You eatin'?' Mrs Gilliam asked when she heard the phone being returned to its hook.

'Yes, ma'am,' he called. 'Do I have time to get a shower?'

'I make time fo' musty men to get showers befo' they set at my table,' Mrs Gilliam assured him loudly. 'You go 'head.'

Earl hurried into the shower and lathered himself under the hot spray. He felt the tension being soaked away and realized for the first time all day that he was bone-weary. For Earl, being bone-weary was quite different from being tired. It was a state in which he found himself after having to do a great deal of work in a short period of time. After stretches like this when the work was completed his bones turned to lead and his muscles to rubber. He needed to sit down. He found when he stood he was sure that his bones and organs would slip into fatty pouches and vacuum caves within his frame and be dragged into a bed and allowed to redistribute themselves. He was sorry that there would be no bed waiting for him within the next few hours.

The shower completed, Earl stepped from behind the dripping curtain and dried himself with the rough-grained towel. He then slipped into his house robe and brushed his teeth, gargled, and flip-flopped back out into the hall. The downstairs cuckoo was chiming. Earl counted. Seven bells.

Before he could get to his room Zeke poked his head out of his doorway.

'There's two professors here to see you,' he said seriously. 'The coach and another man.'

'Where are they?' Earl asked.

'Downstairs. You know Miz Gilliam wuzn' gonna let 'um up here 'til you said it was okay.'

Earl nodded and walked to the banister that overlooked the first-floor alcove and sitting room. Below, Coach Edmund Mallory and the head of the History Department sat discussing something between themselves.

'Hello . . . how are you?' Earl said, attracting their attention. 'Come on up. I was in the shower . . . Mrs Gilliam never lets people into anyone's room.'

The two men smiled uneasily. They picked up their coats and walked up the thirteen spiraling stairs to the second floor.

'Won't you come in?' Earl asked, showing the faculty members into his room. 'I'm not really prepared to handle a great deal of company, but I do have a couple of chairs.'

'That's fine,' Coach Mallory said warming a bit. 'We don't want to take up a great deal of your time, but we received the notes that you put in the faculty boxes this afternoon, and we have been tryin' to get in touch with you or MJUMBE all day . . .'

'I was a little hard to catch up to,' Earl admitted.

'Well, we were curious about this meeting,' Mallory continued. 'Because we don't think that the proper thing's bein' done. The truth is, we wanted to do somethin' constructive befo' we even learned that Calhoun was closin' school. What can we do?'

Earl smiled as he thought the question over and lit up a cigarette. There was a bit of comedy to be felt in the scene. The ever-serious football Simon Legree posing a sensitive question; the quiet, studious history professor sitting bolt-upright in a disheveled brown suit, sporting a red nose that indicated a taste of too much whisky. Mrs Gilliam had probably smelled it too. That meant a night of phone calls to inform all of the neighbors that McNeil had visited Earl drunk. He would have to ask her not to mention to anyone the fact that McNeil and Mallory had come to see him. Because of their jobs, he would say.

'I don't suppose you could do anythin',' Earl finally said, sucking on the cigarette. 'I had planted those notices before Calhoun announced that school was closin'.'

'But the meetin' was called . . .' McNeil began.

'To find out if the faculty as a separate entity thought our demands were unfair,' Earl supplied.

'Some of us don't,' McNeil said. 'A few of us are in positions where to agree or disagree means little because we are the head of a department,' he tapped his own chest, 'or a coach with a winning record for eight straight years an' a Sutton alumni.' Mallory was indicated. 'There are others, mostly the young white members, who also agree, but I'm afraid it's really not enough of the cross-section that you would need to make a big impression.'

'Yes,' Mallory grunted. 'Your agreers are all either political radicals or Phys Ed teachers who aren't supposed to have a brain in their heads.' He laughed without humor at the thought.

'Then there'll be no meeting,' Earl said with finality.

McNeil set fire to a cigar. 'We'll go 'round an' get some signatures in the mornin',' he said, puffing to make sure he was lit. 'If there is anythin' to say, come to the meetin'. Otherwise, we'll just know that nothin' positive has happened.'

'What will the signatures be for?' Earl asked.

'MJUMBE has issued a statement referring to slanted reports being made to distort the facts to parents. They insist that the parents could help the student cause if the students were not being type-cast as hoodlums an' thugs. Our letter will back up their earlier notes and statements, and perhaps some literature of yours, and be sent to the parents. This might include a plea that school not be reopened without a community hearing to discuss what punishment, if any, your group and MJUMBE should receive.'

'What punishment, hell,' Earl snorted pulling on a T-shirt. 'We won't be allowed back fo' a hearin'.'

'What I'm sayin' is that it should be petitioned or added to the list of demands. Something like: "No punitive measures shall be taken against the students who participate in this strike."'

'Calhoun would laugh at somethin' like that if he laughs at the things we have down there now,' Earl said without enthusiasm. 'But there's a long way to go befo' we get to that.'

'Howzat?' McNeil asked.

'Befo' Calhoun can *keep* us off of Sutton's campus,' the SGA president said, 'he's got to get us off.'

28

Destruction

The Strike Communications Center on the third floor of the fraternity house issued a six-thirty plea to all female students. It read as follows:

Dear Sisters,

The members of MJUMBE, Ralph Baker, 'Speedy' Cotton, Fred Jones, Ben King, and Abul Menka are not certain at this time what measures of force will be used to make members of this community leave before the six o'clock deadline for tomorrow. We understand the concern exhibited by both our sisters and our brothers over this issue and we too are concerned. We ask that all sisters who are asking their parents to pick them up notify their parents of a proposed three o'clock meeting in the auditorium where we can explain the student side of the issue. As usual the administration has bottled up the media so that students appear to be nothing more than trouble-making hoodlums. We hope you will convey this message and we ask that you all be present.

ASANTE,
Brothers of MJUMBE

This particular statement was used by Ogden Calhoun to bolster his position when shortly after eight p.m. violence erupted on the campus of Sutton University.

There had been meetings within all fraternal organizations, both male and female, to draw up statements pledging varied degrees of support to the student leaders. On the way back to the dormitories both men and women said that they were harassed by members of the Sutton police force who were patroling the campus area. The reply to this harassment was unleashed fury in the halls of the dormitories where windows were smashed, lounge furniture was thrown through doors and windows, and public address equipment and telephones were ripped from the walls.

Calhoun received a phone call at his home where he was relaxing, dressed for bed.

'Excuse me, sir,' the speaker began, 'but they've gone crazy out here on the campus. They're tearin' up everything.'

'Who? Who has done what?' Calhoun asked sitting bolt upright.

'This is Captain Jones. I don't really know what brought any of this on. My men were on foot patrol an' the police from town were cruisin' in their cars. I was near Sutton Hall an' I heard all this glass breakin' an' people shoutin' an' yellin'. I run down to Washington Hall in time to see a lounge chair gittin' pitched outta the winda.'

'What have the police done?'

'Nothin' but locked they cars, sir, but they scared.'

'Tell them . . .'

'This is Earl Thomas,' a second voice cut in. 'We're in the guardhouse in the parking lot. Call off the damn cops!'

'Thomas? What's goin' on?'

'The police are goin' on. They provoked everything. You're gonna have a real riot if you keep them here.'

'Where is Chief Connors?'

'He's not here, I don't think,' Earl said.

Calhoun muttered a curse. 'I'll be there. See what can be done. Put Jones back on the line . . . Jones! Do somethin'.'

'Yes, sir. You comin'?'

'I'll be right there!'

Before Captain Jones had thoroughly replaced the receiver Earl was already galloping across the campus to his car where the P.A. system remained intact.

Sounds of crashing glass were still echoing across the oval

and lights in the dormitories were being flashed off and on. Earl thought that the flashing lights might be signaling an S.O.S. His car almost backed into the school ambulance being driven by one of the security guards toward Sutton Hall. He paced himself and entered the back half of the oval directly behind a cruising patrol car. He turned the P.A. system up as loud as he could.

'Brothers and sisters. This is Earl Thomas. I have notified the president of the university about the harassing tactics used by members of the Sutton police force and he is on his way to the campus. I am askin' all of you to cease the destruction of our own property.' Earl's drive was interrupted by the opening of his car door on the passenger side. For a moment his heart seemed to stop. He felt sure that it was a member of the Sutton police. It was Abul Menka, carrying a .22 caliber rifle with a box of bullets in his hand.

'Keep drivin' an' talkin',' Abul breathed.

'Brothers and sisters. This is Earl Thomas. I am askin' for peace. Please stop tearin' up our homes. Please do not respond to the police by destruction an' vandalism. We can hurt no one but ourselves that way. I am askin' too that the Sutton police drive over to the Administration Building and wait for further orders from their superior. I am askin' for peace.'

'You layin' to get a piece a lead from one a these devils,' Abul said lighting a cigarette. 'Man, who you think you are? Martin Luther King? Talkin' all this peace shit . . . these devils baitin' the brothers an' sisters, jus' doin' they damndest fo' an excuse to shoot yo' people down!'

'Our people,' Earl reminded Abul.

'Yours if they crawl on their bellies!' Menka snapped. 'I'm down here to defend.'

'Hi many can you defend wit' one .22?'

'Hi many guns did we have at Jackson State? If we'da had one .22 Black people might not a been the only ones that died.'

'Or mo' Black people mighta died,' Earl said. 'Brothers and

sisters.' The SGA president turned his attention back to the P.A. Abul was silent.

'At leas' turn yo' light out so you won' be such an easy target,' Menka said.

Earl doused the lights. They watched two patrol cars pull up in the driveway next to Sutton Hall. There were still two more somewhere.

On their third turn around the oval the sound of breaking glass and screaming had subsided. Outlines of people were stretched across the screens in the windows of the dormitories.

'Please turn off yo' lights an' stay away from the windows,' Earl said, continuing to drive slowly with his lights off. 'Stay away from yo' windows an' keep yo' lights off.'

All four patrol cars were accounted for. The only people seen walking out in the open were the security guards. Earl's car was caught in a blaze of headlights as he started his fourth cycle. Both Earl and Abul recognized the car as the Lincoln belonging to Ogden Calhoun who sat stiffly behind the wheel. Calhoun passed by them as though he had not seen the Oldsmobile. Earl sighed his relief.

'Misser Big Nigger,' Abul sneered. 'A plague on his people. A fuckin' star-gazin' parasite! A curse on the race!'

Earl cut the engine off and sat quietly for a minute in front of the path leading to the fraternity house.

'We all got a long way to go,' the SGA president breathed.

'You can' git but so far runnin' off at the mouth while you on yo' han's an' knees.'

'You cain' git nowhere dead.'

'Better dead than a slave,' Abul spat, lighting another cigarette.

'Is that the way you felt last May when I saw you an' yo' guest at that bar on 211?' Earl asked lighting his own cigarette.

'I wuz waitin' fo' you to bring that up las' night,' Abul said, his anger and sneering tones dying.

'I asked you a question,' Earl said.

'Do you wanna know if a white bitch turned my head around?'

'I wanna know what turned you around.'

'Knowledge, man. I learned where I wuz wrong. Thass all.'

'An' you aren't wearin' dashikis because the fay broad blew yo' program away?'

'She had nuthin' to do with it. I was sick! I was wrong.' Abul was getting angry again.

'Then learn somethin' else,' Earl said softly. 'You don't face a bazooka with a water pistol. You don't fight a tank with a slingshot. You don't risk the lives of future Black mothers jus' because you have an emotional commitment to a .22.'

'All dead bodies that leave this world undefended tonight will be placed on yo' doorstep,' Abul said.

'All brave Black fools who fight when it is not time to fight will be brought to you.'

'We'll see. The pigs will show us,' Abul said as he got out of the car.

While the pig police occupied the minds of the two young Black student leaders, Ogden Calhoun was dismissing them from any further duty on campus, and making another call.

'Yes, I know it's inconvenient. It is an emergency,' the Sutton president was saying. There was a long pause while the man to whom he wanted to talk was summoned to the phone.

'Yes? ... yes, Governor. How are you? Yes, sir. That's the point. I am havin' trouble an' I'll prob'bly get a whole lot more tomorrow ... I asked that the campus be cleared by six ... good ... if they won't leave at six I'll call your men ... They'll be right outside of Sutton? Wait, let me take that number ... yes, I'll call back tomorrow ... right.'

Calhoun reclined in his high-back chair and let the exhaustion that had followed him all through a tense and tiring day take over. He had been assured that a National Guard unit would be available if he needed it for the next night. He felt a fearful certainty that it would be needed.

29

Plans Abandoned

Arnold McNeil was sitting in his living room reading a book when the phone rang. It was answered by his wife, Millie.

'It's Edmund,' she said, referring to the head football coach.

'Good,' McNeil said, coming to take the receiver. He had not been expecting a call from the coach. 'Lo, Ed,' he began. 'What's up?'

'Arnold? There's been some more trouble down here this evening,' Mallory said quickly.

'What's happened?'

'The students tore up some furniture an' things in the dorms 'bout fifteen minutes ago,' the coach breathed. He was standing in the pay phone booth in the lobby of Sutton Hall.

'Where's Calhoun? How did these things get started?'

'Calhoun is in his office,' Mallory said. 'He came runnin' in a few minutes ago with Jones an' one a the men from the Sutton police force.'

'Did he say anything?'

'Not to me, but he seems more resolute than ever about closing the place down.'

'How do you know?'

'He sent the local force home, but Nancy, the girl on the night switchboard, said he made a call to the governor.'

'For what?'

'For the National Guard, I suppose,' Mallory fumed.

'Oh, my God,' McNeil shouted.

'What is it, honey?' Millie McNeil asked.

'I'll tell you in a minute,' McNeil waved to her. 'So what are you sayin', Ed?'

'That I don' know what good any alliance we've formed at this stage will do. I know that Calhoun wants the school closed.'

'We all know that. What can we do?'

'Talk to Admissions the first thing in the mornin'. Try an' see if we can't form an ad hoc faculty committee to investigate the new admissions program.'

'Do you think Thomas added that demand we suggested?'

'I don' have any idea. I wonder seriously if he'll come to that meetin' in the mornin' too. I think the boy's fed up with the whole thing.'

'I didn' feel that way,' McNeil said. 'He's got to do something.'

'Well, whether he comes or not I suggest we go out an' get the signatures of the faculty members who are willin' to serve on the new Admissions Committee to see what happens to Thomas an' MJUMBE.'

'We know what'll happen,' McNeil said. His tone expressed frustration at the prospect of the bureaucratic whirlpool. 'They won't be allowed back. Calhoun will say that they're keepin' the school from operatin' at one hundred per cent efficiency. That was the "catch phrase" in Calhoun's pronouncement . . . and all of the ol' guard will fall in behind him waggin' their tails.'

'Especially after what happened today an' tonight,' Mallory admitted. 'What can we do?'

'Get the signatures from people at that meetin' in the morning,' McNeil suggested. 'That's about all.'

'In other words we really can' do anything,' Mallory said.

'That's right,' McNeil confessed. 'That's exactly right.'

Earl Thomas was not having an easy time explaining the activities of the day to his girl, Angie. He had left the campus minutes after the four Sutton patrol cars were dismissed and had flopped exhausted on Angie's living room sofa.

'I jus' don' want to see your whole college career ruined,' she said, stroking the back of his neck. 'I'm sorry, but you know as well as I do what will happen tomorrow.'

'I'm not leavin' tuhmaruh,' Earl said. 'I'm stayin'. I tol' the women to leave.'

'The women want to stay. You said so yourself. They mus' feel as deeply about the whole thing as you do . . . an' besides, there are more women than men on Sutton's campus.'

'Not the point. The point is that they have to go.'

'An' what if they don't go?'

'Then I'll leave 'cause I won't want to see them gettin' their heads kicked in.'

'You really think that's goin' to happen? Then I don' want you there either. I don' want to see . . .'

'You sound like Zeke an' Mrs. Gilliam earlier this evenin'!' Earl exclaimed. 'What is this? A conspiracy? Get Earl to chump out on his commitment day?' He sat up and lit a cigarette, saying, 'I don' tell you about things I want to do to start a damn debate! I tell you so you'll know where I stand!'

'Or where you lay,' Angie said, walking to the easy chair and reclining in it. Earl could barely make out her features in the darkness. He could see that her head was back and that her eyes were closed. She was rocking a bit and her bare feet were rubbing across the carpet. He got up and walked over to her, standing her up before him and kissing her forehead.

'Nothin' will happen to me,' he said. 'I promise.'

'How can you promise that?' Angie asked. He could see for the first time that her eyes were brimming with tears.

'Nothin' will happen to me that's bad,' Earl said. 'I mean that the worst thing I could do would be to stay away from where I belong. If I'm not there I couldn't do you any good or myself any good. No matter how healthy I looked, I'd be dead inside.'

'Earl! I know something will happen to you. Something always happens . . . Earl! Make love to me, Earl. Please?'

There were mixed emotions in the man's eyes. More than anything else in the world he wanted to slap his woman; feel his palm smack with all the conviction he could muster across her tear-stained face. He wanted to grab her and squeeze her until she begged him to release her. He wanted to turn and walk away from her, leaving her there in torment wondering what she had said to anger him.

'Self-pity?' he asked. 'Selfishness an' self-pity? Something always happens to the things that you love? Make love to you one last time before I die? I should knock hell out of you! Doesn't how I live mean more than whether I live? I'm ashamed of myself, you know? I'm damn ashamed because when I met you I thought you were so stuck up and now I see that it was an ice wall of self-pity; a walking martyr. Angie Rodgers. Her old man is dead. Her boyfriend screwed her and left her with a baby in her belly. She's twenty-two years old and walks around with a foot in her ass that was placed there when she was born. I swear and be damned!'

Angie was stunned. She tried to force Earl to meet her eyes and see the tears that ran more freely now, across her nose, salt water stinging her lips and tongue.

'Is that what it is, Earl? Is that what you think? My desire to make a good home and be a good mother was an "ice wall of self-pity"? My putting aside the things that twenty-two year old women do because I had no man to help me was self-pity? Was it? What can a woman be but cold when she's got to make it by herself? . . . Earl, I love you. I'm a woman . . . Maybe I was wrong to ask you, beg you to make love to me, but I couldn't think of any other way to let you know how much I really love you.' Angie could find no more words to say. She hadn't even looked up during the last part of her monologue to see the pain burned across Earl's face. She hadn't even noticed that Earl was an open book of confusion and agony because of the things he had said that suddenly became obscene and too incredibly wrong to tolerate any balance or consolation. She walked slowly from the room and up the carpeted stairs.

Earl sat under the lamp smoking a cigarette, asking himself where all of the understanding he had thought he possessed was now, when he was faced with a crisis that called for understanding. Halfway through the cigarette he stubbed it out and turned off the lamp. He had made up his mind to go and talk to his woman. He wanted to find out if he could be forgiven for being a man.

Plans Abandoned | 445

Friday

30

Final Word

Mrs Gloria Calhoun, the former Gloria Vernon of Saginaw, Michigan, sat quietly in the upstairs bedroom waiting for the ten o'clock news report. The door had slammed downstairs only minutes before and she had been expecting her husband to come into the bedroom, but now supposed that he was watching the news on the television set in the den.

She felt rather foolish watching television for information about her husband when he sat just one floor beneath her, but she was somewhat afraid of what the news would be. She hadn't been able to help overhearing the tense phone call that had come from Captain Jones at just past eight o'clock. She hadn't been able to ignore the fact that for some reason Earl Thomas, the Student Government president, had cut into the phone call. As a matter of fact it had seemed as though the usually soft-spoken young Thomas was screaming, his words audible from her seat across the room. A disturbance had taken place and had doubtlessly involved the Sutton police. She hadn't wanted her husband to ask them for any assistance. The Sutton students hadn't demonstrated any need to be contained by armed bullies. She crossed her fingers and prayed that none of the students had been hurt. She hoped that a student's injury had not been the reason that her husband had not come up the stairs to face her.

When Ogden Calhoun completed his doctorate in 1946 he went straight to Saginaw to marry the woman he had met during his undergraduate studies at Howard University. Calhoun had been one of the youngest black Ph.D.'s in psychology in America. There had been times when neither of the two thought that he would make it. The war, the money, the pressure on Blacks in the higher realms of the educational system had all been against the young couple, but somehow Calhoun's determination had paid off and brought a ray of hope to friends and relatives who saw an almost fairy-tale ending placed on the Calhoun story when the couple married in the Vernon family church.

Unfortunately that was *not* the end of the story, but rather the beginning of a new phase. The second phase included Calhoun's appointment as the head of the Psychology Department at Small's College in West Virginia, radical contributions on the causes of Black psychological problems to national psychology journals that lost him his appointment, the loss of their only child, Margaret, from polio at the age of two, and a subsequent wall of frustration built between them by Calhoun's long, exhausting work schedule and his wife's boredom.

The appointment of Calhoun as president of Sutton had been a second beginning of the second phase. Neither of them had really expected the appointment because in the fifties there was an open fear of Blacks who spoke out so openly against racism and Black oppression. It had been felt that Calhoun's articles of the fifties would be held against him even ten years later by the white corporations that supplied much of the financing for private Black institutions.

The first year at Sutton had been like a breath of fresh air for the couple. Each became involved with new duties. Mrs Calhoun was a frequent speaker for Women's Day programs at churches in the Black community. Her picture often appeared in the local paper when she was endorsing another one of her many charities.

As a still-life photo of Ogden Calhoun appeared on the television screen, Mrs Calhoun began to regret the very involvement that she had once been so happy to discover. Her community responsibilities had practically severed her ties with her husband. The two of them had lost touch with one another. Their ability to communicate had faded. Their interest in one another had become impersonal. Their sex life had disappeared.

'Sutton University in Sutton, Virginia, was closed today by University President Ogden Calhoun who reacted to a student strike due to nonimplementation of twelve demands with these words: "I have decided to close Sutton University until such time as the university can undergo a readmission program that will insure the community an ability to function at one hundred per cent efficiency." Sources have intimated that the Admissions Office will not be considering new applications received from Student Government officials or members of a new radical student faction call MJUMBE. These student leaders touched off two near-riots today when first they seized the stage at a meeting where Calhoun announced plans to close the school, and tonight when students destroyed an estimated eight thousand dollars' worth of furniture and dormitory equipment. During the interruption of this afternoon's meeting the Sutton students were urged by a MJUMBE leader named Ralph Baker to defy Calhoun and remain on campus. The Sutton police were called in to patrol the grounds, but were asked to leave by Calhoun after the vandalism began. The eighty-seven-year-old institution has been ordered cleared by six o'clock tomorrow evening, but many students have vowed to stay.'

Mrs Calhoun used the remote control to turn off the television when the announcer turned his attention to other news-making events. She was relieved that no one had been hurt, but there was clear frustration and tension etched into the corners of her mouth and around her eyes, frowns penciling crooked furrows across her forehead. She reached for her coffee cup, but finding it empty returned it to the night table beside her bed. She was tempted to switch off the light and avoid the confrontation that would occur when her husband came up for bed, but she did nothing of the sort. Instead, she allowed her mind to wander, floating across the days, weeks, months, and years of which her marriage consisted. She was so lost in thought that her husband startled her when he opened the door.

'How are you?' she tried tentatively.

'Tired,' Calhoun spat out, puffing his pipe.

'Is everything all right on campus?'

'For now,' Calhoun shrugged, sitting on the edge of the bed. 'I went over and did what I could.'

'Was anyone hurt?'

'Of course not. I don't think there was any real reason for the entire incident. Probably started by MJUMBE.'

'You think so?'

'Glo, if you had seen them this afternoon you would have no doubt at all. Savage! Ripped the microphone right out of my hands this afternoon. Tore the wires out of the control panel and threw it on the floor . . . student leaders . . .'

'You couldn't talk to them at all?'

'That's why I'm closing,' Calhoun snapped. 'I had them in my office and tried to talk them into negotiating the demands. Damn if they'd have anything to do with anything I suggested.'

'What did they say?' Mrs Calhoun asked, sitting up.

'Said they'd bring me some things we could bargain with after I'd done what *had* to be done. Ain't that rich?' Calhoun stood and removed his coat, shirt, and tie. He dropped all three articles into a plastic laundry bag that hung from the closet door. 'Tell Arnie that I'll need these things Saturday at the latest when he comes by . . . do I have any shirts down at the laundry?'

'Yes. He said he'd bring them by when he picked up tomorrow. In the meantime you have plenty of shirts in the bottom drawer.'

'Good,' Calhoun replied. He took a fresh pair of pajamas out of the middle dresser drawer and proceeded into the bathroom.

Mrs Calhoun stared blankly at her husband and in her mind's eye she could see the years of her life turning to water and swirling down an hourglass-shaped drain. What had happened to them and to their lives? she wondered.

Where had *her* Ogden Calhoun gone? How long had he been gone? Where was Gloria Calhoun, the woman who had saved herself for this one man?

Her musing was interrupted by a clap of thunder followed quickly by a jagged snake of lightning that blazed across the darkened sky, as drops of silver-paint rain appeared on her windows. She got up and closed the huge windows that looked out over the back of the yards, her carefully tended gardens, and down perhaps a quarter of a mile where a thousand lights still shone bright inside the dormitories on Sutton's campus.

The lightning flashed again causing the lights in the Calhoun bedroom to blink. The wind was picking up. Once again the vision of the young Calhoun, the young Black radical, the advancer of new psychological theories based on the experiences of Black people, danced through Gloria Calhoun's mind.

'It's so sad,' she was thinking, 'to think of what has become of my knight in shining armor . . . my knight in rusty armor.'

31

Faculty Only

Ogden Calhoun enjoyed the luxury of an extra hour's sleep on Friday morning. He had ignored the seven-thirty alarm that generally started his day and informed his wife to wake him at eight thirty instead. He was expecting a long and trying day on the campus once he got there, a day crammed with meetings, conferences, phone calls, and unexpected problems. Upon arriving on campus shortly before ten o'clock, however, he was happy that he hadn't elected to report to work any later. Fenton Mercer, the portly second-in-command at Sutton, was sitting in his office fidgeting with a damp handkerchief.

'Mercer!' Calhoun exclaimed with his best everything-is-roses greeting. 'So early in the day and you're here already. What's up?'

'There's a meeting I think you should know about,' Mercer said nervously. 'I recalled when I heard about it what you had said about my not informing you about the last impromptu meeting that was called and . . .'

'My God, man!' Calhoun snapped, placing his attaché case down on the desk. 'What in hell is it?'

'There's been a Faculty Only meeting called in the Dunbar Library,' Mercer managed. 'I went over there, but they didn't admit me.'

'Who?' Calhoun asked. He had greeted his vice-president with a bit of sarcastic comradery, but now he was all business. 'Who wouldn't admit you?'

'Well, they didn't exactly bar me,' Mercer admitted, 'but they told me that I wasn't welcome.'

'They who?'

'Arnold McNeil . . . I heard about the meeting when I first got here this morning, but when I tried to call you your line was busy and Miss Felch had told me that you weren't expected to be late so I waited. I called again 'bout ten minutes ago, but the line was still busy.'

'Gloria was probably talking to somebody,' Calhoun muttered. 'What time was the meeting scheduled for?'

'Ten.'

'It's a little after,' Calhoun said checking his watch.

'I went over at ten, but they hadn't started.'

'Who called the meeting?' the president asked.

'I didn't find that out,' Mercer admitted. 'Nancy said there were notes placed in all faculty members' mail boxes.'

'Probably Thomas or MJUMBE,' Calhoun said, placing his case on the floor and searching through the papers on his desk until he came up with a pipe cleaner. 'Let's go.'

The meeting hadn't started on time because the assembled faculty members were waiting for Earl Thomas, the man who had called the meeting. Arnold McNeil and Edmund Mallory stood at the entrance to the library talking quietly. Both were hoping that Earl would appear, and neither of the men felt that the Student Government leader would come late.

They were wrong. Just as McNeil was about to take matters into his own hands Earl came through the library door with Lawman and Odds at his side. He smiled vaguely at the two tense faculty members and then slid inside where the rest of the professors sat talking among themselves and smoking.

Earl wasted little time. He went directly to the small table that was in front of the audience and put his notes and papers down. Odds and Lawman sat in the seats where the secretary and presiding officer of a meeting generally sat. Earl never sat down when he was speaking, and did not do so now. The SGA chief waited until everyone present had been seated. McNeil and Mallory were in the last row waiting. Earl lit a cigarette.

'Good morning,' Earl began. 'I had given serious thought to not attendin' this meetin' at all even though I called for it. When the thought of a meetin' with the faculty first occurred to me several things had not taken place that have become overwhelming factors in the student stance during the current crisis. First of all, when the meetin' was called school was still open. That has a great deal to do with our stance.' Earl smiled a bit, realizing that he had stated an over-obvious fact. 'But more important, when I called for this meetin' I wasn' aware of the lengths that our president would go to, to make sure that Sutton University stands still.

'Granted that perhaps President Calhoun considered himself under attack when presented with our "proposals", I still deny emphatically the fact that these issues had never been broached by students at Sutton. I will remind you all of the proposal last year presented by then SGA president Peabody that Sutton go on the meal-ticket system to cope with the inadequacies of the food served up by the Pride of Virginia Food Services. In brief, this was a system where students would buy a monthly meal ticket with a certain amount of holes that could be punched out when a student attended a meal. At the end of the month the tickets would be turned over to the central SGA office and another ticket would be issued. At the end of the semester all holes not punched would be refunded from the initial fee paid by boarding students.

'This is an example of the type of thoughtful proposal that President Ogden Calhoun says he is in favor of. Yet this proposal was rejected and the students were never informed in detail as to why. The only explanation given was that it might be difficult to keep track of food tickets; that some might be lost or stolen and that other students who were not paying might be eating on a friend's meal ticket. I agree that in case of a lost or stolen ticket the university might suffer, but only if the lost tickets were unnumbered and the hole puncher in the cafeteria was not given a list of tickets that had been reported lost and were no longer valid. In other words, all of the objections to the tickets were things that could've been easily worked out. The real reason that the idea was rejected, I suggest, is that the Pride of Virginia Food Services is aware of the quality of their meals and knew that no one would eat in the cafeteria if they had an option.'

Earl paused to light a cigarette. 'Perhaps that's enough about the food. Issues two, three, and four called for the resignation of Gaines Harper, Professors Royce, and Beaker. I suppose that everyone here has read the newsletter published yesterday by members of MJUMBE, but for those of you who haven't, it simply states that Gaines Harper is not presentin' the image that students need to see in order to confide very personal information. I'm sure that some of you will remember your college careers an' a lack of finances that made some of the goin' extremely rough. I'm sure that you didn' relish the idea of discussin' your family circumstances with *anyone*, but I assure you that you would find it doubly difficult to discuss these matters with Gaines Harper . . . As for the two professors referred to, I will take this opportunity to assure them that it is not a personal condemnation. What the students seek is a way to be better prepared for what awaits them after graduation . . . I have here a petition signed by ninety per cent of the majoring students in both the Language Department and the Chemistry Department who feel that new department heads are needed for progress.'

'He's a diplomatic bastard, ain't he?' Odds asked Lawman.

'He has to be,' Lawman said. 'But he's sincere.'

Odds nodded and lit up a cigarette of his own. He was beginning to relax a bit. Earl's diplomacy and ability to articulate had surprised even him, and he had sworn that nothing Earl would do could surprise him after the upset SGA election victory. He took a drag on the cigarette and leaned back. The issues of the demanded resignations from Beaker and Royce had been the matters that had troubled him all night. He had wondered how Earl would enlist the faculty support while asking for the dismissal of two of their most respected colleagues. The whole meeting would be a snap from here.

The next snap Odds heard, however, was the snap the entire

assembly heard as the door to the auditorium had its lock sprung and Captain Eli Jones of the security guards ushered Ogden Calhoun and Fenton Mercer into the meeting. The only man in the room who responded was Arnold McNeil, who was instantly on his feet.

'You were not invited to participate in this meeting,' Calhoun was told by McNeil.

'I'm well aware of that,' Calhoun remarked openly. 'But as the president of the university I am also the chairman of the faculty until such time as a replacement is found for me. Any meeting of this sort should definitely be of interest to the chair . . .'

'Then I so move,' McNeil said fuming.

'Motion denied, I bet,' Odds quipped behind his hand.

'The purpose of this meetin' was to inform faculty members of some things that the students consider important,' Earl said, facing Calhoun at the top step of the elevated platform.

'Let me tell you somethin', Thomas,' Calhoun said pointing a finger at the younger man's chest. 'I hold you and Baker personally responsible for damages to this university that may yet total more than ten thousand dollars. Did he talk about that?' Calhoun asked, turning to the assembly. 'Did he bother to go into the actions taken against Sutton yesterday at our meeting?'

'That's not the point!' Arnold McNeil said, rising from the seat he had slumped into and coming toward the stage. 'I, for one, am tired of being forced to see every issue from your point of view. I think that faculty members have as much stock in this community and in the particular situation that has come up as anyone else, and that our feelings and opinions to this point have been based primarily on hearsay and biased reports. I think,' he said, turning to his colleagues, 'that we need to hear the other side of the story.'

'Could I ask a question?' Mrs Pruitt singsonged above the hubbub of the gathering.

'Please do,' Calhoun said as though he were chairing the meeting.

'Just what do you hope to accomplish, Mr Thomas, or should I say did you hope to accomplish by calling this meeting?'

Earl paused. Lawman nodded to him. All eyes were on him.

'We had hoped to enlist the aid of the faculty,' Thomas said.

'I mean,' Mrs Pruitt interrupted, 'there had to be more to this than simply informing us about things . . .'

'We wanted to suggest two possible alternatives,' Earl said. 'I will be glad to go into them if this meeting is returned to its former state. I mean faculty only.'

'What have you got to say that I can't hear?' Calhoun asked defiantly.

'This is not a debate!' Earl said facing Calhoun squarely. 'The purpose was not for you an' I to argue points here. You know my perspective an' I know yours. You called a meetin' yesterday morning an' Captain Jones had his men on the door. That was not an open meeting! This is not an open meeting!'

'I think we should hear Thomas out,' McNeil suggested. 'Doesn't anyone want to hear the students' side of this?'

'I do!' Coach Mallory said speaking out for the first time.

Unfortunately the coach was the only faculty member who chose to speak out. Earl couldn't decide whether the others were speechless because of Calhoun's presence or because they simply had nothing to say.

'I was goin' to ask members of the faculty to go on strike with us,' Earl said through the icy silence with a weak grin on his face, 'or suggest that certain faculty members safeguard the readmission program in order to establish a buffer for the repression. But I don't suppose the questions I wanted to raise are relevant any more . . . how can you seek protection from a fellow victim?'

32

Exodus

Friday on the campus of Sutton University was generally a day of preparation for weekend activities that almost always included a mixer of some description that night and post-mixer parties in the dorms that lasted far into the morning. The student body would open its collective eyes by noon on Saturday, eat a hurried sandwich in the cafeteria or canteen, and get a good seat from which to cheer the football team (in the fall), the basketball team (in the winter), or the track team (in the spring). If the events were on other campuses, there would be cars loading on Friday night or Saturday morning to take students to the contests.

The cars and buses were leaving on Friday afternoon this week. The Saturday game had been cancelled. The students were milling about in front of the dormitories and the Student Union Building discussing the campus developments and waiting for a break in the depressing atmosphere.

The clouds hovered gray and forlorn over southern Virginia, reminders of the showers that had fallen the previous night and threatened to return.

Aside from the emptying resident facilities there were three centers of action on the campus early that afternoon. Sutton Hall, the administration building, was one. Carver Hall, where the student government was housed, was another. The third was the Sutton fraternity house's third-floor Strike Communications Center.

The five members of MJUMBE were closeted in a closed meeting at one o'clock in the back room of the Strike Center. They were planning what had become for them the most important phase of their strike program: a meeting with the parents of female students who were coming to deliver their daughters from the campus. It was now the most important phase because it would be their last opportunity to gain a measure of protection against the force that Ogden Calhoun was bound to use to clear the university buildings.

'Is it clear to everybody why we're usin' the same papers that we passed out yesterday?' Abul Menka asked.

'I still think it's gonna be a little tight on the oldies, man,' Cotton grumbled. 'Especially dudes an' chicks who graduated from here because they come off like a buncha Toms . . . when you be rappin' 'bout how ain' nothin' gone on here since they opened this crypt, man . . . whew! I don' know . . .'

'Some of the things we said won't be very acceptable,' Abul admitted. 'But you heard 'bout what happened to Earl when he tried to hol' a closed meetin' this mornin'. Ol' Assbucket broke in on the set an there wasn' nothin' nobody could do.'

'We could use the enforcers,' Ben King griped.

'No good,' Abul said stiffly. 'That would never get over wit' Calhoun-type people. We gotta face some facts, man. The folks who comin' to the meetin' is only comin' because their daughters is tellin' 'um to. They basically don' wanna come, think it's a waste a time, an' ain' gonna like the looks of us from jump street.'

'What you sayin' is that we really ain' gonna do no good to have the meetin',' Baker said.

'I s'pose thass the truth,' Abul said, sitting back down to the table. 'But we can't possibly give out new statements. One a them administratin' flunkies is boun' to point out the diff'rence. So there can't be none.'

'We definitely be sunk if Calhoun come over an' rap all the bullshit that the parents wanna hear,' Cotton said with a sigh.

'He won't be there,' Abul said. 'That may be a point in our favor. The bastard's confidence may be gettin' the best a him. All we really need is a handful a chicks. Then everybody in the community would be poised to leap on his shit if he sent big guns after us.'

'How you know he ain' comin'?' Cotton asked.

Abul fished around in his dashiki's breast pocket. He brought out a package of cigarettes, a book of matches, and a piece of folded paper. He lit a cigarette and unfolded the paper. 'It sez here,' he began, 'if you wanna know why school is closed an' you wanna talk wit' us, schedule an appointmen' wit' the secretary for nex' week.' Abul took care to slow his speech into a drawling slur to mock the president.

'Man, these folks ain' comin' back out here nex' week. Thass a lotta bullshit an' Calhoun knows it. I think we should move on all these bastards!' Ben King got up and paced the floor for a minute pounding a huge fist into his palm. He seemed on the brink of an explosion. Even more so than usual.

'Jobs,' Cotton mumbled to no one in particular. 'People got jobs to go to. They prob'bly think comin' out here *today* is a pain in the ass. An' anybody who ain' got no job an' can afford to live nowadays ain' sendin' his daughter to Grade D Sutton University.'

'Thass the point,' Abul said. 'All they gonna know is what we tell them. Unless they run inta one a them flunkies like Mercer.'

'No-Check Mercer,' Baker laughed. 'Thass a worthless muthafuckuh.'

There was a period of silence while members of the group pulled their thoughts together.

'We have ta do a heavy sympathy thing,' Baker commented. 'Otherwise we get our asses kicked t'night.'

'We need to wipe out all a them pigs from Sutton,' King urged.

'We can deal with t'night when it gets here,' Abul said. 'Let's list a few things that we want Baker to rap about when the party starts. After we do that Ralph can move off to the side an' organize the stuff in whatever order he wants to present it.'

'I don't buy it,' King said. 'I don' buy all a this crawlin' aroun' an' sayin' this instead a that an' doin' this instead a that like we in the wrong. Man, this iz some bullshit!'

'You gotta face the truth some day Ben,' Abul said as though to calm the fuming giant. 'Everything that we after you can't take. Everything you wan' ain' available jus' 'cause you're bigger than the nex' cat or you got some "enforcers" to back you up. Some things depend on yo' ability to convince people with words that you're right. When you bang somebody in the head they may go along wit' you, but they always layin' for a chance to go up 'side yo' head too. Thass why people who take things by force can' never sleep.'

'No lectures,' Ben King snarled. 'I don' know whuss goin' on wit' *you* anyway. It's only since the deal got under way that you started openin' yo' goddamn mouth! An' it's only the las' couple days that all a the ideas we had have started fuckin' up.'

Abul Menka got to his feet. 'I'm gonna forget that you said that the way you did,' he said slowly, tossing his cigarette away and freeing his hands. 'I'm gonna attribute that remark to pressure, because my balls are out there on the line jus' like yours. I started speakin' up because I knew I had jus' as much to lose as anybody else an' I wuzn' gonna let some big mouth bluffin' get my ass kicked outta school. I was determined that if I left, it would be because we planned things out an' jus' didn' make it . . . you dig?'

'Fuck you!' King said turning his back. 'You guys can doodle an' dally an' meet an' pray like a buncha en-double-ay-cee-pee niggers if you want to, but I'm gettin' my guns together fo' t'night . . . I'll see yawl at three.'

'Without the gun,' Baker said to King's retreating back.

King said nothing. The only sound from him was the echo of his footfalls as he thudded heavily down the stairs.

Sheila Reed was writing a check for twenty dollars for an impatient coed who stood in front of the secretary's desk with a hat box in her hand. Sheila had been working since nine o'clock that morning with no break to speak of. Earl had asked a couple of times if she wanted Odds to take over while she prepared to leave, but she had assured him that the few belongings she was taking were packed and ready. Her parents had been informed by phone that she would be at her job in the SGA office when they arrived.

'When will the last bus leave?' the coed asked when Sheila gave her the check.

'There's a special bus scheduled to leave at four forty-five,' the secretary replied. 'That gives you plenty of time.'

'What time do you have?'

'Two minutes past two.'

'Good. Thank you.'

The phone rang, but before Sheila had a chance to answer it the extension light at the base of the phone went off, signifying that Earl had answered it in the inner office.

'Thomas,' he announced, leaning back in the swivel chair with a cigarette clamped in his mouth.

'Earl? This is Lawman. I'm in Garvey Plaza. We got 'bout fifty dudes left over here. Mosta the people either leavin' soon or on the border line between stayin' an' goin'.'

'What 'bout the women?' Earl asked.

'Pretty good. I haven' heard a woman yet say that she definitely wasn' goin' home. Mosta them whose parents are comin' said that they goin' to that MJUMBE meetin'. You gonna speak?'

'No.'

'Why not?'

'Because it's MJUMBE's meetin'.'

'I think you coppin' out,' Lawman said.

'What? Coppin' out? How?'

'If you're makin' a split wit' MJUMBE you gotta speak up. You can't tell the women to leave an' then have their parents show up an' have a buncha so-called studen' leaders who're bein' identified wit' you tell them the opposite.'

'The women know how I feel. They heard me yesterday,' Earl retorted.

'The parents didn' hear nothin'.'

'MJUMBE knew how I felt before they called the meetin'.'

'You made them call it when you wen' aroun' las' night,' Lawman persisted.

'I didn' call . . .'

'You the president, man!' Lawman exclaimed. 'I'm trippin' out behind all these moral games you play wit' yo'self that seem to relate to some unknown group a sacred principles. Too much goddamn thinkin' is bein' done when there ain' none necessary. I tol' you a long time ago about how niggers is the only people in America who get hung up on them bogus Democratic ideals like the right to assemble. Fuck a right to assemble! You want the women gone? Then bes' you be there to tell their parents to take their crazy asses home! 'Cause you know as well as I do that if anything happens to any one of them you gon' be the man with the pipe up his ass when they start handin' out the blame.'

'Maybe I'll go,' Earl said wearily.

'Maybe hell!' Lawman said with his temper subsiding a bit. 'You better back yo'self up. It's all the help thass comin'.'

'The way I see it I back myself up if I give 'um busfare.'

There was a pause, an empty hole in the air that neither man bothered to try and fill with words. Lawman knew that he was pushing his friend. Earl was definitely not the type of politician or man to throw his weight around. He had won the election and was carrying out the job in the best way he knew how. When he told people something he was giving them his opinion and what they did after that he generally didn't influence. Lawman had never heard him say, 'I told you that wouldn't work,' when something failed, or 'I told you that would work,' when a venture was successful. It occurred to Lawman that the reason the post-operative statements were never needed was because Earl was generally such a forceful speaker and so adept at bringing people over to his train of thought that his policies toward campus political issues were never challenged. But now it was time for Earl to be more forceful. He could no longer advise as though he were objective about the entire project. He had to make people see what he was talking about whether it appealed to them or not.

The problem facing Sutton University's student body was one of face-saving and adventure. There were many people whose departure had been made very quietly. Some of those who stayed were staying because no one wanted to be considered a coward unwilling to face whatever force Ogden Calhoun sent against them. The adventure that the situation was presenting was obvious. Most of the students at Sutton were the post-civil-rights-marches generation of Black students. They hadn't been old enough to take part in the marches on Washington and the march against Selma. They had never been actively involved in the Black revolution on any level. They were still inside the educational womb and their discussions were all hot air and rhetoric based on television revolutionaries and imported upheavals from Franz Fanon or Mao.

Six o'clock looked like excitement from their viewpoint. Chances were that very few of them had ever had a billy club come crashing down on their heads or mace sprayed on them or tear gas choking them and setting their lungs on fire. Lawman knew that it would be no picnic, but he had agreed with Earl when the SGA president had told the men to make up their own minds while the women were asked to leave. The thing he thought he had to impress on Earl was the fact that no one who had never been involved in a confrontation would want to be on campus to pay for resisting arrest or refusing to vacate private property. He decided that he would try and find some clippings that he had cut out of various Black magazines depicting the true possibilities in the picture for those who had some romantic notion about a revolutionary picnic on Sutton's campus when the law arrived. He smiled when it occurred to him that the sight of those pictures might turn Earl's head around.

'When you comin' over here?' Earl asked. 'Hey! Lawman! You still on?'

'Yeah, man,' Lawman said, cutting his daydream short.

'When you comin' over here?' Earl repeated.

'About quarter to three,' Lawman said. 'Where's Odds?'

'Out front buggin' hell outta Sheila last I saw,' Earl laughed.

'Well, I'll see you.'

'Yeah,' Earl said, 'I'll see you.'

Earl dropped the receiver back into the holster. He lit a ciga-rette and finding it to be the last one in the package he crushed the container and tossed it into the trash. As he stood up to stretch his legs the sound of honking car horns drew his atten-tion to the back window. There were three cars trying to get out of the driveway next to Garvey Plaza. No one could decide who was going to go first. Earl pulled the shade down.

Deep inside he knew that the things Lawman had said were true. Not going to the three o'clock MJUMBE meeting *would* be a cop out of sorts. If he had any responsibility at all to the people in the community and particularly to the women, perhaps it was an obligation to describe Selma, Alabama to them or some of the things that had happened to him as a Freedom Rider.

His hand automatically went to the crown of his head when he thought about the Freedom Rides. He had been only a boy of nine traveling with his college-aged brother. Their first stop had been a small cafe just outside of Charleston, South Carolina. As far as they knew no one, not even the members of the press, had known where they were to stop. But there had been a huge reception waiting for them in the cafe – policeman, rednecks, and Kluxers. Their best move would have been to move on to the next stop, but once they got out of the bus their retreat back into the vehicle was blocked by a stick-swinging, rock-throwing mob. Earl had been kicked to the ground and when his brother had tried to shield his body by crouching over the younger Thomas, a broom handle had crashed into his skull and the last thing Earl remembered was the salty taste of his brother's blood as the red ooze from the gaping wound covered his face.

'I gotta go to that meetin',' Earl decided. 'I'm damned if I know what I'll say. Maybe I'll just recount my own experiences for them, but I gotta do somethin'.'

'Earl?' Someone was calling him and knocking on the closed door to the inner office.

'C'mon in!' Earl said.

It was Odds. 'I wuz on my way over to get a sandwich,' Earl's sidekick informed him. 'I wuz wond'rin' if you wanted somethin'.'

'I'll go,' Earl said reaching for his jacket. 'I need a pack a smokes.'

'Damn!' Odds said, 'you smoke like they ain' makin' no mo' a them things.'

'Yeah,' Earl flashed. 'An' it's gonna get worse befo' it gets better.'

Ogden Calhoun was having a meeting all his own. He had literally dictated the names of the young men that he did not want readmitted to Sutton University. His recommendation to the Board of Trustees had merely stated that certain members of the community would not be readmitted because of activities that endangered the lives and property of the Sutton family. The $8,000 damage (not including labor for replacing damaged equipment) and the takeover of the Thursday afternoon meeting were cited in detail as examples of the activities of these students.

The list of names placed on the desk of Charles Hague, Admissions Director, came as no surprise to either Hague or concerned faculty members who drifted into the Admissions office to find out the particulars of Calhoun's decision.

The list read alphabetically:

> Ralph Washington Baker
> Everett McAllister Cotton
> Roy Edward Dean
> Frederick L. Jones

Benjamin Raymond King
Kenneth C. Smith
Earl Joseph Thomas
Jonathan Wise

Those who didn't know were informed that Roy Dean was called 'Lawman' on Sutton's campus, and that Everett Cotton was really the backfield ace 'Speedy' Cotton. Few people had ever heard Earl's private nickname for Ken Smith – 'Odds' – nor had they heard the term 'Captain Cool' from anyone other than Arnold McNeil and a few students. But there was a fretful, worried frown on the face of every faculty member and administrator who saw the list. They had good reason to believe that these eight men would not leave Sutton without a fight.

33

Explosion!

The only member of MJUMBE who was wearing a dashiki for the three o'clock meeting with Sutton parents was Abul Menka. The tall, bushy-headed New Yorker wore a corduroy dashiki with red, green, and black patches symbolizing the three colors of the Black liberation flag. He was sitting alone in the far-left corner of the stage, smoking a cigarette, eyes hidden behind gold-framed sunglasses.

Three members, Ralph Baker, Speedy Cotton, and Fred Jones, were standing huddled in the opposite corner. They wore sports shirts open at the throat and jackets.

Ben King was standing at the base of the stairs that led up to the stage. He wore a pair of blue jeans, a sweat shirt, and a very casual pea jacket with one pocket missing and the collar ripped.

The auditorium was little over a quarter full at three o'clock. Recognizing the twelve-hundred-seat capacity Baker was reluctant to start before so scant a turnout, hoping that there were more people on the way.

In the assembly were women and parents, male students who had remained on campus, and members of the faculty and interested administrators. Earl, from his vantage point between Odds and Lawman, who were leaning against the door in the far rear of the room, estimated a total of maybe one hundred coeds. The interesting thing about their clothing was that few of them were dressed for a normal day's activities. Most of them were wearing traveling clothes.

The gathering stopped its low hum of conversation when Ralph Baker approached the microphone.

'Excuse me,' he began a trifle nervously. 'I am sorry to have added additional stops on people's schedules, but I feel that too many times things are taken for granted by 'student leaders' that would amaze many parents. But this info'mation is never relayed. For this reason the things that have happened here at Sutton this week would seem to be vague an' mysterious. This meetin' is to perhaps clarify a few things fo' parents as to what our strike has been about. Maybe things will then be clearer as to why we are takin' the stands that we have.

'We men of MJUMBE are all seniors. We are representatives of what is mosta the time the mos' stagnant, cautious section of the studen' body. We see ev'ry possible distraction as a possible delay from graduatin' on time.

'Unfortunately there comes a time when the boat mus' be rocked. In this case President Calhoun is indicatin' that we were intent on sinkin' the boat. No one wants ta drown. Especially,' Baker added with a smile, 'if you've been on it fo' three years an' only have one mo' to go.

'We have handed out a copy of our requests and our reasons for askin' that these changes be made. I read once in a magazine an interview wit' a former political leader at Howard University who said, 'It's not enough to hol' a gun at an administrator's head. You have to pull the trigger.' At Sutton we didn' even do that. We called for a studen' strike to impress our sincerity, our unity. We wanned to show how committed each an' every studen' was to these issues.

'President Calhoun tipped the boat over. Not only did he turn away our demands with only token interest, he sent for the police force that is known in this county to be the most brutal and racist. I know, 'cause I'm a native of this county. The police came out an' threatened us wit' their sticks an' their curses. They acted jus' like everyone knew they would act. They acted white.

'There are several ways of lookin' at our request for studen's to remain here at Sutton. It can be looked at as a personal plea from the members of MJUMBE since all five of us will prob'bly be expelled. But that's not our primary concern. Our concern is that only three of our deman's will be instituted. We will only have, as I said, a token response, and our submission to pressure will intimidate those who follow. There will always be studen' leaders on their han's an' knees insteada their feet.

'Fo' that reason . . .'

Anyone present in the room could have testified to the weight that Baker's words were having. Even though he was reading most of the time from a typed sheet and sounded somewhat stilted, the young man was being effective. But just as he began to draw his suggestions to a close and call for the support that most people felt he most surely would have received, an explosion shook the building.

The explosion came from somewhere behind the building, shaking the auditorium with quick, jerking vibrations. Baker raced to a side window even as the first scream was being drowned by the chaos that was unleashed by the frightened crowd. He reached the door just in time to see a school bus engulfed in a shield of flame; tongues of orange and blue fire lunging skyward from the hull of the vehicle.

The crowd pushed through the exits and toward the streets. The first three men to leave the building had turned the corner in the direction of the blast. They could feel the warmth from the charring and smoking metal, see the melting tires allow the skeleton of the vehicle to collapse around the white-hot wheels.

'A plastic bomb,' Odds said surveying the ashes.

'A son-uva-bitch,' Earl Thomas declared.

34

MJUMBE Discovery

It was after five thirty. The men of MJUMBE had watched all but a very few members of the Sutton community depart by car or taxi or bus, through the narrow passages between buildings, around the oval of dead and dying flowers, and through the cast-iron arch with its proclamation, SUTTON UNIVERSITY.

The last two hours had seen their last plan destroyed, seared by flames and as easily pushed aside as a puff of the black whorls of smoke that had been carried away by the brisk winds hurtling across campus from the east.

The revelation by Victor Johnson that a unit of National Guardsmen was camped just south of Sutton was another setback. Somehow pieces of information about a unit of soldiers never hit solidly home until the last station wagon, with suitcases of clothes bulging out of the storage space, had disappeared from view.

There had been no discussion about the bomb or the Guard. No one had said a word except to confirm the fact that when the five o'clock bus left it would be time to arm themselves. When the last of two late buses belched a stream of black smoke and accelerated southward the five men each got up slowly and started to take his position. Baker was trying to make a last-minute call to the SGA office when he realized that the telephones had been cut off for the day. He cursed and ripped the phone out of the wall. He figured he owed Calhoun a favor.

'The barricades up in back?' Baker asked Cotton.

'Both door an' windows,' Cotton said.

'Jonesy an' I decided we'll lay here,' Abul said, gesturing toward the positions facing the oval near the front door.

'Need somebody up top,' Baker said. 'Ben, you got that scope?'

'Yeah.'

'Why don' we have Ben on the third floor with the scope, you an' Cotton on the secon' floor with the two high powers, an' me an' Jonesy down here since we don't have much range?' Abul said to Baker.

Baker nodded and collected his case.

'Rub Vaseline on yo' face when you take yo' positions. It fights mace,' Abul said. 'An' use the handkerchiefs soaked in vinegar to fight the tear gas. It's boun' to get in here once the windows get broken.'

''Bout that time,' Baker pointed out.

The five men picked up their arms and ammunition to depart. There was no fanfare or commotion. Jones had a .38 Special Rossi from Brazil. Menka had a Winchester .22 rifle. Baker and Cotton had identical .30–30 rifles with a case of Norma cartridges and *bandoleras*. King had a 30.06 with a huge track scope. He carried two metal boxes of ammunition. When the meeting broke up he sat at the base of the stairs and put his gun together smoothly and turned, almost anxiously, to the front window where three of the four panes had been reinforced with metal strips. He nodded to Fred Jones and departed.

There was no final word from anyone. All five men knew what they had to do. Abul was tempted to shake hands because it seemed that only in the past two days had he really gotten to know them, really gotten to be brothers to them. He couldn't find a way to acknowledge this bond without seemingly confessing that he felt death near them. He remained flawlessly cool, crouching behind a sofa and lighting a cigarette.

Barricades had also been placed in front of the entrance to Carver Hall. Earl, Lawman, and Odds sat in the front office armed with a bottle of rum and two quarts of Coca-Cola.

There were no guns, no sticks, no knives. They had been drinking since the explosive ending to the meeting with the parents. Their eyes were red, their jokes becoming less and less funny and yet receiving larger laughs, and their underarms were soaked with nervous perspiration, but they considered themselves ready.

Ogden Calhoun was on the line to the security office. Reporters had been running all over campus and a television crew complete with camera was staked out in his outer office. They had been waiting for a statement from him for over an hour and he had been waiting for a call from the security guard for almost that long. Miss Felch had been brewing coffee and making small talk since the reporters had flocked to Calhoun's office from the scene of the explosion. There had been a dictated paragraph at three thirty stating that the explosion was only further evidence that the institution had to be closed. There was less than a word for the next two hours.

'Hello? Jones? This is President Calhoun. I was waiting for . . .'

'I just got here an' listed the things you wanted, sir,' Jones said breathlessly. 'There are only two occupied buildings. One is the fraternity house and the other is Carver Hall.'

'I want you to direct the Guard when they come in,' Calhoun said icily.

'Yes, sir,' Jones mumbled. 'An' stay wit' the Guard unit?'

'Every damn second! I want to know everything that happens in an instant.'

'Yes, sir,' Jones agreed. 'It's ten minutes to . . .'

'Right,' Calhoun cut in. 'Come on over.'

The intercom buzzer went on.

'It's your wife,' Miss Felch said.

'Tell her I'm busy,' Calhoun snapped.

'I told her that, sir, but she's insisting.'

'Then hang the damn phone up an' call the Guard number. Don't take any more calls. Tell the press I'll make a statement when the Guard arrives at the front door. Tell them I'll speak then. I know they'll complain about the lighting an' all, but kick 'em out of my office an' bring me a cup of coffee, please.'

'Yes, sir,' Miss Felch replied in her monotone. 'What shall I say to the Guard?'

'Tell 'em I said to come on.'

As Miss Felch dialed the numbers that would bring National Guardsmen onto the campus of Sutton University for the first time in the institution's eighty-seven-year history, Abul Menka was making a startling discovery on the third floor of the fraternity house. He had gone up to the top floor to demonstrate the use of the handkerchiefs-soaked-in-vinegar to Ben King. What he discovered was that one of the two metal boxes that he had seen on the first floor did not contain the supposed clip of 30.06 shells, but instead a plastic bomb.

'What in hell is that for?' Abul screamed. 'Oh! I get it! You stupid bastard! You're the one who blew up that goddamn bus! You stupid muthafuckuh! Where's the goddamn timer?'

'This is for an emergency!' King declared picking up the bomb in his hands.

'Like the goddamn bus two minutes befo' we coulda stayed on this muthafuckuh with fifty parents an' seventy women. Right?'

'All right! I won' set it!' the huskier man exclaimed, putting the bomb on a table.

'Set it? You think I give a fuck? What do I care? All I know is that you fucked everythin' aroun' today.'

Baker, Cotton, and Jones all seemed to arrive at the third-floor door at that time. They were speechless. Fred Jones started to wipe Vaseline from his face with a towel. He threw down the handkerchief soaked in vinegar and pocketed his .38 Special.

'Hard bombs to fuck wit',' he said softly as he zipped up his peacoat. 'Them's the kind that blew up them Weathermen in New York. Hard to trus' somethin' like that.'

'Where you goin'?' King asked him.

'I'm leavin', man,' Jonesy said in his ever-quiet manner.

'Why? I made a mistake! You never made a mistake? I thought the meetin' wuz gonna flop! I wanned everybody to know that we meant business. All right! I made a mistake! I couldn' go out there an' undo the fuckin' thing jus' because the meetin' wuz goin' all right . . . I . . . look, I took a chance, man! I made a mistake. All right?'

'Fuck you!' Abul sneered. 'A silly-assed one-man power play! We wuz a team! We wudn' fuckin' aroun'. You fucked it all up!'

'Team? You never been wit' a fuckin' team in yo life. Man, you always by yo'self,' King flashed.

Jonesy walked between the two men and looked questioningly at Baker. Baker nodded and followed him out of the door followed closely by Speedy Cotton and Abul Menka.

'Chicken out, muthafuckuhs!' King raged, running halfway down the landing that led to the third floor. 'You all jus' scared a them whiteys! Thass all! You can't hand me that too-disappointed-to-fight story.'

The Black giant evidently had known very little about the point to which he had driven Abul Menka. When King pulled up next to him and pointed an accusing finger in Abul's face the man in the gold dashiki turned and landed a right hand flush in the center of King's face. As his victim stumbled backward, Abul leaped at him, landing punishing blows on the heavier man's face and neck. King tumbled into the corner of the landing covering his face with his arms until Baker and Jones subdued Abul from behind.

King was spitting blood. He made a slight move as though he would attack Menka when he regained his balance, but Baker proffered a restraining hand.

'I wish you would!' Abul declared, shaking loose and adjusting his sunglasses. 'I'd love to beat yo' fuckin' brains out.'

King turned from the four men and walked back up the stairs. 'I'm stayin'!' he shouted as loudly as he could. 'They'll have to kill this stupid Black bastard while they pry yo' asses from between yo' legs!' He shook a fist at them from the top of the stairs. 'Fuck you cats! Fuck you!'

'That nigger is crazy,' Abul said to Baker as they went down the stairs.

'Maybe,' Baker said collecting his gear. 'His mama was raped by a white man six or seven years ago. He hate 'um now. You should see when he git a chance to block one or tackle a whitey. He's a mean muthafuckuh, man. He sees red.'

'I hear tell some is comin' fo' him to tackle,' Menka said pointedly. 'They gonna have U.S.A. on their jerseys. He should play a helluva game.'

'I hope so,' Baker said.

35

Downhill Snowball

Miss Felch never had a chance to stop Gloria Calhoun from entering her husband's office. Mrs Calhoun came through the open door to the outer office and barged by the startled secretary before a word could be exchanged.

Ogden Calhoun was both surprised and annoyed to see his wife intrude on him. He was putting the finishing touches on his press statement and having a last cup of coffee when the interruption took place. He leaped to his feet and held out a warning hand to his wife.

Mrs Calhoun's face was bitten with anger, her dark eyes flashing too much despair to withstand the tears she felt about to boil over and smear her carefully prepared makeup. Her hair was glistening from the raindrops that had started to sprinkle the air.

'I just came to tell you something important!' she declared ignoring her husband's hand. 'I came to tell you that I'm leavin' you tonight. Right now! I swear to God in heaven, Ogden, that if you send those troops down on those boys I'm through.'

'I have no choice,' Calhoun said, rushing to the door to be sure that it was closed and locked.

'That's a lie!' his wife objected. 'That's as much of a lie as anything else that's gone on this week. There is a choice. You've always had some kind of choice. But you're old. You don't want to see. An' now the choice is almost life or death.'

'I have my duty to . . .'

'Stop! God, I hate to think that I'm really hearin' *you* sayin' those sort of things. I hate to think of you callin' on clichés and lies when I'm practically down on my knees askin' you to take a look at what you're doin'.'

'I know.'

'Stop! I said stop!' Mrs Calhoun almost screamed. 'I'm very tired. I didn't come here to argue. I didn't even come here to change your mind. I was leavin' without a word, but when I called to talk to you as usual you were too busy for me.' Mrs Calhoun sat in the chair facing the president's desk.

'Gloria, you don't know all the facts.'

'Maybe not,' Mrs Calhoun agreed. 'But,' she added as she struggled for composure, 'I do know that there are boys out there ready to die for what they believe in. Boys that are takin' a stand that you would have taken when you were their age. But, God that must have been a long time ago. And they have to face this, this death, because you're an old man. Not really old. Not too old to see as I see, but all you have been able to see for a long time has been yourself. Any idea that wasn't conceived by Ogden Calhoun is not a good idea.'

'They're wrong,' Calhoun said heavily. 'You're wrong. We never did things like this. There was communication an' we faced everybody like a man. We sat down an' argued an' fought.' Calhoun was flustered beyond his frayed nerves and late hours. The mask of rock-hard calm had split like fabric stretched too tightly against its subject, leaving him feeling old and tired and open.

'We never did,' his wife snapped. '*WE WHO?* We, in the thirties? *WE WHO?* We, at Howard? For nine years I've watched you fool people and lie to yourself, using Sutton University as an example to show everyone that the same tough man who was fired for speaking his mind about Black psychology is still as tough and as hard to overpower as ever. All I've read about is the history of collective thought you've been in favor of here at Sutton. That's another lie! Everything that you have implemented here that *wasn't* your idea has been used and publicized as though you had conceived it. Threatening students. "My way or the Highway Calhoun" . . . I feel so sorry for you Ogden. And me, too. I feel sorry for me too. Because I never said anythin' though I saw it all happening a long time ago. But I thought you knew you were acting. I never suspected that you believed that liberal façade that you exposed an' the talk about being on the students' side. I thought you knew that you were only on your side.'

'You're wrong,' Calhoun repeated.

'And you really think I'm wrong too,' Mrs Calhoun said, standing up as though she had just had another revelation.

'I know you're wrong,' Calhoun said weakly.

'I'm leaving,' Mrs Calhoun said turning for the door. Her husband didn't look up as she departed. 'Good-bye,' she concluded.

Minutes tick-ticked by. Ogden Calhoun stared out of the window watching darkness engulf the campus. He saw the sparkling shadows of the raindrops dancing across the path of the light outside his second-floor window.

Miss Felch cut into his thoughts by way of the intercom.

'Yes?' he asked, getting up.

'The Guard is here,' Miss Felch said.

'Where are they?' Calhoun asked.

'Their commander is downstairs with Captain Jones. The rest of them will be pulling in in a few seconds.'

'Good. I'm coming out.'

Calhoun straightened his tie in the small mirror on his desk, finished his coffee, and smoothed out his hair with his palm. When he came through the oak door into the outer office Miss Felch was throwing a sweater over her shoulders. Together they went down the flight of stairs onto the first floor and then out into the misty Virginia evening.

Captain Jones was standing on the second step talking to a man in an army uniform. Flashbulbs went off in the president's face. Huge rows of illuminating camera lights were turned on and the night television cameras started to roll.

'This is the Guard commander, General Rice,' Captain Jones said introducing the two men. 'This is President Ogden Calhoun.' Calhoun shook the general's hand and more pictures were taken.

'I'll be very brief, gentlemen,' Calhoun said to the assembly of reporters and photographers and interested by-standers. 'In the past forty-eight hours Sutton University has been the scene of over twenty-three thousand dollars' worth of damage. We have lost ten thousand dollars' worth of equipment in our resident facilities and today, a thirteen-thousand-dollar school bus, formerly used to transport our teams to athletic events, was blown up. The members of the community were asked to leave in order that we might establish a readmission program, but there are certain members of the community who didn't leave. I think, and Captain Jones will correct me if I'm wrong, that the men responsible for the majority of the damage, the Student Government Association heads and members of a militant group called MJUMBE, are the only students who insisted on staying. All other students apparently saw the sincerity and responsibility from my office to bring peace to Sutton. Therefore . . .' President Calhoun was interrupted by the large roar of motors as the six huge transport trucks carrying the Guardsmen wheeled around the oval and pulled to a stop in front of the office. Flashbulbs were fired at the halting trucks. One man from each truck dropped off quickly and trotted through the rain toward the building. '. . . therefore,' Calhoun continued, 'I have summoned the National Guard unit placed at my disposal by the governor, and I am asking them to clear the buildings here at Sutton. That's all.'

Had Calhoun looked up just at that moment he would have seen one last student car leaving the campus. It was a late-model Ford station wagon with Fred Jones at the wheel and Speedy Cotton and Ralph Baker sitting in the back seat as passengers. The other two MJUMBE men were not in the car.

Ben King was sitting in a chair on the third floor of the frat house. He couldn't see through the darkness and mist across the oval to where Calhoun stood in front of Sutton Hall, but he had heard the roaring engines of the transport trucks as they arrived on campus and then idled in front of the administration building. He was readying the 30.06.

Abul Menka heard the trucks entering too. He was standing at the side window of Carver Hall knocking on the glass window, trying to summon Earl Thomas. Abul had turned down an opportunity to ride with Fred Jones and had even got as far as revving up the motor for his own car to leave, but the lights in Carver Hall, just across the parking lot from the fraternity building, made him think of Earl and the reason why he was leaving. He saw no reason for Earl to die because of King's stupidity either.

'Earl,' he was calling. 'Earl!'

The SGA president finally heard him above the transistor radio that was playing on the desk and went over to the window and opened it.

'Abul. Whuss up, brother?' Earl asked.

'This whole thing,' Captain Cool replied. 'Baker an' Cotton an' Jonesy already left. We found a bomb that Ben King had made. He was planning to use it this evenin'. He was the one who bombed the bus.'

'So you leavin'?'

'What the hell?' Abul asked. 'When I realized that whatever those parents saw and felt during that meetin' explosion really *was* our fault instead a jus' somethin' that someone had planted to blame us, it really took the wind outta me . . . thass why I came over here to tell you to split.'

'No can do,' Earl laughed without humor, turning his face up into the mist. 'The money you guys bet over the las' couple days is comin' to be collected. My signature was on the bogus check.'

'You don' have ta stay,' Abul complained. 'Man, King fucked everything aroun'. Thass part a the reason the ol' man is sendin' the Guard in. You don' have to pay for *that*.'

'Look, man. I know how you guys got those papers that Baker made up the demands from. Sheila tol' me everything . . .'

'What?' Abul asked.

'That Baker took the papers from my desk after she loaned him the key. She tol' me today.'

'I didn't know that . . . either,' Abul said sincerely. 'Baker convinced us all that you wuz jus' another bootlickin' ass-kissin'-type-cat.'

'Doesn't matter,' Earl said. 'Somebody had to start it.'

'It was like a snowball, man,' Abul continued blankly. 'One lie led to the nex' one.' Abul looked up again suddenly as the truck engines began to rev again. 'They comin', man,' he declared. 'Why don' yawl c'mon out. Can't you see that ain' nothin' like we thought it was?'

'But regardless, man,' Earl said calmly, trying to peer through the density of the rain now falling heavily, 'the things on that paper was comin' to a head, an' this was the inevitable result.'

'What you're sayin' is that you gonna pay fo' our mistakes. You know that if you had been runnin' things they would a been diff'rent.'

'Maybe. It don' matter now.'

'Move aside,' Abul said climbing through the window. 'I'll wait with yawl.'

There was little room in the cramped office. Odds and Lawman were sitting on the floor because all of the furniture had been propped against the door.

Abul was welcomed. He sat in the middle of the two SGA appointed workers and poured himself a drink. He didn't have time to enjoy it.

The first burst of fire came from the direction of the fraternity house. It was a series of four shots echoing like firecrackers to the men in Carver Hall. The return fire shook them where they sat. There was a repeating-rifle burst, followed by a thundering from guns. The last explosion was a mammoth roar that none of the four men in Carver Hall would ever believe had come from a gun. Abul Menka dropped his glass when he realized the truth.

'They hit the bomb,' He cried leaping to his feet. 'One of those bullets hit the bomb. Oh, God!' he raced to the side window to see the fraternity house being swallowed by flame leaping toward the stairs starting at the top floor and running quickly down the front of the old wooden structure.

Earl, Odds, and Lawman were rooted to the window unable to react. They could scarcely accept the fact that Ben King was somewhere in that building.

Abul Menka was still screaming as he tore the barricades from their prop positions at the door. He threw the chairs behind him in his haste to leave and shoved the desk far enough away from the door to exit. Earl and his companions arrived at the door just behind him, too late to divert him. They stopped. Through the rain they saw his running figure disappear across the parking lot headed toward the fire.